MEMBERS
OF THE TRIBE

Books by *Richard Kluger*

WHEN THE BOUGH BREAKS (1964)
NATIONAL ANTHEM (1969)
SIMPLE JUSTICE:
A HISTORY OF BROWN V. BOARD OF EDUCATION (1976)
MEMBERS OF THE TRIBE (1977)

MEMBERS
OF THE TRIBE

Richard Kluger

DOUBLEDAY & COMPANY, INC.
GARDEN CITY, NEW YORK
1977

ISBN: 0-385-12989-0
Library of Congress Catalog Card Number 77-70982

in memory of
Abe and Libba Abramson
and
Harry and Fanny Kluger

. . . May the same wonder-working Deity, who long since delivering the Hebrews from their Egyptian Oppressors planted them in the Promised Land—whose providential agency has lately been conspicuous in establishing these United States as an independent nation—still continue to water them with the dews of Heaven and to make the inhabitants of every denomination participate in the temporal and spiritual blessings of that people whose God is Jehovah.

—President George Washington to the Hebrew Congregation of the City of Savannah, 1789

I
Seth's Book

ONE

Savannah, July 25, 1913

Attended Mickve Israel tonight for the first time since Yom Kippur—almost a year. I was uncomfortable about the timing, although I refrained from beseeching the Almighty to water my forthcoming effort with the dews of heaven: one cannot be so selective in applying for divine intervention. I have no doubt it is both sinful and supremely arrogant to solicit that potent reinforcement only on special and convenient occasions rather than to rely on the Grand Dispenser Himself to decide when to intercede and on whose behalf. I venture that Tunney, our devoted Monday-morning adversary, will be sending up his own dispatch for supernal guidance when he warms the pew Sunday at Wesley Monumental. Which of us, if either, shall the Lord favor? On what ground may I pray for the happy disposition of my entreaty? That I am a Jew, defending a Jew unjustly charged with butchering a Gentile child who wore a dainty yellow dress? (Perhaps I should have given thanks that they do not claim he did it to drain her virginal blood for sacramental use on the High Holy Days.) Surely in His infinite wisdom He knows all of this already. Can this episode to Him be other than one more diurnal test of faith of the Chosen People? Someday, I trust, He will lift this burdensome singularity and assign the less righteous a modest share of our ill fortune.

But I did not go to *schul* to complain, either—that's another form of insolence and particularly unseemly in intermittent worshippers. I went tonight because the circumstances that threaten Noah Berg's life and cast me as his reluctant savior seem to cry

3

out for acknowledgment that mere mortal skills will not suffice to beat back the waves of alien sentiment rolling down upon his beleaguered soul from the red hills of a land so materially impoverished and spiritually askew. Not that this display of humility yields me either comfort or strength; quite the opposite, to be honest. Yet I remain enough the devoted son of Israel not to overlook the possibility, however meager, that a last-moment visitation from on high may quicken my wits at the bar of temporal justice or—an entirely acceptable alternative—disarrange those of our foe. Not to try for either advantage would have been the sin.

Our synagogue seems to me more like a church than ever (and I have watched it from the start, having arrived at this port—by no divine design, so far as I can determine—on the day of its consecration thirty-five years ago). This is no private apprehension: they are plainly doing it on purpose to ingratiate the congregation among the Gentiles. The English Gothic design, the steeple, the vestigial transept, the organ and chorus, all were present that April sabbath when the doors were first flung open. (and I entered, wondering earnestly if a crucifix would materialize on the roof for the duration of the prayers lest passersby of other faiths be puzzled, and then offended, by the exotic chanting within). Now, although still forbearing the cross of Christ, they have gone much further. The congregants worship hatless, largely in English, using Wise's decorous *Union Prayer Book,* and with one eye fixed on the hymnal board on the wall of the nave to note the Torah reading for the service—a feature filched directly from the bulletins displayed in high-church interiors. Gone is the *chuppa* at the wedding ceremony. Gone is the Reverend Isaac Mendes these nine years and with him nearly the entire Sephardic *minhag* save the profound *El Nora Ah Lee Lah,* still precariously preserved at the close of our Yom Kippur service. Verily, it is churchly if not quite a church, and our Reforming Rabbi Weisz moves ever more zealously to promote the unity of the Judaic-Christian tradition. Jesus, for the moment, has not appeared among us or in our prayers, but his coming seems imminent. What preoccupies the rabbi is that we be good Americans all, reducing ritual to nuance and thereby presenting the Christian community scant cause to depart from its admirable tolerance of the Hebrews' faith. I find it an antiseptic and sadly defensive form of worship. And despite its studied harmlessness, Noah Berg is apprehended as alien and loathsome and judged before his trial begins. How much gore shall we have in the name of love?

Part of me has known, since the day I fled the menace that I sensed gathering about me up North and arrived here seeking sanctuary with the sunshine, that I would sooner or later have to confront this immemorial enmity directly. Oh, I have had my encounters on this score over the years, but these were private matters, not public exhibitions of massive antagonism. On Monday, I myself shall be in the dock with Noah Berg—and Shylock and Fagin and Isaac of York, not to mention two millennia of other assorted blood-sucking, plague-spreading, gold-grabbing, blasphemous, lecherous, and otherwise deformed killers of Christ, whom we doubt to be or to have been the son of God. God does not have sons—or, as my Grandpa Harry would have said, brothers-in-law, holy ghosts, or other *mishopocheh*. Not even a pet. God is One, not a Father and Son, like the proprietors of a grocery, or Three or a multiple thereof. I am sorry Christ was killed, but I truly did not do it. Nor, in refusing him, do I re-kill him. My heresy thus unabated, prudence ought to have directed the engagement of purely Protestant counsel to defend Noah Berg. As much was suggested to his family, but they insist upon my potent participation.

And so I am named defender of the local remnants of the twelve tribes. No easy chore, that. Though irreparably scattered, they persist in their assignment as God's contentious hostages, obliged till kingdom come (barring a presently unexpected reversal in the species) to bear witness to man's bottomless capacity for beastliness. Playing history's grim jester, even under sanctified auspices, has not of course earned the Jews generous applause, and the faith has therefore widened its repertoire. It was not enough to announce that the Decalogue—and every other known code of moral stricture—had fallen into universal disregard. No, the Jews, perhaps weary of dispensing so many unheeded reminders, managed finally to excite a warm response by presenting themselves to the throng as luscious fodder for its most vile impulses. On the least of pretexts—their vulnerability excused all need of serious justification—they were named the lurking *agent provocateur* in the culture dish whenever the times turned sour. The traits and trades they were required to assume for survival amid such alien corn were defamed as grotesque, and they would be boxed to the ground where the godly and ungodly alike joined the stampede. It is a therapeutic if unconscionable practice, this casting of one's victims as society's tormentors who deserve nothing better and are therefore unworthy of grief. And what else is this trial of ours on Monday but such a staged excuse for savagery?

Shall we thank the toxic Old World for shipping us a Dreyfus Affair of our very own? Or have we cultivated a native strain every bit as virulent as the more seasoned variety? Either way, there seems to be no immunity from the hateful contagion even in this blessed land, which has proven otherwise so hospitable to the yearning progeny of Moses. For myself, I would like nothing better than to exempt America from the ranks of monstrous persecutors and to dwell incessantly instead on her open and generous soul. My own dear father, believing passionately as he did in all the radiant promises of liberty and equality for all, went off to fight in Father Abraham's war and died heroically in Union blue. My mother never forgave him.

II

It was from the seaside that I had my first eye-filling glimpse of Savannah at mid-morning on that limpid tenth day of April in the year 1878.

The trip south by steamer from New York, on a line operated a trifle randomly by the Georgia Railroad, had consumed the better part of a week, and I was anxious as we turned past Tybee Island into the marshy mouth of the river for the final leg of the journey to be swiftly covered. The pace, instead, turned maddeningly slothful. The current, collecting down off the Carolina Appalachians from ten thousand square miles of red hills and valleys and ravines and swollen by the heaviest rainfall on the continent, thrust against our hull. The water itself seemed unyielding—a sluggish, rusty soup. Our upriver progress, however modest, was cheered by treble anthems of birdsong, the welcoming whine of a universe of insects, occasional ricocheting croaks from a vigilant bullfrog, and even the barely detectable plash of an alligator gliding off the bank. (I thought the reptile quite the most hideous and fearsome creature I had ever seen and despaired of fending it off, should we have sunk on the spot, without immediate loss of limb; I pondered which one was the most expendable.) Soon I saw pine and cypress and live oaks of an intensely gnarled disposition sprouting on the shore, which bloomed a greener green than I had known could exist. The air itself gave off so fecund an aroma and dazzling a brightness that it appeared nearly to shimmer with promise of regeneration for all who breathed it. Here was the perfect place to transplant a young life.

The pace of the river traffic matched my heightening spirit. The heavy water was churning now with the wakes of sturdy little coastwise packets, of darting pleasure sloops under full spinnaker, of hulking paddle-wheelers and stately clippers borne by acres of blossoming canvas. It became a spectacular procession of outsize swans to the transfixed eyes of a seventeen-year-old Chaim Yonkel. Suddenly to port, the bluff that the resident red men once called Yamacraw slanted steeply out of the river, and on its crest rose the roofs and chimneys and towers—I saw minarets—of Savannah. Reaching for the cloudless sky, it looked to me a toy town, and all the more benign and beckoning a prospect.

I came upon this picture-book place at almost precisely the age that my father, and his father before him, had struck out similarly for a fuller, freer life in a new land. Grandfather Solomon Adler had come from Ichenhausen, a sullen town in Swabia that tolerated, just barely, two hundred Jewish families. A middling scholar at *cheder*, a better but not sterling one at the *Gymnasium*, Grandpa Solly was not admitted to a university, was not admitted to citizenship—only the eldest of his three older brothers qualified when their father died—and was not admitted beyond the boundaries of the *Judengasse* without paying a "Jew toll," as the burghers delightfully dubbed it. Indeed the Jews in Germany of that era, like so many battening geese, seemed to be there for no reason beyond plucking by the ever-practical state. They and all their earthly goods were taxed within an inch of extinction; they were taxed even for the privilege *not* to serve in the military, a blood sport that the authorities had no intention anyway of permitting them to join in. And all the while they were denied a right to practice any but the most humble of trades, to own property other than their own cramped dwellings, even to marry without benediction of officials who viewed the birth rate in the ghetto as a civil peril not second to a recurrence of the Black Death.

Solly tried working in a bakery, tried grinding cutlery, tried selling spangled yarn door to door, and found them all less than profitable and not the least ennobling. When, on top of this unhopeful history, the duchies and principalities east of the Rhine began to ignite with anti-semitic rioting, young Solomon Adler gathered up the few coins he had put aside, brushed himself off briskly, kissed all his family farewell one sunrise, and marched off to discover if there were not perhaps friendlier *goyim* somewhere in the world. He had to pay, of course, to leave.

Earlier that very year, the first steamship ever to cross the Atlantic—it was called (and I acknowledge nothing providential in the name, although I am no doubt being stubborn) the S.S. *Savannah*—stirred the imagination of restless young Europeans pining for open pastures, and especially of Jews hungering for a sliver of dignity. Most of them headed for America. Solly Adler went, via Hamburg, to London.

A Rothschild he did not become, but life was better by far for him in England. He took a clerical position with a Jewish shipping firm, learned serviceable schoolboy English, developed a luxurious Spencerian pen, conquered the elusive geography of the Baltic Sea and most other European waterways, and absolutely mastered ciphering. In time, he rose to principal scrivener on the premises in addition to his duties as flawless bookkeeper and was able to put by enough to marry and settle into a semi-upholstered flat on one of the less disreputable streets in Whitechapel. There, in 1837, Aaron Victor Adler (the middle name being Sol's expression of gratitude to the Throne) was born, the second of three children.

My father has always been more wraith than flesh for me, but his boyhood, I have learned, was a sustained exercise in longing and escape—as his father's before him, and his first son's would prove. When Sol Adler contracted consumption in his forty-second year and was unable to work steadily thereafter, life in the family household soured and what benefits could be afforded fell mostly to Aaron's older brother, a scholar, and younger sister, the jewel of their mother Minerva's eye. Through boyhood friendships acquired while attending classes for a time with a tutor near Russell Square, he was admitted to several of the grander Sephardic town houses of London, but as his family's fortunes declined with his father's health, Aaron felt the clothing on his back turning tatterdemalion under the very scrutiny of his betters. Soon the lad was dreaming of America. He consumed the *Leatherstocking Tales* and Franklin's almanac, scoured the newspapers and learned that Jews were prospering like everyone else in many parts of that still wild land, and when the great Crystal Palace exhibition opened in Hyde Park in 1851, he haunted the American section of the great hall, hoping to encounter a blackamoor, Mohawk, or some other exotic breed on display for the occasion. The sea was wide, but the far shore so radiant and his English prospects so bleak that within two years Aaron Adler set sail, promising to write regularly of his adventures and send what money he might spare. Lodgings were arranged in advance with Sol's second cousin Lottie off Lafayette Street in New York—"near the Cooper Union." The boy knew all about Lafayette and Cooper.

The city bustled like London but was smaller and gayer, its streets always on the verge of turmoil. The town was growing too big for its pantaloons, as anyone could see—a seaport becoming a great metropolis. Aaron loved its sounds and motion. His distant relatives kept their distance while overseeing his essential needs. A sturdy enough boy, he found hourly work as a messenger in the financial district, flying around Bowling Green like a shuttlecock and wrestling on the grass now and then at noontime with other courier lads who were invariably Irish. Disheveled as a result, he once nearly lost his job; rather than curtail the horseplay and sacrifice the camaraderie, he learned to regroom himself with comb and kerchief before his next assignment. In short order, he was reciting the *Sh'ma* at temple Friday nights with a detectable brogue.

On Aaron's seventeenth birthday, Cousin Lottie's husband accompanied him to the offices of J. Seligman & Brothers, Merchants, at No. 5 William Street, around the corner from Wall. An interview with the office manager had been arranged through a mutual acquaintance from the synagogue, and the boy, promising fleet and faithful execution of his every charge, was taken on at twelve dollars a month as a runner between the office and the

9

docks. If the work itself did not present much of a challenge to him, Aaron took genuine pride in his association with the Seligman enterprise, a rising power in the city's financial circles. An infinite variety of merchandise channeled through the office to the family concern's retail outlets in St. Louis, San Francisco, upstate New York, and Alabama. The business was truly like a national bazaar, although swinging over more and more to commercial banking as gold bullion flowed into the firm from the hills and streams of California. Bearded Joseph Seligman, a bulky, formidable figure in his top hat and cane, and relays of his brothers and retainers marched in and out of the office in a steady, purposeful stream all day long on errands that Aaron told himself were directly linked to the urgent messages he carried to and from the wharves and to the firm's curbside traders dealing in the nation's growing bounty of commodities: Western grains, ore from the Great Lakes region, the South's huge cotton harvest, and pelts and hides and fruits and timber from all over. The air Aaron breathed was alive with the heady striving of hard bargainers and the buoyant shouts of oceangoing men. Salt breezes blowing in off the bay penetrated the streets and lanes and alleys of the Wall Street district, which had not as yet begun to take on its canyoned aspect, and a scurrying pace seemed to turn each passing business hour into a kind of frantic mission to prevail over the vagaries of the wildest marketplace.

In such surroundings, it was unthinkable for a young man not to aspire, and my father applied himself as his father had to the science of self-improvement. He studied accountancy and other business skills at night classes and began to read up in the newspapers on worldwide commercial activity. He soon knew more about the history and current level of tariffs around the globe than any teen-ager in the city and devised strategies to disclose, in conversations over lunch pails in the Seligman shipping office, that he had brains as well as legs. They moved him up to handling elementary paperwork on the docks—checking out bills of lading, transmitting documents to customs officials, and the time-serving like—and, by the time he was twenty, to an inside clerical job at William Street. People on the top were beginning to know his name, and Mr. Seligman himself paused by his stool on one occasion to commend him for a suggested simplification in the paper forms that swirled about the place in a perpetual blizzard. As the firm devoted itself less and less to commodities and ever more to banking, Aaron immersed himself in stocks, bonds, and every other species of negotiable instrument. He read up especially on railroads, spreading their iron tentacles in every direction now, and began to submit, unsolicited, modest communiqués to the inner office. By 1860, he had won a desk in there and a future of genuine promise—provided the Seligmans ever decided to invite someone from outside the family into their most intimate councils. But there would be time for that: he was still a very young man, and while there was gumption burning inside him, he was not about to let it consume him. He did his work, took a bride (the daughter of a neighbor), found a flat just off Christopher Street, went to hear Abraham Lincoln deliver a campaign address at Cooper Union in his old neighborhood, and wondered, along with everyone else, if the nation were about to be sundered by war. On weekends he debated the ethics of slavery with his father-in-law, Harry Popiel, a tailor on Rivington when he could find work (a formidable practitioner of *pilpul* the rest of the time). The stern old Galician insisted that the Torah had not condemned slavery altogether, and besides, he asked, "What would we do with so many *schvartsas* running around loose?" He fought back a tear or two when his daughter Laura—my loving mother—read *Uncle Tom's Cabin* to him aloud but, finally composing himself, said, "A 'for instance' is not proof."

III

When the war came, the Seligman office was converted into a semi-military zone. The credit of the government in Washington was seriously undermined by the Southern secession—cotton, quite simply, was the nation's collateral in world markets—and would-be suppliers of the Union's war needs held back for fear of never being paid. Out of mingled patriotism and opportunism, the Seligmans stepped forward, and through brother Isaac's ministrations in the capital were awarded substantial contracts for uniforms to outfit New York units. Early displays of strength by the Rebel forces disclosed the urgency of the military situation, and Aaron was pressed into temporary duty as a superintendent at one of the Seligman mills, humming now on a seven-days-a-week basis (*Shabbos*, too, was a casualty of Bull Run). Joseph Seligman, meanwhile, was rendering the North yet more essential service by embarking for Europe to peddle tens of millions of dollars of federal "7.30" bonds to fuel the Union military machine—no easy task despite the high rate of interest, which financiers in Amsterdam, Frankfurt, and virtually hostile London viewed as a confession of panic in Washington. Seligman, nevertheless, persevered, as the orders flowing back to William Street testified, and the firm won high esteem with the President and Secretary of the Treasury Chase. My father derived a measure of vicarious accomplishment from these Seligman exercises, but his life seemed to be marking time while the armies of the Confederacy ran amuck. Aaron and Laura decided to contribute to the Union's numerical superiority: I was blessed Seth Abraham Adler at a *briss* the very morning of the debacle at Manassas Junction; my brother Benjamin Isaac followed by fifteen months.

It was shortly after Benny's birth when word reached the Seligman office that one of Lincoln's generals had ordered every Jew removed from northern Mississippi and the sections of Kentucky and Tennessee lying to the west of the Tennessee River as part of the preparations for the siege of strategic Vicksburg. The Union commander was opposed to all commercial traffic in the vicinity but had been forced to yield to Treasury Department policy, which, in response to the mercantile clamor for goods, attempted to regulate trade. It was a forlorn hope. Profiteers swarmed over the area, paying in gold for cotton that had climbed to more than five times its pre-war price. Seeking and often pocketing quick fortunes, the speculators—a portion of them Jewish—defied Treasury orders against shipping bullion into Rebel regions by corrupting Union officers with bribes or a share in their illicit enterprises. In the eyes of the Union commander, there was but one solution. The order, No. 11 from the headquarters of the Thirteenth Army Corps of the Department of the Tennessee at Holly Springs, Mississippi, was issued on December 17, 1862, and read:

> The Jews, as a class violating every regulation of trade established by the Treasury Department and also department orders, are hereby expelled from the department within twenty-four hours from the receipt of this order.

Post commanders will see that all of this class of people be furnished passes and required to leave, and any one returning after such notification will be arrested and held in confinement until an opportunity occurs of sending them out as prisoners. . . .

By order of MAJ.-GEN. U. S. GRANT

"The Jews, as a class!" Did it not matter that only a minority of the culprits were Jews? Did it not matter that the great preponderance of Jews in the region were law-abiding and entirely innocent of any such disloyalty? Why were the Jews, in contrast to all other peoples, forever judged by the lowest of their lot and subjected to mass calumny? Here was an order by an official of the American government quite as horrific as any imperial ukase executed by the *bulvans* of the tsar. My father was staggered. The Seligmans were especially distressed in view of the fact that, in the late Forties, First Lieutenant Ulysses Simpson Grant of the Fourth Infantry had passed many of his off-duty hours playing checkers, poker, and whist on the premises of J. & H. Seligman, Dry Goods, in Watertown, New York. Filling the air with cigar smoke, he would confide to Jesse Seligman his secret scorn of the temperance activities of the new Mrs. Grant. Here had been a man, for certain, kindly disposed to the Jews. And now this.

My father helped a group of Seligman employées draft a fiery letter of protest for prompt transmittal to the President. Could this goodly man who had only a few weeks before announced his intention to emancipate the black bondsmen of the South at the turn of the year now countenance so blatant an act of persecution toward a different group of Americans? Jewish businessmen from loyalist Kentucky, rabbis of national renown, simple citizens professing the old faith—a flotilla of *landsmen*—repaired to Washington seeking the ear of the Great Emancipator. He gave them their answer in a dispatch to Grant from the War Department on January 4, 1863, three days after the Emancipation Proclamation had gone into effect:

A paper purporting to be General Orders, No. 11, issued by you December 17, has been presented here. By its terms, it expels all Jews from your department.

If such an order has been issued, it will be immediately revoked.

The meaning of this reversal was profound for Jews from the North and South alike. In the midst of a war going not at all well, one of the government's more popular generals had issued an order to facilitate his combat maneuvers; that it was an unjust, un-Christian, and, to be sure, anti-semitic measure would have caused it to be greeted, in almost all other lands at almost all other times since the Babylonian Captivity, with scarcely a blink. But here and now, the presiding official of the government, haggard and hard-pressed as he was by battlefield setbacks, chose to countermand the inhumane edict upon direct appeal by its victims. If the blacks had been freed in law that January, the Jews of America were freed in spirit. Here was a land they could truly call home. Aaron Adler decided to enlist in the Union army.

"They're dying like flies out there," my mother, babes in arms, said to him. "It's *Gehenna*, this war."

"I have a duty," my father said. "This is my country."

"Killing is not a business for Jews," said my mother.

"For true Christians, neither," he said. "But someone must do it."

"Why must it be you?" she asked.

"Why should I be excluded?" he asked back. "Besides, soon there will be conscription, and everyone will go."

"I read where it will be permitted to buy an exemption or find a substitute," she said. "Surely the Seligmans will advance you the money—."

"A coward's way out—I won't have it," he said.

"What's wrong with being a coward in the face of death? Who are you—Judah Maccabee all of a sudden?"

"He had something to fight for, as do I."

His father-in-law paled upon hearing the news. "But there are *kinder!*" he said. "You are needed here. War is for Cossacks."

"Sometimes for Jews, too, Papa," Aaron said gently.

"*Meshuggener!*" said the old tailor and turned away with glistening eyes.

And off my father went with the Cameron Dragoons, a New York regiment, and declined a commission in the quartermaster corps. They gave him a Seligman-made uniform (two sizes too large, he estimated), a gun and bayonet (showing him which way to point it), and two mess kits (one for meat dishes, one for milk). After some perfunctory drilling at a fort outside of Washington, he was sent into battle. He wrote with reassuring regularity, advising the family that "I have heard of but a single instance in which a Jew was wantonly insulted on account of his religion, and that was by a drunken Scotchman. His wrath was of short duration, however, I am told, for the Gentile soldiers who were present took umbrage at this verbal tarring of the Israelite as a cheat and a thief, all of his faith being so, and collectively flung this besotted wretch into a certain capacious receptacle for liquid matter." His letters said that he was allowed to wander off to some solitary spot not far behind the lines to say his prayers on the Sabbath, and no one commented when he fasted on Yom Kippur or passed by the pigmeat at mess. As incidental information he reported that one of the earlier famous battles of the war derived its name from a Jew: "In the mountain passes of Virginia, there once stood a small lodging house, where travelers used to tarry overnight on their journey to Richmond or to Winchester, and as its location was central it became quite a famous place in the days before the railroad largely replaced the stagecoach. The proprietor was called Menasseh, hence on inquiring whether there was a place halfway to stop at, you would be told, 'Yes, at Menasseh's.' The junction has retained that name, though now it is spelled Manassas. That is what they tell me at any rate."

It has been estimated that six thousand Jews fought on the Union side, perhaps four thousand for the Confederacy. Seven of the former were awarded the Congressional Medal of Honor. My father was among them. I have worn the medallion around my neck on a slender chain for all thirty-five years that I have lived in the Southland. The citation stated that he had been awarded the medal for "conspicuous gallantry displayed in the Battle of the Wilderness, May 6, 1864, in rallying and forming disorganized troops under heavy fire; also for bravery and coolness in carrying orders to the advance lines under murderous fire in the Battle of the Mine, July 30, 1864."

He survived until October. At dawn on the morning of the nineteenth, the Confederate general Jubal Early led a surprise attack on Lieutenant Aaron Victor Adler's bivouac near Cedar Creek, twenty miles south of Winchester in the fruitful Shenandoah Valley. Whether by shot or shell or bayonet, the government never advised, but my father fell forever in that place, where I have never gone. He was twenty-seven.

"Don't be *farbisseneh*," my grandfather the Rivington Street tailor told his daughter my mother. "They will make him an angel."

IV

And so I grew up with a phantom father, who had died not to help free the *schvartsas* or preserve the Union but out of gratitude that America was kind to Jews. And relatively speaking, that has been true ever since.

But there gnaws within the soul of every Jew in every land the undying suspicion that there gnaws within the soul of every non-Jew in every land the ingredients of a pogromist. There is no telling when these latent elements might, whether out of frustration or debauchery or simple monstrousness, coalesce. And it has happened often enough, in enough places, to suggest that the persecution complex afflicting the Jews generally is not groundless. Indeed it is said to be largely contributory to the state of anxiety in which they live, even in nations that do not badger them for a pastime—constantly suspended between security of person and livelihood and belief, on the one hand, and premonition on the other that patrols will come in the night bearing tapers and drag them away to the dungeon and the pyre. And if not tomorrow, then next month or next year or ten years from now, but sooner or later. Now it may well be, as I myself believe, that such chronic anxiety promotes behavior in Jew and Gentile alike to keep exactly that bestial instinct alive, at whatever subterranean level of being. Instead of socializing easily and openly as if he views the hideous prospect as unthinkable, the Jew withholds a full margin of comradeship from his Christian acquaintances, certain as he is that it will not be reciprocated or, if extended, will in time turn to scorn. Thus, in the commendable name of self-defense, many Jews are wont to veer away from the common concourse and to appear, without intention, clannish and aloof from other men: their differences are thereby accentuated, exaggerated, and perpetuated. The process has never yielded wholesome results.

My family's euphoric hope that this cyclical plague might pass over America forevermore died with Abraham Lincoln. Forgiveness and contrition did not follow the four-year massacre between the states—only rancor between the regions, it seemed, and rampant appetite among the people for self-advantage. Not surprisingly, amid such universal unbenevolence, events antagonistic to my faith occurred at more or less regular intervals as I approached manhood. Soon after the war, I remember, a report that the Hartford Fire Insurance Company and several other leading insurers would no longer extend coverage to Jews—*any* Jews—was authenticated. The action was defended or explained away in surprising sectors of the press, including the New York *Herald* and *The Nation*, and was thereby compounded. The unmistakable implication that Jews as a class were statistically prone to self-inflicted arson was a slur not merely on their honor but on their skill as businessmen, a nearly worse insult. A yet more personally painful incident to us was the news in the *Times* that a Jewish young man, from a family well known in my grandfather's synagogue, had enlisted in A Company of the Twenty-second Regiment of the New York State National Guard, taken the oath of allegiance to serve as a soldier in defense of his state, and then been summarily thrown out because of a regimental regulation excluding those, whether native or foreign-born, "of the Jewish persuasion." The lilies wilted at my father's Virginia graveside.

The national financial crisis of 1873 seemed to make all New York edgy and blue. Jews may not have been any more or less vulnerable to suffering from it than anyone else, but for some of their efforts to alleviate the pain they were prone to being isolated as a group and vilified. My grandfather's closest friend, a felt-hatter named Bromberg, was among the instigators in a group of workers who, having had their wages cut in half over a three-year period while the cost of living rose perhaps by half, organized to relieve their plight. Calling themselves the Hat and Cap Makers' Protective Association, then changing it to the bolder and more provocative Central Union of Capmakers, they took out two thousand workers on strike in the middle of winter. No more than one third of the strikers were Jews, but the leadership was largely so and the workers' command post was a hall on Orchard Street operated by the B'nai B'rith. All the talk was therefore of "Jew agitators," the newspapers ranged from caustic to antagonistic in their coverage and commentary, and the police did not hesitate to bring their truncheons down on picketers of their choice, few of them the colleens who had signed up with the union. Grandpa's friend Bromberg was dragged off to jail bleeding late one afternoon after someone dumped over a charcoal brazier that had been set up to keep the workers from freezing. The strike collapsed after about a month with very little having been gained and a good deal of incendiary anti-semitism in the air.

The hard times did not spare our small household. It was said that fully one quarter of the workers in the city could not find employment. My mother, unable to manage on her pension as a widow of the Grand Army of the Republic and the interest from a modest endowment kindly established in father's memory by the Seligman firm, liquidated part of the principal of the latter and invested it in a sewing machine, on which she began to take in piecework. Her apparent partiality to stitching boys' knickerbockers seemed odd until it dawned on me that the mill must have permitted her to buy the finished pairs at a favorable price and thus keep her two sons, who were profligate at shredding them, decently covered. The machine was rarely idle, often chattering away into the night as she struggled to keep the roof over us and avoid the shame of charity. On the Sabbath, however, she never worked but took Benny and me to the synagogue in her father's neighborhood, to which we had now moved, and coming and going preached the gospel of education. That was the only escape route from drudgery, she insisted, and if we malingered in our schooling, we would have no one to blame but ourselves when fortune came looking for us with a club. It became her strident love song to us, crooned above the dancing needle of her cast-iron Singer. And somehow or other, she and we would find the money to pay the way. Our advancement was the crusade of her life. Benny, fortunately, was a stellar student, and at a precocious age conceived the vision of one day becoming a doctor. The very picture turned mother rhapsodic; the Singer darted on till dawn. My own academic record was less promising, but all agreed that, with less time devoted to the pursuit of hopscotch, baseball, horseshoe pitching, and other sugar plums, I also had the makings of a professional man. A taxidermist, perhaps.

While I somewhat dreamily tried to unravel my future during the summer of 1877—between working as a delivery boy, delving into Homer, Byron, and the forbidden mysteries of the New Testament, turning into a shortstop of nearly acrobatic agility during twilight games in a rocky riverside lot, and consuming countless gallons of lemonade to slake my boiling pubescence—a tawdry event took place that, I think more than any other, pointed me in the direction of my life. Among the wealthy, blueblood, fashionable, or otherwise celebrated crowd that went to take the waters of the famous spa at upstate Saratoga was our eminent benefactor Joseph Seligman. An international financial wizard by now and an honored patriot who was known to have declined President Grant's invitation to become the Secretary of the Treasury, Seligman was in the habit of renting a private railroad car for his family and taking a number of suites at the Grand Union, the queen of Saratoga's hostelries and reputedly the largest such establishment in the world. This summer, he was advised that the hotel had adopted a new policy and no longer wished to accept "Israelites." The incident made headlines across the nation. If the great Seligman, a man of indisputable achievements and unquestioned integrity, could be thus declared outcast, what Jew in America could henceforth be insulated from humiliation?

The Seligman affair sparked other such incidents of which New Yorkers were made especially aware. The New York Bar Association blackballed a Jew. The president of the Long Island Rail Road, then seeking to develop Coney Island into a summer resort, announced publicly: "We do not like the Jews as a class. There are some well behaved people among them, but as a rule they make themselves offensive to the kind of people who principally patronize our road. . . ." It was then that I myself began to hear slurs on my faith at the sandlot and elsewhere. "An anti-semite," went the favorite jape at the Christian-owned grocery for which I delivered, "is someone who dislikes Jews more than necessary."

All of these unpleasantnesses had occurred in and around New York, reputedly tolerant of diverse thought and mingled ethnic strains. But the Jews, apparently, had become numerous and important enough in the city to stop being thought a curiosity and to assume their immemorial function as plump scapegoat. I did not like the whiff of it. I had also begun to feel cramped in our small flat and on those narrow streets. Since my hormones were racing now as well, I read through the papers hungrily in search of a new horizon. It took no Columbus to discover it.

The last federal troops had evacuated the South that year as part of the bargain struck in the election of President Hayes, and a genuine reconciliation between the regions appeared to be in the making. I was both drawn to and repelled by that kingdom of cotton, magnolia, and charred porticos gone to weed. The gallantry it had exhibited in defending its cursed way of life was already legendary. And Jews, I knew, had been prominent in the former Confederate states, prospering as planters, brokers, merchants, and statesmen, doughty Judah Benjamin of Louisiana the most noted of them. The lush, jewel-like aspect of the land itself, the more I read of it, also worked its seductive appeal upon me: all that sun and sky, all those gurgling freshets and green leaves springing from the earth, and the people, thriving among the elements, living a heartier, more nourishing life than seemed available on or off the stale, crowded streets to which I had been confined. And yet—it was these selfsame, swaggering, slave-flogging sons of bitches that had put my father in the ground. They had to answer for that. Somehow, though, to me they were not the enemy camp, not still. For their overbearing, over-reaching manner they had been smitten, and I nearly sympathized with their struggle to reassemble the pieces. With the exodus of the Union army and its camp followers, opportunity would abound now in Dixie for a dutiful, personable young man "of the Jewish persuasion"—or any other. So I told myself.

My mother's predictable opposition to the scheme was blunted by my enthusiasm and, more, by my pledge to send home every extra penny to help pay for Benny's higher education. He would enter the medical college at the University of Pennsylvania the following fall, and it was agreed that he should not dissipate his energy, and imperil his future, by having to hold down a job while pursuing such an arduous course of study. That autumn and winter, I took every sort of odd job available so that I might become self-sufficient when I resettled; what spare time I could manage was spent in the library, reading up on the South and trying to select the most promising territory for my great expedition. A port would be most desirable, I calculated, because of the mercantile activity that could be expected to grow rapidly now throughout the demilitarized region. Charleston, from what I read, had been too devastated by the war and also lacked extensive rail connections. New Orleans was too large and too far away. Memphis had appeal but seemed more a way station than a depot and too raucous by half. But Savannah—Savannah was not too big and not too small, was ideally situated to serve as turnstile and *entrepôt* for the imminent economic renaissance of the southeastern states, and, from the accounts I had read of Sherman's rapine, had survived occupation with its charm relatively intact. A Jewish congregation, I learned, moreover, had existed there since the founding of Georgia, and the first white child to be born in the colony was recorded as an Isaelite.

My mother, Benny, and decrepit Grandpa (who had moved in with them in my place and contributed his previous rent money toward Benny's schooling) saw me off on the boat. I wore my only suit, a gray flannel outfit guaranteed to promote sunstroke but rated very practical until I might afford something a bit more tropical, and a tweed cap that my grandfather had fashioned for me himself. "Inside out," he said with a twinkle, "it makes into a *yarmulke*. It will be the only one in town, you'll see." Then my mother placed father's Congressional Medal into my palm, locked my fingers around it, and said, "Never lose it—or yourself." She refused to cry. I had less luck, and brother Benny altogether dissolved in tears as he hugged me mightily. I turned, hoisted my Gladstone bag (for ballast it held a Bible, a copy of *Great Expectations* that Benny had bought me in a burst of drollery, and Mrs. Trollope's *Domestic Manners of the Americans*, which I judged a sound investment), and hurried up the gangplank. I had never been south of the Battery before.

TWO

Our ship, the *Oglethorpe III* (the first had perished trying to run a Union blockade, the second from fire five years later), offered three declarative blasts of its whistle and subsided. A line of hansoms awaited us at quayside, but my budget provided for no such luxury. I set out on foot for a rooming house recommended to me by the first mate, a kindly disposed fellow with whom I had grown acquainted on shipboard. Half the young people in the nation, to hear him tell it, were on the move, exploring, go-getting, or simply afflicted with the wanderlust. Apprehensive and lonely, I drew comfort from what he said and felt myself part of a mighty trek into the thrilling but (there could be no doubt) ultimately rewarding unknown. My head was high as I came off the gangplank and, as a result, nearly tripped over a wayward rope.

The street was awash with veritable drifts of sand, through which I had persevered no more than a few dozen feet when a black boy of perhaps twelve whirled out of the thinning crowd and reached for my bag with a hopeful "Porter, suh?" I drew back at once, and he did the same. I told him I had no money for that, and he said, "That ain't no-never-mind," and relieved me of the bag anyway. Would he dart away now as quickly as he had come upon me? He would find me a swift pursuer. But flight was plainly not on his mind as he bobbed alongside me, and I marveled at the merest outcropping of fuzz on his head—a cooling tonsure, no doubt. I asked him if he knew where the Belleport Arms rooming house was. He looked uncertain. "Habersham Street and Jones," I offered, and he nodded and swung our line of march to the left. We dodged among the lumbering drays, vehicles unfamiliar to me with their two low wheels, wide tires, and heavy iron axle drawn by a brace of mules that struggled through the sand under a load that had to be a ton or more. I remarked to my guide that the animals seemed to be bearing a remarkably large burden. "That's what they was born fo'," he said. So much for Yankee sentimentality.

We moved up the cobbled ramp that led to Factors' Row, the brick buildings packed together along the top of the bluff where most of the brokerage and warehousing of Georgia cotton was managed, and crossed Bay Street, aswirl with a minor sandstorm of its own. A horse-drawn sprinkler down the block was trying to combat the dust—a welcome if plainly inadequate sign of high civic intentions. I asked my colored companion what his name was and, without frown or smirk, he told me Plato. I thought that entirely hilarious but had the presence not to let on. Then I told him my name and he let out a joyful bray. "Seth!" he piped it. "Sounds like it goes with a girl." He laughed again and then must have noticed that I did not share his amusement. "Ver' nice name, though," he offered tactfully and proceeded to lecture me on who, more or less, the original Plato had been.

My friend was by no means entirely misnamed. Indeed he proved an encyclopedic guide to the local flora, much of which was unknown to me, while we passed through the progression of parks and gardened squares that were the glory of the city. I asked after and learned the names of all the trees—sweet bay and holly and mimosa, laurel and ginkgo and pecan. The Judas trees were frothy with pink-purple blossoms against their heart-shaped leaves. And the lilac-budded shade trees marching in pairs down either side of South Broad Street threw off a remarkably pungent perfume. "Those ones're chinaberries," said Plato. "Dey keep de pluffers poppin'." I looked puzzled. He explained that in a few weeks the chinaberries would be out—green and longish and about the size of a cherry and, when half-ripe, the perfect ammunition for bamboo popguns, known locally as "pluffers," that boys fired off at one other at a distance of thirty or forty feet with a sound as explosive as the report of a small pistol. The effect, as near as I could make out, was achieved by compressed air. Plato left me in no doubt, though, that he was a nonpareil among plufferers.

The houses fringing the wooded and meadowed squares were stately without proclaiming haughtiness, and even the less grand quarters bespoke quality, with their trim little gardens of oleander and plumbago and sweet viburnum behind low brick walls that invited rather than forbade the wayfarer's glance. Many of the homes, otherwise clean and stark in their lines, dressed up in a flourish of lacy grillwork, of the sort I had seen in Gramercy Park. But here the sinuous metal was alive with creeper and wisteria and bright golden masses of jessamine. All together it was a festival for the senses.

Plato left me at the front step of the rooming house. Though I had not bargained for it, I felt obliged to give him a ten-cent piece for his trouble, his company, and his knowledgeable introduction to my new surroundings. I said I hoped we might meet again; he settled for the coin.

The Belleport Arms proved a trifle ramshackle but a definite value. For two dollars and a quarter a week, payable in advance, I had myself a small but snug enough room, with a big window and shade, a serviceable wicker rocking chair, and easy access to the washstand and bath. The privy was out in the rear. The rent covered coffee and rolls for breakfast and a full supper every evening at six. The landlady, whose face looked a bleached white beneath a headful of hennaed curls, was entirely cordial, inquired not at all beyond the minimal civilities, and volunteered only, appraising my wool outfit, "You'll be a mite hot in those, I expect."

I left my jacket in the room, opened my collar, rolled up my sleeves, and set out to roam the city from end to end. That I could in fact do this on foot was greatly satisfying, for it meant that the scale of the place was not overwhelming and that there was pleasing proportion among its human, vegetative, and inanimate elements, which all fell together in a natural symmetry. It made me feel far less a stranger as I wandered this fragrant arbor of a city.

Only the churches intimidated me. They were so numerous and imposing. The Georgian steeple of the Independent Presbyterian, commanding the intersection of Bull Street and Oglethorpe Avenue, pointed so insistently to heaven that my jaw unhinged in awe of it. In New York, such a building would have been too hemmed in to exert its full spell. The First Baptist on Chippewa Square and the far grander Christ Episcopal on Johnson Square were in the Greek revival mode and therefore, to me, a good deal less menacing by their very invocation of a pre-Christian paganism. But the Lutherans' solid stone Church of the Ascension in Wright Square, with its massive Romanesque doors and windows, seemed at once a bulwark against heathenism and a warning to all infidels. And on Lafayette Square, quite the most enormous structure that I had seen in all of Savannah immobilized me—the splendid Cathedral of St. John the Baptist, of French Gothic grace and elaboration, with a large, lush rose window and twin steeples almost fanciful in their adornments: it struck me as having been assembled in monumental tribute to sanctity in general rather than in adoration of Christ in particular. Still, the collective weight on me of all these lovely temples to Jesus had a demoralizing impact. If Christ were not in truth the son of God, why all the bother? Would the Lord have permitted such a lavish expenditure of masonry to perpetuate so impious a hoax?

It was thus with some relief that, on entering Monterey Square, I discovered the cream-colored, stucco structure on the east side that I took at first for yet another church but proved, on inspection, to be the brand-new home of Congregation Mickve Israel— "the gathering of the Israelites." From a workman oiling the hinges on the Gothic front doorway I learned that the synagogue was to be consecrated that very evening. I had arrived just in time to play Elijah.

After finishing my first supper on Southern soil, I had a redemptive, as well as celebrative, purpose for hastening to the new synagogue. For the first time in my life, I had partaken of the forbidden flesh of swine—a great thick gray-pink slab of baked ham, redolent of molasses and ginger, and surrounded but not destigmatized by sugared yams, okra fritters, tomatoes, and bell peppers. To compound the felony, the meal began with bisque of the *verboten* oyster and flaky cheese biscuits and concluded with jam cakes and blazing hot coffee. I was so shriven with guilt at having variously defied the mandates of *kashruth* at the first opportunity that I tried to ignore the thrilling message from my

25

taste buds. But they kept sending it. They said: this is the most thoroughly delicious meal you have ever eaten. The ham and bisque especially. Yet how could that be? Perhaps it was just a sugar-coated ruse, for why should the Lord our God deny to the mouths of His chosen people such succulence?

It was not, of course, a question that sprang at me totally unexpected. We had often considered it in our home. Why, Benny and I would ask our mother and especially grandfather, did chickens and goats, as filthy beasts as lived on the earth, qualify as *kosher* while cats and dogs and eagles and lions did not? Grandpa was not sure but he conjectured in stimulating ways. Dogs and cats were too familiar to human beings, he guessed, and eating them would be close to cannibalism. And taste bad, too. Eagles and lions were notoriously rapacious, a trait that would perhaps transmit itself through their flesh to any who feasted on it and turn them into predators. Of pigs, though, he spoke with authority: "You will die from eating them," he said flatly. "They are infested with vermin and *dreck*. The Torah knows what it is talking about." Benny, being of a more scientific bent than Grandpa, did some medical research on the question and, to our surprise, corroborated more than a little of the old man's warning. Trichina, Benny reported, had been discovered in a London dissecting room some forty years earlier by a surgeon who noticed that minute granules in the muscle tissue he was attacking dulled the edge of his scalpel. Investigation disclosed the coiled worms within each abrasive cyst; breeding in the intestines, they produced symptoms often mistaken for, variously, cholera, typhoid, and rheumatism. Principal carriers, it had been conclusively demonstrated, were rats and pigs. In the latter, the parasite often survived mere smoking and pickling; only a thorough cooking would render it harmless. "And where you're going," Benny added helpfully as my departure for Savannah neared, "they hold a match over the pork for eight seconds and then gobble it down with a pitcher of warm hog's blood. I don't see how you'll survive a month."

But since it was evident that pig-eaters the world over had got on well enough for ages (though at what sacrifice to their life expectancy we can never know), I resolved that I would avoid pig-meat when possible but not starve myself when there was no ready alternative. Surely God would understand. If not, perhaps on arising I would find a koshered chicken under my pillow every *yontif* as a divine sign. Having now committed the unthinkable transgression, however, I was less glib and hurried to the little Jewish basilica to save my sated soul from purgatory.

II

It was not the first church-like synagogue I had seen. Temple Emanu-El, whose membership included the likes of the Seligmans and other families of wealth and power, had opened on New York's Fifth Avenue when I was nine. While its façade had a nonsectarian Moorish look, its interior, I had been told, with its formal pews and pulpit and chandeliers, made it seem very like a cathedral. Families, moreover, sat together, the men hatless and the women bonneted and sitting beside them instead of segregated behind a curtain or in a balcony as was the custom in orthodox *schuls* the world over. But I had never gone inside Emanu-El to look for myself, partly for fear of being thought a gawker or a social-climber, partly out of suspicion that the *shammus* would grab me from behind and make a genuflect midway down the center aisle.

I did not hesitate now at the threshold of Mickve Israel. To do so would have invited being trampled. Every professing Jew between Factors' Row and the Okefenokee apparently wanted to be on hand for the dedication of the new home of Georgia's oldest synagogue. All the seats were taken, and in the excitement nobody noticed a lone newcomer in his heavy gray suit; he, in the farthest corner, was just as pleased.

The sights and sounds of worship here were so different from those I grew up with that I had to keep reminding myself that these were in fact rituals of my tribe, Southern division. The Gothic superstructure, the pointless transept like little wings on a milk-cow, the absence of skullcaps and *tallises*, the stained-glass windows above the altar depicting the harp of David, the *shofar* of the High Holy Days, and a pair of prayerfully uplifted hands— all that strangeness proved mere backdrop once the service itself began and seemed even less Jewish. The organ, which I had never heard in a temple before, was a mind-drenching marvel of sound,

27

swooping from dirge to crescendo in one swift pneumatic flight that prevented all possibility of meditation. Many of the prayers were offered in English, a clear gain in comprehension so far as I was concerned, though I suspected that God would mark us off for not troubling to use His language. And what Hebrew remained in the service was pronounced with a decidedly non-Ashkenazic intonation and cadence. Most striking of all to me, though, was the decorum maintained throughout the worship. The synagogues I had attended always throbbed with an undertow of noise and disorder: the congregation materialized by degrees, clusters arriving as long as half an hour or more after the *davening* began; people floated in and out during the service as whim moved them, they buzzed to their seated neighbors during the endless reading from the Torah, they participated in the responsive reading at their own pace, so that a dissonant drone seemed to prevail at all times, especially when the liturgy called for prayer in unison. But here in Savannah, everyone arrived on time, stayed seated, prayed instead of chatting, responded on cue and decipherably, and gave thanks because, among their other blessings, the service did not last forever. Again, I approved. But reflecting on my supper ham and oyster bisque, I wondered if I were not being too silkily seduced and whether this agreeable, streamlined, Anglicized form of Judaism was really official.

The rabbi must have read my mind. His remarks on that memorable occasion have remained with me since, and they strike me now as when I first heard them as a compelling ode on the pleasing dilemma of the Jew in America. I do not call him the American Jew, or the Jewish American, for those terms, given the primacy of nouns over their modifiers, suggest that either faith or nation is the predominating force in one's life, whereas I have become convinced that it is the interplay between the two—the temporal and the timeless—that shapes us. In the case of the Jews for the past several millennia, however, there was no interplay, only eternal vigilance, for there was no nation, before America, that granted them something more than asylum and extended to them full and enduring membership in all its pursuits.

It was not so in the American beginning, Rabbi Mendes reminded us. Just as Peter Stuyvesant had scorned the first boatload of Jewish refugees from formerly Dutch Brazil who sought a home in New Amsterdam in the middle of the seventeenth century, so the first Jews sailing for Georgia were nearly refused entry. The group of London investors who had financed the 1733 expedition of Colonel James Oglethorpe to create a buffer colony between the Carolinas and Spanish Florida peopled by debtors, ne'er-do-wells, and the other available flotsam of the realm (of whom convicts and past convicts formed the merest handful, legend to the contrary notwithstanding) had not bargained on a boatload of Jews, financed by the London Sephardic community, arriving at Savannah just five months later. So large an infusion of Semitic character, the trustees stated in their official proceedings, "may be of ill consequence to the Colony." Governor Oglethorpe had a problem—in the form of a floating community of Jews—on his hands. Faced at the same moment with a raging malaria epidemic, he welcomed the news that among the Jewish arrivals in the harbor was a Dr. Núñez and invited the healer alone to come ashore. Whether the fate of those waiting on shipboard was to depend on the efficacy of the doctor's skill is unclear; what is not is that Dr. Núñez told Oglethorpe that the colony could receive all the Jews or none. It took them all. The trustees back in London, upon learning that the governor's humane choice was a *fait accompli*, still hoped to minimize this pollution of Hebrews: the good doctor Núñez, they wrote, was to be recompensed for his troubles but under no circumstances were he or his unsavory co-religionists to be allotted free the good Christian earth of the new colony in the manner that it had been to the other settlers. Interpreting his instructions somewhat loosely, Oglethorpe sold for a modest sum rather than gave the Jews their land. But to be able to buy land of their own, even when others received it gratis, was a large improvement over their few and fugitive rights in the Old World—and so in rapid order Jewish farms were blooming in Georgia. Several of those earliest arrivals flourished as vintners. Mickve Israel was founded the following year.

Ever since, the standing of the Jews in Savannah, observed the rabbi, had been relatively secure, flowing and ebbing with the fortunes of the population as a whole. Early setbacks led to heavy emigration to Charleston, site of the largest concentration of Jews in the colonial era. During the Revolution, Georgia Jews were strong for independence, the Sheftall family played a particularly heroic part, and Benjamin Nones won glory by leading the French through the woods to relieve the siege of Savannah. Her Jews stayed loyal to the South during the tribulations of civil war, and in the ensuing, painful period of so-called reconstruction, the Jews of Savannah had risen to positions of substantial respectability in the commercial and civic life of the port.

"On what spot in this habitable globe," exuded the rabbi upon concluding this chronicle, "does an Israelite enjoy more blessings or more privileges, is he more elevated in the sphere of preferment or more conspicuously dignified in eminent stations? Have we not ample cause to exult, with hearts full of gratitude to Him who rules the destinies of man and forgets not the children of misfortune?" Indeed, remarked the rabbi a trifle archly, the lone thorn still afflicting the congregation was not rancor between Jew and non-Jew but the remnants of enmity between Jews of Portuguese and Spanish extraction and those from Germany. The former had viewed themselves, from the establishment of the congregation, as the more venerable and cultivated; the latter proclaimed themselves more pious and faithful upholders of Torah and the protocols of the prophets. "The time has long since passed when such displays of pride and prejudice can be countenanced between us," the rabbi called out with prosecutorial vigor, and heads nodded all about me in assent. "Installed now in this splendid new house of worship, we might pause a moment to reflect not upon what drives us apart as Jews but upon what binds us together—just as we ought to dwell upon what brings us closer to our tribe of fellow Americans rather than what distinguishes us from them. These twin conceptions can, I believe, be fruitfully explored in tandem. And the exploration can begin, I submit, by considering the question that a number of our congregants have put to me. 'Why is it, rabbi,' they have asked me, 'that our new synagogue more nearly resembles a church than any temple we have ever seen?' I would begin my answer by saying it is because nowhere else and at no other time have the Jews so nearly resembled, in every facet of their lives, the rest of their society. The essence of the American people, my friends, is to be found in that marriage of idealism and practicality that every Jew is born with—or else risks early extinction. Has there ever been a people more industrious yet more given to laughter, more stubborn or tougher-minded yet more prone to attacks of sentiment, than the people of America—or the Jews throughout history? Just as the American system of government functions to provide maximum liberty and mobility to each of our citizens, so does Judaism grant the most generous license to each of its adherents. It has been well said that every Jew, spiritually if not literally, is in business for himself. So, too, every American. In return for this unexampled portion of freedom, our nation and our faith both ask in return only that each of us in our own way pursue justice for all men and righteousness in every heart."

I thought that fine, even thrilling. But what were we to do about Jesus? True, the American government had not mandated a state religion, even shrank from the very concept, but had there been one, its emblem would assuredly have been the crucifix and not the seal of Solomon. "I do not argue, my friends, that Jewish and non-Jewish Americans are therefore indistinguishable," said the rabbi, anticipating me. "I suggest, rather, that the distinctions are of less account than the similarities—and that Jews have flourished on these golden shores precisely because of that alikeness. Here we have never been confined to the *Judenstrasse*, forced to rummage in old tomes for promises of eternal redemption on Judgment Day. Here we live in the open, we live in the present, participating fully and proudly. Is it not thus to our interest, I propose it to you, that we conduct our lives and our worship in a manner least calculated to offend our neighbors? Was ever a proposition founded more equitably on self-advantage and consideration of others? At once, some of you will ask, 'But, rabbi, surely you do not suggest that we barter our souls merely to seem companionable?' And surely I do not. I suggest instead that we need not cling to outmoded ritual in the mistaken notion that it is the form and not the substance of our faith that establishes our singularity. Times change, and Judaism to survive through so many long, dark centuries had had to be flexible as well as constant."

Ah! Sublime unguent for a scorched conscience. I walked slowly back to the rooming house, lost amid the trees and vines and shrubs that looked so silvery and fey now under a full moon. It was good that I had come here. A whole new world was unfurling for me. I wondered if God, blessing as He did a resilient Judaism, and (it followed) protean Jews, would present me overnight with a Southern dialect. It would make things ever so much simpler.

III

That first Saturday and Sunday I set aside for acclimatizing myself to my new, lustrous, and powerfully disorienting surroundings. On Monday I would seek work in earnest. The weekend was for browsing, chatting with whomever I might, reconnoitering. Saturday I lingered mostly about Factors' Row and the iron walkways connecting it to Bay Street—clearly the nerve center of the community—to sop up whatever I could among the topics of pressing local concern. The most edifying of these proved to be speculation on the current level of bawdy activity at the Pulaski House, where the long, dark private rooms once catered to planters, in town for a day or night, or both, of carousing, but were now given over to the humbler activities of card sharps, sporting women, and transients either seeking to patronize the other two sorts or blissfully ignorant of their presence on the premises; it was not, at any rate, where I would first apply for work.

Sunday was preternaturally quiet save for the caroling of the ubiquitous church bells. I found myself sauntering south under the lethal chinaberry trees arcading East Broad. Without destination I swung east through the Yamacraw section and out along the road toward the little settlement of Thunderbolt on the Wilmington River, a lethargic branch of the Savannah. The houses thinned, and farms fanned out on all sides. The road rose and then dipped beside a small hollow. Shouts rang out from the far end, where a clump of shacks clung to a knoll above the meadowed field. Nearing it, I made out the scampering forms of boys at play. Of varying sizes but all barefoot, with their denim trousers rolled up to not much below the knee, they were joined in a recognizable variation of baseball. The four bases defined the playing field unmistakably, but there were only six to a side—pitcher, catcher, and four highly maneuverable fielders—and the bat, three or four inches wide and perhaps two inches thick, seemed more a paddle with a handle notched out of the bottom than the round stick I had known in my New York playing career. The ball, of rubber and about the size of a small orange, was friskier than the sodden leather ovals I was used to, and the rules here seemed to provide that the batsman was counted out if his hit was fielded on the fly or one bounce or, failing that, the base was tagged with the ball before he arrived at it or, more treacherous, a fielder hit him directly with the ball while he was en route. One of the small group of spectators lolling beneath a live oak told me it was called townball.

Aside from an occasional squall of protest over a close decision at one of the bases, the game proceeded in good order, thanks mainly to the sandy-haired beanpole who pitched for both sides with faithful impartiality. Perhaps a few inches over six feet, he was a perpetual windmill of arms and legs who appeared to take as much pleasure from a good poke off one of his deliveries as from a slick play in the field behind him. In the peppery, occasionally truculent chatter among the players that ceased only when the ball was struck, the fielders call the pitcher "Billygoat," or so it sounded, and urged him to throw with more speed or deception. Occasionally he responded by whistling one in at high velocity and leaving the batter baffled. But his chief concern was to keep the contest close and moving, and all the action proceeded to his steady rhythm. There was animation in that angular face of his, flushed from fluid exertion, and his eyes seemed to glint shrewdly in sizing up each of his ten rotating opponents. It was as if they were his playthings, and he were toying with them but not unkindly. I wondered what there was goat-like about this lanky, tousle-headed fellow who appeared to be about my age and was the very picture of what my grandfather Harry called a *langer loksch*.

Several innings after my arrival, one of the players tripped over the jute bagging that served as third base and gave his ankle a nasty sprain. Billygoat scanned the sidelines, spotted my city pants, and looked elsewhere for a substitute. The rest of the onlookers were either too old or too dark, and his eyes came back finally to me. "Y'wanna?" he asked. I stood there paralyzed. "C'mon," the tall boy urged, "it's only fo' one inning. But just roll up them bloomers." A brief chorus of hee-haws went up behind him. A hundred excuses sprang to my tongue—I had never played this game, I had no other clothes, I would slip playing barefoot, I was from New York, I was Jewish, I was occasionally troubled by asthma—but none was utterable. In a trance I took off my shoes and socks, folded up my trouser legs, and with eyes groundward and heart percussive, headed for the injured boy's place in the field when the sides changed. I came within a few feet of the pitcher and ventured a sideways glance at him. "You a Yankee?" he asked, more curious than hostile. "Sort of," I said with a dry throat and kept moving. His eyes followed me to the fielding spot between second and third base. "The ball don't bounce any different here," he said with the trace of a smile. "We jes' play meaner—sort of." He managed to cheer and mock me in almost the same breath.

The first batter nearly tore my hands off with a line drive—no one played with gloves in that day and age, of course—that I managed at least to knock down. The ball was rock-hard and stung awfully. I would have to learn how to cushion its arrival and not present myself as an irresistible target. The next batter sent a drive well into the outfield, and when I moved out a ways to receive the relay throw, the runner from first came tearing by and gave my hip a swipe that sent me sprawling. My trousers were now embossed with a green streak. Two batters later I dashed to my left to stop a smoking grounder and began to toss it to the second baseman for the force-out, but the lad was gathering daisies in right field. My duty was plainly to hurl the ball at the incoming runner—only my hand flinched and the ball stayed tight in it. "You gotta wing it, Yank," Billygoat said calmly as I returned the ball. "Worst you kin do is kill 'im." It did not come out sounding exactly savage but his message was nonetheless forceful. At my next opportunity, I let fire with full power, but some residue of charity must have cramped my muscle tissue, for the ball flew wildly past the diving runner, bounded into the outfield, and allowed two more runs to come home. Out of the corner of my eye I saw Billygoat messing with the pitcher's slab and shaking his head in disbelief while the ball was being fetched. Unnerved by the time my side finally straggled from the field, I vowed to redeem myself at bat.

Though it was about the same length as the ones I had played with, this flat paddle of a bat had neither their compact heft nor the whip-like torque. I waggled the chunk of lumber as menacingly as I could manage as Billygoat went into his fanciest windup and sent the first pitch sizzling in at me. I flailed hopelessly late at it and must have missed it by a foot. My ears were reddening now. I held the bat back as far as I could and brought it lashing forward more quickly on the second pitch, driving the ball foul well past third base and leaving my hands with as painful a sting as I had ever suffered. Play stopped for a moment while I hurriedly tried to rub life back into my numbed fingers. I spied a smirk of contempt—or was it plain pleasure?—over my discomfort on Billygoat's face as I stepped back in and tried to check my rising dander. The best I could manage on the third pitch was to chip the ball over toward the second baseman, who promptly sent it whistling at my head. I turned aside at the last instant and thereby limited the damage to a mildly bloody nose.

Despite my negative contribution, our side rallied, and I came to bat again that final inning. The flow from my nose had not altogether stopped and my hands still hurt, but I spit into my palms, rubbed the saliva in well for its full healing power, and seized up the war club with renewed determination. The first two pitchs were temptingly slow but far off the plate. Billygoat's third pitch, though, I smacked squarely on a rising line to dead center field. By the time it was recovered I had come scorching into third base, earning an immense cheer and a symmetrically scraped shin for my effort. My teammates were whooping now on the sidelines, yelling that I represented the winning run. The catcher, a fat boy wearing a cheerless black wool hat, glared down the baseline at me, as if daring me to confront him. The challenge was not long in developing. The next batter grounded to the first baseman. I took off the moment the ball hit the field. That black hat on that moonface loomed larger and larger as I hurtled toward home with the ball in flashing pursuit. The moment of collision sent a flame of pain into my midsection as the two of us went tumbling to the earth in a furious clench while the ball skipped harmlessly by. I lay there gasping for breath as my teammates piled onto the catcher, who, unable to prevent my scoring, had settled for delivering a massive blow to my solar plexus. When the dust settled, we had won the game—the score was on the order of 28 to 27—and my left trouser leg was shredded from groin to heel. The pain I felt all over was incidental.

The players soon scattered, and I was left a bloody, tattered mess, cursing myself for having submitted to such foolhardy mayhem. Behind me then I heard that gently mocking voice of the pitcher: "You sure look a fright, Mr. Yankee Doodle. If everyone up North bled so easy, we'd still be fightin' the war." Then he offered a wide warm smile, said he admired the pluck if not the skill I had shown, and asked if I wanted to fix up and maybe have a root beer at his uncle's store over on the knoll above the field. I accepted gratefully. It proved the most fateful meeting of my life.

His name was William Doak Baxter—Billy Doak they all called him, not "Billygoat" as my ears had registered it—and he lived in Savannah, he said, on East St. Julian Street just off Warren Square. When I told him I was brand new to the city and did not know that section, he asked unhesitatingly if his family might have the pleasure of my company for Sunday supper—unless of course I had a previous engagement. The spontaneity of his invitation flustered me, and I suggested as nimbly as I could that perhaps he ought to consult at home first in case my coming might disrupt his family's plans. "Hell, no," he said. "Sunday's kind of a potluck open house—folks're always driftin' in on accounta my Uncle Gus. He comes by every Sunday 'n' attracts more acquaintances than molasses draws flies."

It was Uncle Gus's store we had repaired to, Billy Doak explained, unlatching the side door and urging me inside. "He's got a whole string of 'em out 'n' around the county an' keeps 'em all supplied from his main establishment down on Bay Street— maybe you saw it? The Adelphi, he calls it—that means 'the brothers' in Greek, only he's got no brother, leastways no live one. The one he had died young before the war, so when Uncle Gus went into the merchant business later, he named his place as if there were still two of 'em—like kind of a tribute, y'know?" He handed me a small earthenware bowl and a towel and led me around to the cistern to wash up. He was at home here, Billy Doak said, because he worked at the store every Saturday, when things were busiest, and brought the weekly receipts into town at the close of business, saving the store manager the trip. He liked this section so much that he made a point of coming out to play ball on Sundays after church. "Y' get to know the customers better that way, too," he said, splashing two handfuls of rainwater into his face and drying it briskly.

He was so friendly and open that I was attracted to him from the start. There was a robust directness to his manner—I caught no trace of condescension—and his clean, manly good looks (aside from those strange pale green eyes that lent a spot of softness to an otherwise sharply planed set of features) added to his appeal. He gave off an air of confidence and competence, here as on the ball field. I asked if he was planning on a career as a merchant. He shrugged and pondered a moment, then finally said, "I'm fixed to go up to Virginia, come autumn—the university at Charlottesville, y' know?—to see what kinda head I got for studies—for *real* studies, I mean, not the sorta diddlyshit learnin' y' get down home here. Uncle Gus, he's a university man himself, though you wouldn't hardly know it—he went up to Athens before the war, only he says Virginia's the best school in the South an' aspirin' young men like myself oughta aim high." He looked at me earnestly for a second. "Between you, me an' the hitchin' post, I don't cotton to studyin' my eyes out—it hurts yo' pitchin' arm, don'cha know?" he said, and gave me a hearty rap on the shoulder. "Say, now, let's get you fixed up with some new drawers." I told him I couldn't afford anything fancy. He said, "That's the only kind we got—unfancy. Here, try these—I'm gettin' pretty good at guessin' sizes." He leaned against the counter and watched with clinical detachment as I lowered my shredded trousers without hesitation and reached for the brown jeans he offered. "Hell, you sure are a bony cuss," he said with mirth. "Those may droop a little, first off." But they proved a decent enough fit, if a bit congested in the crotch. "Wrench yo' pecka' right off if y' move too fast." He laughed and turned to get us each a bottle of Hires from a cool spot in the storage room.

On the trip back to Savannah, he showed me how to drive his family's gleaming black buckboard, asked about living in "a big ol' town" like New York, and wondered why I had come to Savannah, of all places, to find my fortune. "All the money's up where you left," he said. I told him that I had studied up and figured that the tide was due to shift, now that the army had moved out. "Uncle Gus'll be mighty pleased to hear that," he said. "He's reckonin' the very same way."

Uncle Gus, as it developed, was stricken with the catarrh this Sunday, and so the Baxter residence, a snug brick home with a touch of Georgian trim, was quiet as the rig turned into their narrow street. East St. Julian was distinguished from every other thoroughfare I had seen in Savannah by its surface of oyster shells—the handiwork, no doubt, of the resident bivalve king of a bygone era. Our noisy arrival produced a stirring on the porch. A girl with long, straight, chestnut hair bobbed up from her chair, saw there was company, and came skittering down the front steps in greeting. She wore a white blouse and lavender petticoat and moved with the same easy gait as Billy Doak. "That's Mandy," he said, "My lovin' baby sister." He meant the baby part as a joke, for she was clearly in the fresh bloom of early womanhood. "Mandy," he said as we climbed off the buckboard, "I have the pleasure of presentin' Mr. Seth Adler, a new arrival from the city of New York. Mr. Adler, this is the fair Amanda Lizabeth Baxter—and don't take t' heart anythin' she says that sounds tetched on accounta her havin' delusions of grandeur."

Amanda performed a demure curtsy and took in my face and form in a sly glance. "Mr. Seth Adler," she said with eyes averted and cotillion correctness but a tinge of self-mockery, "you are welcome to the proud Southland, and you are doubly welcome to fragrant Savannah, the belle of Dixie. And you are most especially welcome to Jubilation, our humble yet thoroughly respectable hermitage—."

"I wish t' Christ you'd stop callin' it that," her brother said. "Yo' cain't have yo'self a hermitage smack in the midst of a city, Miss Bubblebrain—."

"I am sure Mr. Seth Adler understood that I meant it only in a whimsical manner o' speakin'," she said icily, looking more at me than Billy but mostly at an audience she evidently imagined in attendance behind the bushes. "My brother, while possessed of a certain exterior charm, suffers from vulgarity of language and habitual rudeness toward his sister, who he wishes would merely flutter her fan in abject silence when confronted with guests of his acquaintance. It's no doubt a stage he's goin' through which we all hope will prove mercifully short-lived." With barely a pause, she skipped from scorn to tease, and from Billy to me as her target. "I had no i-dea, Mr. Adler, that folks in New York wore jeans just like the farm fashion 'round here. Or has Billy Doak been outfittin' you special on the Lord's day?"

Billy held up my torn gray city trousers. "Mr. Adler met misfortune on the ball field," he said. "Can we get Abigail to sew 'em?"

"Looks as if yo' mighty strenuous in taking exercise, Mr. Adler," she said, with half-smile, half-rebuke. "You'll have t' adjust to our leisurely ways."

She was quite the most scintillating, self-possessed young woman I had ever beheld. I was not at all certain whether I would have preferred to embrace her fiercely on the spot or deliver her a swift kick in the seat. She was by no means a rare beauty—the nose was a bit excessive, the chin a mite deficient, the mouth too bold and mobile—yet her vivacity gave one little chance to assess her looks in repose. Her brother was the handsomer of the pair. "I shall do my level best, Miss Baxter," I said, trying to attune to her embroidered phrasing.

"No doubt," she said, in apparent relief that I at least had a tongue. "And do, by all means, avoid the summer sun at its beastliest." She turned to her brother. "Abby and mother are thoroughly occupied with supper. Suppose I have a stab at repairing Mr. Adler's damage—?" She reached to take my trousers from Billy. "I've become a passably accomplished seamstress, mother says."

Her brother drew back. "A man's trousers are a highly intimate garment," he told her sternly. "Young women of character—not to mention virtue—ought not to be on familiar terms with such articles."

"Pishtush," she said back. "It's just old cloth—and good Rebel gray at that. When a guest has an emergency, hospitable folk are obliged to ease his distress and not stand on idle ceremony." With that, she snatched the trousers from her astonished brother's hand and skedaddled inside the house, not to reappear until supper.

"A perfect hellion," said Billy Doak toward her vanished wake. "I adore her."

We pitched horseshoes out back while I was offered a synopsis of the recent Baxter family chronicles, narrated with both affection and dispassion. Travail, tragedy, and lately triumph had been their lot for the past twenty years. Before the war, Zebulon Augustus Griffin—Uncle Gus—and his brother Samson reigned over a fourteen-hundred-acre realm known far and wide as Felicity Farm, twenty miles out of Savannah on the western edge of Chatham County along the Ogeechee River. When Sam succumbed to snakebite, the grief-stricken Gus pined for company. Fortunately, his sister Evelyn had married a shrewd young Savannah importer of European finery named Damon Baxter, and the couple happily accepted Gus's invitation to move in at the plantation and help him run the enterprise. Since Gus was a resolute bachelor, devoted more to his hounds, corn whiskey, cotton, and slaves (in that order) than the rustling skirts of Georgia belledom, Evelyn Baxter became mistress of Felicity Farm, where she brought Billy Doak and Mandy into the world almost under the very guns of secession and rebellion. In the conflict, Gus did nobly as a cavalryman until his horse was shot out from under him at Chickamauga; in the fall, the rider's leg was shattered, reducing him to dependency ever after on a stout blackthorn cane. Damon Baxter, directing the Confederacy's covert supply operations in and out of Savannah harbor, was aboard a cargo ship bound for the Antilles when it was blown from the water by an iron-turreted Union warship. There were no survivors. To cap the nightmare, a column of Sherman's troopers left the main house at Felicity a charred husk on their atrocious route to the sea; only a few outbuildings remained habitable.

For a year after Appomattox, Gus Griffin drank himself into a hopeless stupor and his sister grew ever more desperate, watching her children run ragtag through weed-choked fields. Then one day she denounced Gus for his self-pity, grabbed up his blackthorn, and, wielding it like a shillelagh, drove a dozen bottles of bourbon—his entire remaining supply—off the sideboard. It was time to live again, she said. Gus never had another drop. Sober, he saw at once that profit was to be made not in a return to farming but in supplying the pitiful blacks and poor whites who sharecropped the land in fifty- or hundred-acre spreads. He raised cash by selling off half of Felicity, rented out the rest, then borrowed Evelyn's meager inheritance, and brought in supplies to furnish his penniless croppers, who clutched at any reed. By trickles, the cash collected, and Gus understood that he would prosper if he became his own supply merchant instead of paying exorbitant prices and torturous interest to Savannah operators. He rented a waterfront warehouse, began to buy in bulk for his own use, and opened little stores at dusty crossroads all over Chatham County. Everywhere, the land had been atomized, and demand grew for supplies in small quantities, readily available nearby. Nearby meant the distance a black errand boy could cover on muleback in an hour or two over those rutted back roads to nowhere. Gus became a deft manipulator of the notorious lien system, furnishing supplies on credit to the pauperized and ignorant dirt farmers of the region, who paid him dearly for the privilege and pledged him their whole harvest in the bargain. And the more cotton they all grew, the lower the price fell year by year. But the price of supplies and the rate of interest stayed high, and Gus Griffin battened on a countryside growing steadily poorer and malnourished. He, though, became rich, took up bachelor quarters with two in help at the fashionable Pavilion House in Savannah, and ran a veritable empire out of the Adelphi, his Bay Street headquarters. His sister, meanwhile, was able to buy a substantial home on St. Julian Street (which she puckishly named "Jubilation" in semi-mocking memory of the scattered family plantation) and raise her children as decent gentry.

"You ought to go see Uncle Gus tomorrow," said Billy Doak, concluding his account. "He's plenty ornery, but he's always on the lookout for a good man, which means anyone who don't favor liquor or use his fingers and toes to do the times tables."

"Uncle Gus," said Amanda, rejoining us in time to hear her brother's summation, "is a genuine ogre. He always reminds me of those peg-leg buccaneers who ruled the Spanish Main—he's so bold and prickly and merciless, and Lord, the way his eyes gleam! But he also happens to be a dear, generous prince when he chooses to be—and is quite devilishly handsome. Real villains never look like that—their souls are too full of barnacles and tarantulas and—an' heaven knows what else—." A frilly half-pirouette announced she was changing the subject and then, from hands clasped behind her back, she produced my trousers, re-sewn with a skill that had miraculously minimized the world's longest vertical scar. She held them up against her to display the handiwork. "Fit for the palace ball at Whitsuntide," she said, "or whenever they schedule those gaudy spectacles. They *are* a bit baggy and dusty, though, Mr. Adler, so as your self-appointed

costumer may I respectfully suggest you give them a good airin'
out and a thorough pressin' before attendin' the masked gala."

"I am truly and humbly grateful for your adroit effort, ma'am,"
I said.

"She ain't no 'ma'am,'" said Billy, still mildly peeved, "she's a
miss—and well on her way to a career as a public seamstress. Or
we may put her out to a spindle at the biggest, dreariest mill in
Augusta—if they'll have her."

"He knows my preferences in that regard perfectly well," said
Mandy with an artful leer at him. "They are, in order: parlor-
maid, milkmaid, and barmaid. The order, I confess, changes from
time to time. Billy Doak, however, believes I ought to confine my
energies to pickin' camellias, performin' the minuet, and braidin'
my silken hair. We petticoats, sir, are a delicate lot—."

Their edged banter dwindled during supper, a candlelight
buffet served prettily on a brick patio in the rear. Mother Baxter
radiant in yellow organdy, greeted me with just the right blend of
warmth and circumspection so I would not feel too much an intruder amid the dozen or so guests milling about in the gloaming.
Five or six small tables had been set out, but none of the adults
chose to join the one nearest the edge that the young Baxters had
reserved for their private guest and themselves. It was a thoroughly casual arrangement, and I was thus spared a series of formal introductions and probing interviews. Billy and Amanda took
turns drifting among the other tables with practiced ease but at
no point was I left unattended. Before the meal was done, Mandy
had uncovered, with ingenuous curiosity, surgically applied, the
prime features in my biography. The disclosure of my poverty reduced me to an object of merely ordinary intrigue in her eyes, although she professed high admiration for my boldness in having
traveled so far in my quest for the grail. The disclosure of my
religious faith, on the other hand, restored me to her realm of ex-
otica, and before long she was interrogating me as to whether the
tumbling of the walls at Jericho should be attributed more properly to Joshua's military prowess or divine intervention. Since the
Jews were widely held in disrepute as warriors, I offered in jest,
the latter was the more likely. I for one, I added, had never fired a
gun in my life.

They were both stunned at that revelation. "Oh, but it's grand fun!" said Mandy. "We'll have to teach you. Billy, why don't you take Mr. Adler down to Uncle Gus's at the first chance an' blast a few wolf rats out o' the feed sacks—?" Billy promised; I was enthusiastically non-committal. Of far more utility was their joint offer to teach me how to ride and groom a horse. "You won't survive a week 'less you 'tend to that," Mandy warned. It was agreed I would receive my first lesson the next day, right after visiting Uncle Gus to see about a job.

The North may have botched the reconstruction of the South, but the young Baxters, it seemed, were not above trying to turn the tables, beginning with the first pliable Yankee to wander into their net.

IV

The apple-red double doors and mullions on the front windows needed touching up, but the big overhead sign looked to have been freshly painted. "THE ADELPHI," said the bold, elongated capital letters, and underneath, "Dry Goods, Fancy Goods, Hardware, Seed & Grain, Groceries, Drugs, Medicines and Gents' Furnishings." And kitchen sinks, no doubt. All the way at the lower right in small letters you had nearly to squint at to make out, it said, "Z. Augustus Griffin, Prop." Uncle Gus's palace. I prayed the caliph's indisposition the day before had not carried over and left him in a foul humor.

The smell inside was overwhelming. It reeked of a dozen essences—kerosene, onions, new leather, tobacco, ripe cheese, shoe polish, linament, whiskey, soap, machine oil, pine tar, salted fish, all combined in one great organic miasma that you could have put a blade to. The customers, sweating and smoking and spitting and audibly passing wind, added to the indoor effluvium. Counters and shelves overflowed with goods arrayed in what struck me as a hopeless jumble, yet there seemed a purposeful flow to the traffickers who filled the aisles, pawing and sniffing every item. At the candy counter on the side wall, a small boy in overalls without a shirt had his arm elbow-deep in a jar of lemon zanzibars as I passed; he looked up guiltily, as if having maimed too many pieces in his search for the ideal one. At the back I told a clerk that I thought the proprietor was expecting me; in a moment he returned and ushered me to the open doorway at the far left corner of the seething establishment. Gus Griffin was seated at his desk by the rear wall, gazing out the streaked window as I hesitated on the threshold. "Don't dawdle, son," he rumbled without turning to me. "I've only got a few minutes for yo'."

His wide-brim white hat was pushed well back on his head, which he revolved slowly in my direction, revealing an expanse of freckled scalp, bushy sideburns going gray, a shaggy mustache to complement it, and a god-awful scowl that put me not at all at ease. He had propped one booted foot against an extended bottom drawer, and his hands held a gleaming, double-edged barlow knife with which he was laconically cleansing and paring his nails.

I ventured a bit closer and said something on the order of "How do?" He said nothing and offered me neither his hand nor the chair beside his desk. After a moment of attacking a cuticle, he said, "My nephew was by a little while back—gave you quite a buildup." I nodded and felt his eyes starting to roam over me from under his lowered brow. "You come a long ways from home," he said.

"Yes, sir," I said, louder than I wanted, "eight hundred miles."

"Says you reckon the South will rise again—and mighty soon." The voice was rough but resonant.

"Yes, sir," I said.

"'Course some people roun' here don't think it evah fell— maybe jus' kinda stumbled a little—."

I could not tell whether I was supposed to respond to his interlocutory, which seemed more a monologue than an exchange. I kept still.

"Well," he said, confronting me directly now for the first time, "you look too bushy-tailed to pass fo' a carpetbagger—besides which yo' too late. So maybe yo' got somethin', after all. What is it you'd like me to do fo' you, boy?"

"I could use a job."

"What doin'?"

"Anything you need."

He snorted. "But you don' know nothin' 'bout the kinda merchandise we got. Or the customers. Or our ways. An' hell, face it, boy—yo' sound funny to Southern ears. Think that's good fo' my business?"

44

"I—I learn fast," I said, fighting back panic. "I cipher well, I write a nice hand, people tell me—. And I work hard, as hard as you'd want—."

"I expect so," he said, not much smitten, and reached behind him for his cane. He sighted down its length as if it were a rifle, then took up the knife and began to shave away some microscopic imperfection. "Fact is," he started up anew, "I need me a boy right now. Fact is, I'm almost always in need. Fact is, it's hard as the devil's shit to keep good help now'days. Even harder to find it in the firs' place—."

"Yes, sir," I said, joyful at the conciliatory tack he seemed to be taking.

"You don't have to 'yessir' that, boy—I'm jus' making an obse'vation." He blew a few grains of blackthorn off the cane and ran his hand down it again to test for smoothness. "Now then," he said without preface, "Billy Doak tells me you're a Jew." It came out sounding more neutral than accusatory. I said that was so. "Then how come you don't try findin' a job with one of yo' own kind?" he added. "We got any number o' respectable Jew merchants in town—an' you know the sayin' about birds of a featha'?"

My throat constricted. I fought it open to answer, "I don't rightly believe in that."

"Why not? It's nature's way—."

My mouth was suddenly parched. "I've been taught all men are brothers," I managed.

"In a pig's ass," he said. "But I 'preciate the sentiment." He folded his hands under his chin and fixed me with his small bright eyes. "The truth is, I have nevah yet hired me a Jew—."

"I—didn't know that—sir."

"No, I suspec' not. An shall I tell yo' why not?"

I began to flush. "I suppose so—sir."

He leaned forward, eyes narrowing. "Don't sass me, boy. I'm tellin' yo'—I'm not askin'." He slumped back and studied the ceiling for a moment. "I'll be dead honest with yo', son," he said, collecting his odious thoughts. "I fin' the Jews mighty unappetizin' folk. Not that I don' 'preciate the travail they have suffe'd. But don' yo' see how they brought that on themselves? For rejectin' Jesus, they have natu'ly been denied citizenship throughout

Christendom, they have been denied ce'tain desirable pu'suits and occupations—I know about all that, y' see, son—and so bein' thoroughly dishonored an' deprived o' the chance for honest profit, they became all gnarled and wily and in-bred, and they bent all their effo'ts to one end and one only—the accumulation o' filthy lucre. All that pe'secution that sharpened their wits and made them such graspin' thieves to bargain with also did somethin' else terrible—it destroyed their manhood, don'cha see? Real white men, they're full o' vigo', full o' enthusiasm—they're chivalrous an' frank an' open. They love the land and know how t' farm it. They love t' fight and t' hunt. They love t' run an' jump an' piss into the wind. They love t' build an' sing an' write verse an' fuck their asses off an'—an' *live*, fo' Christ's sake, the way man was meant to! But not your Jews. No, suh. They're all clenched up and jittery. They wouldn' know a plowshare from a nutcracka'. They sit in dank co'ners all day countin' up their loot. An' they read and whimper and pray all night fo' deliverance, ignorin' the historical fact that they *been* deliv'ed. An' when they get picked on fo' refusin' the Almighty's glorious message to Bethlehem, they truckle under like craven cowa'ds 'stead of standin' tall an' fightin' back an' takin' what medicine the Lord has ordained. There's not a manly trait among 'em. They make mis'able soldiers—won't hunt—can't stand the sight o' blood. Why, eatin' meat with the blood still oozin' is against their utmost convictions. An' the crownin' blow is they chop off a piece of every boy baby's pecka' in the name of some fancied hygiene. Was there evah a more unnatural savage act inflicted on men?"

It was at about that point that he must have noticed the tears streaming down my face. No sound had escaped from me, though. I just stood there and watched all that poison come spewing out of him, and when he finally paused to catch his breath, the sight of me seemed to suggest to him that he had said quite enough. Carefully I took off the chain I wore around my neck and handed the Congressional Medal to him. A former military man, he examined it front and back with interest. "My father won that," I said softly, "for killing people like you."

Momentarily chided, he handed it back. "Must've been a brave man, yo' daddy," he said and sighed. "I suspect he was the proverbial exception that proves the rule. Yo' should be proud o' him, son."

"Because he killed—?"

"Because he did the manly thing. Because he did not shrink from his duty—."

"And would it have been the manly thing for me to grab that stick of yours and beat you on the head with it for the vile things you said just now—?"

"Yes!" he said, warming to the challenge, "Yes, boy, if that's what you felt. And my duty is t' defend myself—."

I checked my sudden fury. "That's the law of the jungle you're preaching, Mr. Griffin. That's not God's will—or, the way I understand it, what Jesus taught."

He was silent for an endless moment. "You should unde'stand, son," he said at last, "that I'm testin' yo' mettle. But I do get carried away by my own rhetoric every now an' again. I'll be pleased to sit still fo' a rebuttal if yo'a so inclined."

Without invitation I took the seat beside his desk. Then looking this ruddy brute straight in the eye, the way my grandfather had prescribed when I wished to console a friend or discomfit an enemy, I prayed silently for a *choleria* to descend upon him before nightfall and said my piece. The Jews, I told him, were no more or less virtuous than anyone else, but if he insisted on dwelling on their alleged shortcomings as a group, as a class, as a people, fairness dictated that he acknowledge their reputedly characteristic strengths as well. For it was these, not my blood lust or circumcision, that would establish my value to him as a hired hand. No one disputed that Jews were industrious. Or that they were thrifty. And drove a hard bargain. Their high intelligence was legendary, as was their allergy to dissipation: Jewish drunkards, gamblers, and lechers were a rare order of mammal. All these qualities, I concluded, should recommend me to him, so long as his mind was as mired as he revealed it to be. Jews, moreover, were excellent Americans, for they cherished liberty, disdained no man, and earnestly aspired to a just reward for their enterprising ways; it was for such beliefs that my father had fought and killed and been killed, and for such that I revered his memory.

Gus Griffin had taken my measure and now he was appraising

the results. "Yo' said that nice, son, an' yo' provin' right gritty. Only I can't escape the notion the whole world's got about yo' brethren bein' addled on the subject o' money. It's the alpha and the omega of their whole existence—I can see it plain on their pinched faces—and while I surely could use a clerk o' two who knows how to drive a good firm ba'gain, I don' much care to have him drive the customers right outa my stores."

It was a classic instance of the pot calling the kettle black. But I did not discover until later on how cunningly and with what vigor his operations were leeching blood money from the Georgia peasantry by shrouded interest charges that would have made Shylock seem like the Good Samaritan. To have named Gus Griffin the master gatherer of the golden fleece of Chatham County would not, at any rate, have endeared me to him just then: most hypocrites are understandably thin-skinned. It was agreed that, each of us having spoken his piece, we would mull the situation overnight and that if I wished, knowing his inclinations, to pursue the matter, I should present myself at his office the next morning at nine.

Billy Doak and Amanda made light of my report that their Uncle Gus harbored a profound bigotry toward Jews. "You should hea' him on the nigras and the Quaka's," said Billy. "All that cussin' and those insults, though, they're just his way o' seein' what kind o' stuff yo' made of. He don't mean it—beyond maybe a little bit."

I was still so hot under the collar when Mandy coached me through my first riding lesson that I took imprudent chances in coaxing the handsome roan they lent me to a gait well beyond a learner's. Mandy announced that I had the makings of a natural-born equestrian; I urged her to report as much to her uncle, along with the intelligence that Jews had invented horseback riding thirty centuries earlier on the plains of Moab. "Is that the truth now?" she asked, voice arching musically. "As true," I said, "as any of that rot he gave me." She laughed, touched my arm in the daintiest of rebukes, and declared me "a caution." I was uncertain whether that was good, bad, or neuter.

That evening, while listlessly pursuing my copy of Mother Trollope's *Domestic Manners of the Americans* for an hour before retiring, I came upon a number of passages that seemed providentially suited to my circumstances. I brought the book along the next morning to my confrontation with Uncle Gus and asked if I might read a few sentences to him.

"They're by Frances Trollope, the mother of Anthony Trollope —the famous English novelist."

"I'm familia' with Mr. Trollope, son," he said without appearing to take umbrage. "I have even read one o' two of his wo'ks."

That heartened me. "His mother toured America earlier in the century," I offered, "and wrote this account of her impressions. She said of Americans—and I'm using her very own words now— that 'no people on earth can match them at overreaching a bargain.'" Uncle Gus's eyes widened a bit. "Then she accused us of being a money-mad people. She said, 'This sordid object'—she meant money—'forever before their eyes, must inevitably produce a sordid tone of mind and worse still, it produces a seared and blunted conscience on all questions of probity.' And just a bit later, after declaring that 'No American conversation is ever complete without the word "dollar,"' she winds up by comparing the traits of the typical American with those of other people. She says, '. . . in love of lucre he doth greatly resemble the sons of Abraham.' And then she—."

"I can start you tomorra in the dry-goods section," he said. "Eight to sundown every day but the Lord's, an' overtime when need be. Pay's twenty-two dollars a month, take it o' leave it, an' advancement solely at the proprietor's discretion. Any stealin' and yo' get the boot on my good leg impressed on yo' skinny *derrière*. Now good mornin' to yo'."

He never shook my hand.

THREE

My career as a merchant would span the better part of four years, during which I acquired a certain precocious finesse in ministering to the daily needs of my fellow man. This comet-like ascent into the retailers' firmament was fueled by the ardent belief that I was performing a truly pastoral function—and by a complementary knack of forgetting that all the while I was leading the poor dear lambs to slaughter.

The first month, I was plainly on probation, although nobody put it quite so baldly. New boys had a lot to learn and a lot to put up with. My good gray jacket, for example, which I made the mistake of wearing to the store those first few days, was soon the depository of a pocketful of molasses, which had congealed indissolubly by the time I discovered it. Between my split trousers and treaclized coat, I was not precisely the town's central sartorial ornament. After a week of clumsy effort, one of the other clerks succeeded in singeing me with a hotfoot at lunchtime—nearly setting fire to the farm-supply shed as well. I, naturally, was reprimanded for the episode and told to ignite my tobacco in less flammable surroundings or swallow it. Great mirth, too, greeted my attempt to comply with instructions to hammer a number of advertising posters from soap manufacturers into a strategically located post, which, despite its wood-like veneer, proved to be constructed of iron; I must have curled thirty nails before detecting the first derisive snorts from the store manager and his clerical accomplices, witnessing my earnest ordeal through averted but glee-teared eyes.

A far graver initiation, the one that swiftly separated the go-get-ters from the incompetents, was learning the pricing system. Solomon himself would have had trouble with it. "We got at least four prices for every item," the manager explained. "There's one for them that pays cash on the barrelhead—which is natu'ly our preferred type of customer. There's a second price, slightly higha', for the man who pays up ev'ry payday. Then there's a third price, higha' yet, for them that's steadily on the credit, always buyin' and always owin' but at least always settlin' up part. And then we got a special price for them we gotta dun to death or sue to get paid, which makes 'em colossal pains in the pecka' an' so justifies our chargin' half again as much as the basic price."

When in doubt, make them pay dear—that was the prevailing rule. My own instincts were fixed in the opposite direction until I was administered a graphic lesson one afternoon toward the end of my second week on the job. A gent in working clothes but neat and clean came in and, under my scrutiny, began fishing around in the brogan barrel for a suitable pair. The crude, broad, shapeless workshoes, so unlike the footgear in the North, were made of split oak-tanned leather that developed deep, pain-inflicting creases across the toes after a few days' wear; the soles, unpadded to begin with, were fastened with untrimmed hardwood pegs, producing an often unstable tread, and the seams were bound with heavy harness brads that caused their share of abrasions. Since left brogans and right ones were of precisely the same design, great batches of them were dumped helter-skelter into big bins, and the customer was invited to plunge in to find two of these durable if excruciating items of approximately the same length and pay from a dollar and a quarter to two and a quarter for the pair, depending on which category of customer he was. This particular chap soon disdained the brogans and asked to see the finer, fitted footwear. I found him a smart, relatively comfortable pair at three fifty and was in the process of wrapping them up when the customer, explaining he was new to town and would be paid a few days hence but wanted a pair of good shoes for going to church in the interim, asked for credit. Awaiting my own first pay envelope, I was naturally sympathetic. And when he volunteered that he was working at the Georgia Central yards, he all but had me. I told him I would have to check, however, and, bearing the box of shoes with me, went to find the manager, who turned out to be

51

away. So was his senior assistant. That left only a couple of other clerks who had no more authority than I; on my own I decided to grant the shoe customer his credit. Upon hearing of this tender-foot heresy, the manager promptly denounced me as a jackass and threatened to march me by the collar before Gus Griffin's wrath-ful countenance. I promised never again to grant a stranger un-collateralized credit and begged him not to tell the proprietor un-less the customer defaulted. The manager relented. On the assigned day, my treacherous customer failed to materialize. My pay envelope would be docked the full purchase price, I was told, and if I repeated the blunder, I would be out chopping cotton be-fore sunset.

Yet on payday the full twenty-two dollars was handed to me. I reminded the manager of my debt. He looked gratified at my hon-esty. "Oh, that," he said. "That was just a little ol' trick we save up fo' every greenhorn. Them shoes're back on the shelf—been there a week now. Your welchin' customer, that was my cousin Loftus. He come in here with instructions to test you out, boy, and you fell f'r it clean as a whistle."

My second payday was more memorable still. The envelope this time contained twenty-three dollars, one more than I was due. Only when I was back in my rooming house and counted out the money did I discover the error. I counted it twice more to make sure. Was it possible I had earned a one-dollar bonus because of my diligence? Surely they would have apprised me of such a fact to encourage future perseverance. More than likely it was due to two bills having stuck together under the bookkeeper's usually nimble thumb. For a moment, I contemplated the ethics of keeping the wayward bill: I had worked very hard, after all, and was not re-ceiving a princely recompense; who, moreover, would ever know the truth? And I could always claim that I had not noticed the overpayment; the burden of proof to the contrary was surely on the employer's end. But it was impossible. Some deep dread, out of all proportion to the size of the misdeed, told me to confess the error at once.

"An' a good thing," said the manager, pressing his lips and plucking the dollar from my fingers. "Wasn't no accident, nei-ther," he added and sprayed tobacco juice past my trouser leg. The bonus dollar, it turned out, was a dual test of every new boy's character. His second pay envelope always contained an overpayment, and if the lad did not report the mistake at once, he was labeled a petty thief with potential for far worse perfidy; or, to be more charitable about it, he was deemed careless about money or bad at counting, and in either case a dubious risk for promotion. "'Course any guy who don't 'fess up, he gets the extra buck the nex' month, too, and if he *still* don't cough it up, his career comes to a premature closeout, if y' get my drift—."

Not long after, I faced another, but more nuanced test of integrity. Ordered to help out for a spell in the grocery department, I watched the clerk in charge pour a liberal dose of water into the bottom of a two-quart pail and then fill the rest with milk ladled from a twenty-gallon can. He was on his third diluted pailful when I spoke up and asked if that wasn't cheating the customer. "'Tain't," said the other clerk, a fellow in his middle twenties who knew the ropes and had been kind to me. "First off, everybody deacons the milk—so where's the harm? Besides, if y' wanna be such an exac' cuss, this here ain't really waterin' the milk, on account o' the water goes in first—."

But cheating was cheating, and it kept itching my craw. Finally I told the other chap I thought it was plain dishonesty, and he suggested that I take it up with the manager. The latter's eyes widened theatrically when I made my charge and, over my protests, he ushered me into Gus Griffin's office, shut the door behind us, and told the proprietor I had practically accused the establishment of premeditated robbery. Perspiration foamed from my pores like white water in a rapids.

"So," said Uncle Gus, describing graceful arcs in the air with his blackthorn cane, "our resident Isaiah is bearin' witness to false deeds."

I said nothing.

"Is that right, boy?" he persisted.

"More or less, sir," I offered with pained reluctance.

"You been here a couple o' months and already yo' tellin' how to run the place—is that right, boy?"

"Not exactly, sir."

His agate-cold eyes were on me full now. "Well, then what's the problem? Are we or are we not robbin' the customers by yo' lights, Mista' Seth Adler from New Yawk High 'n' Mighty City? Speak or fo'eva' hold yo' codpiece, boy—."

I crossed my arms over my chest as if to ward off the expected blow and said, "What's right is right, sir. Watering the milk is crooked business."

The stillness was complete as Griffin's eyes consumed me. An instant before I threatened to decompose, that look of cauterizing fury turned into a smile. "John," he said over my shoulder to the manager, "you raise Mr. Adler's pay on up t' twenty-three a month from now on, y' hear? An' tell Alec to feed the watered milk t' the sows at Lum Green's pen—no need to go wastin' it." John gave me a pat on the shoulder and departed. Uncle Gus proceeded to allow as how I might have a future in his service. "Y' did the right thing, son. Lotsa places water the milk—a lot of 'em skim off the cream first—and do a helluva lot worse tricks. Some mix farina into the musta'd and chalk into the bread and starch into the lard. Some even cut the flour with plaster. But not us. We bargain tough but fair and square, and the customer gets what he pays fo' and not a lot of gimcrack and chickenshit, y' hear?" I nodded, still numb. "That watered-milk spectacle, we arranged that demonstration 'specially to see what kind o' principles you got. Most new boys watch Alec like they was dumb cows themselves and neva' open their lips that maybe he's doin' somethin' wrong, so we have t' pull 'em in here after a time an' tell 'em right from wrong." He shook his head slowly and with evident sadness. Then he eyed me cannily. "But every once an' again we find some boy who don't have to be told. Those are the ones who get on here, Mr. Adler—you bear that in mind."

If it proved useful to the advancement of my career for me to have spoken up on the occasion of the adulterated milk, another episode occurred not long afterward when I calculated it would be equally advantageous to hold my tongue—no easy trick in view of the callous injustice involved.

A bony black man named Tiger Eddie, a cropper on one of the Griffin holdings in the county and not unknown around the store, had come in to town, he said, to inspect the wider variety of fabrics at the Adelphi than was available at his nearby Griffin-run country store. It was a Saturday, and Tiger Eddie, having been noted, made himself scarce in the throng of shoppers, but while he was still on the premises, the assistant manager discovered that a large bolt of hickory-stripe shirting fabric had had an irregular piece of perhaps two yards snipped from it. A lot of customers had fingered the open bolt, about the most popular in the store, and a heavy cutting shears had been left close by to service the constant demand for the cloth. Attention focused on Tiger Eddie as he settled up his purchase of gray cottonade for jeans-britches, apparently to replace the sweat-stained pair he had nearly worn through, and a card of buttons for the fly. When the assistant manager invited him into the supply room on unexplained business, the black man hesitated, then capitulated as two dozen eyes scalded him. In private, a confession was readily extracted, along with the cloth that, by extraordinary sleight of hand, Tiger Eddie had jammed inside his loose osnaburg shirt.

John the manager was summoned at once and an arrest warrant drawn. But Tiger Eddie, trembling so severely that a giant urine stain began spreading in an irregular circle about his groin, begged John not to turn him over to the authorities. That would mean the prison farm for certain and, under the convict-lease system, an indefinite term of crushing labor, probably in the coal mines upstate. John kept shaking his head and scratching away at the warrant. Desperate, Tiger Eddie ripped off his shirt, fell on his knees, and pleaded with the manager to administer any number of lashes that seemed a just punishment. Mercifully John relented, and they took Tiger Eddie out to the loading platform, tied his wrists to a pair of meat hooks, and, his spindly rib cage heaving uncontrollably, laid open his back with thirty cracks of a buggy whip. Gus Griffin himself applied the thirty-first, and last, blow— so furious that it splintered the narrow end of one of his blackthorn canes—and then cut the negro down. He crumpled, a dazed and bleeding bundle of bones, yet with a smile on his lips, for he was free to go if and when the life juices renewed their flow within him. From the ring of perhaps a hundred onlookers, two black youngsters jumped forward to claim the fallen body lest it receive further abuse from the toes of passersby. One of the colored boys, I saw, was Plato, my erstwhile guide on the day I arrived in Savannah. As discreetly as possible, I brought the fallen colored man a dipper of cool water; Plato, acknowledging the kindness with a slight nod but nothing more, took it from me and brought it to the lips of that inflamed body. My duties obliged me to hurry back inside. Half an hour later, when I had a moment to re-check, the blacks were gone.

I had about convinced myself that such direct application of frontier law was more charitable than sadistic when a similar incident unfolded with so different a denouement that I could harbor no further illusions about the quality of Southern mercy. The culprit this time was a white man, in his mid-forties or so and somewhat down at the heels but pretending otherwise in his fraying broadcloth suit, fawn-colored vest, and high topper of antebellum vintage. He wielded his walking stick with what struck me as particularly gymnastic exuberance as he navigated the aisles, but I thought nothing more of the demonstrative habit until I saw John usher the gentleman into the rear and close the door behind them. That fluently wielded walking stick, it seemed, was tipped with a sharpened nail, and its owner, mixing an occasional lightning thrust toward the shelves among his innocent gyrations, managed to spear a goodly assortment of small, soft merchandise, including several plugs of tobacco, cakes of soap, lemons, and a packet of firecrackers. The total cost of these items compared closely to the price of the striped shirting that Tiger Eddie had filched, but in this case no arrest warrant was drawn or any skin flayed into bloody ribbons. Instead the larcenist was directed out the back way and firmly instructed not to return unless he wished to be separated from his teeth.

What distressed me most about this glaringly dual standard of punishment was my own complicity in the arrangement. Not only did I fail to speak up in protest of the inequity—that was defensible, if reprehensible, as simple and heartless self-interest— but I undeniably derived an indecent thrill upon realizing that I was a beneficiary now of so heinous a system. Whereas the faith of my fathers had distanced me from all the white, Christ-craving knights-errant of hobbled Dixie, our mutually milky skins were a firm bond whenever any in the ocean of black brutes surrounding us needed reminding that the Lord had assigned him perpetual hind teat and had sanctioned a sharp knee in his fevered testicles if he ever forgot his place. I did not savor that protective coloration, but I did not openly reject it. Some instinct should have told me that whoever gains today from justice sullied may perish tomorrow from the same abuse. Perhaps it tried to, and expediency turned my ear. At any rate, I did not count myself a sinner.

II

The fear I had nourished that loneliness might undo me in this far-off new Canaan of mine was routed by midsummer of that first year. Several of the other clerks at the store had befriended me, and I would sail with them some Sundays or patrol the strand after dark in quest of modest adventure. To pass the dank nights we would join in the shanties and dwell over our ale at one or another of the River Street taverns, have a round or two of chess or rummy at our quarters, or gingerly seek female companionship without caring or daring to pay for it. As a result, too, of introducing myself to Rabbi Mendes at Mickve Israel and assisting him with an occasional custodial chore, I was invited now and then as a homeless, neglected, and somewhat raffish refugee to several of the more refined Jewish households of Savannah, where pickled herring and hopping john were served in convivial tandem. But the focus of my leisure hours continued to be the forthright Billy Doak and the exuberant Amanda Lizabeth Baxter, at whose home on East St. Julian Street I had become a constant visitor.

They monitored my progress at their Uncle Gus's and relished it as if I were a favorite performing pet. Billy would drive by the store in the buckboard to fetch me after work sometimes or Mandy would send a merry note, often in a rebus, inviting me to supper a few days hence; Sundays we might ride or picnic by the riverside at Causton Bluff or sail downstream under a blazing sky as far as Elba or McQueens island. There was dreadful little I could do to reciprocate their kindness and slowly I began to shy away from their invitations for fear of being taken for a sponger— a *schnorrer* it is called in Yiddish, I explained, duly noting the manifold shades of meaning it possessed. *Schnorrer, schnorrer!* Mandy kept saying it over and over, delighted with the snouty quality of the word and telling me, "But it sounds jus' like what it means!"

Yiddish was a remarkably expressive language, I ventured, and offered a few more choice morsels, of which *chozzer, schlemiel,* and *mishpocheh* were immediate favorites because of their phlegmy, exotic, and clearly caustic tone. "Of course," I added, "only uneducated Jews use Yiddish. It is the purest slang—nothing more. My mother shivers to hear me use it." It was as the purveyor of just such cosmopolitan oddments that I think they treasured me; surely it was not for glibness of tongue, at which Mandy so excelled me, or my gifts as horseman, mariner, or ballplayer, in which capacities Billy was so supple. Our mutual attraction as opposites was obvious and agreeable, and they took special pleasure in indoctrinating me in local ritual; the more outlandish or alien each new one struck me, the better they liked it.

One suppertime in late August, by way of example, Mandy greeted me at the porch with the ecstatic news we were to dine on ricebird pilau. My response was restrained, even skeptical, for I suspected it must be one of the region's more primitive repasts, else why that boisterous announcement from my young hostess? The rice, dry and grainy, was splendid. The bird part was another matter. They were tiny devils—bobolinks they were called up North—stewed whole, seasoned with salt and red pepper, and served with their inert little heads still very much intact. "They're good 'n' crunchy," Mandy exuded. "Y' just pop 'em down the hatch."

"Like that?" I asked, indicating their heads.

"How else?"

"Well—beheaded—."

She wagged her long locks vehemently. "The base of their brain's the most succulent po'tion of all, silly. That'd be like eatin' the husk and throwin' away the ear o' corn. Now you jus' go on and try one of those tasty darlin's—."

She and Billy witnessed my agony with unveiled mirth. The very idea of decapitating the creatures with my own jaws repelled me far more than the act itself, which produced a taste, as nearly as I can recall, not unlike a slightly bristly chicken liver served on a supremely stale biscuit. One ricebird was all I allowed myself that night. Or have since.

The week after that ordeal, Billy Doak and Amanda invited me along on their annual turtle-egg hunt. I sensed at once that here was yet another indigenous custom of marginal, if not entirely resistible, charm. I miscalculated: it proved a genuine stomach-turner. The hayride to the southeastern end of the county was a tumult of jouncing song, loony laughter, and unabashed spooning in the moonlight, though Mandy held herself aloof from the playful clutches of the randy males and, anyway, Billy never let her out of his sight.

We tied up a little below Beaulieu on one of the coastal streams, divided up into boatloads of four, and followed the shoreline out past the mouth of the Little Ogeechee into Green Island

Sound. Billy Doak, competent as ever, was our intrepid admiral. He mounted a pair of torches in the gunwales and set the pace with his sure, swift oar strokes through the calm, moon-bathed surface of the sea. He led us down the narrow channel between Little Don Island and Raccon Key, across the eerily wide estuary of the Ogeechee herself, and onto the beach of Egg Island to stalk our prey. Several of the more amorous of our companions, feigning fatigue, never strayed from the shore. The rest of us, bearing torches in a suddenly silent procession, snooped along the sand for turtle prints. I asked Mandy what these might look like. She hushed me, grabbed my hand, and whispered that she never had seen any, but someone else—Billy more often than not—always did the discovering. After some twenty minutes of our rimming the island, a single word skimmed back from the front of the line —"crawl." That meant the track of the mama turtle, Mandy hissed to me, and we all moved up onto the dunes. Through a stand of marsh grass our line penetrated, taking care not to let our torches singe it lest the whole field go up. Under a rock ledge the lady turtle was at last detected, more ghastly and enormous than I ever dreamed—a snapping frenzy in the torchlight, clinging to the nest for all she was worth. It took a great deal of dextrous poking and prodding and prying to dislodge that dedicated mother from her brood and take possession of it. There must have been two hundred eggs nuzzling under that giant humped shell. The booty was quickly divided on the spot, each of us scooping up about a dozen eggs and placing them gently into little cloth sacks we had brought along for that purpose. Perhaps fifteen or twenty were smashed in the scramble to finish the undisguised act of cradle robbing. In the abstract, it had sounded like spirited if unnecessary play; in the event, I found it cruel and unredeeming foolery. To cap it off, we tortured the mother still further by taking turns riding her around the beach. "Ringtails go first," one of the arch-tormentors announced, flipping the turtle on its back while the order of riders was established.

"Seth Adler's a ringtail!" Mandy cried out, disloyalty dancing in her eyes.

"What's a ringtail?" I asked, baring my teeth.

"Someone who's never done it."

"I don't wanna—."

"You've *got* to! You'll put the dreadful curse of the sissifiers on the boats headin' home if you don't—."

"You show me how first—."

"But those things're powerful dangerous! They'd as soon snap your hand off as budge an inch—." She saw in my bulbous eyes her words had found their mark. Overflowing with giggles, she grabbed my arm hard and said, "Now you jus' stop pretendin' to be a coward 'n' set yo' tail down on that itty-bitty monsta' like she was an ol' plug mare. Why, yo' makin' more fuss'n yo' do mountin' that roan stallion, an' he's a wild one—."

And so I teetered-tottered across the dune on turtleback for a few dozen yards to the uncontainable glee of the others, who shouted such encouraging japes as: "Ride 'er, Yankee!" and "Don't crush the ol' tart!" and "Hell, she's bustin' his balls!" Only turtle and rider were less than ecstatic. Especially the latter, fearing that if he slithered off, emasculation by the snapping avenger would follow almost instantaneously.

Next day I was invited for supper to Jubilation, as Mandy made a point of referring to the Baxter home. The appetizer consisted, predictably, of a basket of our turtle eggs. Uncle Gus, on hand as was his Sunday wont, took pleasure in Mandy's elaborately distorted account of the hunt—the distraught turtle she turned into a bloody-eyed shark and a slight breeze on the homeward row she promoted into a quasi-monsoon—and helped himself to the first egg in the batch. I watched with gastric revulsion as he pinched a little hole in the shell, injected a squirt of Worcestershire sauce and a dash of salt into the opening, and bolted the whole thing raw, as if he were tossing down a particularly potent physic. Yum-yum, he said and helped himself to another, not noticing, I hoped, that I had nearly disgorged the remnants of my breakfast and lunch. The damned ricebirds had at least been cooked; this was scarcely a step removed from feeding on still living tissue. Billy Doak cracked his egg with more care and ate only the yolk. Mandy, blessedly considerate of my tender sensibilities when Uncle Gus was around, said she preferred hers cooked and I took the hint. Even then, the whites were still runny—"They neva' do firm up," she said—so I downed just my yolk in concert with her, never tasting it, really, but convinced it would start snapping violently once it reached my stomach. She teased me into having two more, hinting that they were beneficial to young men's virility until her mother hushed her.

It was later that evening, the week before Billy took the train north to Charlottesville and life as a dissolute Virginia scholar, that we explored for the first time at any length the barrier between us. Mandy, surveying the stars on that soft September night, plunged us into it by her extravagant speculations on life after death. Resurrection, she made plain, was the central miracle of her faith, and what had been good enough for Jesus would be just fine for her. Billy suggested that she would have to live in closer accord with Christ's teachings if she hoped to make the grade; Mandy insisted she was off to quite a good start, that she was loving toward everyone she knew, with the possible exception of Priscilla Fay Stewart, who was hard to love and not just because of her warts, and that besides, if you were perfect as a child, you could never demonstrate any progress, and it was well known that Jesus was particularly partial to genuinely repentant sinners. "My real problem," she said, "will be figurin' which sins I can afford." I laughed at that, but Billy scoffed and told her that admission to heaven was not arranged by a negotiated settlement of accounts. She asked what made him so sure, and their exchange waxed hotter until Mandy looked to me as the arbitrator. "What does the great God Jehovah advise?" she asked, as if I were a Pharisee.

"I think He gives orders instead of advice," I said.

"Then what does He order about gettin' into heaven or goin' to the othe' place and gettin' yo' gizza'd fried foreva'?" she asked.

"I don't remember any mention of fried gizzard."

"Don't sass me now, Seth," she said, serious and aroused. "What's yo' God Almighty got to say—?"

"My God Almighty is the same as yours, Mandy Beth."

"That's jus' in a manner o' speakin'."

"No, it's from now till kingdom come—."

She pondered that a moment. "Does that make my Jesus yo' Jesus?"

"Well," I said, treading cautiously, "we're both Jews."

"Does that mean you believe in the Resurrection with all yo' might an' soul, Seth Adler—because that is the most beautiful and thrillin' thing there eva' was since the beginnin' of creation—."

61

"I believe—I believe a man's spirit can live on after him in the hearts of others."

"Now yo' know that is an entirely different thing from life everlastin', and that's what I'm referrin' to. Do you believe in that—in the good and the holy dwellin' fo'ever and eva' in bliss and contentment—?"

"The Torah doesn't go into that very much."

"That means you don't believe—?"

"It means it's not something Jews sit around and worry over."

"But what in heaven's name is more important to them?"

I shrugged. "We're supposed to be kind and decent and do the best we can in this life and let God take care of the rest. That's God's Kingdom, and if He wanted us to know about it, I guess, He would have told us—."

"But He *did* tell us!" Mandy said. "He sent us Jesus, His son. And Jesus was slain for the sins of men an' reborn in heaven—."

"If Jesus was God's son, how could anyone kill him in the first place?"

That bothered her. My dispassion on the subject bothered her even more. What kind of God, she wondered, demanded that His flock lead a virtuous life without assurance of heavenly rest?

"A stern God," I said.

"But how can yo'-all love a God like that? My Jesus is so—so warm and so kind an' forgivin'. You can *see* the look in his face, up on that horrid cross, takin' on the sufferin' for all us sinners and never complainin'—. That's so beautiful—I cry my eyes out thinkin' of it sometimes." She looked up at me with a flash of contentiousness. "But yo' Jehovah—why, He's just a burnin' bush! Who can love an ol' burnin' bush?"

"Loving God isn't like loving a sweetheart," I said. "You love Him because He made heaven and earth and you and me—and because if you don't, you are a blasphemer and can expect to be punished sooner or later."

"That's a God to dread, not to love," she said. "I like my Jesus better. There's sweetness in him, you can see it. You can see those agonizin' limbs o' his an' that lovin' face an' those hauntin' eyes. Your God's got no face—no heart—."

I could not deny to her that I did not know what God looked like. And I prayed to no cross, to no statue, to no image. I bore no ikon on my travels. It was hard to know God who never embodied

Himself in material things, and harder still to convince Amanda Lizabeth Baxter that there could be no other God before Him, or after, and so I did not try. I settled for remarking, "If He has no heart, why did He send you Jesus?"

Billy Doak drove by the store a few days later to say goodbye. I did not see him again until Christmas. Mandy, without her brother as chaperone, receded from my life at summer's end, and I was incapable, for many reasons, of taking any initiative, though she charmed and tantalized me exceedingly. We were simply of two separate worlds and there could be no misconceiving it. That view was confirmed in mid-October when Mrs. Baxter placed an order through her brother for a new piano, to be presented to Mandy, I learned through an idle few words upon its delivery to the store, on the occasion of her sweet-sixteenth birthday. I was not asked to the party. I told myself I had no right to expect to be, but I cussed her just the same. A few weeks later, to my surprise, I was asked to Sunday supper on East St. Julian Street; the hiatus had lasted two months.

"I want to explain," Mandy said directly and led me on a turn through Jubilation Gardens, as she beguilingly labeled the little stand of mimosa and viburnum in her backyard. "It was a fancy-dress party, and I jus' knew you didn't have an outfit for it—."

"It doesn't matter," I said.

"It matters to me," she said. "Yo'a my friend."

"Your pauper friend—."

She was unaccustomedly still for the moment, as if to acknowledge at least the partial validity of the charge. "I neva' think o' you in that fashion, Seth—."

"Then how?"

"As a young man not born to privilege, yet strugglin' with true pluck to make his way in the world—."

"Surely your mother disapproves of our friendship—?"

"Mother says I may have what friends I please—."

"Your uncle, then?"

"Uncle Gus thinks yo'a Billy's friend—."

"And Billy?"

She looked away from me. "Billy asks about you in his letters. He writes fine letters—."

"But he worries about—your caring for me—?"

She nodded to the ground, then looked up with eyes ablaze.

"He is exceedin'ly fond o' you, though, you unde'stand. He plans t' write you himself, he says, an' tell yo' all about the university—."

"You mean it's all right for me to be his friend, but not yours."

Mandy sighed. "He thinks he's savin' me for some Galahad—prefa'bly one with the middle name o' Beauregard—."

"Is that what you want, too?"

She glanced at me coyly. "I am but sixteen, Mr. Adla', sir, and neva' been kissed—."

And so I kissed her, behind the spreadingest mimosa in Jubilation Gardens, and we remained friends, though somewhat distant ones. She visited now and then at the store, and I joined her and some companions from the turtle-egg hunt on a long Sunday ride and picnic just after Thanksgiving. For religious scruples, I declined her invitation to tag along with the same gang on a caroling party over the Yuletide, and Christmas Eve I dined with Rabbi Mendes, who opened his home to any stray and lonesome Jews in the vicinity that season of hardly bearable Gentile gaiety. Billy, home for the holidays, sought me out next day and confided in me as if he had never left. He had many other friends, of course, but my metropolitanism made me his favorite and most knowledgeable companion, free of the provincial strictures he now reviled at every turn. In this raillery as well as his running narrative of life in dolorous academia, I noticed the constant accompaniment of a brimming mug of toddy. It was the beginning of his long engagement with strong spirits.

III

Shortly after the turn of the year 1879, Zebulon Augustus Griffin, in all his whittling majesty, summoned me to the office and announced that my golden opportunity was at hand.

"'Bout a month before plantin' time I want you to go on out to McAllister and help Ossie Nesbit run his store," said Uncle Gus. "Ossie's a fine ol' boy and keeps a nice shop an' all, but times're changin' an' a man's got to be more aggressive now'days. Yo' wages'll go to twenty-five, still collectable here the las' Satu'day o' the month." He wasn't asking; he was telling.

I had begun to feel at home in Savannah, where there were rhythm and color to life, and the surge of activity by the riverfront made each day an event. Out in the county, what did they do all day besides listening to the cotton grow? But could an eighteen-year-old whippersnapper spurn the entreaty of the merchant king of Chatham County?

"I believe I do detect a trace of hesitancy on yo' part, Mr. Adler," he said. "I can unde'stand that—Savannah's a lot bigga' pond than McAlliste', I grant yo'. But out there's the real world, son, where all the ass-bustin' sweat turns the earth t' use. Without them, we'a nothin' here. This town's just a funnel. Those country folk need service—an' you can serve them an' yo'self at the same time if yo'a dedicated. Everythin' that goes on out there comes across the threshold, an' I mean everything, which makes yo' a individual they all gotta reckon with. Ain't a blessed thing goin' forward in the community but you don't hear 'bout it. The man who runs the store, he's a combination supplier, banker, broker, politician, news-spreader, social adviser, medical counselor, scribe for the illiterate, character reference—an' burier of the dead. They got special white gloves for that last one." He stood up and came close to me now. "Son, the fastes' way to learn what you gotta know about life is the route I'm proposin'. You'll know more than all the pastors, more'n the sawbones, more'n all the schoolmarms in captivity, about the sins and griefs and follies of yo' fellow man by helpin' run Ossie Nesbit's store." Then he shook my hand by way of authenticating the wisdom of his words and signaling that our discussion was at an end. He had a large hand, and its grip was very powerful.

Ossie Nesbit was in the middling stage of losing his eyesight, but he was still "spry as a cricket and tougher'n green pine," as he told me upon my arrival, but dimming vision was a serious peril to the solvency of a country storekeeper. "Yo' gotta have eagles eyes," he said without self-pity, "or they'll walk out with half the stock in their britches." I was to be Ossie's eyes—and arms, legs, back, and wits as well, it developed.

I was expected to open up the store soon after dawn—which meant starting out from Savannah well before sunrise—and dust off the merchandise, build a fire when the weather was raw, sprinkle the floor with a bucket of rainwater from out back, and sweep out. Before the doors opened for business, there was a brutal spell of pushing and heaving and grunting my guts out of place to move in the fresh goods from the cellar—the hogsheads of molasses and fish and pork, the barrels of flour and vinegar and whale oil, the kegs of nails and buckles and buckshot, the two-hundred-pound packages of spices from Ceylon that I had to tip end over end and to shove on display. Throughout the day I remained a beast of burden, first scooping and pouring and cutting and weighing and measuring and wrapping—everything from a yard of guimpe to a hundredweight of corn meal—and then helping haul it all out to the customers' wagons. But more than brawn was needed. I had to know the merchandise inside out, and I had to know the customers almost the same way. The clerk was expected to bear in mind the girth, chest expanse, leg length, and approximate shoe size of his every customer and provide apparel that fit even (and especially) when he was too busy to come himself and sent a young messenger to fetch it. I was to become an overnight wizard on the needs of human bodies—everything from what was new and most potent to unplug the constipated to how to extract a white bean from an infant's nasty nostril—and of mules and horses, too. I, who not many months earlier did not know dobbin's withers from his martingale, was consulted on the latest nostrum for lameness and whether that big blue bottle of linament worked on man and mare alike. I, who had never grown a radish, was obliged to attain (or at least feign) authority on every phase of agriculture from seed to sod and know the name and use of every plow part in stock. "An' if yo' send 'em out a cuttin' colter instead of a grass rod," Ossie warned with a wink behind his thick lenses, "they'll laugh you right back t' Goshen."

That my time at Nesbit's Store was not a term in purgatory but more nearly what Gus Griffin had promised it would be—a gritty learning spree—is documented by letters from there I wrote my mother, who naturally saved them all. A few excerpts may suggest my ordeal of discovery:

18 July 1879

Dearest Mama,

I am writing with one hand and using the other to chase away the flies with a switch. All you can do is try to drive them off for a while because there are just too many to kill. Mr Nesbit put up flytraps and I hung a dozen curls of sticky arsenic paper, but they don't make much difference. Besides, there is a saying around here that goes, "Ten flies come to one fly's funeral." You can actually hear them hum in a swarm around the dried fruit and spilled molasses and smears of lard. They are all over everything this time of year.

These people learn to live with a lot of things that I doubt if we could bear. To them the flies are part of nature and so is all the dirt they say "ain't no never-mind." No one thinks anything about bringing their animals in the store and letting them lick the lard that we sell to the other customers. The worst thing is the spitting. The men spit all the time, mostly their chewing tobacco but anything else they feel like, too. And not just out on the porch, mind you, but indoors. For years they used to make the stove their target, especially in cold or damp weather, or just the floor between the display cases. Then Mr Nesbit finally got sick of the stove looking like it was covered with barnacles, or worse, so he put in a couple of buckets filled with sand and called them his official spit boxes. But some of the lustier spitters still overshot, he thinks on purpose, and the stove is never a thing of beauty. I asked Mr Nebit why he permits it, and he says it's just a custom that has taken root and his customers believe it is their unalienable right to spit, so long as they don't hit him in the eye. . . .

23 August 1879

Dearest Mama,

These people are always surprising me. Sometimes they can be very kind, as when they share their hospitality with me, even though they have very little to share, and sometimes they can be plain cruel.

For instance, I never thought country folk would be hideous to animals. But here it seems to be almost a way of life. Kicking them is like second-nature. They do much worse. The other day a customer reached into the turpentine jar and painted some of it on to the backside of a stray cat that lives around the store. For a minute the cat just stood there stunned. Then he dug his claws hard into the floor, let out a dreadful howl and took off like he was shot out of a cannon. Knocked down five displays and three lady customers. Then there's a man named Ansel who is always playing checkers on the porch or strumming a banjo (he does that right well, as they say here) and who is fond of teasing dogs. His favorite trick is to tie a string to a piece of meat and feed it to any canine who wanders by. The dog naturally gulps the meat straight down, but then Ansel starts pulling on the string and not too hard. The dog grunts and growls and scratches in pain each time Ansel tugs, and the other men on the porch slap their thighs and collapse with laughter.

Their own mules they don't treat much better although they would be lost without the dumb brutes. They work them all day in the sun with little rest or drink as if they have no feelings. And they load the wagons with too much for a forty-mule team to pull and expect one or at most two of them to drag it over these dirt roads even when they are up to their bellies in mud and the axles are practically scraping the ground. On Saturdays sometimes I see a pair of them left by our hitching post all day without food or water and by the time their owner remembers them or needs them to drive home, they have eaten the collars, which are made of corn shucks, off of one another. . . .

8 September 1879

Dearest Mama,

The strangest thing has happened, proving to me what a small world it really is, especially down here.

Plato, the negro boy who helped me take my bag to the rooming house the day I came to Savannah, is now living out here with his uncle, who turns out to have been the colored man they whipped for stealing at Mr Griffin's store that time. Plato's home in Savannah burned down, so I have taken him on as helper. He is very devoted and hard-working for the few pennies a week I pay him—a very good investment. . . .

30 September 1879

Dearest Mama,

It's odd how being a Jew in the country here is proving to be anything but a drawback especially with the colored. Everybody in these parts is very religious—there seems to be as many churches as haystacks nearly—and they are all very vocal about loving Jesus yet not very resentful that I do not. I think that is because they know the Jews came before Jesus and he was of them, so naturally I am respected so long as they think I have religion in my soul (as I surely do in my fashion). To the negroes, I am a special prize because they favor the Jewish part of the Bible almost more than the Christian part on account of Moses leading the Jewish slaves out of Egypt to freedom in the Promised Land, all of which they naturally see as themselves and me as a link to the past. They come around to the store to look at me and ask me questions about the Bible as if I am an expert, and I do not want to disappoint them by confessing my ignorance so I sometimes pretend to more than I should (this is bad and I will stop it). For example, they wanted to know exactly how big Noah's Ark was, which I got out of the Torah, and how it sailed (I said it just floated around since the Bible doesn't go into that), and how come with all those hundreds and thousands of animals on board it didn't smell terrible (I said the Ark had portholes and Noah and his family, not having anything else to do, washed the animals with soap, and when they wanted to know where the water came from I said that was the least of their problems). . . .

18 October 1879

Dearest Mama,

They are bringing in the cotton harvest now, and Mr Nesbit looks over every bale on which he holds a lien so as to reckon the accounts as close and accurately as possible. He is a very honest merchant though I have heard much talk about his pricing items too sharply (for which I get a share of the blame naturally). We are selling hundreds and hundreds of yards of jute bagging and bundles of steel ties which the farmers take across the street to the ginnery where the cotton gets cleaned and packed and the work goes on way into the night.

Harvest time here is not at all like Succoth, which

I think of as a joyous occasion. Instead, the farmers are worried sick about the price they will get and whether they will be able to meet their debt to Mr Nesbit and Mr Griffin or fall still farther behind. The work is exhausting but the men say they are having sleepless nights and you can almost see the worry in the deepness of the creases in their brows and the lines around their eyes and in the sudden grayness of their hair (I am sure I am not imagining it, though Mr Nesbit tells me I am).

The problem is that they are all on a treadmill and nobody knows how to get off. In the beginning it was easier for the store owners to keep track of their customers' debts if they grew just a single cash crop. The farmers found that suited them and cotton was easiest to manage since as one of them put it to me, "Any dad-blamed fool can raise it—all it needs is hot days and warm nights, an' we got plenty o' them—and nothin' can kill it, not even drought." So the storekeepers would stake farmers only if they grew cotton, which meant that before long that was all anybody was growing. They don't even grow what they eat, not wanting to sacrifice cotton land for food, so they pay dear for things like corn meal and flour that get sent down here from Iowa and the West and on which Mr. Nesbit and Mr. Griffin and everyone along the line make a pretty penny. . . .

10 January 1880

Dearest Mama,

It is raw and chill here now, although it never becomes outright cold. Things get very quiet around this season of year, and for the first time I am beginning to understand the sense of loneliness of country life that the farmers sometimes admit to. They sit around all winter cooped up in their small, cold shacks with precious little to do. The only part of our store business that perks up around now is the patent medicines. I thought it was because there is naturally more sickness in winter, but I wrote to Benny telling him the names of the medicines that are most popular and asking why. Since many of them are made up in Phila. he was familiar with their ingredients, and he says the reason is undoubtedly that they all contain such things as laudanum, opium, morphine and other narcotics that soothe the farmers and help them while away the hours in a painless stupor. Unfortunately, says Benny, none of the medicines gets to the root of the problem, which is that many illnesses are caused by tiny organisms and not, as everyone around here seems to think, by constipation and night air.

It is no wonder they are always constipated, by the way. You would be, too, if you ate nothing but fatback, corn bread, hot biscuits, white gravy and molasses three times a day and 52 weeks a year. (The molasses by the way is to help you forget about the taste of sowbelly.) Their whole systems get jammed up and their breath is foul, their teeth rot, their skins break out in sores, their backs ache, and their appendixes burst in the middle of the night and they die without knowing why exactly. . . .

19 March 1880

Dearest Mama,

The farm folk are rousing themselves now that the first buds are nearly out, so we are powerfully busy (as they say) around the store getting ready for planting time. To try to be of help to our customers, I have done some reading up in books on agronomy that Benny found out about for me and were in the Savannah library. Also we get a few farm journals in here that pass the latest word on modern farming. Unfortunately, nobody around here is much interested & everyone says what was good enough for their pappy is good enough for them—if only God will smile their way as he used to on their ancestors.

Take the plows, for instance. Different kinds of soil need different kinds of plows but practically everyone gets the same kind—cheap. Where the land is sandy, the plow should not go deep but turn a wide furrow, but in the tight clay land (of which there is a lot in Ga.) a narrower and sharper-pointed plow is required. Only everyone just keeps on using the same stamped iron plows shipped in from Kentucky so long as they hold together. . . .

Later that spring, Ossie Nesbit's eyesight took a turn for the worse, and Gus Griffin promoted me to manager of his McAllister branch (though the store retained Ossie's name and he still drew a small salary) and jacked my wages to a lavish forty a month.

It was a considerable responsibility, for I was not yet twenty and still very much a stranger, but I had learned fast and did not have to strive abrasively to keep the operation solvent; Gus Griffin had built that into the system. The principal margin of error available to me was the extension of too much credit to the wrong parties, and both Ossie and Uncle Gus coached me in the particulars so that I might avoid the pitfalls which lure a generous heart.

My ascension to upper managerial ranks signaled a steady increase in sales at Nesbit's Store, the result of spontaneous—and not a little calculated—outgoingness on my part. The store's real business, I sensed, was not its merchandise, which was standard fare sold at extortionist markups, but the lives of the people who patronized it. It was those I tried to cater to without being a busybody or smart aleck. I had my most success with the blacks, whom I had long since stopped referring to as *schvartsas* in letters to my mother. The countryside was swarming with them, yet I never felt menaced by the fact or the need to establish my superiority over them. Their ignorance was so monumental and their expectations so low that any effort at kindness on my part was repaid tenfold.

Plato, whose last name was Layne, I promoted to the rank of assistant clerk in charge of a great deal of dirty work. This greatly enhanced his standing in his own eyes and those of the colored community in general, while the whites, from Ossie on down, were not offended by his honorific designation because its very humbleness seemed a mocking reaffirmation of the negro's degraded station in life. To Plato, however, the dollar and a quarter he received each week was real enough, and to the blacks in the hinterland I was two steps from qualifying as a young Lincoln. I addressed them as "mister" and "ma'am" when no whites could hear—a duplicitous tactic in which the blacks cooperated by waiting to be served until white ears were absent. Similarly, when no whites were around I allowed them use of the privy instead of the woods or fields, on the theory that bodily elimination was universal to the species and deserved to be expedited without reference to social status. Shit was shit.

My very name—Seth, third son of Adam and Eve, apparently favored by God over the iniquitous Cain and the slain Abel— added to my appeal among these rural blacks. I was an embodiment of the prophets and teachings of ancient Israel. They were forever asking my blessing in Hebrew, the magic language of piety, and beseeching me to perform, in full voice and melody, a sample prayer in that mystically potent tongue. (The favorite was my *brocha* over bread, a reasonable facsimile of which was soon being recited, I learned reliably, over the biscuits in dozens of nearby farm shacks in the hope that Jehovah would especially welcome worship in His native dialect, perhaps even bless the crops as a bonus—or, at the very least, turn the biscuits softer.)

Every Saturday just after closing and before riding back to Savannah, I stuck a few pennies in my trousers, went out to the sideyard where a dozen black children gathered for the ceremony, and stood on my head. If that did not completely empty my pockets, I added six or seven cartwheels to the performance as the gleeful youngsters scrambled in my wake to claim the coins. They had never seen a clown before. To their elders, I was also endowed with the properties of a healer because I insistently denounced their fondness for swigging turpentine as a cure-all. The stuff smelled bad, tasted worse, burned their insides like scalding tar—and therefore, to their thinking, had to be splendid medicine. I read to them, at every opportunity, a letter from Benny, who advised that the principal effect of turpentine, when taken internally, was to turn the kidneys into delicatessen. At least a few of them took Benny's advice that eating cabbage and greens and any fruits they could scavenge was better medicine than all the bottled rotgut on his brother's shelves. He also urged them to "sweep the floors of their cottages several times a week." I wrote back that the "cottages" were shacks, brooms were a luxury item, and that almost nobody had a floor to sweep—only earth.

The white farmers I enchanted less, but that there were so few signs of overt hostility to my faith, my youthfulness, and my outlander's way of talk and thought was all the triumph I could expect. I knew enough not to act haughty, and the genuineness of my interest in their problems and obsessions was plain. I joined whenever possible their porch palaver about everything under the sun, and above it, too. The hottest running debate, as I recall those long summer afternoons, concerned the efficacy of infant baptism; the Baptists and Disciples of Christ were of course strong for full immersion while the Methodists and Presbyterians insisted that symbolic sprinkling perfectly well satisfied the Deity's wishes. At times I was consulted to offer a presumably neutral opinion, but given the perils of antagonizing one or the other group, I generally found virtue in both sides and instead produced the torn old Vulgate that Ossie had left behind to settle ecclesiastical disputes. Invariably, my efforts only compounded the problem, and I would be good-naturedly disqualified from the balance of the debate on the ground of possessing a truncated male member. When I protested, with equal good cheer, that one thing had nothing to do with the other and, besides, Jewish ritual really had not made my organ shorter but only a trifle more conical, they invited me to put it on the table so they could decide for themselves.

IV

Beyond his considerable economic sway, I soon discovered, Gus Griffin had also accumulated a good deal of political musculature in Chatham County. In fact, he ran it. Or to state the matter more precisely, no decision of consequence was taken without consulting and, more often than not, obliging him. No aspirant himself for public office, he oiled the flywheels of local power deftly and operated them noiselessly. His motivation was viewed as benign—the achievement of community-wide prosperity stood as the centerpiece of his platform—but his conception of how the rewards of that process ought to be gathered and distributed began with self-license and progressed no further than the principle of maximum self-aggrandizement. Greed, in short, he saw as a sizable contribution to the art and science of good government.

In his resolve to prevail over the legion of forces that fate had ranged against him in the aftermath of war, Uncle Gus was among the early crop in a new breed of Georgians—resilient (some said unprincipled) freebooters who saw that the plantation days would never come again and that the South would have to fuse with the rest of the Union, or starve. He promptly established amicable relations with the carpetbaggers, whom he found about as variously honest or conniving as the native population. He grasped, moreover, that there was no alternative, for it was their imported money that would have to transfuse economic life back into the South, that would go to operate the plantations and supply the merchants, build the railroads and feed the mills, open the coal and the iron mines, and generally rouse the Confederate diehards from protracted lethargy and bitterness. Because they found no choice but collusion, Uncle Gus and men like him joined in the rebuilding process with open-faced zest and fed well. By tactful collaboration with the carbetbagger-scalawag-negro-Republican-federal constellation of interests, which often warred among themselves, Griffin and his resolute brethren across the state dominated the Georgia legislature, which had never yielded more than one-third of its membership to radical and Reconstruction forces, even at the height of the Union dictates. With their political sovereignty relatively intact, the economic realists had scant trouble dissolving the mindless loyalty of the rural masses to the fast-fossilizing remnants of the plantation aristocracy, who continued to propound the romantic doctrine that industrialism was the scourge of every proud Southern yeoman. Uncle Gus, having concluded that the sole alternative was ruin, concentrated on accumulating capital and improving his rate of return instead of spilling his energies in the forlorn hope of restoring a vanished past.

Since most of the new industrial activity in the state was concentrated in the Atlanta area, Uncle Gus stayed in close touch with the financial and political kingpins there, thus assuring himself of the credit he needed to keep building his operations while monitoring the legislative front to be sure no radical arrangements were introduced to disturb his dominion. Nowhere in that equation was there room for genuine interest in the condition of the dirt farmers who had made him rich. He surely took no satisfaction in their poverty; it was just that he could not conceive of jeopardizing his own position even a fraction to help theirs. The Lord, it was universally acknowledged, helped those who helped themselves, and Gus Griffin was, by that measure, indisputably earning divine sanction in his plundering of the help-less.

I asked him one Saturday night, after bringing in an especially plump boodle, why the gap between our cash and credit prices was so large. I had tried to use consummate tact in framing the question, but he saw through me to the implied rebuke. The credit charges he himself bore at the insistence of Yankee-backed Atlanta and Cincinnati banks were no less extortionate, he said, than those he imposed on his clientele. That the latter, due to tumbling cotton prices, were unable to accumulate the where-withal to dig themselves out of debt was unfortunate, he agreed, but the supplies the farmers needed were not going down in price, so the merchants who furnished them could hardly be expected to do so on a charitable basis.

There was no way for me to challenge his claim, but my having raised the question at all must have alerted him to the desirability of convincing me he was at heart a humanitarian. Or, at the least, not a predator. He saw himself, rather, as a non-elected servant of the masses, helping them to meet their elemental needs on terms consistent with fiscal prudence. To demonstrate his sincerity as a businessman-statesman, Uncle Gus invited me to spend my three-day August vacation accompanying him and his nephew to the state Democratic convention in Atlanta, where he was to serve as a Chatham County delegate to pick the gubernatorial candidate. The idea more than likely originated with Billy Doak, who, in the absence of his mother and Mandy, then off on a nine-month grand tour of Europe, had been urged by his uncle to join him in what promised to be a spirited interlude in an otherwise quiet and somewhat lonely summer. Billy, though, insisted that the sugges-tion I come along as well had been his uncle's and betokened high personal and professional regard. Whatever the truth, the occa-sion marked the first time I had broken bread with Gus Griffin outside the Baxter house, and he proved an engaging host and col-orful narrator of the political warfare then unfolding.

The party machinery was in the firm grasp of the so-called Bourbon faction, of which Gus Griffin was a mainstay in the con-servative southeastern part of the state. "Bourbon" was plainly a misnomer for the group; "bourgeois" would have been more apt, for no Georgians were less wedded to the feckless past or more dedicated to the roseate future than these lawyers, bankers, brokers, merchants, railroadmen, and leather-lunged speculators. Shrewdly, they had attracted to their ranks and posted up front as standard-bearers men of golden voice, flowing beard, and courtly demeanor, many of them heroes of the late Confederacy and said to embrace the most cherished sentiments and ways of the ante-bellum age. Such a one was Alfred H. Colquitt, completing his first term that summer of 1880 as governor of Georgia and favored by the new masters of the state for re-nomination. Since Georgia was ruled overwhelmingly by Democrats, the nominee of the convention was thus virtually assured of election. But opposition to Colquitt was brewing, and although Uncle Gus dismissed it as trivial bickering by the yokels, Atlanta was alive with reports that rural interests would fight efforts to ram through the governor's re-nomination and seek in his place a compromise candidate more kindly disposed toward their needs.

Scion of a leading planter family, son of a legislator-judge-Methodist minister, Colquitt was a polished graduate of Princeton who had been an influential member of the Georgia Senate, outspoken states' rights Congressman in the mid-Fifties, and a brigadier general in the Confederate forces—he was hailed affectionately by regional orators as "the gallant hero of Olustee"—before enlisting as a suave industrial promoter who welcomed, indeed embraced, Northern financiers. He was known to have been associated with a multimillion-dollar syndicate invested in Southern railways, a New England textile mill, a Tennessee fertilizer factory, and far-flung coal-mining operations. Alongside him, Gus Griffin was a penny-ante piker, but by both such men had the alliance between the old planter class and the developers of the new industrial order been forged. What differences persisted between the two groups were generally resolved without open contest, thereby denying to the disaffected but largely leaderless and politically inept lower-class farmers of both races a meaningful voice in the affairs of state. Governor Colquitt, however, had opened the door to dawning public suspicion that the Bourbons were perhaps not entirely dedicated champions of the greatest good for the greatest number. Indeed, an investigation of his regime had resulted in the impeachment and resignation of the state treasurer, the impeachment and conviction of the comptroller general, the resignation of the commissioner of agriculture, and the disclosure that certain intimates of the governor were profiting

77

hugely from the brutal employment of convicts, whose labor they rented from the state at a cost per body not exceeding seven cents a day. Such abuses had hitherto been overlooked by white Georgians on the understanding that any issue dividing them along class lines could restore the negro to the status of political importance he had enjoyed for a time before the reclamation of white supremacy at the beginning of the Seventies. Ballot boxes were stuffed with impunity and black votes bought like corn meal whenever the racial issue threatened to surface; it was a rare party platform that contained any words beyond the gelatinous platitudes that all Anglo-Saxons were agreed upon. This time, though, the party machinery threw a gear. The clatter was deafening.

Billy and I sat in the jammed gallery, drenching in our own juices, as the speeches for and against the governor rattled on with the persistence—and range—of a snare drum. Only when it was proposed that Colquitt the heroic bungler step aside for a new candidate mutually agreeable to the ins and the reform-minded agrarian bloc did the tiered chamber begin to stir. Then, as the dissident elements seemed to be gathering strength around the floor, up rose redoubtable boss Patric Walsh, owner of the Augusta *Chronicle* and bare-knuckled defender of party orthodoxy, to try to crush the rebellion. Dewlaps aquiver, he spewed out the staccato phrases like Vulcan showering sparks from his anvil. They had stood together two years earlier to put this distinguished son of the South into high office, he thundered, and they must do so once again in the name of party harmony and Christian civilization—"and we do not intend to depart from the city of Atlanta until we have nominated Alfred H. Colquitt! We have come here to do that, and we shall do so if it takes till Christmas!" The hall vibrated with obedient cheers, and the uprising seemed on the verge of extinction.

As the last echoes from Walsh's cannonade subsided, an extremely young, extremely slender man with a splash of red hair atop his even, freckled features could be heard addressing the house in a voice shrill and ringing with conviction. Standing on a chair, his chest proud but so narrow it looked as if it could be encircled by a pair of grown man's hands, he created a stark contrast to the magisterial presence of the previous speaker. All ears attended him now as he read through a list of possible alternative candidates. It was not what he was saying that riveted them so much as the audacity of so callow and miniature an opponent of the party hierarchy. I guessed him to be in his early twenties, at most. Soon word circulated that the speaker was a delegate from McDuffie County named Thomas Watson, who practiced law in Thomson, a town about thirty miles out of Augusta, and was said locally to dwell in fear of no man. Suddenly, his list completed, young Watson looked over the hall and then toward the chieftain Walsh, who had just delivered the Colquitt-or-bust ultimatum to the convention. "Sir," he said, "I am tired of hearing the cry of generosity when I see no generosity." There was a smack or two of applause. "I am tired of the cry of harmony," the youngster went on, "when I see no harmony." More applause. "I have not come here to be fattened on chaff," he said, voice surging with confidence. "nor filled with taffy. You might as well attempt to gain flesh on corncob soup in January." They laughed, and now he had them awaiting his every phrase. The redhead warmed to the opportunity:

> Mr. Chairman, the gentleman from Augusta tells us that we must yield to him, and that unless we nominate Colquitt this party will permit no nomination. Mr. Chairman, this is not the language which a friend addresses to a friend. It is not the language a brother addresses to a brother. It is the language of a master to his slave.

Cheers to the rafters.

> Sir, the gentleman's position means that we must take Colquitt or the party will be disrupted. Sir, if it must come, let it come. We love the party, honor it, are devoted to it, but we will not yield when the gentleman's speech has made it a loss of self-respect to surrender.

When he was done, the hall shook as the name Tom Watson flew from every lip. The slender young man was engulfed by well-wishers who grasped for his hand, and the anti-Colquitt forces marched around the floor in a demonstration that confirmed the power of Watson's oratory. Even the pro-Colquitt newspapers agreed the following day that the words of the delegate from McDuffie County—at twenty-four, he was the youngest participant in the convention—were the sensation of the conclave. Uncle Gus himself, conceding that Boss Walsh had been a trifle ham-handed in trying to bring the convention to its senses by grabbing for its throat, had praise for the young spellbinder. "A purer piece o' grit never inhabited a slight frame," he said. Then with a nudge in my rib cage, he added, "The outcome, o' course, won't change any."

He was right, naturally. On the morrow, the magic had fled, and Walsh had the votes. Colquitt was re-nominated, but Billy Doak and I had been stirred by the fight and pleased that a fellow only a few years older than we had stood that steaming chamber on its ear. To our delight, and Uncle Gus's disgust, the anti-machine forces decided soon after to buck the Colquitt candidacy and in a rump session put up a contender named Norwood to stand in the election as an independent Democrat. "A nobody," said Uncle Gus. And so he proved as the campaign reports circulated in Savannah through September. Norwood spoke infrequently and ineffectually, and when he did take the stump, he succeeded only in antagonizing colored voters who should have been his strongest supporters. The sole item of interest to me in the campaign was word that Tom Watson was ranging up and down the Savannah Valley, plumping for Norwood with all his might. I wondered why.

One Saturday in October I got the chance to find out. It was a busy morning, when they were bringing the cotton in from all over the countryside. At first I didn't notice him, for he was easily lost in a crowd of three, but then he was next to me, the top of his red head no higher than my chin, and asking in a quiet, friendly way if he might give a little talk from my porch in the middle of the afternoon. "Won't do your business harm," he said. "I'd practically guarantee it." The eyes, pale and narrow, glowed with determination. The mouth and brows were thin and straight, a pair of parallel slashes across that smooth boyface. I told Tom Watson the community would be honored by his presence. He nodded thanks, asked if he might put up a poster or two, and suggested that I consider passing out a few refreshments, the cost of which, he had learned from his season as a storefront Demosthenes, would be recouped many times over from customers flocking the counters before and after the political address. When

I agreed, he wrote "Free Eats" in crayon at the bottom of the posters and "Three O'Clock Today" just above.

It was the largest assemblage I had seen since coming to McAllister. There must have been well over two hundred souls milling about the hitching grounds, and the free cans of sardines, oysters, and salmon on crackers served on the porch were soon exhausted. I felt like a master of ceremonies as the speaker moved to the porch railing and looked out on all those upturned, weather-beaten faces that slowly quieted. They stood as one man, nearly, uniformed in their faded chambray shirts, denim overalls bleached by too many washings with lye soap, blunt brogans caked with manure, and big black wool hats that set off their gaunt, corded throats and, when they turned, the creviced crimson back of their necks. Perhaps two dozen colored farmers hovered on the edge of the gathering.

Watson worked them over like a virtuoso. One after another, he pinked those raw nerve-endings of discontent. He regretted that he was there as a party rebel, he said, but the party leadership had grown so high and mighty it no longer cared what the common man preferred. The men who worked the soil were the backbone of Georgia—its heart as well—but nowhere were they heard or represented in the highest councils of the state. As for the governor, there were all those scandals that had apparently escaped his attention, the high taxes he had levied, the dubious appointments he had made. And the convict-lease system he had encouraged, allowing the state a profit in crime by renting out prisoners for twenty years at a stretch, was a throwback to the barbarism of the dark ages. The blacks in the throng applauded with special animation over the last item. The time had come, the speaker concluded with a spread-eagle flourish of his arms as he squinted into the sun, to elect a governor committed not merely to the interests of moneymen and the railroads but to the hopes and souls of decent men in all walks. And then he was moving among them, shaking their hands and listening to their complaints and gathering up their affection. "A right plucky pissa'," I heard them say as they finished shopping and headed for their wagons, spewing tobacco juice all the way.

He stayed after closing time for perhaps an hour while I brewed us some coffee and asked him what prospects his candidate had to beat the incumbent. "None," he said, "but they'll know they can't jes' stick our noses in it any time it suits 'em." He acknowledged that his decision to campaign against the party hierarchs had no doubt clouded his own political prospects, but principle and expediency were forever colliding, he added without excessive unction, "an' a fella has to decide when knucklin' under once too often makes him gag."

He asked me where I had come from, about how I liked Georgia, about the troubles of the farmers, and about my intentions. I told him I had once hoped to attend a university but there had been no money in the family for that and now I was eager to get ahead. He said he understood, that poverty was no disgrace, that he himself had been unable to pay the sixty-dollar tuition at Mercer, the little Baptist college in Macon, and was known as one of the poor boys, shy and awkward in manner and very plainly dressed, during his two years there as a student. After a number of spirited but low-paying stints as a teacher, he had read law, tried to practice in Augusta and gone hungry, then opened a little office in his hometown of Thomson and handled every case that walked in the door—and went after business in four adjacent rural counties as well. "You get to' work all day fo' two dollars sometime," he said. "An' sometime you get to ride fifty, sixty miles and if yo' lucky win a judgment fo' seven dollars an' costs. An' sometime yo' go a long way fo' nothin'—or worse. I went down to Pope Hill in Jeffe'son County couple years ago an' this Jim Cardue, he calls me a liar in the court room, so I slapped 'im, an' outside he does it again, so I hit 'im again, only he's a sizable cuss 'n' whips me pretty good. I end up with a scratched-up face. 'Course he was black-'n'-blued and had a split nose." I laughed and asked how one set about reading for the law. He said he was pleased I might be thinking about getting out of the merchant business because the storekeepers were bleeding the farmers throughout the South. I gave him Uncle Gus's answer to that. "Sounds like you been listenin' to too many snake-oil drummers," he said. "Usury is usury. Country folk're dyin' on the vine every place I go. Yo' look too honest to pretend you think otherwise." I gave a slight confessional nod as he reached for the small traveling kit he had stowed beneath my counter. "Jus' find yo'self an honest attorney—maybe a retired judge, even—and hope he'll let yo' hunker down in a corner an' answer yo' questions now an' again." He gave my hand a shake, said to look him up if I ever came to Thomson, and sprang nimbly onto his horse. "I'm due to fiddle at a dance up in Jasper," he said, looking down at me for the first time all day. "I betta' hightail it. I'll fiddle fo' the customers next time I come by —I'm pretty fair at it. Meanwhile, I'm much obliged to yo', Mr. Adler."

Governor Colquitt won sixty-five percent of the popular vote that election and Mr. Norwood managed thirty-five percent— thirty-four of it attributable, I warranted, to the efforts of Tom Watson.

He did not personally appear on my horizon again for nearly two years, but the picture of him, a bantam of rare courage and compassion, was never far from my thoughts. Meanwhile, I persevered. Sales at the store continued to grow, and Gus put my wages up to fifty-five a month. Then he learned that I had ordered ten gross of baby dolls for the Christmas season at a dollar and a quarter a dozen. "That's a mighty hefty investment in doll babies," he growled, looking at the order slip as if I had lost my senses. But I loaded up the store window with them, put up posters all over the county announcing their arrival, and soon had wagons pulling in from far and wide to buy the irresistible little critters at a quarter apiece. We sold them all except a threesome I held out and brought to Gus, who grudgingly put them in the window at the Adelphi. They lasted twelve minutes.

Beckoning me to his quarters on New Year's Day of 1881, Uncle Gus offered extravagant (if not entirely unmerited) praise for my industry, ingenuity, and unimpeachability and promoted me to the managership of his new outlet at Sunbury, in neighboring Effingham County. It was his largest undertaking to date and its plans, he confided, called for inclusion of a fertilizer-manufacturing department. His thoughts were more and more directed to converting the entire operation into a wholesale supply house and abandoning the retail outlets altogether. Again he advanced my wages—they stood at eighty-two a month now, generous pay by prevailing standards and enough for me to put some by in the bank in addition to what I sent my mother—and I was able to appear at the Baxters' Easter gala in entirely presentable apparel.

Amanda had come in for the occasion from Charleston, where she was completing her first year at Miss Melaney's Classes ("for Chantilly Lasses," she added *con brio* in detailing their endless charms), and Billy Doak had returned a week prior from Virginia under somewhat cloaked circumstances. I thought at first the cause must have been his studies, about which he would caterwaul to me in his intermittent letters; a fellow of abundant physical presence, he possessed a mind hostile to abstract conceptions and indifferent to the civilizing arts. Greek he found elusive, rhetoric tedious, and Shakespeare and the poets bombastic. Only his discovery of fencing, in which he was coached by an itinerant French master, had stimulated him at Charlottesville. At Christmas, he had demonstrated his progress to me by wielding the blade with flashing aplomb and thoroughly dispatching a scarecrow he had enlisted for practice. It was the swordplay, I suspected now, that had been his undoing at the university. His uncle disparaged him, within my earshot, as "our addled D'Artagnan," and I learned much later that Billy, while in his cups, had crossed swords with a fellow student and lacerated the poor lad's windpipe. Happily, the blow was not fatal, but Billy retreated homeward in shame, stashed his épée in the attic, and declined all invitations to exhibit it. The only change I noted in him, aside from a generally subdued and occasionally morose mood, was a tendency to have a wineglass perpetually in hand before and after dinner and his insistence that everyone now call him "Bax," as he was known at the university. A few months after his return, he took a position with the Georgia Central, shuttling triangularly among Savannah, Augusta, and Macon in the freight department. Within the family circle and among outside intimates, it was understood that the railroad job would serve as Bax's apprenticeship before joining, as heir apparent, his uncle's thriving enterprise.

In Sunbury, a town up the Ogeechee River, where the falls provided hydropower for several new mills to which the farmers herded for work after laying down their hoes in despair, I managed nicely. Uncle Gus's new emporium recorded sales nearly three times as heavy as anticipated. A machine I installed to separate the customers from their funds more pleasurably—"Ritty's Incorruptible Cashier," as the first cash register to be sold in Georgia was designated in its patent—was an instant popular success. The paper roll on which each sale was posted to the accompaniment of a merrily ringing bell rewarded both customer and proprietor, the former by announcing his acquisition to the world, the latter by holding the clerk to strict account for the cash and providing a running record of the number and size of sales and the daily totals. Gus ordered one for the Adelphi two months later and stormed over its interminable non-delivery; finally, he requisitioned my machine, which was a somewhat rickety demonstration model, and I did not get it back until the new improved model arrived in Savannah from Ohio. To pick up business, which seemed to slacken off, coincidentally or otherwise, with the forced evacuation of the register, I began to advertise heavily and perhaps even a little diabolically in the Sunbury weekly *Vindicator*. In heavy-breathing prose of my own composition, we featured the latest in frippery and gadgetry, from lacquered rice-paper fans to the most elegant of velocipedes, while in smaller type announced sale prices for the most unenthralling of items—earthenware chamber pots, for example, at twenty-nine cents each (a mere 100 percent markup instead of the usual 300 percent rooking). Enticed by novelties they did not need and could not afford, our customers compensated by loading up on chamber pots and similar necessities. Sales leaped. Gus again followed suit. He cleared out a whole warehouse of rusting hardware and moldy dry goods in one heavily advertised marathon sale that I was brought down to Savannah to direct. Gus claimed you could hear the clatter of departing pots and pans up as far as Charleston.

By the end of the year, I was spending more of my time at the Adelphi, helping coordinate operations for all the stores, than up in Sunbury. Gus invited me to join him in drawing up the orders for the spring line, and at Easter of 1882 he took the climactic step in our business relationship. It was preceded by a superb dinner at the Yamacraw Club, the exclusive oasis on Bull Street of which he was a founding member. The soirée, in a private dining room, was attended by just the two of us. Over brandy and cigars, Gus Griffin spoke expansively of a golden future. The gunsmoke of the Sixties and the rancor of the Seventies had dissipated, he said, "and if we can jus' keep Hotspurs like young Tom Watson treed—or maybe somebody'll jus' lay a pole-axe to 'im one night— there's gonna be enough riches to make everyone happy. We got the raw materials. We got low-cost labor. We're gettin' the railroads put in everywhere yo' turn. An' folks're fed up with all the stale feuds and sorry combat of yeste'day. All we need now is the money to put it all together—and the brains an' fortitude to carry on through. That's what you got, son—guts an' gray matter —and that's why I want yo' with me now that I'm mappin' out big plans." Having tantalized me, he then suggested I drop by the offices of his attorney the next morning to read a proposition he had had drawn up in properly convoluted legalese. "Gene'll explain anything that you can't unpuzzle on yo' own," he said with a small smile, "though I suspec' he'd have to get up pretty early to pull the wool on you, son. I hope you'll think hard on what he shows you."

Eugene Montrose Venable was an admirably direct, which is not to say abrupt, counselor-at-law. He was as crisp and precise as Gus Griffin was sodden and haphazard. I had seen him at the store often enough to nod to as he marched by, his immaculate white head and matching suit evidently immune to contamination by the surrounding vapors. But we had never spoken to one another before that memorable interview in his second-floor office on Factors' Row.

"Mr. Griffin is well pleased with your work for him, Mr. Adler," he said. "He tells me he has had few other employees so able and dedicated. He wishes to assure himself of your future services and has accordingly instructed me to draft this formidable-looking document. To cut through the voluminous legal phraseology, I should say at once that it is a proposal of partnership. A very junior partnership, I hasten to add, but as you have only recently attained your majority, this would seem a highly commendable beginning."

It was a quite simple proposal on its face. I was to draw from that time forward an annual salary of not less than two thousand dollars, to be considered an advance against my share of the partnership's net profits. That share was to be two percent at the outset and to increase by one percent every two years of continued satisfactory employment until my total share reached five percent; in addition, I would be entitled to buy into the partnership up to the point matching the share given to me as compensation. Thus, by the age of twenty-seven, I might own as much as ten percent of the enterprise, provided I found the funds to purchase half that amount at a figure agreeable to all the partners.

"Those other partners," Venable added, "consist solely of Mr. Griffin's sister and her two children, who I believe are well known to you and who have been apprised and are entirely approving of this arrangement. Their aggregate share of the partnership, I have been authorized to disclose, is twenty-five percent." He folded up his copy of the draft as I continued to study it in glazed disbelief. "It is, I think you'll agree, a remarkably generous proposition," said the attorney. "It is unique within my experience, let me assure you—and in view of the substantial size of Mr. Griffin's organization, extraordinary by any standard." I meekly concurred, and the attorney went on methodically, "Mr. Griffin has instructed me to say further that as a token of his admiration, he plans, upon the consummation of this arrangement, to nominate you to membership in the Yamacraw Club—which is tantamount, may I insert, to assuring your acceptance—and to assume, as his personal responsibility and gift, the annual dues for a period of five years." My head was swimming now. "The cuisine there, as I believe you know, is the finest in Savannah," he said.

Then the attorney shifted uneasily in his chair and looked out the window at the quay for a moment as if rummaging through his mind for precisely the most fitting words in which to frame the final portion of the proposal. "I must add," he said, spacing his phrases, "that this arrangement has but one condition attached to it from your side of the bargain—namely, that you privately renounce your affiliation with the Hebrew faith and embrace, within twelve months, any of the Protestant denominations. Mr. Griffin's preference would be the Presbyterian faith but he appreciates that decision must be left solely to your discretion—."

"Tell him thank you but no," I said at once, a sudden hollow within me.

Venable formed a small Gothic arch with his fingertips and studied me in silence for a time. "Yes," he said then, "Gus guessed you would probably say just that. He therefore asked that you take a week to reflect on the proposition—."

"I don't need a week."

"Nevertheless he asks you to take it. He believes the matter too important to be dealt with in peremptory fashion. He suggests you vacation in Charleston for the week at full salary."

"I see," I said. "He seems to have thought of everything."

"In keeping with his regard for you, Mr. Adler—."

"If his regard is so great, why does he condition his proposal on a matter utterly extraneous to my ability as a businessman?"

"Precisely because he believes your adherence to the Christian tradition will open many doors to you and make you that much more valuable an asset to the firm."

"That's candid, at any rate," I said. "Does Mr. Griffin have no regard for my spiritual well-being? For my peace of mind?"

"He believes the tranfer of your religious denomination will put your soul in no great jeopardy on Judgment Day," Venable said drily. "He believes you to be, above all, an intensely practical young man who, for all your pride in the faith of your fathers, has not benefited much from it. Your success here, he feels, has come in spite of it. To put it bluntly, Mr. Adler, he doesn't think you give all that much of a damn about being a Jew so long as no one calls you on it."

"He's calling me on it—."

"He's making a business proposition to you—."

"He's trying to buy me."

"Without a doubt," said Venable. "The question is the fairness of the price—."

He phrased it in a way precisely as offensive as the proposition itself. It occurred to me he had done so intentionally. "And what is your view of the bargain, Mr. Venable, if I may ask—?"

He was not surprised by the question. "My view is of no consequence whatever," he said.

"Let me judge that."

"Mr. Griffin pays me a fee to represent his interests. These, at the moment, include my soliciting your agreement to his proposition—."

"Does that mean he has bought you as well?"

I saw a glint of anger streak across his face and then its composure returned as rapidly. "I've enjoyed our meeting, Mr. Adler," he said, rising to shake my hand. "I look forward with interest to our interview a week hence. I wish you well in your deliberations."

Despite myself, I took the proffered week to decide. Part of it I passed, as proposed, in Charleston, where Mandy walked me from one end of the Battery to the other not less than a hundred times and begged me to relent. "I have prayed to Jesus for this to come to pass," she said, "and now you won't even hear of it. Why, Seth?"

"Because you pray to Jesus," I said. "Jesus was a man, Mandy—a flesh-and-blood man."

"But the Lord was in him, Seth, usin' him—."

"Like the Lord used the burning bush—?"

"Yes," she said, "yes! yes! Just like that—."

"But nobody prays to a bush, Mandy Beth. Jesus was a man, a teacher, a saint even—but not a god. The Lord said, 'Thou shalt have no other gods before me,' Mandy, don't you see?"

"You can learn to love Jesus, Seth—."

"I love him already—or what he teaches, at any rate. But your uncle wants me to worship Jesus as well."

"Isn't that what love is, Seth—a kind of worship?"

I took her by both hands and spun her toward me. "I love you, Mandy Beth—on my honor I do, and you know it. But love means cherishing, not worshipping."

She squeezed my hands hard. "Yo' jus' splittin' hairs, Seth. It's not becomin'. If you love me, then love Jesus."

"If you love me back, don't ask me to."

"I think yo' afraid to love, Seth."

"If it means I have to choose between you and God."

She struggled against her tears. "Your God, yes," she said.

In Savannah on the weekend, Bax and I rode out to Thunderbolt and the meadow where we had first played ball together four years before. "You're being invited to join the family is what it means," he said. "I think that's the finest tribute yo' can pay another human bein'—."

"Don't you think the price of admission is a little steep?"

"I suppose it all depends on yo' convictions, Seth. Does a man's religion really matter all that much if you subscribe to the notion we'a all God's children?"

"Why ask me that? Why not ask your uncle?"

"In case you don' know, Seth, we-all agreed to Uncle Gus's proposal—."

"Including Mandy?"

"Especially Mandy. She said if we don't mean that much to you, then yo' place is elsewhere."

A letter came from my mother the next day saying that Grandpa had died. On his deathbed, she wrote, he pronounced a *choleria* on the tsar of all the Russias for the new edicts against the Jews, word of which had just reached America. "They are termed the May Laws," she explained, "and they require the expulsion of the Jews from all the villages and rural centers, even in the Pale of Settlement. Only in the ghettos can the Jews of Russia now live. Travel and trade are forbidden. The bandits do this, Sethela, because they say if the Jews were permitted to enter the life of Russia, they would dominate it. Sometimes I believe God is on holiday. Your Grandpa went to his rest an angry man. I thank Heaven for our America and pray for both my dear sons. . . ."

My second interview with Eugene Venable turned out differently from what I suppose either of us had anticipated. My connection with Gus Griffin was at an end. Instead, I would read law with Venable for no wages during the first six months, attending court with him and being instructed on the pleadings and proceedings, in return for serving as scrivener and all-purpose lackey; the next six months, I would clerk at fifty dollars per. In a year I would seek admission to the bar; the possibility of my joining his practice was held open but nothing more.

FOUR

If every worthy Jew is, as has been said, at heart a Talmudist, then every worthy lawyer is at heart a Jew. The best of both breeds share the reflex to worry a proposition into the ground after examining it from five dozen angles and detecting its every peril. Finally, though, it is not that propensity to fret a problem to death en route to solving it that distinguishes the ablest of legal practitioners (whereas it is precisely that obliterating pertinacity that immortalizes the most gifted students of *pilpul*); it is, rather, their knack for casting the problem before them in such a way as to assure a satisfactory solution. No one, after all, long prospers by winning medals in losing causes. The trick is to reduce hapless undertakings to a minimum. Eugene M. Venable, Esquire, made this my first lesson at the bar.

"Can you tell me, Mr. Adler," he asked, folding his arms across his chest, "how to discover the height of a building by using a barometer?"

I weighed the question carefully. My brother Benny, indefatigably fascinated by such instruments, had actually constructed a working model of one when we were lads, but my interest in it had been limited to the remarkably frangible nature of the quicksilver he kept trying to insert in it (and which I kept removing to make into mushy pellets). Rather than offering an absurd guess, I confessed total ignorance to my mentor.

"Well, sir," he said, "you go directly up to the owner of the structure in question and ask, 'Will you tell me how high your building is if I give you this barometer?'"

His face, for the instant, was as blank as mine. Only when he allowed himself the merest crinkle around the edges of his thin mouth did I detect his purpose and permit myself to laugh out loud. It was quite the shrewdest, most economical piece of pedagogy I had ever heard. And the more I thought about it, the harder I laughed. Mr. Venable smiled a bit more openly over my appreciative response (although his teeth never made an appearance) and then waited with swiftly restored solemnity for my enthusiasm to subside.

"Let me not belabor the point," he said, folding his long, bony fingers together and fixing his look at the wall just above my head. "Neither limitless industry nor bolt of insight nor the timely intrusion of the gods—or all of these—can be relied upon for the excellent performance of this craft. Note, if you will, that I say 'craft' and not 'trade' or 'profession' or 'calling' or some yet loftier term. 'Craft' is precisely what is involved, no more, no less. Your native intellect and the natural responses of the barnyard will likely prove more enlightening to you in the pursuit of this work than fully mastering the letter of the law. Let me, therefore, venture to reduce the entire lawyering process to three seemly steps. First, my friend, define the matter at issue with the utmost clarity of which you are capable. Let it shimmer before your contemplation. To proceed before the shimmering stage has been reached is little wiser than to advance upon hostile ramparts blindfolded. Second, take pain to assemble all the tools at your disposal and to understand their various uses—barometers included. Third and finally, prepare what documents you do as if every iota must withstand the severest scrutiny by the justices of the Supreme Court of the land. No piece of work worth doing in the first instance, Mr. Adler, is too small to be executed with high devotion." He unclasped his hands. "End of sermon."

Never again after that first day did I hear a homily drop from the man's dry lips. His mind and manner were entirely hard-edged; he was ill disposed to vaporous maunderings and grand pronouncements. And while he was far less theatrical than almost every other member of the Savannah bar and tastefully undemonstrative in and out of the court room, his practiced astringency worked well to his advantage. That very spareness of utterance assured rapt attention for whatever he did manage to say, which proved invariably acute and often totally demolishing.

At the outset, I was put to reading for two months when I was not performing relatively mindless chores such as copying documents by hand or letterpress in the office and tracing unindexed title conveyances in the nethermost bowel of the county courthouse. My texts were three: Blackstone, for the basic architecture of Anglo-American jurisprudence; the Constitution of the United States, for grasping the ingenuity of the federal compact; and the Georgia Code, for earning a livelihood.

"All else follows from these," said Mr. Venable, guiding me to his shelves. His Blackstone was a four-volume abridgment. He flicked out the first in the set. "You will find in here what a superb foundation we colonies had to build upon," he said, flipping through the pages. "You will savor the style and cadence of the law—its structured sense and pleasing symmetry. Why, a deed, for example, is nothing more than a single long sentence, but so painstakingly composed and integral at its best, that no more than one is needed—." He cut himself off before succumbing to adoration of what he had insisted was no more than a craft. The Constitution he told me to master inside out—"It is not an exhaustive task; it is a miracle of brevity and conciseness." The codification of the Georgia statutes, on the other hand, filled so fat a volume that I needed both arms nearly to transport it from the reading stand it normally inhabited beside Mr. Venable's desk. "Familiarize yourself with it," he said, "don't memorize it. Learn to find your way around. The index, of course, is your touchstone. Unfortunately, it is an abomination. I think the Mad Hatter himself must have perpetrated the thing—I believe he has in mind that equity is an exalted form of horsemanship. But once you get the hang of it, you'll discover a certain internal consistency to it, at least."

I dizzied myself putting down the foundation. Wanting to learn it all in an instant, I found my mind racing ahead of what was on the page before me and thereby too often losing the thread. The mental excitement was so great that it took me two weeks to figure out that in my haste to cover ground, I had entirely overlooked the contour of the terrain. I started again, this time tethering my attention to the text at hand. Like bits of mosaic, patterns formed. I no longer expected the law to reveal itself to me in one grand, luminous design; the merits of each piece and sliver were quite enough to sustain me, and when I discovered them interlocking with frequency, my ecstasy was muted but nonetheless genuine.

By midsummer, when the activity of every law office in Savannah had been reduced to intensive immobility and Mr. Venable was free to ask after my progress, the second stage of my legal education began. My teacher may have been a poor Polonius but he made a more than passable Socrates, with a touch of Torquemada added for catnip. My lessons took the form of thrice-a-week dialogues, lasting between one hour and two and growing for the most part out of recent cases in which Mr. Venable himself had participated.

I had demonstrated enough progress by summer's end to be promoted from exploration of the hypothetical to the substantive daily concerns of the office. Mr. Venable allowed me to look over his shoulder as he prepared an action in behalf of the First National Bank of Sunbury against the Mayor and City Council of Sunbury for the recovery of $2,639 in taxes levied against it—in plain violation, the bank contended, of the Revised Code of the United States, which exempted national banks organized under federal laws from taxation by local or state authorities. Starting in 1872, the city had imposed a one-hundred-dollar license fee against the bank; starting in 1878, it had assessed a tax of one percent upon its capital stock. The bank protested in writing each year but nevertheless paid the fee and taxes, so that it might avoid, it said, a sale and seizure of its property by the municipality. I was assigned to gather the grounds upon which we might move to recover the bank's payments; Mr. Venable, meanwhile, would pursue the same course independently. He proved rather better at it.

At our first strategy meeting on the case, I hesitantly proffered as a useful precedent the Supreme Court's well-known decision in 1819 of *McCulloch* v. *Maryland*. The justices, in that famous instance, had outlawed a state's power to tax the local branch of the nationally chartered Bank of the United States. Voice aquiver with conviction, I quoted from Chief Justice Marshall's resonant opinion:

> That the power to tax involves the power to destroy;
> that the power to destroy may defeat and render useless
> the power to create; that there is a plain repugnance in
> conferring on one government a power to control the

constitutional measures of another, which other . . . is declared to be supreme over that which exerts the control, are propositions not to be denied. . . .

"Yes, yes," said Mr. Venable, "a fine old chestnut and nobly put. And how precisely does this help us?"

The *McCulloch* decision seemed so plainly apposite that I was certain he was ragging me. "Why, I believe, sir, that it deprives the city of Sunbury—or any city or state or territory or what-have-you—of imposing a tax upon any creation of the federal government or institution chartered by the United States—."

"*Any* creation or institution, you say?"

"I—so it would seem, sir."

"Seeming is not knowing. Why, just ten years ago the justices of that selfsame Supreme Court were called upon to decide whether the Union Pacific Railroad, which was chartered by the Congress, was immune to taxation in the states through which it runs. And do you have any conception, sir, of what conclusion they reached?" He paused the merest fraction of a second. "Let me tell you, then. The Court said the railroad was not immune—*not*, sir, immune from state and local taxes. Read, for your elucidation, the Supreme Court reports at 18 *Wallace* 5." He crossed his arms in mild perturbation with me. "I fear that you grant far too much sway to *McCulloch*. More to the point, sir, I fear you misconstrue the nature of our assignment. We are *not* attempting to prove the illegality of the city's tax upon our client. The city is in indisputable violation of section 5214 of the federal code, behind which *McCulloch* stands as a useful beacon insofar as it applies to local taxation of a federally chartered bank. Our problem is not that our client has been wronged but how are we to *recover* his illegally taken funds. You will see that this is a different question entirely."

I saw. Back I went to the library shelves, and before the day was out re-presented myself before Mr. Venable with a mildly hopeful air. "The supreme court of Georgia held," I reported, "in 48 *Georgia* 309, that in general a tax levied without authority of law may be recovered, and nowhere do I discover a federal or state statute authorizing a municipal tax upon a federally chartered bank." Now, I thought, we were getting somewhere.

"Yes," said Mr. Venable, "but your case did not decide that a *voluntary* payment could be recovered or that a recovery could be realized unless the payment was compulsory. Had you been a shade more diligent, Mr. Adler, you would have come upon 50 *Georgia* 304, in which the state supreme court held that a tax voluntarily paid, *even though* illegally assessed by the taxing power, cannot be recovered unless some artifice, deception, or fraudulent practice was involved." He looked hard at me. "And do our facts justify any such claim, Mr. Adler?"

"I—I would have to investigate further, sir, but so far as I now know, they do not."

"Correct. And where does that leave us, then?"

"Dependent, I suppose, on how the courts have defined 'voluntary' payment."

"Correct. Go find out. You might have a look at Mr. Dillon's treatise on corporations—the third edition, I should think."

I went one better: I found not only the definition propounded by the sage Mr. Dillon but several recent opinions of the United States Supreme Court that embraced Dillon's language and cited him. Having labored long into the night to make my discovery, I appeared before Mr. Venable with authentically bleary eyes first thing the following morning and read to him:

> Where a party pays an illegal demand, with full knowledge of all the facts which render such demand illegal, *without an immediate and urgent necessity therefor,* or unless to release (not to avoid) his person or property from detention, *or to prevent an immediate seizure* of his person or property, such payment *must be deemed voluntary,* and cannot be recovered back. And the fact that the party, at the time of making the payment, files a written protest, does not make the payment involuntary.

"Exactly," he said.

My face dropped. "You know these cases, then?"

"I know them," he said. "It is my business to know them."

I looked up sadly. "Our prospects of winning, then, are remote, I take it—or have I overlooked some miraculous device that will rescue us?"

"I think not," he said. "I've chased down every conceivable avenue. I believe the bank's case for recovery is hopeless, and have so advised. They wish me to litigate, nevertheless, and so we shall put the best face we can upon the facts. Meanwhile, I have instructed the officers to withhold future payments and to institute an injunctive action at once if the city persists in trying to collect its illegal tax."

He carried the case with remarkable adroitness to the Georgia supreme court, where our client was roundly thrashed. The bank, said the court, had not properly resisted the illegal levy "by the exercise of that diligence that the law favors." The bank was obliged to act "within the strict rule the law has fixed"; otherwise, it had to abide the consequences of its own default and negligence.

"Admirable," said Mr. Venable, studying the court's ruling without a flicker of resentment. "Please note, Mr. Adler, that the court finds duress or coercion to have been merely 'shadowed forth,' to use their words, as the impelling power or motive for the bank's payment. Shadows are rarely helpful creatures in the eyes of the law. Indeed, they are generally classed as invisible." He put the court's opinion to one side and reached for new business. "I have no doubt," he said, scanning a pile of correspondence, "that the bank will disburse its fee to us at the earliest possible moment."

II

He was, by turns, properly patient and impatient with me, excusing the inevitable misapprehensions, deploring the inexcusable lapses—an ideal taskmaster, now guiding, now cajoling, always accessible if not always joyful at the intrusion. For me it proved a relationship fruitful beyond any expectation. If it lacked the dimension of personal solicitude, I could not complain. I had not, after all, enrolled in a nursery. Our association was entirely a professional one in those months, and in that regard he was as open and generous with me as any man could be. His private life he kept thoroughly guarded, and not merely from me, I learned. In and around the courthouse, Eugene Venable was considered a distinctly cold fish, albeit a masterly practitioner. So clenched and meticulous was he said to be that he had been unable for some years now to find a clerk he could tolerate long. That marked me as rare merchandise.

As if to acknowledge the impersonal tone to our dealings, Mr.

Venable encouraged me to haunt the county courthouse, to meet and mingle with fledgling lawyers of my generation, and to watch and make note of the virtuoso performers of his own. He himself was of that breed of attorney who holds the client to be best served when his case never reaches the courtroom; Mr. Venable's best efforts were thus devoted to thrashing out a matter in his or opposing counsel's quarters—or down by the old mill stream if that would prove congenial to settlement. I admired this cerebral preference, but it was a seemingly juiceless variety of practice for the lawyer-in-training who much prefers histrionics and naked confrontation before judge and jury. Young bloods crave action. Two and three times a week I therefore attended the courtroom, hanging on the fiery (and deploring the soggy) exchanges between counsel, jotting down impressions in my now bursting notebook and grading the performances. My own estimate was so often at odds with the findings of the jury that I rapidly concluded blarney and bluster were far more essential gifts in that arena than a knowing or nimble brain. The most successful of that courthouse corps were simple thespians. I saw why Eugene Venable kept his distance from forensic folderol.

I observed with special interest a case pitting a train engineer named Whitehead, who had lost his leg on the job, against the Augusta, Macon & Savannah Railroad, reputedly the sootiest line in the South and surely one of the most arrogant, judging by what Billy Doak Baxter, who worked for it, had confided to me. It was a plain case of David v. Goliath, to my view. I listened with bleeding heart as Whitehead's counsel, an especially mellifluous mouthpiece, recounted how the trainman while straddling the engine and the car behind it had reached down to uncouple the two cars even as the train was in motion—a standard maneuver, to hear the lawyer tell it. But the drag bar on the engine pilot gave way as Whitehead landed on it and tumbled him onto the track, where his leg got so mangled that it had to be amputated. Who was at fault? Whitehead was, said the railroad's attorney. No one had ever instructed him to uncouple a moving train. The engine, moreover, had been leased two weeks prior to the accident from the Georgia Railroad, and its safe maintenance was clearly the responsibility of Whitehead, who was in charge of the engine crew. Not so, countered the amputee's spokesman: the railroad had no more forbidden Whitehead to uncouple a moving train than it had specifically charged him with the safety inspection of the engine. Somebody was plainly negligent but not the engineer. So much for legal nicety. Plaintiff's counsel proceeded to recount, in gruesome detail and with undeniable eloquence, his client's bloody agony. He rendered by suggestion every groan and blast of pain the man had had to endure and declared him entitled to compensation equivalent to his suffering. "This unspeakable torture," he said, "must be placed on one side of the scales and on the other, money—money, money, and more money, until they in even balance hang." Moved, the jury awarded Whitehead fifteen thousand dollars. I was thus not surprised to discover that for its next appearance in that court on a negligence matter, the Augusta, Macon & Savannah line had retained the services of Eugene M. Venable.

I felt odd on the side of the industrial oppressors. My superior shortly disabused me of that uneasiness. The plaintiff, he insisted, was a fool and deserved not a cent of compensation. Belvedere was his name, and he had been riding his spirited stallion Bismarck along a highway adjacent to the railroad track. As they approached the crossing, along came a train, which at the required distance of four hundred yards gave a shrill blast of its whistle. Trouble ensued, however, when the engineer, whether overzealous or playful was not known, offered another sharp rasp of the whistle at a distance of only ninety yards from the crossing and kept on with the blasts until Bismarck was quite frothingly beside himself and dumped rider Belvedere to the ground, where fractures and contusions resulted. He sued the railroad for five thousand.

Belvedere's lawyer offered the usual lachrymose performance, though he was handicapped by his client's retention of all principal appendages. Mr. Venable, at his dispassionate best, unmasked Belvedere for a perfect jackass. The horse, he produced witnesses to testify, was a highly temperamental beast, known to bolt under circumstances far less dire than the explosion of a train whistle scant yards from his ear. No prudent man had any business riding such a highway. And surely when he saw and heard the train approach, he ought to have ridden away from the tumult and not toward it. Witnesses at the scene reported, furthermore, that the horse had dislodged its saddle and sent it flying, though the straps remained unbroken—evidence that the saddle had been carelessly put on. The jury sent Belvedere packing without a farthing.

In addition to his fee, the grateful railroad presented Mr. Venable with a small but lucrative portion of its regular business thereafter as well as a lifetime pass. The first time he made use of the latter, I went with him to Augusta on an expedition in Gus Griffin's behalf. Uncle Gus had decided firmly now to move into the guano business and sought at once to become the undisputed fertilizer king of southeastern Georgia. He hung on to his stores for the time being and instructed his league of managers and co-owners to push guano sales hard as the farmer's sole hope for salvation. For those who could afford or be persuaded to go yet deeper into debt, the cotton yield rose accordingly. But since cotton prices continued to slide, the farmer who fertilized was lucky to hold his own. Only Gus could not lose in that equation.

Having launched his new enterprise out of a makeshift shed adjacent to his store in Sunbury, close enough to Savannah for him to oversee its operations, Gus bought a small but thriving fertilizer operation in Macon and had his eye now on a good deal larger factory in Augusta; if he could land it at a fair price, he would be master of the guano industry from the Savannah midlands to the sea. And his nephew, whose duties for the railroad caused him to shuttle among the cities in which the mills stood, could be counted upon to look in on each outpost regularly and report back to the major-domo. Indeed, Bax joined us for the three-hour ride and was authorized to sit in with Mr. Venable, Gus's emissary plenipotentiary, in the exploratory negotiations with the Augusta guano prince; I, meanwhile, was at liberty to take in the sights and look into, for instruction's sake, the proceedings at the Richmond County courthouse.

Augusta, I had been told, was kissin' kin to Savannah, both having been the brainchild of the inexhaustible Colonel Oglethorpe, but aside from a few external similarities, I found the upriver city far less beguiling and widely befouled by slag. Its Broad Street was very broad indeed, though—a good deal more so than the Broadway of my boyhood that now seemed as distant in time as it was in space—and I strolled its length to the northern end before doubling back and hunting out the courthouse a few blocks from the river. The regional bar, I learned there, was aflutter about the upstart who was campaigning hard for the nomination to represent nearby McDuffie County in the state legislature but had not bothered to obtain the blessings first of the party organization. Tom Watson was at it again. And he was being uncourtly enough to appeal openly for the black vote, which remained sizable in the countryside; his standing with the white farmers, meanwhile, continued to rise each time he wangled an acquittal for one of his forlorn clients. He had become so persuasive a defense advocate in those rural parts that his appearance at a local courthouse was enough to lure the peasantry from its plowshares and fill the gallery with scuffed manure and hayseed. In fact, he was due to display his dark powers the following morning out in Warrenton, thirty-odd miles distant, in defense of a thoroughly worthless lout charged with criminal assault who nevertheless managed to wind up with a behind full of buckshot. Bax, who remembered Watson's derring-do in Atlanta two years before, joined me in urging our senior colleague to take the coach to Warrenton that evening so that we might watch the redheaded little dynamo in action. Since the other party to the guano negotiation had asked a few days to mull Uncle Gus's initial overtures, Mr. Venable welcomed the interlude as propitious; off we clattered into the sunset.

It seemed as if the court calendar had been arranged to suit Tom Watson's circuit-riding practice, he was in such demand at so many courthouses within a fifty-mile orbit of Augusta. He had four cases on the Warren County Court docket that morning, bunched like clay pigeons for his sharpshooting. The first three were nothing special, although one of them—in defense of a reprobate charged with pig-stealing but on the flimsiest of evidence—stimulated his robust talent for hyperbole in the rural idiom. He directed it toward the plaintiff, whose ability to identify the purloined porker in question Watson sought to impeach. "Why, gentlemen," he said, cozying up to the jury box, "our outraged friend here wants you to believe that if a piece of the missin' animal's middling were boiled with collard greens, he could tell it was his by testin' the potlicker. Why, I presume from what he says, gentlemen, that he could with all ease tell you the sex of a hog, male or female, merely by smellin' of the gravy." They laughed the plantiff out of court.

Watson's final case of the morning involved a disreputable local fellow who boarded the train to Augusta one day in an intoxicated condition, resisted his expulsion by an overzealous conductor, and wound up with a carcass riddled by buckshot and a charge of assault and battery. His young lawyer made a passionate plea for justice, insisting that the defendant had been the wounded party and had ended in the dock only because he was poor and ignorant. But even such as he, Watson orated, had their dignity and rights. The jury did not even trouble to retire. The slope-shouldered reprobate was free, a hero, even, for the day at least, and Tom Watson was submerged in a tidal wave of admirers who all but swept him down the courthouse steps on their shoulders.

He was only twenty-six, but there were those ardent ones among his followers who were already calling him a tribune of all the people. I could see by Mr. Venable's face that he at first regarded young Watson as merely a precocious rural practitioner of that tawdry courthouse oratory that he found so contemptible. Yet as we rode with Watson back over to Thomson, the nervous energy spilling out of him, he convinced the three of us, without trying, that he had meant every word he said in court that day about the unruly passenger. "I indulge in no mere literary license, gentlemen, when I say these fields and woods are filled with such men in their wool hats and homespun, their eyes downcast because they have had hope beaten out of them," he said as the day coach rattled toward Augusta. "They are forever being collared and booted about by arrogant young conductors—and just as surely by all these railroads that charge them such outrageous rates to carry their cotton." I saw the color drain from Bax's face as the accusation cut into him. "They are so much disposable trash in the view of your Wall Street moguls—of city folk all over who rob them of the fruits of their labor and expect them to receive the larceny with gratitude. The countryside, I tell you, will rise up if this long continues—." It was clear why the young firebreather was both feared and ridiculed at the courthouse in Augusta.

Mr. Venable proposed that the overproduction of cotton was the root of the farmer's problems; Watson begged to differ with him. "It is the lethal lack of credit that locks them in, sir," he said. "Your banks and supply merchants—they will back only cotton. The treadmill is running in reverse; these people have to hurry to stay in place." He looked over at me. "Well, I'm glad you at least have reformed," he said, recalling our last meeting (to my disbelief) at the store in McAllister two years before when he stumped against the governor. "As a lawyer you may aspire to becoming an honest scoundrel, anyway." I told him I would have him to thank in that event, due to the counsel he had given me on that prior occasion, and he smiled. We spoke of his own current campaign, and I reported that the courthouse crowd in Augusta was saying that he had stolen the negro vote by endorsing the Republican platform. It was not precisely news to him.

"I am not one of the dearly beloved in Richmond County," he said without regret. "They will say or do anything to see me thrashed. I produced five affidavits from leaders of the negro caucus that endorsed me, and all verified that I did not embrace the Republican program. I spoke in favor of free schools for the colored people—there is no other way to lift them from barbarism—and against the convict-lease system, which I have decried up and down the Savannah Valley as the vilest sort of public policy." Confronted with the testimony of black participants, Watson's opponent for the nomination had withdrawn the charge and then himself from the race. In no time, the party machine produced a new rival, more formidable than the first, and pushed to have the nomination decided at a closed-door convention of white Democrats rather than by an open race at the polls. Watson had to muster his wool-hat throng from every dell in McDuffie County to a mass meeting at the courthouse in Thomson to prevent the decision from being made in convention, where the bosses would plainly preside and prevail. In the weeks since, he said, he had tasted political combat morning, noon, and night, addressing every district barbecue that would put up with him and at the end leaping with the young ones off balance rock into the nearest swimming hole. "I stop in every sort of place imaginable," he confided with evident relish, "and receive every sort of treatment from extravagant praise to malignant abuse. I have my devoted friends and arch-foes. My spirits volley back and forth between hope and doubt, elation and despondency. It is all very thrilling—and very exhausting." He urged us to join him that evening at a barn dance in Dearing where he was to play and speak. His willing captives, we went.

As he fiddled away for dear life, the furies chasing him along some precipice only he sensed, you could not tell that he had already put in a day active enough for six men. His chieftain in that district, a white man named Hadley, bent down in front of Watson and beat the bass strings with straws while one negro played second fiddle and another knocked the hide out of a tambourine. Their collective sound was as irrepressible as Tom Watson himself. They ran through the likes of "Polly Wolly Doodle," "It Ain't Gonna Rain," and "Billy Magee Magaw," with Watson and Hadley taking turns at calling. At first intermission, the candidate played to their heart strings with renditions of "Beautiful Dreamer," "Old Folks at Home," and his best, "Buttermilk Hill," in which he sang only the haunting refrain, "Johnny has gone for a soldier. . . ." Having reduced them to emotional dishrags, he swung snappily into "Old King Cole" and got the dancing started again. At second intermission, when he seemed on the verge of collapse, he asked for their vote.

"They will tell you I am for the nigra," he said, his voice muted by now to an insistent rasp. "It's all right for Colquitt to get it, y' see. It's all right for Stephens and Brown and the rest of the organization crowd to get it, y' see. But when I get it, that's all wrong. Well, let me tell you something, my friends, and I want you to remember it. You—we—all of us out here, black and white—they try to keep us apart so that we may be separately fleeced of our earnings. You who doubt me are deceived and blinded so that you may not see that this race antagonism perpetuates a monetary system that beggars us both, the white farmer and the black alike." His gift for self-dramatization served him well. The cry against him from the bosses was nothing but persecution, he said, and whom were they really after, those citified political henchmen, but the country folk they would discard as always like old whiskey bottles once the vote was in. "No, gentlemen," he said, winding up at precisely the limit of his listeners' endurance, "they are in for anything to put me—and you —down. But with the fine support I find in your midst, they'll never do it. I hear the tread of the people, aroused up by this crusade. They come to see that justice shall be done. The whole people shall decide this contest."

Before we drove off into the night, Mr. Venable put a fifty-dollar bill into the candidate's pocket in the interest of good government, Billy Doak Baxter whispered into his ear that he planned to leave the employ of the railroad before the year was out, and I promised to seek the intervention of Jehovah in his behalf. Eyes aglitter, he thanked us all warmly and saw us to a waiting rig.

Two months later, we read he had won by 392 votes. We drank his health.

III

There was but one Jew among Eugene Venable's clientele, though at no point did he intimate that one was enough. No doubt he honored my tenderness on that score, to the point that I do not remember our ever discussing the topic of religion after our first encounter. Yet events toward the close of my first year in the office propelled me into intimate contact with his client Richard Mordecai Lazarus, proud son of an old Savannah Sephardic clan and the only Jewish cotton broker extant on Factors' Row.

A handsome, cordial man of limber torso, Lazarus moved with social ease and physical grace through Savannah's financial and civic circles. He had served by turns as a director of the Cotton Exhange, vice-chairman of the Board of Trade, and member of the Board of Education; his stately wife, the former Miss Jane Pinto Myers, was prominent in charitable causes, having risen to the eminence of first directress for a term of the Savannah Widows' Society, which provided quarters and a small stipend for destitute women and their families, as well as first vice-president of the Industrial Relief Society and Home for the Friendless. Both were prominent in the affairs and functions of Temple Mickve Israel, and their dark-haired, blue-eyed daughter Ruth was regarded within that congregation as the loveliest gem in all of Southern Jewry. Lazarus himself, moreover, was a sportsman of some accomplishment: he sailed with finesse, rode with abandon, played tennis and badminton with acrobatic flair, and swam with endurance said to be nearly Byronic. If there were any objections to him among Gentiles, they were that he did not drink and he did not hunt (and no true gentleman abstained from either) and that his evident pride tended to shade over now and then into arrogance—as if he were a fully endowed white man.

On an otherwise uneventful afternoon in the spring of 1883, one of Richard Lazarus's more or less steady customers in cotton futures appeared at the broker's office in what all on hand later agreed was a semi-inebriated state and placed, as he was wont, a substantial order on margin. Seeing the man's condition, Lazarus tactfully inquired if he were quite sure he wished to proceed and suggested that the market appeared to be in a particularly volatile mood just then. The customer took umbrage and threatened to transfer his business elsewhere until Lazarus soothed him by recommending a reduced order, which was duly placed. And indeed prices had dropped by the time the sell order was executed through Lazarus's New York agent, and the broker billed his customer for $478.76 to cover the loss on the transaction. Whether from annoyance with his fortunes as a speculator or displeasure with Lazarus for having tried to prevent his folly, the customer declined to pay the bill, charging that the broker must have misunderstood him and was now attempting to laden him with the debt. More than likely, the man reckoned that Lazarus would not risk his dignity and high standing by suing to recover so relatively paltry a sum. His integrity as an honest broker thus impeached, however, Lazarus never hesitated despite Mr. Venable's advisory that the case was not a promising one and advice to absorb the debt with as small a commotion as possible. Lazarus argued that, on the contrary, the last thing he could afford to open himself to was the inference of fraudulent dealings, and the knave in question was certain not to be discreet if he were allowed to get away with his welshing. "Mr. Lazarus appears to be burdened by a hyperactive sense of honor," remarked Mr. Venable as he set me to work on the matter.

It was while I was assisting in the preparation of the legal papers in his case that Mr. Lazarus, crossing paths with me on Bay Street as he headed home for dinner early one afternoon, invited me to his home for the following Sunday. The event was marked by a family musicale, featuring Mrs. Lazarus on the harpsichord, Miss Ruth on the harp, and a houseful of cousins and aunts and uncles performing in relay on assorted other instruments. It was Bach and Mozart, mostly, and they were thoroughly earnest about it. The quality of play was necessarily uneven, but the virtuosity of the Lazarus women shone through in each piece, I thought, although I was perhaps partial to Miss Ruth, who in no way acknowledged my presence after we had been introduced.

Dinner was an oyster roast in their yard. An immaculately liveried colored man popped the shells on the open fire by the dozens and gashed them open in flawless legerdemain as the guests kept coming by for refills. Heaping portions of hopping john, a salad with vinegary dressing, hot biscuits, and frosty pitchers of apple cider completed the menu; for those with room, a lemon custard came at the end, along with the strongest coffee I had ever tasted. Amid such a *gemütlich* setting, Mr. Lazarus ushered me dutifully from group to group, identifying me as "the bright lad in Venable's office" and all but ordering them to put me at ease. Late in the afternoon, I joined a foursome that included Miss Ruth in a demure croquet match on the side lawn; with consummate tact, I managed to finish last, winning neither admiration nor sympathy from the group. Ruth, in a cordial aside, recommended that I swing with a bit more tempered stroke as I was overshooting each wicket by a good three yards. Her breath was faintly apple.

As I prepared to leave with the others, Lazarus urged me to linger for an hour so that we might get to know one another a bit better. His wife served tea and cakes, and Ruth, changed to a fresh dress of green velvet with a touch of lace at the throat and cuffs, hovered on the edge of the conversation. We discussed the lawsuit only obliquely, since the subject was plainly not fit drawing-room talk, but Lazarus did not hesitate to expound his theory that liquor, which had caused the unfortunate incident, was mankind's foulest discovery. Drink, through the ages, had produced very little good and a great deal of bestiality, he said, and charged the red-eyed Gentiles with criminal indulgence; the abstemious habits of the Jews, by contrast, had contributed significantly to their high ethical and material attainments. I thought that somewhat self-serving and even rather narrow-minded; all such categorical pronouncements earned my scorn. Surely, I ventured, there were enough non-drinking Christians and afflicted Jews to mitigate his theory.

"You're young yet," said Lazarus. "It's a fact of life—not a philosophical proposition."

Even if his view were statistically supportable, I said, perhaps the abstinence of Jews from alcohol was due less to their highly civilized state than to their fear of losing self-control, with all the attendant risks in a world so often and widely alien. It came out, though, sounding like an accusation.

"You mean to suggest that Jews don't drink out of cowardice?" he asked, turning suddenly grim.

"Out of caution," I quickly countered. "They cannot afford to let down their guard when confronted with so much hostility. They cannot appear as buffoons or behave witlessly."

That calmed him somewhat. "But there's no hostility here, for example," he said. "None of us in Savannah lives in apprehension. We have our temple. We serve in civic capacities. No one abuses us—."

"Yet you are uneasy over this legal matter."

"Any businessman of integrity would be."

"You deny that your faith compounds the problem?"

"I—I do."

"You deny that such an incident might unravel everything you have built?"

"Only as it might any man's—."

"And the situation is not especially acute because you are a Jew in a Gentile world catering to an overwhelmingly Gentile clientele that might, at the merest hint of underhandedness, abandon you where it would not a Gentile?"

He paused to consider. "I have not viewed the matter in quite so brutal a context before."

"Or perhaps, sir, you have not willingly acknowledged it because it runs so against your eagerness to belong fully to your community."

"It is a splendid community—these are fine people. They do not discriminate as your innuendo hints—."

"And yet *you* do, sir—unless your earlier remarks about Gentile partiality to alcohol were offered in commendation—."

I had mocked a man of pride before his own family; no matter that his pomposity and shortage of candor had spurred me to it. A drawing room is no place to hone one's skills as a cross-examiner.

"You have a bold tongue for so young a man," said Lazarus, now plainly offended.

"Forgive me, sir," I said, "I meant merely to explore a dialectic and not to tender disrespect, I assure you—."

"I fully understand."

The frostiness of his manner made it plain that he did not. Only his daughter's intervention prevented my immediate dismissal.

"Oh, daddy, you are too stern with Mr. Adler," said Ruth Diana Lazarus, my savior and captor, in a voice that spread balm over the room. "I think he was trying only to suggest that you cannot have it both ways—."

"I fully grasp his drift," her father said with a sharp look to her.

"I think this entire legal mishmash has you somewhat out of sorts, Richard," said his wife. "And surely, we must attribute Mr. Adler's zeal to debate to the exuberance of youth—."

But the forgiveness was not forthcoming. There were no more invitations to their home, and later that spring Richard Lazarus lost his lawsuit despite Mr. Venable's most assiduous efforts (my own being still no more than incidental); the judge held trading in cotton futures to be "pure speculation, contrary to public policy, and where parties engage in illegal transactions, the courts will not interpose to grant relief." The Georgia supreme court affirmed. That seemed to seal my estrangement from the Lazarus household. Ruth's eyes and mine met occasionally at temple on Friday evenings thereafter, but neither her family nor I attended with sufficient regularity to convert that brief flicker of recognition into a sustaining event in our lives.

The following spring, however, she and I were hurled back together—in sorrow.

Early each April, the shrimp-boat fleet that operated out of Thunderbolt would huddle in the harbor on a Sunday morning to receive the blessings of the clergy for a fruitful catch during the ensuing season. Later in the day, by tradition, the crowds swelled along the shoreline to watch the Savannah River spring regatta, a more or less amateur affair that was nevertheless promoted with fanfare by local boosters and undertaken with perhaps excessive passion by the participants. A passable sailor, I chose to watch and learn in the not very ardent hope of entering in some future year. Sailing to me was a way to relax, not to intensify my life. My vantage point that spring, by chance, placed me very close to Jane and Ruth Lazarus; Richard Lazarus, who had done well in the small-craft event in prior years, was considered one of the favorite entries in his ketch *Pinto*. I myself was partial to Billy Doak Baxter in his sloop *Amanda II*, though Bax was credited with scant chance to place among the leaders. The odds-on favorite was the defending champion, Richardson Supplee, a prominent rice planter, marksman, and womanizer.

The wind was up and the start fast as about three dozen craft began the zigzag course downriver. Lazarus was among the early leaders but he seemed to lose serious ground rounding the buoys and at one point appeared to be entirely suspended along the edge of the course. Yet he kept rallying and coming back with a rush until the race narrowed to a contest between him and Supplee on the last leg. Supplee hung daringly close to Lazarus, trying to pass him to windward and deny him the breeze. In desperation, Lazarus luffed momentarily, then swung sharp to leeward and must have caught a swifter rush of the current, for in seconds he had made up the lost distance and was surging into the lead. He won by more than a length. Ruth hugged her mother, then me, and might have embraced half the shoreline crowd in her ecstasy; ingrained decorum reclaimed her all too promptly, however, and she apologized to me and then her mother for her lamentable impetuosity. I thought it entirely fetching.

I trailed them to the docks where they went to greet the victor. He smiled amiably enough upon receiving the silver urn emblematic of his triumph, but as he strode down the planking, I saw him wave the trophy with a sharp gesture and declare to his family, "The bastard tried to run me right off the course!" By the middle of the following day, all of Bay Street had heard the charges: Supplee had attempted to drive him into the buoy on nearly every leg (twice succeeding and thereby requiring Lazarus to honor the rules by circling the marker an extra time) and forced him into the big mud bank off Barnwell Island for a precious few moments. Supplee's defenders countercharged that he simply sailed hard and stole Lazarus's wind at every opportunity, thereby reducing his opponent's control and maneuverability; besides, Lazarus had won, had he not? Yes, by the same power that had parted the Red Sea, Lazarus confided to intimates. In no time the charge had reached Supplee's ear. The sportsman at once dispatched a messenger to Lazarus's brokerage office demanding to know if the charges had been accurately reported and, if so, that they be promptly and publicly retracted. Lazarus replied by putting the charges into writing and threatening to lodge a complaint against his tormentor with the regatta officials to prevent his participation the following spring. Supplee's messenger returned within the hour with a challenge to a duel on the Brampton plantation outside of town two days hence.

It was Jane Lazarus who visited our offices and hurled herself within my hearing upon Eugene Venable's shallow reservoir of mercy. "Madam," he said, doing his best to calm her, "this is an entirely extralegal matter. The law explicitly forbids the practice." Then surely the sheriff will intervene, Mrs. Lazarus hopefully suggested. "No sheriff, to my knowledge, has ever interfered with a rape, a duel, or a lynching throughout the history of the state of Georgia," the lawyer responded. "I believe they call it frontier justice at the Harvard school of law." But it would be plain murder for her husband, who had practically never fired a pistol in his life, to be faced by this expert killer, she wailed. "May I suggest, then, madam, that Mr. Lazarus consider either withdrawing his charges as inadvertently overstated—or practicing up his marksmanship with great dedication these next two days." Her husband's honor would not permit the first alternative, Mrs. Lazarus declared and quite collapsed with grief. That show of despair yielded a promise from the attorney to consult with the challenger's seconds to learn if there was any bloodless way out of the dispute.

Rationality seemed about to intrude as it was learned that one of Supplee's seconds was to be none other than Billy Doak Baxter, who often hunted on the Supplee plantation and, it was said, had been invited to whore with him from time to time. Bax came willingly to our office at Mr. Venable's urging. The situation had got out of hand, he acknowledged. Mr. Venable prodded him for the truth about what had happened on the race course. "There was some jostling," Bax acknowledged but would go no further. "Lazarus won—he should have held his tongue." I suggested that it was precisely because he had won that he spoke out; had he lost, any complaint would have been dismissed as so much sour grapes. Bax nodded at that. "But it was not so glaring a thing," he said, "or others would probably have seen it, too." I cast doubt on that, given Supplee's skill, and wondered, in view of his social and financial standing, whether any witness to the mischief would have dared to cross him by coming forth. Bax agreed to try to arrange a face-to-face meeting between the two men in strictest privacy. But the next day he advised us of his failure. The duel could not be averted short of Lazarus's yielding. Mr. Venable went to the Lazarus home the final evening in an effort to reason with him; he came away only with a codicil to the broker's will.

It was a misty, drizzling dawn on the Brampton heath, where I found myself in attendance as a second nominated by Mr. Venable, who firmly declined to be present at the lawless event but wished to be informed fully of the particulars. Lazarus seemed pale and dazed as he was helped off with his coat. His adversary appeared utterly unruffled as he prepared for the critical moment by emptying a small crystal goblet of whiskey.

The event proved unendurably prolonged. The formalities were executed in due order, the foes took up their weapons, stood back to back in rigid symmetry, walked off at the signal their prescribed twenty paces, turned simultaneously, and—I could not believe such barbarism was unfolding in the year 1884 of the Christian era—fired. Both shots missed. Poor visibility no doubt contributed to that felicitous result. A great sigh exploded within me. But the affair was not yet done.

The seconds met at the center of the field, and one of our party said, "Our friends have exchanged shots. We trust you are satisfied. Is there any reason why this contest should be continued?"

Their chief replied: "We have been deeply wronged, and if you are not disposed to repair the injury, the contest must continue."

"Bax!" I burst out. "It's madness!"

He looked up at me, stunned by my breach of Southern etiquette. They were all children, playing a deadly game and unwilling to be scolded to their senses. Bax merely shook his head and retreated with his group to the other end of the killing ground.

Again they fired; again they missed. This time I led our party to the center spot. I had in fact researched the code of dueling and learned the proper lines for all eventualities. Suspecting that our opponents knew less, I spoke the words prescribed for the challenger's side upon his wishing to end the hostilities. "The point of honor being settled, there can, I conceive, be no objection to a reconciliation. I propose that our principals meet here on the middle ground, shake hands, and be friends."

Their chief second looked at me with disbelief. Bax drew him aside before he could answer, and the two spoke heatedly with their backs to us. In a moment the leader turned to me and said, "Nothing has been settled—except that they are foul marksmen in this weather. Mr. Supplee would prefer to die than yield."

We trudged back to our ends of the field. Lazarus was looking paler by the moment. "You have shown your valor," I said to him. "This is a waste." He bared his teeth at me and asked the others in our party for my removal.

They fired a third time, and missed.

The man was bent on murder, I said to Lazarus in a voice loud enough to be heard at the other end of the heath. Lazarus, in a voice no softer, ordered me from his sight. They fired a fourth time, and missed. From behind a tree, where I feared Lazarus might fire at me, I hissed: "God has done His best."

On the fifth round, they raised their pistols with special care and fired. Lazarus grew rigid, the pistol fell from his hand. He staggered forward a foot or two and then dropped to the ground. The surgeons at once attended the hole in his side. He was dead before they could get him to Savannah. Supplee was arrested by the waiting sheriff, charged with murder, and released on $25,000 bail pending trial a week later. The conclusion was foregone: not guilty by reason of self-defense. I had never seen Mr. Venable argue in court with less vitality. He ought to have prevailed upon the authorities to stop the duel, I told myself; that was his duty as a civilized man. On reflection, however, I came to understand that, for all his rectitude, he was yet a man shaped by his heritage and that he had done what he could to overcome his client's obstinacy. Besides, I supposed, Supplee would have contrived his revenge in some other, no less deadly fashion had the duel been avoided without his detractor's having recanted. It was Lazarus himself, in the end, and his misconception of honor that were at fault.

"Because he was a Jew," Ruth told me at their home after the funeral, "he felt he must not retreat."

"Because he was a Jew," I said, "he should have known better."

"You are too harsh on him."

I looked away from her with tears in my eyes. She took my hand

and said, "You did your best—I was told." I nodded. "We all did our best," she said.

Ten months later, Ruth Lazarus became my wife.

IV

We worked hard, Mr. Venable and I, at making a lawyer of me. I had, in common with many new to the law, a tendency to jump too rapidly and too far in one direction or another before I had properly digested all the facts and legal possibilities. "Every case has a specific center of gravity," my teacher remarked one day when I had wandered from the hub of the matter. "Our job is to locate it and live with it—not pretend it is inoperative." He taught me, too, to bear in mind not only the law and the facts at play in each case but also the atmosphere generated by the first two—"Who are the parties to the action, why are they really here, and what will they settle for?" is how he put it. "The rest is rhetoric."

Only a dullard or gross malingerer could have failed to gain early admission to the bar with such a mentor. The clerk of the Superior Court administered my examination with all deliberate gravity and presented the results and his recommendation to the judge, one of Eugene Venable's oldest friends and keenest admirers. His honor summoned me to his chambers, said I had done justice to my teacher, discussed at length a problem of particular complexity in the lien laws that he was struggling with in a case currently before him (the statutes were severely lacking in equity to the tenants, I remarked), and concluded that I knew more law already than seventy-five percent of the practitioners in Georgia. He signed my certificate of admission with a flourish, sent for a notary to authenticate it, and while we were waiting, offered me the mightiest shot of bourbon I had ever confronted. We toasted jurisprudence and then one another, and I put the liquor down with three gulps. I recall distinctly, just before losing consciousness, thinking how much I liked the taste. On my recovery, the judge in his kindness said he supposed there were some things in life that took longer than the law to get the hang of, and presented me with the remainder of the bottle.

On the first of January of 1885, I was officially advanced from clerk to associate in the office of Eugene M. Venable. My modest salary, even substantially augmented by Ruth's inheritance, would not have been enough to provide my bride with the sort of surroundings to which she had become accustomed. More to the point, the large Lazarus home on Taylor Street would have become a petrified hollow without her presence, and her mother would have withered with loneliness. I moved in, and Jane Lazarus, with her exquisite sensitivity, yielded the master bedchamber and retired to the farthest quarters in the household. It was an altogether congenial and prudent arrangement, sustained by mother Lazarus's willing grant of sovereignty to the younger generation. The sole dispute among us, at the time, was the morality of putting out the Lazarus legacy at interest.

"So long as it is done at modest rates, I see no harm," I said. "What else would you do with it—hide the funds in a cupboard and dissipate them as need be?"

"It's just the image I have of—moneylenders," said Mrs. Lazarus. The word fell harshly from her lips. "I don't relish the picture—."

"Of becoming Mrs. Shylock, as it were."

"Precisely."

"No one is recommending you go in for usury," I said. "Interest is merely fair profit on a transaction—a rental of sorts."

"The line between the two is not always clear. I think it behooves our people to exercise great restraint in these matters."

"The banks will do that for you."

"I cannot control the policies of the banks."

She was every inch as proud and anxious about her Jewry as her late husband, perhaps more so given the happenstance of his demise. Her concern, though, seemed to be misplaced in this particular regard. "One reason the Jews have made such good and useful Americans," I argued, "is their antipathy toward hoarding their gains. They put their money to work. Without that vital flow, the land would never flourish. The Jew is the ideal capitalist —except, perhaps, for his periodic twinges of conscience, which he generally accommodates by acts of charity."

The contest ended in a draw. It was agreed that Mr. Venable and I should keep an eye alert for a promising enterprise into which to funnel the Lazarus money; meanwhile, the banks would put it to use at seemly rates.

At the office now, I began to pull a bit of weight. I drew up wills and deeds on my own, subject, to be sure, to the unblinking scrutiny of the head of the firm, and I argued several motions in court without disaster befalling. Given Mr. Venable's reluctance to fritter his time in the courtroom, my chores in that department soon multiplied. In the process I made a horrifying discovery: I adored the sensation of filling a room with the sound of my own voice. Not that it produced a notably sweet serenade or especially stirring anthem; in truth, it was merely the delicious expansion of ego at work in thus occupying the psychic territory of any number of captive listeners. Self-gorged, I would rise to my feet, survey the scene, suffer a fraction of a moment of nausea, and then launch my speech, taking too many too frilly words to say what I needed to. I began to fancy myself the reincarnation of Daniel Webster. Then one morning, while hanging out my most glittering arabesques, I forgot altogether where I was going, grew flustered, lost all confidence, and subsided in helplessness. By that single setback, I learned that style can too easily become overwrought and too often misapplied, with a resulting fatal loss of clarity and rigor. Pledging to keep my tongue from clicking out of joint, I re-dedicated myself now as a logician, and rather than preparing my remarks to the illuminated letter, I settled for committing to memory the few central points of my argument and left the precise phraseology to the moment of delivery. The results were salutary.

My coming of age as an attorney, in my own view, was signaled by a case to which the court had unmercifully assigned me—a criminal action against one Hiram "Quick" Culver, charged with robbing five dollars from the pocketbook of a local taverngoer. He was known as "Quick," the state managed to put on the record by means of improperly admitted character witnesses, because of the infamous speed with which his hand was able to extract money from any billfold within his range. Culver insisted he had won this money in a game of three-card monte. The state charged that he had sweet-talked the victim into buying him a drink; when the latter produced his pocketbook to pay and removed the rubber strap he used to secure it, the corner of a five-dollar bill was revealed. Quick as a wink, Culver allegedly yanked the bill free and passed it to a confederate, who speedily departed. Culver's quickness was not so remarkable, though, as to escape detection, and charges were pressed. The alleged victim's account, reinforced by the testimony of a half a dozen witnesses who declared that Culver's character was so bad that he was not entitled to credit on his oath in a court of justice, produced a finding of guilty by the jury. The court sentenced Culver to ten slow years of hard labor.

Stunned by the severity of the sentence, I carried the case with determination to the state supreme court. My client may or may not have unlawfully taken the five dollars, I argued, but the worst he was guilty of was larceny, a misdemeanor, and not robbery, which was a felony and far more reprehensible. Find him a common cheat or swindler if the evidence so discloses, "but the essential element of robbery—namely, force or intimidation—was wholly wanting," I said. There had been no scintilla of evidence that violence or the threat of violence accompanied the alleged act; it was like sentencing a man for committing rape when the worst charge the evidence would support was fornication. The trial court had further erred, I charged, by allowing the character witnesses to defame my client, who had merely exercised his own well-established right to make a statement not under oath in his own behalf without undergoing cross-examination. The prosecutor was free to attempt to impeach the veracity of the defendant's unsworn recital of the happening but not to introduce testimony of the general shady character of the fellow.

The highest court in Georgia agreed with me. Culver won a retrial, which resulted in a two-year sentence. Every thug and flimflam man in south Georgia must have heard about my triumph, for criminal cases immediately started flooding through our office door, to Mr. Venable's evident displeasure. It was agreed that I must be highly selective in taking these on; charity, after all, was my mother-in-law's specialty.

One indigent client I could not refuse: my erstwhile black guide and assistant assistant, Plato Layne, who had changed so much since I had last seen him in the country four years previous that I scarcely recognized him when he greeted me on River Street one noonday, not far from the site of our first encounter. He was tall and well muscled by now and very much a man of the world. My successor in charge of the store in McAllister had dispensed with his services, Plato reported, and farm life being as grueling and entrapping as we all knew it to be, he had returned to Savannah to look for work. At the moment, he was serving as a hand at the largest livery stable in town and hoping to become a coachman; meanwhile, he was trying to acquire some skill as a repairman as well as a groom. He had ever been a willing lad and not without intelligence. He had sought me out now, he confessed, to help him with a big problem.

Plato's father, it seemed, had been sentenced to nine years and nine months of hard labor for having borrowed a white neighbor's horse without authorization—or so the white man testified; the black man's explanation of mitigating circumstances was discounted. More than ten years had passed, Plato explained, and his father was still not at liberty. So far as the family knew, he was being held unlawfully at Smithsonia, the notorious Jim Smith's gigantic convict-lease farm upstate outside of Athens. They had written his father several letters, but no answer ever came. I was wanted to gain his freedom by proper legal means. His family had no money to pay for this priceless service, Plato said, but he would offer his own services to me personally or to the law office without compensation for however long a period I thought fair. I could not decline him.

Investigation of the courthouse records corroborated Plato's account. His father George had been held in involuntary servitude for the past six months, by my calculation; I moved at once for an injunctive writ in the United States District Court, charging Smith with violation of Layne's right to liberty under the Thirteenth Amendment. A federal marshal was sent to deliver the document. Two weeks passed without any word. On inquiry I learned that the marshal had been told there was no such person as George Layne listed on the roster of Smithsonia inmates. "'Course that don't mean he ain't there," said the clerk of the court. "Smith is one smart son of a snake—that's how he made his fortune, whippin' all those black asses into line."

My problem was intensified by the plain fact that the state itself really had no penal system. That service had been rented out, in the name of governmental economy, to private enterprise. To poke my nose into the Smith place was to risk getting it shot off—perhaps even guarantee it. In my futility, I turned to the one man in Georgia who knew most about the subject.

Tom Watson had served with distinction, and nearly total frustration, during his single term in the lower house of the legislature at Atlanta. True to his word, he introduced many measures to widen the rights of the downtrodden and the dispossessed. His very first proposal was an amendment to the state code to relieve the farm tenant in temporary default of his rent or debts of the requirement to post a bond of twice the amount owed in order to contest the landlord's right to seize his crops or equipment (and thereby assure his permanent disability). The proposal got nowhere. Nor did Watson's efforts to empower counties to tax railroads running through them. Or to fix responsibility more directly on the railroads for accidents along their rights of way, where the carnage was appalling. But his fiercest wrath was directed at the convict-lease system, which he declared "commercialized the state's sovereign right to punish her criminals by ceding it to money-making companies whose only interest is to maintain the convict at the lowest possible cost and to work him at the utmost human capacity." The atrocities performed by the whipping bosses, he said, were legendary. But Watson was too shrewd a politician to demand the outright abolition of the system. Instead he proposed a special investigation by the legislative committee in charge of penitentiaries. In a rare paroxysm of humanitarian concern, the proposal passed. But the investigation, completed within a month, was a travesty. Even the most brutal of the farms and camps won commendation. Watson, at least, had gained statewide recognition as an authentic champion of the underclasses before he retired temporarily to private practice back in McDuffie County, one of the few places in Georgia where impersonal business interests did not dominate the affairs of men. The legislature, he told his constituents after leaving it, was the plaything of plutocrats, utterly without tolerance for the grievances of the lowly.

He answered my plea for help within the week. "Coercion will not avail," he wrote. "I know Jim Smith and his place; it is the very model of purgatory and he a vainglorious Beelzebub. One must knock politely at the gates and practice gentle persuasion. I will join you in the effort if you wish."

The venture took me from the office for three entire days. On the train ride from Augusta to Athens, Watson left me with no illusions about the potency of our prey. Smith reigned over forty thousand acres of the most fruitful and superbly tended farmland in the South. He operated his own cotton-oil plant, his own fertilizer factory, his own sawmill, his own blacksmith shop, and his own railroad, consisting of a locomotive, eight freight cars, and his own private luxury car for excursions throughout the state. If the rest of Dixie had followed his lead in the use of the soil, it would have battened instead of plunging blindly toward impoverishment. Smith grew corn as well as cotton, ground his own meal, raised his own meat and vegetables—was altogether self-sufficient in his endeavors, which were subsidized, to be sure, by muscle power that he rented from the state for but a few dollars a day. Insurrection he discouraged by a judicious blend of bread, circuses, and the lash. Victuals were ample for everyone on the place, be he overseer or life-term cutthroat. The prisoners were invited to get sizzling drunk on Saturday nights, provided no damage was done to the property (including, most especially, each other); on Sundays, the entire work force was ushered aboard the Smithsonia Cannonball and given a rip-roaring trip up and down the ungraded tracks, whistle blasting at every cowpath on the route and blurring awareness that all the while the train had never moved beyond the boundary of Jim Smith's land. One night a week, Smith climbed up on a platform in a small building next to the big house and dispensed justice as he alone saw fit to all who violated the protocols of this earthly paradise. Anyone who ran for it, he hunted without let-up, had the dogs chew to pieces, and then put on tattered display as a chilling lesson.

We arrived late in the morning, expecting to state our business and obtain its swift resolution one way or the other. Smith, a man of evident high learning, greeted us cordially and insisted we join him for dinner as his price for looking into the matter without delay. He flattered Watson for his labors in the legislature, agreed that the investigation of the lease system had been a mockery of justice—"Joe Brown's mines grind up the niggers like corn meal," he said matter-of-factly—but disputed the charge that he himself exercised heavy influence over the appointment of judges and prosecutors in order to assure his farm a steady flow of nearly free labor. "No need for that," said Smith. "We perform a public service on this place." He yielded to a small smile. "Well, perhaps two or three judges around the state feel indebted for my recommendation in their behalf. I am, after all, though, gentlemen, a civic-minded Georgian."

After the meal, we retired to the veranda and watched as several dozen black women, wives and children of the prisoners, assembled on the lush lawn. At a signal from their leader, they broke into jigs and other rhythmic capers choreographed evidently to gladden the master. "My happy harem," said Smith offhandedly. "Lovely wenches, all. These are the pick of the place. But I'll restrain my appetite for the moment—." He eyed us shrewdly. "Unless, of course, you gentlemen care to—?" Watson, prim and unsmiling, said he feared we had no time. "I suspect you disapprove," said Smith. Watson insisted it was not his place to approve or disapprove. I looked away.

On inquiring of one of his foremen, Smith advised us that there was no George Layne on the premises but there was a large darky everyone called simply "Little Bit" whose last name was listed as Lane. They went to fetch him for us. "He may not have been aware his time was up," said Smith, adding without a smile, "and sometimes our overseers forget to remind the boys. Most of them, you know, have it better here than whatever they'll find outside. Some bring their families in rather than leave the place. All I ask in return is the minimal *droit du seigneur*." By his own outsized testicles, it would appear, he was promoting miscegenation to the status of a civic improvement program.

"Little Bit" Lane proved to be every bit George Layne. Smith ran him through the litany before settling the matter. "How we treatin' ya here, Little Bit?" he asked the big, brooding, and intensely wary black man.

"Fine, suh."

"You like the train rides, Little Bit?"

"Yassuh."

"The grub?"

"Yassuh."

"Clean enough for you, Little Bit? We keep the floors swept like new, don't we, now?"

"Cleanest flaws I ever seen, boss."

"Little Bit, you know what year this is?"

He scratched his head in practiced consternation. "Not fo' sure, boss."

"These men here, Little Bit—they tell me your time's up."

The black man's face remained impassive.

"How do you feel about that, Little Bit?"

"If they say so, boss—."

Smith sat back in his chair and drummed the tabletop for a moment. "Little Bit, how'd you like your family to come on up here from Savannah way and you-all be together in one of the private cabins? We'd sure like to have you stay on—."

The pain of his dilemma now wrote itself over the black man's face. How could he be sure the whole interview was not some trick? He was speechless for a long moment as he studied Watson's eyes and then mine for a sign. "If it's all the same to you, boss," he said finally, "ah'd as soon take my chances—."

Smith pursed his lips, turned his hands over, palms up, toward us, and said, "He's all yours, gentlemen."

The reunion of the Layne family at the rail depot in Savannah would have brought a smile to the Medusa. Plato served as janitor, messenger, and all-around blithe spirit at our offices for three months without pay—two of them in fulfillment of his bargain, one of them out of gratitude. When it was plain we had no real need of his services, a new place was found for him: as coachman and general outdoor factotum to Billy Doak Baxter, a young man of boundless prospects.

FIVE

Having remade my life independent of them, I renewed my acquaintance with Billy Doak and Amanda Baxter but on a somewhat more guarded basis than formerly. We had fully forgiven each other, even trivialized the incident over which our first closeness had broken, nor did I shrink from my rôle as junior counselor to their uncle, who by the late Eighties had been all but officially canonized as the grand vizier of Savannah.

Gus Griffin's wealth must have grown exponentially in that decade after he extricated himself, by prudent degrees, from the storekeeper trade—"I am fed up bein' pawnbroker to the ass end of humanity" is how he put it to the blanching Mr. Venable—and transferred his funds into banking, railroads, and the fertilizer-manufacturing business. His nephew served as the dashing yet dutiful caretaker for Uncle Gus's prospering guano enterprise. If the challenge in that was none too taxing, Bax had his compensations, to judge by his wardrobe, the gleaming phaeton that Plato drove him in everywhere, the bacchanalia he hosted at the Yamacraw Club each Thursday evening, and the general hauteur he began to don with all but the closest of his associates. "None of it makes up for the indignity," he confided to me one time, "of that birdshit stench every time I set foot in Gus's mills. And it clings to you forever—I could bathe twice a day in a vat of lye and still reek like a privy. Why, Seth, I swear my dreams are filled with mountains of the stuff—great, soaring Alps of snowy dung that I can never quite reach the top of—and I wake up in a sweat, my nostrils quivering with those vomitous fumes—." On other occasions, when Bacchus had cast his spell upon Bax, he could exclaim no less poetically over the odoriferous charms of the guano mills, which he recognized were also piling up a sizable fortune that would one day be partially his.

If his current occupation had its unrespectable features, Bax was nonetheless an exemplar of the New Southerner who had found in industrial activity and not dominion over black bodies and exhausted land a compelling life drive. The indolence and arrogance of the old cotton kingdom had dissipated, and its blindness lifted. Thousands of the rising generation, not to mention the more resilient of the ebbing one, were consumed by the vision of Dixie being spread across America by the Atlanta newspaper editor Henry Grady, who wrote, "The South found her jewel in the toad's head of defeat. . . . I see a South the home of fifty millions of people; her cities vast hives of industry; her country-sides the treasures from which their resources are drawn; her streams vocal with whirring spindles. . . . We have fallen in love with work." A slightly more accurate reading of the situation would have held that the South had fallen in love with money, which provides infinitely more groceries than pride.

Gus Griffin, for one, was not inclined to romanticize the profit-making impulse. His nephew, however, perhaps because he was not a self-made success and therefore needed to apply a somewhat more richly burnished patina to his attainments, took to proclaiming the acquisitive instinct as nature's noblest gift to mankind since Prometheus made off with fire. Profits were the quickening life force of Western man, Bax declared in a rosy-hued toast every Thursday night before quitting his banquet at the Yamacraw dining tables. Beyond routine profits, Bax began in time to sport a gleam in his eye for speculative ventures that would demonstrate his valor and vision far better than the methodical cultivation of seafowl droppings and other choice varieties of manure. It was at this point that he turned to me for professional counsel.

"I don't want this to have anything to do with Uncle Gus—not at first, leastways," he said, explaining why he had lured me from the office and earshot of Eugene Venable. "Gus respects guts, Seth," Bax went on earnestly. "That's what he's always admired in you—not just your wits—and even if he still thinks you crossed him at the end, that took guts, too. I've got to show him my brand, don't you see? I'm not about to spend my manhood toadyin' to the man, however kindly he may be to us." There was, no doubt, merit in his motivation; the vehicle he had chosen, however, revealed a want of caution I could not commend.

For sixty thousand dollars, Bax purchased a large iron steamboat of light draft and great speed from a firm in Wilmington, Delaware. The vessel was ideal, in his view, for carrying cotton and passengers down from Augusta to Savannah and fertilizer and passengers upriver from Savannah to Augusta. Traffic in both commodities and both directions was on the upswing and the number of craft available to carry it had not kept pace, Bax calculated. From his own cash holdings, augmented by those of his mother and sister, who thought the investment safe and the show of independence from Uncle Gus wholesome, the purchase was made outright under my watchful eye. Ours was by no means the leading admiralty firm in Savannah, but Bax said he would have no other lawyer but me; that I was associated with Mr. Venable, his uncle's counselor, moreover, kept the new venture all in the family, so to speak. The boat was rechristened the *Savannah Blossom* and, after being refitted to offer a modicum of passenger comforts but nothing overly luxurious, began her run in the summer of 1887. By harvest time, she was a river fixture. By November, she had repaid her price of purchase.

On the strength of the *Blossom*'s performance, Bax assembled a little fleet. He added a second, smaller steamboat, capable of holding about twelve hundred bales, to the Augusta run for twenty-five thousand dollars and named it the *Evelyn* for his mother. For ten thousand more he picked up a small wooden steamer, dubbed the *Felicity* after the old Griffin plantation, for the Ogeechee run, and then filled out his flotilla with the *Adelphia* (after Uncle Gus's empire) on the Canoochee run and the *Damona* (after his father) on the Altamaha run to the docks at Darien, about fifty miles below Savannah. The total investment came to nearly $175,000, most of which had been recouped by the middle of the second harvest season. Bax had taken to spending far more of his time at the tiny Baxter Lines steamship office off Bay Street than at overseeing Gus's guano business. His uncle, with only slightly grudging acknowledgment of this apparent whirlwind triumph, began to cast about for a new executive assistant.

That was the fall when Bax took me out and taught me to shoot. In view of the fate that had befallen my wife's father, I saw

125

no great virtue in clinging to my ancestral abhorrence of gunplay. Mr. Venable, moreover, made minimal competence in marksmanship a requisite for my elevation to full partnership in the firm. "It is the touchstone of your continued upward professional movement," he said. "Mere technical virtuosity at your craft is helpful but not imperative in the view of the true Southern gentleman." I said that I failed to see what blasting the feathers off a beautiful bird had to do with true sport. "I should say it was more a matter of blood lust than true sport," he said. At my dubious look, he added, "Your Joshua was every bit as mean a general as Grant. Your David had blood in his eye when faced by a giant adversary. Your very own father shot to kill Johnny Reb—." They all had justification, I offered. "So do you," he said to me, "—avoidance of famine for want of clients."

So off I trooped into the marshes near Tybee, at the mouth of the Savannah, with the new mercantile prince of Georgia. Bax was understandably heady with success as he waded into the water, the certain conqueror of man and beast. That liquid motion of his athletic boyhood had not yet altogether abandoned him. His every movement was fluid and purposeful. We led the dogs out at daybreak and unerringly flushed a covey of plump quail. On the first rise, he brought down two. "They call that a crack shot," said Bax without preening. "If you nail one on that first rise, they call you a wing shot. It takes a while." My progress that day was limited to not emptying my stomach at the sight of the retrievers, their mouths smeared with bloody feathers, bringing in the bag.

I won my badge as a blood-sport novitiate the next day. We went out after doves. "They're fast and smart and fly high as hell," Bax instructed. We baited the field with care and kept low and still for what seemed to me endless hours of immobility. I was certain my joints had rusted. But Bax's eyes and ears took in the whole throbbing panorama where I apprehended only a still-life in lavender and silver-gray and wondered if my muscles would ever uncramp. With a sudden bolt, he fired and the whole field was all at once a slowly gathering swarm. Instead of making a dart for it, though, the birds seemed to slough off toward the edges of the field and hang close to the horizon. But one rose at too sharp an angle and presented a fat target for Bax, who brought it right down. I fired off toward the perimeter and felled a pair with a single load—a feat that totally astonished both of us. "To Georgia's newest wing shot," my colleague said in toast, passing me his whiskey flask.

Billy Doak Baxter made a pair of confessions that autumn of 1888 while turning me into the least deadly marksman at large in the Southland (if not on earth). Once, after he had finished the dregs of the day's whiskey ration, he told me that there were times, when he peered down the sight of his long lustrous Winchester, that he saw his uncle's fierce face at the other end. "And still I want to *pull*, Seth—I want to *pull*! Yet the man has been a father to me—I have no cause." He appeared deeply disturbed by the specter and retreated into a heavy gloom as we made our way back to the rendezvous spot, where Plato picked us up in the carriage. I dismissed it as the sort of perverse hallucination all of us are afflicted by from time to time but have the sense to keep to ourselves.

Less easily dismissed was the disclosure to me on the eve of his wedding, as we made camp preparatory to his final bachelor hunt, that he was not greatly smitten by the charms of Miss Cecilia Fawn Dabney, his bride of the morrow. Not that she was lacking beauty, grace, or intelligence, or that he feared she would prove less than passionate in bed or serviceable at child rearing. It was just a certain spark that was not there.

"The law forbids you to marry Amanda," I said, only half in jest, and he sensed my meaning. Truly, she had spoiled him for every other woman in the country.

"You ought to have had her, you know," he said softly.

The kerosene lamp caught his fixed, far-off look while leaving the bottom of his face in shadow. Night sounds off the marshes and the noiseless whirring of insects filled the momentary void in our exchange. "Perhaps," I said at last, "but I've done well enough." I reached across then and gave him a fraternal slam on the top of his bare shoulder, saying, "And so have you, you peckerhead. Cissy is a splendid woman. Besides which, it's time you stopped playing the stallion. A man of your means—."

"Oughta have a lovey-dovey home and rear a big ol' family and toast his balls by the fireside when the wind's up—I know," he said in gentle mocking. "You sound like ol' Evelyn. She's been lecturin' me at the full moon for five years now, which is why she sees less and less of her dumplin' boy." He gave a snide little laugh and hiccoughed. "You sure don't hear her tellin' Uncle Gus about the joys of wedded bliss and—an' all that chicken-shit." Bax shook his head with conviction. "Say what you will about Gus—he's a free man, the freest man I know—."

Also brutal, vain, arrogant, and a mite foul-smelling—all qualities traceable to his unfettered, indeed scarcely house-broken existence. I thought it best not to note as much just then. Instead I indulged Billy Doak his final night of fantasizing the life of a perpetually potent rake, heaven-sent a harem of disposable lovelies with lubricious thighs whom he consumed at the rate of a dozen per evening on a bed of silken cushions and rose petals to the accompaniment of a fifty-dulcimer orchestra. For there remained about him, despite all the trappings of worldliness, a good deal of adolescent passion to swallow the entire planet. He was likewise afflicted still by a mindless innocence of the dark powers of fate and adversity hovering above all our long route to the grave. He had in place of the hardness of his uncle a portion of sweetness and charity that I saw then as his salvation.

To register his rage at being reduced to a state of legalized captivity, he showed up the next afternoon half an hour late for his own wedding. He blamed it on the quail, which he said were flocking in such profusion he had lost all reckoning of the time. My Ruth was having none of that. "Sometimes," she said to me, "you must kick a client in the seat of his silly pants."

II

As her brother moved toward a more settled and conventional existence, Amanda Baxter, radiant (if a trifle plump) in her middle twenties, swung around in the opposite direction. I fell occasionally into her path of departure from orthodoxy.

Eminently nubile, with a body ripely rounded but a hellion's tongue that repulsed the advances of all but the most confident suitors, Mandy was plainly not the early-marrying kind of woman eager to serve and service a man and brood. "No one's going to own me!" she once told her brother at the top of her lungs, and she meant it. She did not set out actively to shock polite Savannah but she declined to withhold her impulses for fear of hissing tongues. There was the matter, for example, of her bicycling. Mandy had bought one of the first low-wheeled bikes with gearing and chain drive to be shipped to America by its inventor in Coventry; within a year, the machines were everywhere, and women had joined the men at pedaling furiously away. But by the time the more vigorous sector of Savannah matronhood came out in its long black bloomers, languidly circling the broad shell walks off Bay Street, Mandy had abandoned such demure outfitting as a restraint on her movement and taken to wearing comfortable skirts that revealed all but an inch or two of her graceful legs south of the kneecap. Even that, however, she soon found an impediment to working up a good head of steam as she pedaled away with the fury of a marathon racer and in blatant contrast to the stately gait of swoon-prone belles out for a touch of pink in their cheeks before teatime. So Mandy took to donning jeans for her biking forays, tying her long, shiny hair back with a stout white ribbon and whizzing about the city as if tomorrow would never come. Overgrown tomboy was the kindest term Savannah socialites used for her outlandish get-up; hussy was the more common label. The men merely followed her arrow-like passage with protruding corneas.

Such antics invited more cutting whispers. That so well bred, healthy, and undeniably voluptuous a woman should have reached the marrying stage and passed right on through it toward spinsterhood with her spirits apparently unbroken suggested to every echelon of local society that Amanda Lizabeth Baxter was genuinely abnormal and perhaps even certifiably perverse. Opinion, however, was divided as to whether she fornicated too much or not at all. Given her demonstrative nature and certain exhibitionist tendencies, the preponderant view, not surprisingly, leaned much toward the likelihood of promiscuity. They had her bedded with a long list of natural and unnatural partners, ranging from the wealthiest of resident bachelors, flashiest of itinerant medicine-show drummers, and lustiest of crewmen from the Baxter steamboats (on which she was known to relish traveling on occasional sweltering days) to her handsome brother, her insatiable satyr of an uncle, and any of a number of athletic young women with whom she was seen cycling, sailing, riding, or cozying with in a booth beside the soda counter at Rosen's Pharmacy, where she had become a mid-afternoon fixture. Not a grain of evidence, to my knowledge, lent substance to these seamy reports.

But even the most charitable of her acquaintances did not assume Mandy celibate.

And yet she held herself with such unshrinking dignity and radiated so powerful and disciplined an intellect that the chosen object of her workday energies—the Baxter Academy for Young Gentlemen and Ladies Between Ten and Sixteen Years of Age, No. 12 Telfair Square—was a well-accepted addition to the Savannah cultural landscape. It enrolled some four dozen of the quicker-witted young free spirits in the county, who, by common assent, acquired an education superior to anything else available. The school, however, was attended by no less controversy than that surrounding the character of the headmistress herself. For in addition to routine courses of rote learning, Miss Mandy's Classes, as the Baxter Academy was generally called, were enriched by an unusually vivid pursuit of geography, replete with Zulu spears and as many other artifacts, however unsettling, of far-off cultures as Mandy could commandeer from friends and museums; by British and French history taught from a decidedly anti-monarchial perspective; by training on the recorder in Gregorian music and English country airs; by miniature dramatic offerings lifted from the likes of A *Midsummer Night's Dream,* Jonson's *Volpone,* or Milton's masque, *Comus;* and best of all, by a diet of literature judged most likely to stir youthful imaginations and open them to the adventure of life. She had them reading the *Iliad* and all lamenting for the noble, fallen Achilles, *Ivanhoe* and all pounding down the greensward in full knightly regalia, *Billy Budd* and all quaking in fear of the hateful Claggart. She fed them the gothic tales of Mr. Poe, the poetic gems of Miss Dickinson, the pulsing free verse from *Leaves of Grass,* and Samuel Langhorne Clemens' wonderful new story of lost innocence—*The Adventures of Huckleberry Finn.* And she nourished their sprouting bodies as well as their hungry minds. Classes were required in social dancing, country reels, Scottish flings, and other respectable steps. An open lot behind the school was rented for outdoor exercise, including tennis matches on a makeshift court, townball for the boys on a foreshortened field, archery for the girls, and tag and foot races for all. Rather than distracting them from their studies, the athletics were found to release the pupils' bursting physical impulses and produce far more attentive scholars when classes resumed.

Such innovative pedagogy caused uneasiness among even the enlightened and riled the narrow-minded. Much of Miss Mandy's licentious reputation traced to her inclusion of Walt Whitman among the school readings, the intimations of biracial fellowship in *Huck Finn* drew added protests, and the requirement of athletic exercise struck some as downright deviltry and an open invitation to physical intimacy between budding (and perspiring!) youngsters. But Mandy would tolerate no interference with her regimen; parents were always free to withdraw their offspring and ask a pro-rata tuition refund if they judged the academic fare overly stimulating. The few withdrawals that did occur were accompanied by convulsive protests from the children, who swore their undying love of Miss Mandy and Mr. Gray, the tiny withered schoolmaster who shared the teaching duties. She was such a spellbinder, in fact, that the least inhibited of Mandy's detractors went so far as to locate the playing out of her secret proclivities within that schoolhouse on Telfair Square, where she was said to draw upon the pitifully scarce sexual resources of Mr. Gray and even to lure the more pubescently advanced boys and girls within her web. Mandy herself laughed away every such gross innuendo and kept on about her business with an inner serenity I found admirable.

Indeed, and in candor, it was more than admiration I felt for her. No doubt my ardor toward Amanda Baxter would have subsided far sooner in the wake of my happy marriage to Ruth Lazarus had Mandy herself taken a spouse and thus become altogether inaccessible to my way of thinking and, more pertinent, of feeling. Her unattached state, however, made her an object of intermittent allure to me and, it was apparent, every other potent man in Savannah—and therefore an already convicted Jezebel in the eyes of every wife. To reduce temptation, I kept a seemly distance from her for the first several years of my marriage, but this denial of fondness proved more difficult when she hired me as her attorney to handle the legal arrangements in starting up her school. I tried to meet her needs on a strictly-business basis. Her needs, it happened, were not so readily restricted, nor were mine at the time, which, as if the fates had presided, proved to be the last week of a three-month abstinence surrounding the birth of our first child. I offer this information by way of mitigating the nature and extent of our subsequent relationship, not absolving it. (Indeed, what application for forgiveness of moral transgression makes sense when it can be granted only posthumously? For I am determined, of course, that no word of these memoirs shall see public print, even if judged worthy, until the death of the generation following every principal herein.)

We met that afternoon, at Mandy's suggestion, beside the soda counter in Sam Rosen's pharmacy. She said she found my office stuffy, as it surely was, considering the cubicle I had been assigned until my business warranted something larger; anyway, she said, she did not want dear, dreadful Mr. Venable nosy-parkering into her business and reporting back to Uncle Gus, who was stern enough already with her about how she invested her money. She was determined, at any rate, to go ahead with launching her school and confident enough about attracting pupils to have me proceed with vetting the lease. She wanted my opinion now of the wisdom of allocating dear, dour Mr. Gray, who would carry a good deal of the teaching burden on his nearly vertical shoulders, a small but symbolic portion of the ownership of the academy. My advice was short and swift: wait a bit and see if he warranted it.

Having disposed of business in a jiffy, we seemed to have a few moments to spare for refreshment. Mr. Rosen's soda counter was easily the most elegant in town, in the state probably. I had gladly granted him a little free counsel about import duties and exchange rates while he was outfitting the fountain along the lines of the finest continental *Trinkhallen* and *buvettes,* and as a result he became a loyal client. Every detail of the refreshment counter was deluxe: the creamiest Italian marble for the counter top and dispenser, the sturdiest of copper and tin-lined carbonators and coolers from England, the finest of French gas lamps and mirrors with cut scrollwork, and a whole rainbow of flavors in a dozen crystal-clear syrup holders, each in its own imposing niche, arrayed along the base of the huge looking glass on the back wall. At the top of the mirror, etched in an arc, it said, "S. Rosen Pharmacy," and inside the arc in smaller letters, "Est. 1854." The soda counter had turned his establishment from a prosaic service shop into a convivial showplace and doubled his income. "And the more converts the temperance movement makes, the better business gets," he reported while ushering Mandy and me to a booth. His only mistake, he said, was having put in a white marble counter. "White is for Versailles," he reflected. "In here, it stains every time somebody orders blackberry cream or raspberryade— my two favorite flavors, naturally. The counter top has to be scrubbed with soap, water, and oxgall every half hour or it looks like a battlefield." He gave me a wink. "Next time we get brown."

"A nice man," I said to Mandy after he had left us, "though I understand he is a gentleman of the Jewish persuasion."

"I wouldn't know," she said.

"Oh, yes," I said. "You can tell because they're always complaining about something or other."

"I never noticed," she said.

"Oh, yes," I said. "It's designed to throw you off guard. They're fiendishly clever businessmen, you know."

"I hadn't heard," she said.

"Lawyers as well, although they sometimes drive too hard a bargain and thereby lose the game—."

"Seth, must you?"

"Must I what?"

"Abuse me so cheaply? That was long ago, and I was very young."

"And now?"

She looked directly into my eyes for a moment and then away. "Now I know who I am," she said.

"Are you still in love with Jesus?"

She would not meet my eyes. "Jesus is a comfort," she said.

"Is he God?"

She was upset by the profound turn our banter had taken, and the lines around her mouth showed it. "A manifestation of God, surely," she said.

"We're all manifestations of God—."

"Seth, what difference can it possibly make?"

"I told *you* that once. A big difference, you said. So we went our ways. A parting of no great consequence, to be sure, in the larger scheme of things—."

She sat with her hands clasped and eyes closed till I stopped the torture. In another moment I was the one discomfited by the crudity of my unprovoked onslaught and the tender depth it had struck in her. My eyes were nearly brimming when she said, "They have the most marvelous concoctions to drink in here," and signaled to the counterman, who promptly produced a chalk board itemizing the flavors of the day. These included Grape Nectar, Cold Blast, Wina Vina, Melaroma, Vanilla Ambrosia, Tokay Lemonade, Sarsaparilla, and, of course, the local favorite, Blackberry Cream. The Raspberryade was on re-order. Mandy had a dish of orange ices and the ambrosia; I, the lemonade. She lapped up the wet confections with a most unladylike relish, finishing before I was half done. "I guess I was hungry," she said, "and thirsty. And to be honest, indulging myself here is the sole vice of my otherwise immaculate life." She contemplated ordering a refill of the soda but thought better of it. I offered her the balance of my drink, which had me all but effervescing out the ears, but lemonade she held in low regard as semi-medicinal.

Out in the sun, she urged me to walk with her as she cycled slowly to the schoolhouse so she might show me the interior arrangement she had planned. Her enthusiasm was so contagious that I found myself marching double-time across Barnard Street to Telfair Square. Except for a few leftover rugs and odd pieces of furniture from the previous owner, the spacious brick structure was empty, but her hopes and dreams for the place tumbled joyously from her as she romped from room to echoing room, imagining them rampant with churning young bodies and open minds and fervent babble. She demonstrated how she would lecture with effulgent command of their heretofore roving attention, wielding her pointer with emphatic slashes at the air and threatening to run it through the first little bugger who dozed off. "And here," she said of the arts and theatre room, "we shall re-produce, with astonishing fidelity, the most wistful of Gregorian music on the recorder. And over there we shall embrace Shakespeare—and perhaps Jonson—and over there perform the dances of the Highlands—and—and, oh, Seth, this is quite the most glorious thing I can imagine pouring my life into just now!" I was so happy for and with her— it was impossible not to be swept up in her projected passion— that catching her in my arms and drawing her to me seemed more a spontaneous act of celebration than an overt act of love. Our kiss was long and deep and full and left me unmistakably tumescent. "The thing," she said, catching her breath and drawing her mouth a few inches away, "is to do something worthy with your life. It doesn't matter what, so long as you love it." Her forehead rested against mine. "I'm so glad you've become an attorney, Seth. I should have hated your being a merchant all your life—and don't start in on me again about the mercantile genius of the Hebrews—."

It was a moment of such exquisite intensity and open warmth between a man and a woman who had no business expressing at last what each had for years felt for the other that I have no sense how long that moment endured. It was consummated, though, I recall with minute detail, in a moist and pliant embrace on a mauve divan in the recessed corner of a third-story bedchamber. "Have you ever beheld such a perfect pair of breasts?" my partner asked directly after our last ecstatic thrash had subsided. "Did you notice how round they are and unblemished? And see how they stand straight at attention and point neither out nor in? Superb specimens, I've been told." I said my experience did not qualify me as a connoisseur in the matter but that appraisal was no doubt accurate and she ought to consider entering her glories in the state fair. "You insufferable bastard!" she howled and made me pay with an intense contraction of her clasping loins. Our laughter went clattering down the steps and through every hall in the house.

It was understood, when we parted, that we would meet for future dalliances but at a time and place to be decided when the spirit mutually moved us. "I cannot plan these things," she said. "The whole essence of it is spontaneity. To have to spread my thighs on an arranged schedule would reduce me to a machine—and that I'll never be for anyone." I asked if that was why she had not married. "In part," she said. "And in part because I treasure my privacy and integrity too much to abandon either. I don't need anyone else to confirm my existence, Seth. My ambition is to know myself, to do so totally and with all my parts in harmony, and to keep growing, not trade my possibilities for the incessant needs of a randy phallus and bottomless belly, not to mention the soiled underlinens of mewling babies. And if I am overcome by sexual tension that has no other outlet, I practice autoeroticism without the slightest apology. It serves." I said hers was the most selfish outlook I had ever encountered. "Self-sufficient," she corrected me. "It's for strong people. Weak ones need each other to know they're alive." Was she denying the heightened emotional vibrancy of shared experience, like the one we had just known? "Not at all," she said. "But they're only glorious instants—the spark of a glowworm in a very long night. Mostly there's only yourself."

Our random liaisons recurred for years, but always on so casual and irregular a basis that I never felt myself to be in spiritual violation of the Seventh Commandment or that our illicit intimacy undermined the solidity of my relationship with Ruth. Mandy was merely an added dimension, of highly volatile substance, in my life. Her reciprocated fondness for Ruth, furthermore, startled and at first confused me, it being so radical a departure from the usual "other woman" arrangement. But because neither of us was the polar emotional force to the other's being but at most a stimulating diversion, we were able to mingle socially without discomfort on our part or suspicion on that of others. Indeed, my wife and I were frequent guests, along with Billy Doak and Cissy Baxter, at East St. Julian Street for *intime* dinner parties over which Mandy presided with perfect composure; her partner for the evening might be someone as inoffensive as the mousey Mr. Gray from her school or a strapping seminal vessel of a sea captain, generally of foreign extraction and registry. Still, no social evening passed without our exchanging a whispered vow or hidden touch of devotion. Yet she would openly embrace Ruth and chat animatedly half the evening with her, sharing what I soon came to learn was a joint disdain for Mandy's decorative but sluggish sister-in-law.

"And she holds her brother in only slightly higher regard," Ruth told me after one such dinner, "though she loves him dearly." I said I thought Bax was proving an able enough businessman. "His fleet won't last," she said. "Mandy's sailor friends tell her it's manned by drunkards and poorly paid, highly unnautical types." I suggested that envy had perhaps poisoned such assessments. "Seth, the fellow's a mental vacuum and an incipient alcoholic, and we both know it," Ruth said. "I really don't understand what there is about him that attracts you so."

I looked coldly at her. "He is a decent, honorable man," I said, "easy to be with and generous with his wealth and skills. You must not dismiss a man as a subhuman, Ruth, if he would prefer slaughtering doves to listening to a recital of Chopin. A bit uncouth, perhaps. I need him, Ruth, to keep from being refined to death." I did not explain why I needed his sister.

One grand Sunday in the late summer of 1889, after Bax and I had sailed on the river, we joined our wives in Mandy's backyard —the "Jubilation Gardens" of her girlhood years—for what would prove a memorable event in the history of Southern, and indeed all of American, industry. At the time it was a mere frolic, and we all joined in the antic proceedings without self-consciousness.

For the annual Christ Church harvest fair, Mandy had volunteered to provide the liquid refreshment, but instead of the usual tepid lemonade she had taken it into her head to arrange a soda counter on the order of Sam Rosen's elaborate oasis, only somewhat miniaturized. Sam had assured her that it was technically feasible and promised to look into the leasing of portable carbonating equipment. Out of deference to Ruth and me, as well as Sam, Mandy conceived the undertaking along interfaith lines, suggesting that if the fountain was well received at Christ Church, the entire arrangement might be shifted over to Mickve Israel's *Succoth* festival the week following. To make the fountain more charmingly original, she proposed that each of us concoct a flavor of our very own invention, which we might name and would be so labeled among the fountain offerings. Toward that end she provided each couple with a three-legged iron pot as well as one for herself and her mother, who stayed young by joining in as many of her daughter's activities as seemed appropriate, even the loonier ones. Heaped on the patio tables were a colorful variety of fruits and fruit extracts, herbs and herb extracts, bowls of sugar and pots of honey, and half a hundred other ingredients she had assembled the week previous from the spice and condiment counters of local markets and, in several of the more exotic cases, directly from wholesalers at the quayside. She presided over the project as if we were a slightly overgrown (and decidedly backward) group of her school pupils.

"For professional guidance," she said, hefting a fat tome, "I have consulted this splendid and authoritative work. It is titled *A Treatise on Beverages* and bears the sub-legend 'Full Instructions for Laboratory Work with Original Practical Recipes for All Kinds of Carbonated Drinks, Mineral Waters, Flavorings, Extracts, Syrup, Etc.'"

"The 'et cetera' is not alcoholic, by any chance?" asked Bax.

"We are preparing refreshment for good Christian temperance men and ladies," said Mandy, "and Hebrews—."

"Well known," I said on cue, "for their habit of abstinence, present company excluded." Bax offered me a complicitous wink and attended to our bourbon and branchwater.

"Our text," Mandy continued, "is by Charles Herman Sulz, who is described as a technical chemist and practical bottler. His work, running to nearly nine hundred pages, was just brought out in Philadelphia last year and is regarded, I'm advised, as the last word on the subject. May I therefore offer you this cautionary word from dear Mr. Sulz? He tells us at page 609, and I quote: 'Successful syrup-making depends foremost upon the freshness and purity of the ingredients, the intelligent care with which they are combined, and the cleanliness of the utensils employed.' The ingredients, I can assure you, are the freshest and purest that money can buy. The cauldrons I have scrubbed to the point of exhaustion, and the boat oars I have provided to do the mixing have been sanded free of splinters and all unsightly detritus. The rest is up to you. A blue ribbon will be awarded to the tastiest blend— even if it's mine, as is most likely."

Mandy scampered around among us, coaching and coaxing, reading us pertinent passages lest we muck up—"No, no," she explained, "it says, 'Never add the fruit or other acids to the syrup either before boiling or when perfectly cold'"—but after an hour or so it was clear that we were botching the thing quite dreadfully. Two cauldrons of dark, acrid sludge were all we had to show. The four of us voted to abandon further effort and constitute a jury of tasters for Mandy's own brew.

She set about it with studied care. Her point of departure, she declared, would be the formula for Belfast ginger ale—without the ale, "a most invigorating potion, well known for its delicious bouquet." Working closely with the text at first, she ground up fifteen ounces of first-quality ginger root and laced the bottom of the pot with them. Next she added six drams of cut-up Mexican vanilla beans, six ounces of sliced orange peel, an ounce and a half of nutmeg and a similar portion of Ceylon cinnamon, which she bruised first in a mortar, and fifteen or so grains of capsicum. At this juncture she began to introduce water heated to exactly 95 degrees and stir it all up with her oar gently but steadily. Next came a dash of attar of roses, a pinch of dandelion—"for its tonic properties," she said knowledgeably—and a vial of lime juice.

"No, make it lemon!" Cissy Baxter insisted. "Lemon is ever so much more refreshing than lime." Mandy shook her off quite firmly and consulted her book. "Science, my dear, must be our guide," she said. "The lemon, containing as it does much more sugar and mucilage than, for instance, the lime, is far more prone to rapid deterioration. We must not invite the likelihood of rot." Triumphant, Mandy then crumbled in a few dried green coca leaves—"valued in the tropics and South America especially for their narcotic and aphrodisiac properties," she said with a raised left eyebrow—and sprinkled on peppermint extract, bitterish and cooling. Now she made a major innovation and altered the whole balance of the elixir: six ounces each of cherry and raspberry juice and four of honey, guaranteed to derive from non-toxic blossoms. As a fillip she blessed the percolating stew with a tablespoonful of sarsaparilla root, with a perceptibly earthy odor to it that she had us all sniff—"a well-known purifier of the blood and bowels," she said, "and almost never contained in drinks dispensed under its name."

She took a ceremonious step back and contemplated her handiwork. "Before the moment of supreme trial by human taste buds," she said, reaching for a small packet on the bench beside her, "I must add this final element, which I fetched at virtually no expense from beside the Thunderbolt Road a few miles from town." She emptied the packet into her hand and displayed a few stalks of dried, uninteresting weeds. "Our next-door neighbor, you see, is a studious amateur botanist and collector, and the other week he invited me to glance through his mounting books. It was not the most stimulating few hours I have ever spent, I'll warrant, but my patience and good-neighborliness were rewarded when I came across this entry. It has no medicinal value and no flavor and no anything else to get excited about—except its name, which is 'Juba's bush.' 'Juba' happens to be what some of the more primitive blacks call a ghost or unearthly spirit. More to the point, the word evokes another, more satisfactory word—'jubilation,' which is the name we have used in jest for this house for all our days in it. I therefore add these harmless shreds of Juba's bush to this magical liquid and dub it—Jubilee!" We all applauded and rushed forward for a taste.

"Too sweet," said Bax.

"Too tart," said Ruth.

"Too strong," said Cissy.

"Too neither-here-nor-there," said I.

"I like it," said Mother Baxter.

"I adore it," said Mandy, "but really we must give it forty-eight hours to steep."

We came by two days later for the critical test. It was unlike any other flavor I had ever tasted—nutty-rich, fresh-fruit tangy, sweetish but not cloying, bracing yet mellow, and altogether delicious. We each put aside our earlier reservations and agreed it was a taste triumph. Mandy alone dissented. "A touch more sugar, I should think," she said and carefully sifted in four ounces. She stirred vigorously for a few minutes and then had another spoonful. "Ah," she said, "better. Much better."

The world agreed. Offered from a porcelain keg labeled "Miss Mandy's Jubilee" and mixed with carbonated water, the syrup was the high point of the church fair, which I attended as co-counselor to the warden and vestry and Mandy's friend and attorney. The line at the soda counter never shrank, and Mandy's invention was in greatest demand of all. One of the few unstrained smiles ever to light the lips of Eugene Venable followed his first sip of the stuff. Uncle Gus himself, a teetotaler to the day he died and always on the lookout for a pleasing new beverage, pronounced his niece's mixture twice as sassy as Hires root beer, his carbonated favorite. "I hope you got the formula written down good somewhere, girl," he said, "'cause I'll wager a jackrabbit to a stallion your little ol' Jubilee is gonna outlive us all."

It seemed, at the time, an excessively euphoric prediction by a flattering uncle. Mandy, viewing the whole activity as a lark, had not in fact bothered to write the formula down, but enough premeditation had gone into the brew so that she had no trouble reconstituting it from memory. On advice of counsel, she listed the ingredients and their amounts on a clean sheet of paper and deposited it in her bank vault. Turning the stuff into a commercial product was just a pipe dream, and even when Sam Rosen agreed to carry it as one of his featured flavors for a month, Jubilee (without the "Miss Mandy's" prefix) did not precisely set the world on fire at first. But as of this writing, twenty-four years distant from the event, Uncle Gus's expectations for the drink seem certain to come true. To be sure, he had more than a little to do with that fulfillment.

Within eighteen months of the birth of Jubilee, Billy Doak Baxter's fleet went down. The two events were of course casually unrelated, but as a consequence of both, all our lives changed.

The *Savannah Blossom*, flagship of Bax's line, ran onto a sandbar within sight of Augusta in November of 1889 and broke in two. The steamer had been covered for fifty thousand with the reputable New World Insurance Company, which unhappily failed at almost precisely the same time, and so Bax recovered not a cent. A month later, the *Evelyn*, moving downriver from Augusta with a bulging load of cotton and a full passenger list, caught fire about a hundred miles from Savannah. The blaze spread with such rapidity that there was barely time to tie up at a landing and get the passengers on shore; the boat burned to the water's edge and nothing survived but the iron hull. The insurance, enough to replace the ship itself, was inadequate to cover the cargo and passenger property claims, which ate up the payment and more. In the spring of 1890, the *Felicity* struck a snag in Cat Finger Cut on the Savannah and went down—an unsalvageable wreck. The captain, to whom Bax had leased the ship on a profit-sharing basis, had failed to renew the insurance despite his promise to do so. That September, the *Adelphia*, on a run down the Oconee from Dublin with five hundred bales and thirty passengers aboard, rounded Sapelo High Point with a sweeping ebb tide under her and ran into a heavy northwest wind blowing a fair-sized gale directly toward the Atlantic. As she rode into the sea at Sapelo Sound, the top of her whistle blew off and let out all her steam. Anchors were quickly thrown overboard but did not hold. A boat was put over the side to tie ropes to the beach, but the crewmen fastened the stout lines to what they thought was a stump of a live oak set firmly in the ground, but the stump and roots pulled right up at the first tug from the foundering ship and left her at the mercy of the tempestuous wind. The passengers were rescued by a passing steamer with a skilled and courageous captain.

To pay off the multiplying debts thus incurred, Bax had to sell the *Damona*, the last of his fleet. The calamitous sequence had unfolded with such swiftness that he was left a crestfallen wraith. His family and friends anticipated that once the shock had passed, Bax would rally his energies and start anew, perhaps in some other area of enterprise. But the total obliteration of his plucky little fleet seemed to have gelded his acquisitive impulse for the time being; he drifted back into overseeing Gus's fertilizer business a few days a week and feeling sorry for himself the rest. His alcoholic intake rose alarmingly until all of us close to him stopped pretending it was a temporary aberration and tried to find a new outlet for his manly faculties.

It was about then that Gus Griffin took a sizable permanent suite at the elegant De Soto Hotel, which opened just in time for the holiday season at the end of 1890 and became at once the social hub of Savannah. Named for the *conquistador* said to have first explored southern Georgia and points west, the hotel was a monument to the taste and trends of its time. Designed by a staid Bostonian evidently fixated by a fear of earthquakes, the De Soto had the solidity of a sepulcher. The squat Romanesque *palazzo* was enlivened on its exterior by elaborate but non-bearing arches, crenellated brickwork, and terra-cotta ornamentation of a cautious formality. Inside, all was a riot of sumptuousness. Deep dark carpets enveloped one's tread. Throne-room-high chambers gained majesty from the massive mahogany furnishings. Corridors wide enough for three stagecoaches to pass were aflicker with brilliant sconces and astir with the constant tinkle of service bells. Gilded and beaded portieres lent grandeur to every entranceway, and great crystal chandeliers of the most intricate design bathed the main dining room in a ceremonial light. And everywhere in the building, at every hour, there was activity—in the gymnasium, in the solarium, in the game rooms where the whist and bridge tables were always thronged, on the verandas where dowagers rocked and gossiped till dusk. The grand ballroom, with its golden draperies and Belgian lace curtains, was the site of every important event on the Savannah social calendar. And the dining room, featuring the finest and most extravagantly served cuisine east of New Orleans, was a hubbub of radiant women in gowns of flowing pink satin and blue brocade and gentlemen of obvious means in the latest word in formal attire; the chimes of merriment and clatter of service trays continued till well after midnight when the last of the guests returning from an evening performance of *The Barber of Seville* or *Macbeth* at the Savannah Theatre took their late supper. Visitors came to the De Soto from across the nation, especially Northerners fleeing the cold weather, and stayed for weeks and sometimes months. Cabs with silk-hatted drivers hurried in steady concourse from the rail depot to the De Soto, where the air was punctuated by the thud of heavy, round-topped trunks and quick with the rustle of ladies arriving in taffeta dresses and braid-trimmed capes cut short to reveal their tiny, strangled waists. The whole city was enlivened and aggrandized by the coming of the De Soto.

To fit in, Uncle Gus underwent a radical restyling. He took to gray suits—only gray, by way of tribute to the Confederacy—with lapels and collars cut high in the London manner, and on Sundays and for dress occasions he donned frock coat and silk hat but clung to his trademark, the blackthorn cane, instead of a more dapper model. He was in frock coat for the housewarming affair he gave for no fewer than two hundred acquaintances in his velours-hung apartment; the buffet that Mandy arranged offered oysters on the half shell, terrapin soup, pheasant, filet of red snapper, roast beef and English plum pudding, and a cornucopia of vegetables, fruits, pastries, and desserts. The evening was an auspicious one for me as well because earlier in the day Mr. Venable had elevated me to full partnership and extended the firm name to reflect my exalted status. Uncle Gus, in an expansive mood, announced my promotion with proprietary gusto to the assemblage at the height of the feast; champagne glasses were raised in my direction from all corners of those crypt-like chambers. It was, no doubt, a generous gesture by my erstwhile employer and benefactor, but its principal effect was to make me aware that Ruth and I were the only Jews in attendance.

That fleeting thought was given substance over cigars and brandy when Gus edged me into a corner and said, with his usual bull-like tact, "I don't know what you've heard about the guest policy here toward your illustrious kinsmen—."

I had in fact heard a few rumbles at temple to the effect that several Jews had been turned aside at the De Soto on the claim that the house was filled. But so great was the demand for accommodations from the beginning that the story might well have been true. "Well," I said, "it being well known that my illustrious kinsmen were notoriously slippery characters, I hear they are not much wanted, for they'll soil the bed sheets and stain the curtains."

Gus gasped on cigar smoke in the midst of his laughter and nearly had to be taken out onto the balcony for an airing. When his choking fit subsided, he tearfully resumed his posture of confidentiality and said, "I want you to know, son, that before I took my quarters here, I had this thing out with 'em. I said to 'em, pretending sympathy, y' see, 'What's yer policy on kikes?' An' the manager, who's one of them long-nosed peckers from New England, says to me, 'Kikes we do not welcome; gentleman Hebrews, of course.' I said I'd buy that."

"And what," I asked Z. Augustus Griffin, newly minted humanitarian (and Beau Brummell), "is the management's test for distinguishing between the two?"

He looked at me hard, as if I had broken the rules of the game and the mood of the occasion. "Gentlemen don't ask questions like that," he said finally and moved off. There is none so righteous as a reformed varmint.

Respectable Jews were not the sole beneficiaries of Gus Griffin's arrival at the De Soto; boosted far more was that ruby-red potion to which he was rapidly growing addicted—Jubilee. Gus proceeded to put it on the map by tirelessly spreading word of its virtues as both a refreshment and a "blood purifier" (the euphemism of the age for a bowel-cleanser and headache-combatant). He served it daily in his own apartment, winning so many converts that soon the hotel was obliged to list Jubilee on its menu and beverage card. And when a soda counter opened in a corner of the lobby, Mandy's drink was spotlighted under the caption "Savannah's Own."

Demand for the drink at the De Soto was gratifying but scarcely enough to justify producing the syrup as a full-scale business operation. Its reception there gave Mandy ideas, though. During the summer of 'Ninety-one, as the temperature soared, she told Sam Rosen that his exclusive franchise on the stuff was at an end and arranged to have it dispensed at the three other soda counters in town as well. Sam not only was understanding but even offered to invest a few hundred dollars if Mandy decided to market the drink more widely. Shrewdly, she gave away or sold off nothing she did not need to; instead, with her own funds, she had coupons printed up and mailed, via the city directory, to every homeowner in Savannah, entitling the bearer to one free glass of Jubilee at his or her favorite soda counter (the expense of which Mandy of course reimbursed to the fountain owners as the coupons were redeemed). The campaign worked marvelously well, and the supply of the syrup, still being brewed in the Baxter back yard on East St. Julian Street, soon fell behind the damand for it.

It was then that Mandy invited her brother to join with her in the infant enterprise. In view of Uncle Gus's delight with the drink and the fact that production was slumping at his fertilizer mills, Bax saw no harm in setting aside an idle corner at the Sunbury factory for manufacturing the syrup in a more orderly fashion and on a larger scale. He studied the cost of the ingredients and the time it took to mix and steep them, added in the expense of bottles, cartage, and advertising, and came up with a price of a dollar and ten cents per gallon jug. This produced an estimated profit of 175 percent on each unit, not counting anything for rental of the premises. The numbers were presented to me for inspection and counsel. What pleased me still more than the projected profitability of the operation was the lilt in Bax's voice as he outlined the undertaking. Here, I sensed, was the germ of an enterprise that might flourish sufficiently before long to command his full allegiance and maximum effort as a businessman. And since his love for his sister had never, to my knowledge, slackened, he was anything but resentful over the provenance of the product. Mandy, for her part, recognized all this and asked me to draw up the briefest and most informal possible partnership agreement between brother and sister, with the profits to be split equally. Besides his enthusiasm and financial acumen, Bax donated the services of Plato Layne, who divided his time thereafter as coachman and manservant to his young master and chief brewer and deliveryman of Jubilee. Mandy rode with him weekly out to the mill to test the latest batch before the black man carted the fresh jugs off to the customers and picked up the empties. She called it her Jubilee Summer, and before the year was out, they had sold just over twelve hundred gallons of the pleasing syrup.

My own involvement with Jubilee passed the point of casualness the following spring when I accompanied Mandy on a sales and negotiating trip to open up what we banteringly called the Tybee Territory. Ever since the Georgia Central had taken over the short line that ran not quite eighteen miles from the Randolph Street depot in Savannah down to the ocean beach at Tybee in 1890, the seashore there had turned into a gold coast. Vacationers flocked to it from up and down the Savannah valley, and before long it was the most popular ocean resort in Georgia. Could there be a more promising market for a refreshing new beverage than throngs leisurely working up a lusty thirst under a blazing Georgia sun?

The train to Tybee was a joyride all the way, starting with the fare of a penny a mile for adults and a dime ticket for children—the lowest rates in the South. The rollicking hour was passed in song and mirth as mustached blades in their ice-cream suits jollied sweethearts who had packed heaping hampers for the beach picnic. Youngsters, and not a few grownups, poking their heads out of the window to see the back of the train as it whipped around a curve, had no fear of being guillotined by a passing engine, for there was just one track on that playland Tybee run. Mandy was as giddy and gleeful as any of the fillies in our car as we set out on our two-day excursion. Before the ride was over, she had sold the candy butcher on the wonders of Jubilee and extracted his promise to sell it up and down the aisles if and when she decided to turn it out in bottles.

At the Tybrisa Pavilion, focal point of the beachfront activity, Mandy was greeted as a conquering heroine. The management was fully cognizant of Jubilee's appeal and of the great esteem it had won by then at the De Soto—and if it was good enough for the Empress of the South, as the hotel had taken to calling itself, it would surely bring pleasure and prestige to the bobtailed crowd at the shore. I drew up a letter of agreement for a dozen Jubilee coolers to be placed at strategically dispersed food counters along the boardwalk and arcade; in the bargain, Mandy provided free wastebaskets for each spot and a polished tin circle with "Jubilee" embossed upon it in the swirling Spenserian script that was fast becoming a part of the Savannah landscape. The signs, loosely attached to the wire sides of the baskets, were soon removed as souvenirs of Tybee (and evidence, presumably, of satisfied customers); by summer's end each refreshment stand carried instead a Jubilee sign overhead and out of harm's way. Everyone at Tybee was soon swimming, it seemed, in the ocean and Jubilee as well.

Mandy and I on that trip took discreetly separated rooms at the Tybee Hotel, arranged for the owner to offer Jubilee to his guests, and then went crashing into the surf in robust celebration of our happy hunting. She did not swim like a delicate buttercup dabbing a toe in the water and squealing at the coldness; she plunged in all the way, breasting the waves like so many furrows that needed turning. She sprang in and out of the water with porpoise-like arcs of her rejoicing body—no easy maneuver in view of the deadweight imposed by the voluminous swimsuits of the period; even her own somewhat trimmed style covered far more of her than it exposed. On the way back to our rooms, she whisperingly pointed out which of the women were wearing corsets underneath their bathing outfits. Stimulated by the salt air and the gleaming sunscape, our lovemaking was strenuous and a bit sandy. "There was a time," she said afterward, "when I was afraid of the outdoors. I mean the country, fields, the forest, the ocean. Maybe it was growing up knowing that my other uncle had died of snakebite. I guess I thought there were always things lurking in the grass or behind the next tree or over the next rise, ready to pounce. And now—now it's just the opposite. The bluer the sky, the broader the field, the thicker the trail, the swifter the current, the choppier the ocean, the more I adore it. It's like one—enormous—coital explosion—may I say that? Will you think me a hopeless deviant? I can't help it, you see—life is orgasmic for me. I often think no one should take such pleasure from it."

But take she did, and gave in return. There is no telling how many of us there were who loved her and fell beneath that jubilant, mesmerizing spirit she rained upon all the world.

IV

For all its promising start, Jubilee remained a brother-sister hobby—Mandy was still devoted to her classes, Bax to hunting, fishing, and other compulsive forms of recreation—until outside economic forces exerted themselves uncomfortably upon the family. And if any one man can be said to have catalyzed and channeled those forces in a way that served to bring Bax back to earth and turn Jubilee into a thriving nationwide institution, it was that fiery little Jeremiah of the Savannah River valley, Tom Watson from McDuffie County. By 1892, he was the most radical—some said visionary—member of the United States House of Representatives.

In the previous half-dozen years, no one had been more active in spearheading the potent agrarian uprising known as the Farmers' Alliance. Watson shouted to the benighted masses that unless they stood together against the mighty industrial trusts and banking interests that were picking their pockets clean, they deserved their dreary lot. Everywhere in the Southland, cooperatives sprang up so the farmers could supply themselves with seed and jute bagging and the other necessities of their livelihood at something less than extortionate prices. Guano suppliers like Gus Griffin were being squeezed from two sides—competition from the low-cost Alliance cooperatives and depressed cotton prices that left the growers with less money than ever to invest in fertilizer. Gus began to think hard about selling out while there was still something to sell. His only likely customers were the big Northern outfits. In the spring of 'Ninety-two, I joined Bax on an expedition to Baltimore in quest of buyers. The trip proved inconclusive; on the way home, we stopped off in Washington to see the most feisty man in the capital.

Six of the ten members of the Fifty-second Congress who represented Georgia were elected on the People's Party ticket, or the Populists as they were widely known. Watson led the Georgia "Pops," as they endearingly called themselves. The party, Southern and Northern, had joined with the Knights of Labor in a platform that demanded the end of the tight-credit policies favored by the conservatives who commanded both major parties. The rebels also called for the end of giveaway privileges and indulgences to the business leviathans. Among the radical proposals now introduced to the Congress were the free and unlimited coinage of silver (an inflationary measure to aid debtors); outlawing of speculation in futures of all agricultural and mechanical products (to assure the farmer and laborer a fair return on their work); reclamation of excessive land grants and sales to corporations, especially the railroads (because giveaways even to stimulate regional growth were rank favoritism); government ownership of all means of public transportation and communication (to prevent the farmers from being gouged by astronomic freight rates); and a graduated income tax (to take more from those best able to pay). Every plank in that platform frightened the bejesus out of

Wall Street and its banker cohorts across a nation that was sliding toward financial panic. And most frightening of all was the fervent spokesman of that diabolical program.

Tom Watson came to Washington in his soft Southern hat and won the ear of even his most militant detractors with his touch of dialect of the old South, a language that traditionally bespoke gentility and favored fixed ways, not the uprooting of the sources of power. He was small and thin and hyperactive amid so many large and lumpish scoundrels, and his face still looked perfectly beardless. But there was no mistaking the bright resolve in his eyes, any more than they could miss that abundance of dark red hair pushed back from his face lest it hide him in a thicket.

He had not endeared himself to his fellow federal legislators, Watson confided to Bax and me over a cold beef-plate dinner in his quarters, and his assignment to the least weighty of the House's standing committees was ample testimony to his low standing. But he would go right on proclaiming the truth as he knew it, he said, and submitting reform bills no matter how unlikely of passage.

On the House floor that very afternoon, Watson fricasseed a bill proposing the outlay of three hundred fifty million dollars to bring the American navy up to the standard of those in Europe. Directing his windmill delivery at the Speaker, a fellow Georgian and political foe who responded by probing busily about his bicuspids with an after-dinner toothpick, the redhead asserted:

> . . . Sir, the real truth is that the enemies we have to dread in the future are not Great Britain, not France, not Germany, not Italy, not Mexico nor Chile nor the Dalai Lama of Tibet, but our own people. And what do I mean by that? I mean bad laws here at home. I mean class legislation here at home. I mean overgrown and insolent corporations here at home, and the greed of monopolies. . . .

At the close, he moved the chamber with a graphic account of the misery in working-class Atlanta, where wage earners took home thirty-six cents a day if they could find any work at all and were succumbing to pestilence just then in such numbers that there was no time to give them a proper burial.

No one who heard him was more moved that day than my colleague and client, W. Doak Baxter (as he signed his name), the kindly-natured boy-man and undeniable beneficiary of the system that Watson so tellingly accused of unbridled avarice and monstrous inhumanity. His uncle, of course, had never supposed his economic purpose to be other than to seek his own maximum advantage on earth. Bax, by contrast, weaned on the golden gospel of the Eighties, had fused profits and chivalry within his conscience and assured himself he was up to the Lord's business as well as his own. That he did not blindly oppose Tom Watson for flaying him and his ilk as loathsome predators was the truest measure of Billy Doak's compassion. In truth, he was too decent to wear the spurs of a robber baron, or even an equerry, with comfort. "We pay our people no more than the Atlanta mills," he confessed to me after Watson's speech. "We prosper by imposing wage slavery. It's what Tom says—despicable and evil. Yet I have not turned my back on it. Sideways, perhaps, is how I've taken from it—but I've taken nonetheless."

He did not become a mendicant overnight by any means, but he did reduce the more ostentatious forms of his self-indulgence (to Cissy Baxter's mingled joy and alarm) and pledged himself to Tom Watson's cause to whatever extent possible. The redhead had few other adherents in cautious Savannah, with its window on the world and feckless social whirl. But by the autumn of 1892, the economic slide had reached avalanche proportions in much of the nation, and there was cold comfort in waltzing to Strauss at the De Soto cotillions or prancing to Blue Steele's lilting rendition of "The Girl of My Dreams" under the refracted colored lights on Tybee's wind-blown dance floor. A sense of social urgency, of things pulling asunder, arose on all sides, and the issues Tom Watson had first raised were suddenly on everyone's lips. Watson himself was singled out as the most dangerous man in Congress, and funds from the North flowed out to help his foes unseat him in the eleven-county backland that comprised the Tenth District of Georgia. Bax resolved to work the other side of the street.

His heart high, he hit upon a way to help Watson, who was locked in the grimmest battle of his flamboyant career, and at the same time tool up the vehicle Bax was now sure would carry him to a happy and noble destiny—even if the contraption ran on soda-water. The scheme was short and sweet: he would follow

Watson's campaign trail in a decorated wagon that sold Jubilee at a break-even price of two cents a cup to the crowds that always collected for the candidate's stirring appearances. Refills would cost just a penny. By all but giving the drink away, he would be adding a cheerful note to the Pops' anthem and avoid any charge of exploiting the masses. It might even draw more listeners to the hustings. At the same time it would spread the Jubilee gospel into new territory, where folks of a very different sort from the customers in Savannah could test the virtues of the beverage. And if the Tenth District took to its taste even half so avidly as Savannah had, Jubilee could be sold in any semi-tropical zone on earth.

"We've found the stuff is good for headaches, too," Bax said in proposing the idea to Watson after one of his rallies.

"Then I'd say you've come to the right place," the candidate answered somberly and then brightened a bit. He seemed in need of something to lift his dark mood, even momentarily. "All right," he said, "provided you slip a Mickey Finn to every Democrat and heckler in the crowd—."

Mandy was delighted at the notion and dispatched one hundred twenty gallons of syrup—half the entire Jubilee inventory—and Plato Layne to drive and operate the soda wagon that Bax rented and outfitted in Augusta the next morning. Each of us knowing a thing or two about the display of merchandise, we transformed the wagon into a gay but not gaudy fiesta on wheels. On both sides it bore the identical sign in red, white, and blue:

> Have a
>
> # J U B I L E E
>
> the gen-u-one

I thought the bottom line, of Bax's composing, an abomination and said so. Unswayed, he said the literary license in the family belonged to Mandy and he would leave it to her to decide the motto's fate; for the moment, though, it seemed perfect to tickle the fancy of rural folk who were not the purist users of the language. My huckstering days long past, I yielded graciously, and so one of the great slogans of American marketing was born.

At the rail depot, Plato came tumbling off the train with that filmy, unsmiling look he had taken to wearing since attaining adulthood. The sight of Bax and me brought a flicker of a smile to his dark, high-cheeked face, but as we began to move off toward the baggage car to collect our crated jugs of Jubilee syrup, Plato appeared to hesitate. Bax asked the matter. "I done somethin' I maybe shouldn'ta, boss," he said, hooking a thumb back over his shoulder toward the train. On the platform, in faded overalls and a dented straw hat, stood an old black man who had evidently followed Plato off the train but paused before joining him. He seemed familiar to me. "I brung my daddy," Plato explained. "He say he want to do somethin'—anythin' in the world —to help Mr. Tom Watson. He say Mr. Watson save his life— and you, too, Mr. Adla'—an' now he wanna pay back. He heard tell Mr. Watson might gonna get his ass shot up from folks what hates his speechin' and the truth he tells, so he come here to pertect him—." Which is how Little Bit Layne joined the campaign trail.

No other contest for federal office that year, not excepting the presidential race between Cleveland and Harrison, generated more intense national interest than Tom Watson's fight to hold his seat in Congress against the American Borgias, big and small. There were furious speeches from every stump, daily fistfights and nightly gunfights and about fifteen murders before it was over, and even in the single week I could afford to follow along in person, one could not fail to detect an emotional undertow ready to boil over at every next turn of phrase. (Among the victims of that heated climate was the Jubilee wagon we had outfitted: the drink proved so popular an added attraction to Watson's appearances that his foes conspired to tip over the traveling dispensary soon after its arrival in the district and spilled its entire contents.) The issues were elemental, and the ignorance that for so long had blighted Watson's pliable agrarian masses was lifting in the light of revelation; their bond of common misery had linked white and black paupers in a desperate fraternity. The election outcome would hang on how many black votes got counted.

Where the colored people's sympathy lay was never in doubt. Tom Watson was, without question, the first native white Southern political leader of any magnitude to acknowledge the negro's aspiration to be treated as other than a two-legged beast in sack-cloth. His speeches now called openly and frankly for a reversal of the immemorial Southern repugnance toward black sweat and black blood and black semen. He did not, of course, go so far as to espouse social equality of the two races, but he did cry out against the hatred that blinded poor whites from seeing how much more they had in common with impoverished blacks than with their paleface betters. He repeatedly addressed racially mixed audiences from the same platform with negro speakers, he nominated a negro to a place on the Pops' state executive committee, and he constantly demanded, "Tell me the use of educating these people as citizens if they are never to exercise the rights of citizens."

And yet the outcome of the election was entirely in doubt be-cause the blacks were not free to vote as they chose. Their ballots, like their beings, were still bought and sold, coerced and ter-rorized, and they were marched to the polls as if on the chain gang and their marks made under the direct scrutiny of political operatives with the full power of the law at their disposal.

Plato Layne went home with Bax and me two weeks before the campaign ended, but his father stayed on to help Watson among the colored people of the district any way he could. Mostly, that meant serving as bodyguard for the black preachers who talked up the Watson candidacy any place they could gather half a dozen potential voters. Three of the negro orators were mangled by white toughs despite the nearness of Little Bit Layne's large fists. Elsewhere in the district, black campaign workers were shot at and one wounded mortally.

On election day, the carnage was out of control. Plato re-counted his father's version of what had happened to him near a polling place at a schoolhouse in Elbert County. "My daddy an' a white man, they was leadin' a flock of our people, whites and coloreds, up to the votin' when this white fella Mr. Head and a bunch o' otha' Democrats come along and reco'nize a lot of our folk. This hyar Mr. Head, he say they used to crop fo' him and owed him still and he knowed what we was up to, so he run ova' and pick up a standa'd from his wagon and swings it at the oldes' darkey in the bunch and knocks 'im down. The old man's son, he hit back at Mr. Head, who don't like that and hies hisself off across street to his house and come out again with a shotgun goin' from both barrels. One of the otha' whites, he starts with his pistol an' our people is fallin' and screamin' all ova' de place. Two of 'em was killed, five hurt bad, and my daddy—my daddy—he reached up and where his right eye used to be was nothin' but blood—."

Plato slumped against the carriage that Bax had sent to pick up the old negro at the rail depot and sobbed openly after telling his story. Bax waited a respectful moment and then offered his bourbon flask to that devoted servant. Plato clawed his tears away, took a long drink, and returned the flask with a nod of thanks. Bax lifted it, in tribute to Plato's father, and had a swallow himself. He had the grace not to wipe away the black man's spittle.

Tom Watson ran up a large majority in the rural counties, but in Augusta and surrounding Richmond County, the Democrats belied their very name. Federal marshals had been posted at several polling places, but they were no match for or curb on the local police. The ballot boxes were stuffed all day long by repeaters, by minors, by negroes shipped across the Savannah from South Carolina and hauled to the polls in four-horse wagonloads. Disgruntled millworkers were intimidated or bribed or both, and whiskey—not Jubilee—flowed in buckets in the Augusta wagon yards. Black, Watson's foe, was credited in Richmond County with more than double his total in the other ten counties in the district combined—and some two thousand more than the number of all legally qualified voters in Richmond itself!

Tom Watson has not held public office since.

V

The Populist prophesies of 1892 had not been overstated, events rapidly revealed.

Too much raw material and too few finished goods were being produced in America; commodity prices dropped drastically, and none worse than cotton, which fell to four cents a pound by 'Ninety-three. Country crossroads were growing into towns, and towns into cities, and what the increasingly complex urban markets needed most were finished products. But the nation's businessmen, having fattened for a generation on the opening of the West, cheap raw materials and cheaper labor, were not eager

154

to change their ways. Intensively machined goods, for one thing, required vast infusions of capital, and the tight-credit policies universally endorsed by the entrepreneurial class served to stunt the expansion of that vital nutrient. Foreign investors, moreover, began to flee the American capital market as the severity of the problem became apparent. Farmers, who had known depression for the better part of a decade, were joined now by armies of unemployed mill hands and factory workers as production in all areas fell off sharply. Companies closed, banks failed, money disappeared; whites as well as negroes walked the roads seeking relief. In Georgia, where Tom Watson had been clubbed off the political stage, poverty, hunger, and misery were more widespread than at any time since Sherman's marauders had cut like a plundering scythe from the red hills in the north to the sea at Savannah.

In the very severity of conditions in the South, Billy Doak Baxter saw his opportunity. He summoned Mandy and me to a meeting with Uncle Gus at his De Soto apartment. The South's worst problem, Bax began, had been its maniacal devotion to cotton, as all now recognized. The rest of the nation and Europe had long fed off Southern commodities, but the real profits always went elsewhere—to brokers and bankers and railroaders and manufacturers with their high value-added pricing. To meet its everyday needs, the South had paid dear for imported goods despite its own wealth of resources. "It's time all that changed," he said. "It's time we turned the tables."

"I'll surely amen that," said Gus Griffin, brushing a stray cigar ash from his gray lapel.

"It's time Cincinnati started buying from us instead of selling us blind," Bax pushed on, vigor rising to his voice. "It's time the whole damned nation began taking Southern products—only we've got to make 'em in the first place and ballyhoo 'em in the second place and then send out our drummer boys to every town between here and Oshkosh—an' hell, right on up the Oregon Trail!" We all nodded but Bax scarcely noticed. He stood up now and went over to the sideboard where Gus kept a tall siphon of carbonated water, a covered dish of ice, and a small bottle of Jubilee syrup. "Brand-name goods of every kind are catching on all over," he continued, dropping a few ice shards into a tumbler and dousing them with the syrup. "People don't just ask to buy a watch any more—they want an Ingersoll. They don't just ask for soap—they want Pears or Ivory—or the new flakes Charlie Fels makes up in Carolina—where is it at, Gus, Yanceyville?" Gus nodded, his expression as fixed as the cigar clenched in his jaw. Bax splashed seltzer water into the tumbler he was holding and handed Gus the finished concoction, all fizzing on top. "Well, hell, now why shouldn't they all be sayin', instead of 'Let me have some sody water' or 'Let me have one of them Hires,' why shouldn't they all say, 'Make mine a Jubilee, partner—I crave the taste'? We've got a winner right here on our hands in Mandy's little recipe. Gus, you like it just fine. Half the guests in the hotel swig it all day long. The crowds at Tybee can't get enough of it. Every soda fountain in town sells out before we get around to 'em with the refills—."

Gus downed a huge gulp of the stuff and in short order emitted a prodigious belch. "Sure, I like it fine," he said. "I'm yer star salesman, ain't I? Only it's just plain sugar-water and you're sellin' it local. You know what's gonna happen the minute you try peddlin' it out of this neck o' the woods? First off, it costs you an arm an' a leg to haul the stuff. Second place, twenty-three other guys pop up sellin' their own brand o' the stuff, so why's some Dapper Dan in Kansas City, say, gonna hold out for a Jubilee when the local fountain man is pushin' Grape Whoopee or some such?"

"Because Jubilee is better," said Bax. "You said so yourself."

"Maybe I'm partial to the inventor."

"Maybe so, but the rest of Savannah doesn't suffer that handicap. Look, Gus, we'll tell the world. This isn't like guano. Guano is guano, an' only farm folk need it. A beverage is different. Everybody gets thirsty—."

"Everybody can drink plain ol' water when they're thirsty," Gus snapped, reinstalling his cigar. "They don't gotta pay good money for some sweet swill."

"Everybody can also rinse off his hands and face and ass with plain ol' water instead of usin' Pears or Ivory—."

"Soaps clean better than plain water—."

"And Jubilee tastes better. And that's what we're going to tell the whole blamed United States of America. We're goin' to sell 'em Jubilee from every soda counter in the Union. We're gonna hire us the smoothest-talkin', freshest-smellin', fastest-movin' set o' salesmen as ever traveled this land. And then we're going to make it in bottles out o' mills in every city and town that'll have us—and advertise it from every fence and gate and doorpost and lamppost and put it in every home in the land where people work up a thirst. It'll come cascading out of the South like a ruby-red waterfall and quench a whole nation, Gus. It'll be the premier product of the Old Confederacy, an' the world's gonna know it—."

We all stared at the tiny beaded bubbles flying up through the deep red liquid in Gus's glass and winking at the brim. "The boy surely does work up a head o' steam," said Gus to no one in particular. He tossed back his mane, and stared up at the ceiling for a time and then began tapping his blackthorn cane against the floor Morse-code fashion. "Well," he said finally, "I like your pluck, Billy, an' the general drift of your thinkin'. It's just I wonder if we got the right product. It don't somehow seem essential enough. It's like some kinda toy thing—."

"That's just why it's perfect, Gus," Bax shot back. "It's so cheap and pleasant you don't have to think twice about a purchase. You may put off buyin' a new plow—an' maybe you'll hold off on the guano if you can't lay in enough to do your whole spread—but a little ol' glass of soda pop—hell, no! A man needs a squirt o' pleasure to get him through a long hot afternoon—."

"And in the bargain," Mandy put in, "he's clearing his forehead and cleansing his clogged bowels."

Gus nodded slowly. "Course, it's not entirely plain to me whether the stuff's a tonic or a physic or champagne without the alcohol—."

"We'll push it as all three," said Bax. "Nobody thinks he's indulging himself that way."

Undeniably, Bax had thought through every argument. He was ready now when Gus served up his final reservation. "I don't know, Billy—times're mighty rough. You got people genuine starvin' from here to hell an' back. Maybe this ain't the time to try to sell 'em all fizzy water—."

"It's *just* the time!" said Bax. "It's practically all they can afford —an' they might as well get something happy out o' life. Besides

157

which, times aren't ever gonna get any better if we all sit around and mope about 'em. Somebody's got to get up and start movin' with new energy and new ideas. And we've got one right here. If we go out and shout it to the rooftops, nobody's gonna head us off!"

I would have sworn I was listening to Tom Watson deliver a barn-burner. Billy Doak Baxter had set his mind to the thing and he was going ahead with it, he confided to me later, Gus or no Gus. But as the head of the family and the reigning financial figure in southern Georgia, Gus's presence among the guiding hands of the ambitious new enterprise would make it substantially more formidable and resolute. "All right," said Gus, removing his cigar and checking its sluggish ember, "how much?"

How much depended on how. Bax proposed that they generate what cash was needed from the family and close friends and stay out of the credit market as long as possible. "Every penny's got to count," he said and then sketched out a marketing plan for the foreseeable future. He had had enough of whirlwind success followed by headlong disaster. Now he would build solidly and by stages. The first year of the operation would be devoted to saturating all of Georgia with the drink; the next year, the adjacent markets of Alabama and South Carolina; then outward in tiers, until by the end of the fifth year they would have drenched all Dixie in the stuff. And once the Southern stronghold was secured, they would move on to the Northern and Western markets in concerted fashion—presumably without need or benefit of rebel yells.

"We'll debut in New York at Delmonico's," said Mandy, nearly as effervescent as her brother.

"Coney Island might be a better bet," I offered.

Within a fortnight, the financing structure was arranged. Ten stockholders would put up ten thousand dollars each; no bank credit would be sought until after the second year of operation, when the solidity of the company would be apparent to all. If not, it would be dissolved. Gus, Bax, Mandy, and Evelyn Baxter each took a hundred shares of one-hundred-dollar par stock. Eugene Venable, for himself, and I, representing the Lazarus interests, each took another hundred shares. The general manager of the De Soto, the president of Gus's principal bank, and the most affluent broker on Factors' Row came in. The final hundred shares Bax offered to Tom Watson.

"It's him or me," Gus had said, upon hearing the proposal.

"Why?" said Bax. "Because he was right?"

"Because he's a rabble-rousing, two-faced little pissant!"

"The man's a prophet without honor in his own land."

"And that's the way he's gonna stay if I can help it—."

"His time is coming," Bax said calmly.

"You make him sound like Christ," said Gus. "If he's so Christ-like, how come he's got ten thousand to spare on a sugar-water speculation?"

"I don't know as he has. But I hear his plantation is well run and growing steadily." Bax shook his head. "You've got him all wrong, Gus. You always have. Watson's the best thing business has going for it anywhere in Georgia. All he ever said was that capital can't keep taking; it's gotta give something back to labor besides slave wages."

Gus was unmollified. "He's still a pissant."

"So was Napoleon," said Bax.

"And you saw how he wound up—."

But Bax held his ground, and when Watson wrote back that he would be privileged to be among the founding stockholders, the roster of investors was complete. It was left to Mandy, who had invented the drink and christened it, to name the company as well. With characteristic cheek, she said it would be called the Jubilation Plantation Corporation. And so it has been ever since.

SIX

Measured by the mighty molten flow from the furnaces at Homestead and Gary and Bethlehem, by the torrential outpouring from the petroleum fields of Ohio and Oklahoma, by the bursting golden harvest from the sundered sod of Kansas and Iowa, or by the pillars of dust from the longhorn herds crashing across the Cimarron, the product of our little company in a dank corner of Georgia was the most puny imaginable—of no more consequence to the stuttering national economy, it seemed at the time, than the beat of a hummingbird's heart in the midst of a hurricane. That today, after but two short decades, it is well on its way toward becoming the single most American thing in America is a tribute to the consuming energy of the thirty-four-year-old visionary who saw in Jubilee not some new brand of soda pop but the Holy Grail itself. W. Doak Baxter burned with a white flame in those early years of the company.

My own function as counsel to the corporation was limited at first to riding out every other day to the factory site on Longstreth Way at the western city limits and producing small but audible sighs of wonder as the three-story brick fortress materialized with awesome speed under Bax's driving lash. Bax himself was a flurry of perpetual motion throughout the process. When he was not overseeing the pipe fitters and bricklayers or interrogating glassmakers and coal-suppliers or plowing through mounds of specification sheets showered upon him by manufacturers of carbonating machinery, he was trying to fend off swarms of the jobless contending for the fifty or so positions to be filled by the time the plant opened in May of 1894. Amid this ceaseless swirl, Bax's sweet temper was tried daily by delays and mistakes and misunderstandings and all the thousand snags likely to be suffered when the driver is far keener on reaching his destination than the team that is drawing the burden.

In his zealous attention to every phase of the newly expanded operation, Bax overlooked only one thing, so far as I could see. But it happened to be the most basic ingredient in the product. I asked him about it one evening when he and Cissy had come by for dinner during the middle stage of the factory-building. "How's the water supply out there?" My tone was casual. Urgency would have turned him defensive.

"The table's plenty high," said Bax without concern. "I can stick a screwdriver in the ground and hit water 'most anywhere."

"I was actually thinking more about its cleanliness," I said. "You can't rely on the fountain owners for that any more. Once you put the stuff in your own bottle, you've got to vouch for it."

Bax dumped a refill into his glass of bourbon. Since the company was formed, he had cut down sharply on his alcoholic intake by way of acknowledging the fresh responsibility he bore: he took nothing at all during the working day and a highball or two after dinner for relaxation, a great deal better reason for putting it away than self-sorrow. He set down the bottle I had parked next to his chair and studied his drink for a moment. "Well," he said, "I've tasted it, and while it may not be as good as this stuff, it seems fine to me. It looks clean when you hold it up to the sunlight. It smells clean. I'd say water's the least of our worries."

I thought otherwise and wrote of it to my brother Benny, with whom I had remained in continuous correspondence over the years. Of late he had given up a portion of his private practice to work for the barest minimum in compensation with the renowned Dr. Hermann Biggs of New York City's board of health. Having studied in the laboratories of Koch and Pasteur, Biggs had returned to America and launched a one-man revolution in the field of public health. Benny had eagerly offered his services when Dr. Biggs introduced diagnostic tests for cholera throughout the city. At the time I wrote him, Benny was assisting in experiments with a diphtheria vaccine and pioneer treatments for the "white plague" of tuberculosis. "Dr. Biggs is convinced we should do far

161

better," he had written me soon after the turn of the year, "to work at purifying the water and milk supply of the city than to seek remedies once the diseases have taken hold. 'An ounce of prevention is worth ten tons of cure' is how he puts it. The man is the inspiration of my life."

At my urgent invitation, Benny agreed to come to Savannah to survey the water supply at the factory site. With him he brought the necessary testing paraphernalia, which he set up in a miniature laboratory in one of the sitting rooms at our house. Bax, edgy at any intrusion and eager to get production under way at the first possible moment, greeted my brother's arrival reluctantly. "You are a perfect jackass," Mandy told him when his coolness to Benny manifested itself in a cutting remark about "laboratory crackpots." She took Benny in tow herself and made plain her gratitude to him for his voluntary labors. His discoveries soon brought Bax around as well.

Having relied on surface wells and the river itself for drinking water until well into the Eighties, Savannah had lately paid tribute to modernity by passing an ordinance that required residents to sink artesian wells as their chief source of potables. Public health, ever a problem in the city, improved markedly (although Savannah's severest perennial plague, yellow fever, did not abate until Dr. Reed's splendid work in the tropics became widely known after the turn of the century). In the outlying sectors of the city, however, in which the Jubilee factory was rising, the drilling of deep wells had lagged, and so when Benny began his inspection of the countryside, he found mostly shallow wells, no more than ten to fifteen feet deep, available to supply the plant. He came back to the site shaking his head. "In New York," he said, "the board of health has banned all use of well water, even deep ones. Here you're practically taking the surface runoff."

"The surface is a whole lot cleaner here than you've got up there," Bax replied. "You've piled people into boxes and let 'em foul the earth by the ton each day. We've got fields here, mostly—."

"Also stable yards, privies, dung heaps, and slaughterhouses, all within a mile or two of here, not to mention a graveyard with suspiciously toxic drainage. My advice is to test."

We all gathered in the makeshift laboratory in our house as Benny explained carefully what he was up to. The key test for detecting organic impurities was made, he said, by introducing per-manganate of potash into a sample of the water supply. Against the backdrop of a white bedsheet, Benny set up four test tubes, one filled with distilled water, the other three with water drawn from wells in the vicinity of the factory. Into each he put six drops of the permanganate solution, which at once communicated a bright violet hue to the water. "The color comes from the oxy-gen in the solution," Benny noted, "which, whenever it comes in contact with easily oxidizable substances, such as decomposed or-ganic matter, loses its oxygen and consequently its color. Over two or three days, infested water usually changes from violet to pink to scarlet, then a duller scarlet, then a muddy scarlet, and finally no color at all. The distilled water will of course remain this con-stant beautiful violet, so we can tell by contrast at any point how our tests samples are progressing—or retrogressing, as the case may be. The more and faster the color changes, the worse the infestation." He also arranged a less ornamental test for sewage contamination by filling a well-scrubbed pint bottle three quarters of the way, dissolving a teaspoonful of granulated sugar in it, cork-ing the bottle, and sitting it on a windowsill in the sunlight for two days. "If the well water turns milky or cloudy," Benny said, "it's unfit for human consumption."

Not to keep us in painful suspense, he performed a third test on the spot. Into a beaker of well water from the factory site, he added a few drops from a solution of nitrate of silver he had brought along for that purpose. The water at once turned a pale brown. "This is called the Leffmann test after the scientist who perfected it," Benny said. "The color here indicates, beyond any doubt, the pollution of the water by urine."

Bax was unconvinced. He suggested the silver nitrate had trans-formed the color. He would await the results of the other two tests before even beginning to acknowledge that they had a prob-lem. My small daughter Judith, who had been posted to watch the progress of the other two tests, excitedly reported the next day that only the tube of distilled water retained its bright rosy hue; the well-water samples had lost their color altogether in barely twenty-four hours. By the following day, the bottle of sugared water had turned nearly opaque.

"The combined results are conclusive," Benny informed us. "I could also test for sulphuric acid and any number of other contaminants, but I should think this would be enough to convince you of the wisdom of seeking some other source of water."

Bax pouted for days. Mandy, on the other hand, sought a solution. "What about rainwater?" she asked Benny. "Lord knows, it rains enough around here to keep us supplied." That would be better, Benny said, but not problem-free. Outdoor cisterns were natural attractions for organic matter like bird droppings and wind-blown bacteria and microscopic plant life, all of which was subject to decomposition in the sunlight. Indoor storage tanks posed comparable problems such as attracting the vapors from dust-bins and gas-works and other sources of refuse. "And ponds?" asked Mandy. "We have ponds and ponds." No, Benny said, ponds were worse. Not only did pond water abound in vegetative life but because of shallowness in many cases, the water in ponds warmed rapidly and hastened decay at a rate well beyond the purifying power of the dissolved oxygen drawn from the air. Mandy shook her head. "What about ice water?" she asked, a trace of desperation creeping into her voice. "I've heard that freezing water purifies it—though heaven only knows how we'd find ourselves enough ice." An old wives' tale, said Benny. Frozen water was no purer than the liquid state; all it did was disguise the offensive contents while perfectly preserving them until they thaw.

"What's left?" asked Mandy resignedly.

"Boiling," said Benny.

"All of it?"

"All of it," he said. "But if you sink artesian wells, it won't take all that long—an hour, I'd say, for boiling a vat of a hundred gallons, and you'd be perfectly safe."

Bax grimaced and grumbled and griped but he acquiesced. He stayed up all night with the blueprints and redesigned the entire interior layout of the factory to accommodate three thick oak vats, bound on the outside by galvanized iron hoops to withstand the pressure of two hundred bubbling gallons each. To keep the building as cool as possible, he located the water-purifying vats on the third floor next to a smaller one already planned to supply the steam-washing operation for the bottles on the second floor. The rest of that floor would be given over to inspecting and labeling the bottles, brewing Jubilee syrup, and administrative offices; the actual carbonating and bottling process was to be conducted on the ground floor to keep the hauling of filled bottles to a minimum. Bax showed the revised arrangement to Benny, who studied it with care, suggested shifting a pipe or two around to facilitate the flow of the purified water to the carbonators, and then praised it warmly. "You've done yourself and your customers a very large favor," he said.

"Not half so large as the one you've done us," said Bax. "I hope you'll accept my profound apologies—."

Benny waved off the expression of gratitude as excessive. But in the privacy of our dining room that evening, his last with us in Savannah on that trip, he registered puzzlement over my preference for *goyish* associates.

"It's not a matter of preference," I said. "It's just the way things have worked out for me down here."

"But they blow so hot and cold. One minute Baxter is ready to drop me down a well so I can get really close to the water. The next he is charming me to death with kindness. There's nothing constant. They're so hard to trust—."

"They say the same of us."

Benny sipped at his tea and slowly shook his head. "Sethie, Sethie," he sighed. "I think you're bamboozling yourself. You're two steps from conversion without knowing it. You crave their food. You don their dress. You talk their language. And your synagogue! I wonder that they haven't replaced the tabernacle yet with an ikon of the *shammus*'s favorite saint. A church, Sethie— that's what that is—."

"Faith takes different forms in different places," I said oracularly. "Naturally I eat and dress and speak as local custom dictates. It's what's inside a man that counts—."

"And what's inside you, Sethie? Pigs' knuckles and shrimp creole! Me—I'm a man of science. I'm allowed to experiment. I can even be excused for straying from the fold because I'm so busy healing bodies and figuring out the Lord's mysterious ways that sometimes I forget what day it is, *Shabbos* included. But I don't go waltzing off with the Gentiles every time they start fiddling a pretty tune—."

I was not insensitive to his charge. But I had, long before that moment, reconciled to my satisfaction the contrary tendencies of form and fundament. And here was my beloved brother dismissing that painful resolution as simple convenience. My first impulse was to defend myself. In another moment, however, I was seized with the suspicion that over the passing years it was he, the worldly metropolitanite, who had become the provincial and not I in my outpost by the sea. "The Gentiles call that tune, Benny—haven't you noticed?"

"Noticed? They never let me forget—not in my profession. It's as if they're afraid we'll contaminate their blessed holy water by looking cross-eyed at it. One Jew gets into medical college for every fifty qualified applicants. And why? Because they are afraid of our competence. They want to penalize us for our merit. And when we lack it, they mock us as dunderheads. You can't win. And the immigration has made everything worse. I hear even my enlightened professional colleagues, when they think I'm out of earshot, denounce the city Jews as so many animals jammed into their filthy hovels and merrily rooting about for a bite of *kishka*—as if we take pleasure in our poverty. We're either too rich or too poor for them, Seth—too smart or too dumb, too kind or too vile. It makes me bitter." He pushed the last of his peach cake to the side gently. "I've stopped falling all over myself trying to embrace every *goy* who smiles at me. I keep looking for the bat he's got behind his back—."

Perhaps my judgment of him had been too harsh, as his had surely been of me. If we were not each other's keeper, we were obliged at least to seek mutual understanding. "I think you miscalculate the world down here," I said to Benny. "I don't go out of my way either to embrace Christians or to flee from them—any more or less than I do Jews. I find pleasing people in about equal proportion in each group, only there are few Jews to choose from among. I don't mean that the two are not different—I've never pretended that, or deluded myself that Christians believe that, even the ones I'm closest to. But that difference doesn't obsess me, Benny, the way I'm afraid it may you. What we have in common with them—minds and hearts and navels and kneecaps, loves and hates and yearnings—and death, your ghastly specialty, Benny, that no one else will attend to—those matter more than how we differ. That's what I believe. Do you believe that, Benny?"

"To a point," he said, unprepared for the ardor of my response. "But I cling to my faith much harder than you because finally, my dear brother, men may function as their common humanity dictates when things go well, but they *feel* as their separate upbringings teach them the moment things go sour. And the world I know is more sour than sweet by half. A Jew risks his neck daily in such a place. Yet I would not disguise my faith—."

"Nor I mine," I told him. "But I refuse to be defined by it, as if to say a man is a Jew—or of any faith or tribe or nation—is all one needs to know of him to judge his worth. I am neither ennobled by the creed I was born to—that is not what belonging to 'the chosen people' means to me, Benny—nor diminished by it, however long or far or hard the world hounds us for possessing it. No, what my Jewishness does is to distinguish me. It tells me what is just and right no matter what or how the heathens holler. It orders me not to grovel before what I know to be false, to be merely ornamental, to be a debasement of the sacred word. I may not profane the holy spirit even if it is more mystery than enlightenment to me. I cannot turn my back on that, Benny, although it means a kind of living martyrdom, spent in perpetual wariness of the Gentiles by whatever name they go. You abuse your brother by saying otherwise. Yet you dishonor life itself if you hold all men in contempt but your own kind."

We kissed goodbye, as always, at the rail depot.

11

The equanimity I had expressed to Benny toward the factor of faith in my feelings for the community at large was jolted not many weeks after his visit when Eugene Venable succumbed to pneumonia at the age of sixty-eight. My mentor, my inspiration, my partner, he had also turned into my friend in the last years of our association. I cannot say that he ever bared his soul to me, any more than I could conceive of his having ever bared his buttocks to Mrs. Venable, but there are worse sins in a man than remoteness. Gene Venable taught me to think before as well as after I spoke, to tend to both the forest and the trees, and to consider carefully what every man said but to be persuaded by none but myself. We prospered in mutual respect.

That prosperity, however, ended for me with harsh swiftness after his death. While I think it safe to say that a Jew was acceptable as Mr. Venable's junior colleague so long as his competence was apparent to all and his character vouchsafed by the old man, his passing altered that. The warden and vestry of Christ Church, after seeing to his burial without cost to the family, sent me word that its legal affairs would henceforth be conducted by a different firm. That was neither a great surprise nor a financial setback to me, but the man was hardly cold in the ground when the church fathers felt obliged to so inform me. Within days, our railroad, gas company, and banking business had also evaporated, and the wills of half a hundred other clients of long standing were transferred out of the office. Gus Griffin had the courtesy to wait a fortnight before coming by himself one afternoon to collect his papers from our vault. "It's nothing personal, son," he said. "It's just good business. I'll do what I can to send people your way." I thanked him without looking up from my desk, Gene Venable's Chippendale legacy to me.

Gus's niece and nephew, however, remained my clients. Each sent a short note of sympathy and pledged future loyalty. And as if the stigmata of my excessively intimate association with the *goyim* had been koshered away, my Jewish clientele increased detectably. But since one could hardly hope to thrive on a sectarian practice of that sort in the southeastern sector of Georgia, I found myself, out of the survival instinct, taking on many more criminal matters than would ever have sullied the firm's docket under the Venable regime. Hardly a week passed when I did not hie myself to the county courthouse on Wright Square for a morning or two of beseeching the jury to have mercy on my conniving, thieving, or otherwise reprobate clients, ninety-eight percent of whom were guilty as sin but claimed, in nearly every instance, to have been driven from righteousness by the grim economic realities of the age. Rarely did I wheedle an acquittal, but in time I garnered a reputation for honorably extracting the kindliest possible disposition of even my most thoroughly unpromising cases. These humanitarian efforts were most highly regarded, curiously enough, by the constabulary, whose mountainous chief, the florid Weyland Yates, pronounced me a sterling ornament of the bar to all who would listen. I won such a champion, no doubt, because I, almost alone among the defense practitioners of the region, never railed against the police as truncheon-happy bullies or sought to discredit their performance of duty merely because it was directed against some perverse fellow I was trying to get off. As a result, I was awarded easy access to the police station, its personnel, and its records—an advantage that frequently facilitated my work and benefited my caged clients. As in my days at country-storekeeping, I was viewed at headquarters as a co-author of the Old Testament and the living embodiment of the Mosaic Code, in admired contrast to all those other dark-eyed, black-capped, nigger-coddling, lucre-gouging, Christ-killing *momzers* out there. One of the beefier lads on the force took to calling me, to my face, a "good ol' Hebe" until I confided to Chief Yates, after several months of this back-thumping greeting, that I should be grateful for some slightly less demeaning, if no less affectionate, tribute.

Such interludes aside, the mainstay of my practice throughout the Nineties, beyond a doubt, was the service I rendered as general counsel to the Jubilation Plantation Corporation—or "the company" as we all called it for short. Bax and Mandy, who regarded the enterprise as essentially their own, prevailed in their demand that I be retained despite contrary pressure from others among the stockholders. So that I might serve the enterprise more ably, Bax indoctrinated me for endless hours on the intricate network of bubbling gunmetal machinery that was to produce the drink, though it was a subject in which I had not the slightest professional competence or amateur interest. In fact, Bax was educating himself more than me in the process—and a good thing, for while Jubilee was a humble enough product, without moving parts or finely calibrated machining, its manufacture invited human error at every stage of the production cycle. During the break-in period, everything that conceivably could have gone wrong, did. Generator pipes got clogged from too much gas pressure. Vats of caramel overflowed from overcooking. Improperly shut valves caused condensers to explode. Impure marble dust in the carbonators made the drink smell bad, steel- instead of tin-lined cans made it taste metallic, leaking acid made it turn from a brilliant ruby to a stale-looking ocher. And bottles began to shatter from a dozen different flaws. But Bax never lost hope or patience, and finally the product was ready for presentation to a world beyond Savannah.

Leaving behind an uneasy but attentive complement of managers and superintendents and foremen to run that wayward factory, Bax took to the huckster trail accompanied by a pair of personable assistants and determined to sell the world's most delectable beverage from every conceivable outlet—and some outlandish ones as well—in every county in Georgia. As in Savannah, they began with bulk syrup sales as the swiftest way to introduce the drink to the greatest number of customers. Every pharmacy, soda fountain, luncheon and short-order restaurant, hotel, tavern, and resort with carbonating dispensers was solicited, and those not so equipped were told why they ought to be. Enthusiasm among dealers was stimulated by a tempting variety of premiums, both functional and decorative, including prescription scales and medicine cabinets, wall clocks, mirrors, and showcases, as well as trays, glasses, and porcelain urns for the adornment of the fountain itself. After the syrup order was written, point-of-sale signs and festoons were hung, placards posted on fences, free-trial coupons distributed door to door, and advertisements placed in the local press. Town by town, county by county, the volume accumulated steadily.

Once statewide fountain orders for the syrup had surpassed a thousand gallons a month, Jubilee in bottles was given its send-off outside the Savannah market, where the early response had been favorable. Considering the logistical difficulties of handling twenty-four-bottle metal boxes of the drink, the sales effort concentrated on the big cities, especially Atlanta, Augusta, and Macon, where older brands had a head start and grocers and other locally minded storekeepers were resistant to a product so closely identified with Savannah. The orders trickled in at first—two cases here, five there—too few, really, to allow economical pickup of the empty metal cases. To stir business, Bax borrowed an idea from the old Adelphi operation: he gave each account that ordered three dozen cases a free cash register; when it arrived, of course, each one had a sign proclaiming the splendors of Jubilee indelibly etched to its back. Most of the store owners thought that a little sharp but few returned the popular machines, and Jubilee sales bounded ahead. Soon nearly every local freight in Georgia carried its rattling quota of Jubilee en route to or from Savannah. Pleased with so much added cargo, most of the rail lines agreed to sell the drink—for a plump commission, to be sure—in bottles on their passenger runs and from dispensers in the depots. By the spring of 'Ninety-five, the factory on Longstreth Way was operating overtime two nights a week; by midsummer, every night and all day Saturday.

Ever on the prowl for outlets to sell his product, Bax invented them when all else failed. He even ventured back into maritime operations of a sort, although this time he left the steering and travail to other hands. Little steamers emblazoned with Jubilee pennants pushed up and down every river in the state, peddling the drink dockside at any plantation, lumber camp, turpentine mill, or watermelon patch that would let them tie up. So popular did "the Jubilee break" become that the work-bosses, who themselves craved the taste, agreed to gather and store the empty cases till the supply could be replenished on the next trip two or three days hence. The reception was less cordial in the mill towns. The management ran its own stores and was not eager to share revenues with any outsiders. Jubilee wagons thus had to be stationed beyond the town boundaries, at a good distance from the shacks of the waxen-faced workers. Even so, the wagons were mobbed on their semi-weekly visits, and the drink proved especially beloved by the hollow-eyed, bacillus-riddled urchins who put in fourteen-hour days at the spindles and had precious else to look forward to beyond the cool, sweet, bubbly drink. This popularity, siphoning a few splashes of profit from the company stores, caused the Jubilee wagons to be set upon by hired hooligans and overturned in several locations. After briefly considering arming each wagonmaster with a shotgun, Bax concluded that his enterprise had more to lose than gain by such bravado and retreated, for the time being, from this promising territory.

There were other setbacks along the way. Remembering the immediate response to the drink before violence ended it during Tom Watson's ill-fated Congressional campaign, Bax went after colored customers as ardently as whites. They may have been poorer but they got no less thirsty. Good economic sense dictated that they repair to the nearest brook for a palmful of nature's most efficient thirst-quencher. But Bax argued without remorse that his product had a higher and more sociable function and was thus not exploitive of but rather a service to the needs of the masses. Those needs in the Black Belt counties would not be met at the soda fountain and other usual service outlets, where negro patronage was not invited, and so Plato Layne, elevated to the position of Jubilee sales representative throughout the black bottom of central Georgia and recompensed accordingly, began arranging for distribution at the clapboard stores and roadside stands that dealt with colored clientele only throughout the back-country. Accounts were nonchalantly kept at such places, however, and sales figures constantly outstripped actual revenues until Bax required all such transactions to be made on a cash basis, which reduced the volume but enhanced profits at once.

To boost sales, Plato himself painted a large mural on the side of one crossroads store that depicted a colored man in overalls swigging Jubilee from a bottle. The store was overrun with customers, so Plato commissioned similar signs at as many other spots as he could find that were willing to give over a whole side wall for the purpose. The sales increase was gratifying, but by the time Bax shudderingly discovered the cause—"We'll have to boil the bottles for a month once the first cracker sees those signs," he told me—it was too late. Klan and other hostile types splattered the murals with whitewash and painted "Niggerwater sold here" over them. Angry, illiterate letters addressed to merely "Jubilee, Savannah" threatened the smashing of the company's entire output unless the drink was withdrawn from sale to "nigger lips." Within a week, Plato was reassigned to cleaning bottles at the factory; the only colored employée there in a position other than purely custodial, he was twice nearly nudged into a boiling vat by resentful co-workers and soon asked Bax to have his old job back as coachman.

Such casualties notwithstanding, Jubilee advanced on many fronts. And the better the sales, the more Bax spent on advertising it, for he understood it was not a product of necessity and that the demand for it would have to be sustained by other means. Most of the early advertising was uninspired. Our newspaper displays and placards were largely limited to proclaiming the delicious flavor and tonic effects of the drink—"the potion that cheers but does not inebriate" was the most stirring slogan of that era. Bax and Mandy were not wordsmiths, and the Georgia woods did not yield a timely genius. And then the Lord, or someone, sent Gordon Hazard.

Hazard, who made everyone call him "Happy" because of his sunny disposition, blew into town propelled in equal parts by natural ebullience, hot air, and hunger. The last was the chief operative force. He had received splendid training as a copywriter for several of the more skillfully deceitful patent-medicine houses until, in a fit of contrition, he spilled the beans to one of the conscience-stricken national magazines investigating the false claims and doctored testimonials that were standard in the blarney racket. Happy managed to relocate with the impeccably ardent mail-order house of Sears, Roebuck until, in an outburst of candor, he suggested to the egomaniacal boss how to improve a soggy piece of his most prized copy. As a result, Happy had gone hungry for months, or so he said, although his globular silhouette and bouncy step belied the claim. And so when he spotted the classified that Bax had placed in the Cincinnati *Enquirer*, among several Northern papers, Happy showed up in a bowler and houndstooth suit, and announced, "I'm your man," before any responses had been received.

Happy wasted no time expunging the fake-medical content from the sales pitch. "We don't want our drink gathering dust waiting for people to feel lousy," he said. "We don't even want it waiting for people to feel thirsty. Jubilee's bigger than thirst! There's nothing exciting about thirst! And Jubilee's got to be exciting—an event all by itself. It's got to make people feel good! None of the other soda yokels have figured that out yet."

He did more than ridicule the competition. Happy Hazard showed how it should be done. He put Jubilee into beguiling settings and brought each one to life with copy as bold and snappy as the drink itself. Typical was a scene at intermission time in an elegant theater. In the background was a glimpse of the curtain with a fleecy pastoral setting and the milling audience at the head of the aisles comparing notes on the performance; in the foreground a vivacious and stylishly dressed young woman and her gentleman friend were seated at a small round table and hoisting a glass toward each other. Happy's copy read: "A taste of Jubilee is just as enjoyable as the play itself." And below that: "Joyfully in harmony with the spirit of all recreations, it is a flavorful, refreshing tonic beverage, in which a proposal to health and happiness becomes an accomplished fact." Mandy called it perfect.

Bax was no less pleased with Happy's "sweat ads." All manly men loved baseball, and Jubilee was being sold at most ball parks in the South by then, although it was by no means the leading brand. Happy decided to seize first place by enlisting the top players in the game for endorsements, starting with George

"Snuffy" Bean, the ball-hawking centerfielder and ferocious base-stealer of the Cincinnati Red Stockings who was a native of Peanut Bend, Georgia, and the apple of Dixie's eye even though he had not played an inning there since boyhood. The price was a thousand dollars for a year's use of his name; Bax thought that extravagant until he saw Happy's first effort. It showed a bare-headed Bean roaring cap in hand into third base in a cloud of dust as the fielder waited dejectedly for the late throw. The copy ran:

SLIDE, SNUFFY, SLIDE!

Snuffy Bean's on base. Something's bound to happen. Everybody on edge—nerves a-tingle—heads racing—up on your toes. Crack! A drive into left. Go, Snuffy, go! He's burning up the bases. Swoosh into third—safe! Good boy, Snuffy. You shout yourself hoarse cheering him. And when it's all over, you're hot and parched and limp. A cold, delightful quaff of Jubilee will put you right back into the game. Rooters and ball players alike swear by it.

Snuffy Bean says: "I drink Jubilee all year long. But I like it best of all between games of a doubleheader. It lets me start the second contest feeling so vigorous and refreshed that I feel like I never played the first one!"

Bax doubled Happy's salary and gave him a real office. Buoyed, he proceeded to break new ground in the seminal development of billboards. His basic sign was graphically uncluttered so there was no missing the simple message. The rectangular boards were bisected diagonally into congruent red and blue triangles; the printing was in clean, bold white: "Have a JUBILEE—and treat yourself right." Nothing fancy, and just a hint of *double-entendre.* Where Happy showed his *condottiere* style was in the way he seized prime locations for the billboards and repulsed all rivals along key stretches of railroad track, on heavily trafficked streets and highways, and on the roofs of strategically situated office buildings. His most inventive achievement in this form of the art, no doubt, was the seriatim sign—little poems, displayed one line to a signboard and spaced beside the road at thirty-foot intervals. His first such creation went:

When you're thirsty
As a camel
Follow the trail of
The wisest mammal
Not to an oasis
Or up a tree—
Just grab the nearest
JUBILEE!

and early on sent three drivers veering off the road, so attentive were they to that deathless poesy. Safety, if not the doggerel, improved with familiarity, but the idea was soon heisted by other brands, and Happy's fertile mind turned to more spectacular techniques. His masterstroke was the erection of a mammoth electrified Jubilee sign eight hundred feet up the side of Stone Mountain just outside of Atlanta. "Its message reaches more people than any advertisement in the South," he announced after surveying his disfiguring handiwork.

"How do you know that?" I asked him.

"I know it," he said.

"*How* do you know it?"

"You're crowding me, son. I know it the way I know the sun will rise tomorrow. There's never been anything this big before in this part of the woods—in the whole hemisphere, I'll wager. And this is only the beginning. Think of the Grand Canyon when we move west—think of the Brooklyn Bridge when we hit New York. And once we're international, I can see us on the Matterhorn—on Gibraltar—on the white cliffs of Dover and the pyramids. I've even got a little scheme for the Piazza San Marco involving a hundred thousand pigeons and half a ton of bread crumbs spread out into enormous letters—." I remarked that certain legal, not to mention aesthetic, considerations might interfere with such an ambitious program; Happy shrugged me off with "Some people'd ban poontang from a whorehouse." A year later, as it happened, the outraged citizenry of Dover, England, rose up as a single man and, after passing an anti-littering ordinance, smote the giant sign that the Quaker Oats people had put up on the cliffs. On advice of counsel, Bax ordered the Jubilee sign taken down from Stone Mountain before the locals took it into their heads to do it first. Happy was inconsolable for the better part of fifteen minutes.

The surest sign of Jubilee's billowing success was the number of people who began to sue us. Nobody tries to milk a barren cow. Most of the suits in those years were claims for damages from customers who said they had discovered unwholesome and unsightly ingredients in their bottle of Jubilee. Flies, roaches, beetles, spiders, praying mantises, and even frogs were prominent on the list of intrusive animal life; tacks, nails, bolts, iron filings, and "Bryan for President" buttons were among the most common metallic objects alleged. Cigar butts formed a category all their own. Defending against these charges, which were coming in dozens annually by the turn of the century, consumed an inordinate amount of my time until we figured out a way to dispose of them painlessly.

At first, the company was inclined to pay out "hush money" to such offended customers on the premise that it would be cheaper in the long run than contesting the matter and suffering the effects of unsavory publicity, certain to follow no matter what the outcome of the litigation. But to continue to buy off such plaintiffs, I advised after the second or third such instance, was to extend an open invitation to blackmailers to feast on the corporation's bank account. The sooner the issue was faced in the courtroom—and we succeeded in establishing a precedent in our favor and a presumption of fakery by the claimants—the more surely we would discourage all such get-rich-quick schemers. The real fly in the ointment—or bottle, one might say—was the burden we carried of proving a negative (i.e., that there was no crawling, creeping, winged, or otherwise mobile or formerly mobile creature or sharp, pointy, jagged, or otherwise abrasive object in the bottle when it left the Jubilee factory on Longstreth Way). In court I summoned any number of our more mannerly and well-scrubbed employées, who testified at length on the exemplary sanitary condition of the company's premises. But plaintiff's counsel had scant trouble in producing several former Jubileers, as Bax jauntily called his devoted band of workers, who testified that the place was a sty. He evoked the concession from our people, moreover, that any of the less jolly Jubileers, whether out of pique over low pay or protest of the working conditions or plain unspiteful fatigue, might have brushed a foreign object into the beverage. We lost the case and five hundred dollars. More suits piled in. Clearly, another tack was required, and soon.

At the next such encounter, prompted by a petite widow with a brittle henna who claimed to have found three wasps in her Jubilee one morning at the breakfast table, I produced the expert testimony of the leading entomologist at the University of Georgia. He agreed with the plaintiff's identification of the allegedly bottled insects. I then asked what he could tell the court about them.

"Well," he said, "I think the most pertinent thing about them is that they are dead. They appear to have been in that condition for quite some time. And almost certainly, if they were in fact discovered in this lady's bottle, they had drowned long before she uncapped it and made her harrowing discovery. The drink itself, moreover, contains sufficient carbon dioxide to render these insects quite harmless to the human digestive system." This time the jury awarded only two hundred fifty dollars.

We were making headway, no doubt, but I was left to my own devices to squelch the threat that some jury somewhere might soon award a claimant ten thousand dollars and set off a Niagara of such actions. Our landmark defense was waged in Savannah, where I thought our chances best. I had armed myself with advice from my entomologist friend at the university, my brother, and a local authority on exotic cuisine. The plaintiff charged that he had found a medium-sized cockroach in his bottle and asked twelve hundred dollars in damages plus court costs. My defense was short. I put on only the factory manager, who gave the usual testimony about sanitary precautions. Then I approached the offending insect, lying belly up and quite lifeless in a jar labeled "Exhibit A." I held up the jar for careful inspection, then passed it among the jurymen, who made properly revolted faces and swiftly handed it back to me. With great ceremony I then uncapped the jar and grandly popped the bug into my mouth, gave two loud crunches, and swallowed it with an emphatic gulp lest anyone should claim hoax.

"Objection!" roared the plaintiff's counsel.

"What are *you* objecting for?" asked the judge. "He's the one who ate it."

When the courtroom calmed itself, I proposed that the case be adjourned for twenty-four hours, when the jury might inspect the state of my health and decide whether, even if the bug had been present in the bottle when it left the factory, the claimant would have sustained ten cents' worth of damage, let alone the small fortune being sought. The only compensation the plaintiff was entitled to, I said, was his right to patronize a different brand of soda pop, "although none that I know of is half so satisfying." The jury preferred to retire on the spot and voted in our favor.

III

That only passing reference is made on these pages to the modest domestic adventures I have shared with my devoted wife Ruth, our daughter Judith, and hitherto undisclosed son Elihu (a blessing of the Columbiad year) betokens neither indifference nor forgetfulness. Rather, the events of our home life have been so unexceptional—and the general level of prevailing contentment so high—that they seem scarcely in need of recording. Having said as much, I would be remiss not to cite the sole crisis that served to dash vitriol upon so much connubial bliss.

My affection for and later intimacy with Amanda Baxter were sustained throughout the first decade and a half of my marriage, but because they were so compartmentalized and supplementary to the main business of our separate lives, they inflicted scant emotional drain. It was the way each of us preferred it, and a more civilized arrangement I could not imagine. My close involvement with the company, of course, put us into regular contact, but I did not presume that the mere opportunity of easy liaison should prompt a tightening of our ties. I continued merely to wander over to Mandy's schoolhouse toward the end of an afternoon perhaps once a month for a chance social visit. Indeed, I learned more of her from Ruth, who taught music at the school for an hour or two several mornings a week, than from my own engagements with her, which often ended in speechless frenzy.

One soft April afternoon in 1897, I heard the strains of Chopin wafting from Mandy's third-floor office-studio as I approached the school by cutting across Telfair Square. The front door was unlocked as usual, and I let myself in quietly, as I was wont. The music no doubt prevented any sound of my arrival from reaching upstairs, and by the time the piano stopped, I was midway up the carpeted landing to the second floor. My rap on her door must therefore have taken her by surprise, but I could not fathom why Mandy did not answer it after a moment or two. I knocked again and still drew no answer. I called her name and said who I was and asked if anything were the matter. "No," she said through the door, "I was—just daydreaming." I asked her to open up; she said she was under the weather. I then understood there was someone else with her and discreetly retreated. But I could not resist the darker impulse to take a seat on a bench in the square and wait to see who her visitor was. My surprise was all but uncontainable, but I waited until later that evening to reveal my discovery.

"I'm not proud of my method," I said to Ruth after the children had been put to bed, "but I'm aware of where you were this afternoon."

Her glance met mine and then skidded off. "I see," she said.

"I fail to grasp why your being there should have been kept from me—unless—unless your friendship is something other than I had supposed—and I came upon you at a compromising moment—."

"You may think what you wish," she said, barely above a whisper.

"My God, Ruth—were you disrobed? Is that it?"

"Your tact seems to have abandoned you, Mr. Adler," she said, bracing herself now for the confrontation.

"You deny nothing, then?"

She stroked the long graceful lines of her neck while weighing an answer. Her cheeks were flushed and her eyes hot as she stood and began to march from end to end of the room with measured steps. "We shall see about denials in a moment," she said, "but for my part I will tell you what you must already know—that Amanda Baxter is a woman of great magnetism—of profound intelligence and ready wit and emotional dimensions I have encountered in no other human being. What I have come to feel for her has no relevance at all, Seth, to the life you and I share, which I find so rewarding and supportive. Amanda—commands another part of me—in a way only another woman could. It has not—it need not diminish what you and I are and feel toward each other—."

"You wish to continue this unnatural relationship—?"

She shook her head. "That's quite obviously impossible now."

"I should think so."

"But if my relationship with her is unnatural, as you so gallantly put it, what shall we say of yours? Perhaps you'd care to enlighten me as to why you came tap-tap-tapping at the boudoir of the scintillating Mademoiselle Baxter in the quiet of the afternoon—."

"It is *not* a boudoir, Ruth—it is a schoolhouse, and I had some business to conduct with her—."

"What business, Seth?"

Her eyes consumed me. I tried desperately to brazen it out. "Some papers for the company that needed signing—."

"Seth," Ruth said quietly, "she told me—everything."

"There is no everything. We're friends—old friends—."

"Illicit friends, Seth. The infrequency of your fornication does not excuse it."

The breath had all but drained out of me. "Why did she tell you?" I asked finally.

"She said she assumed I would have guessed—from the circumstances—and the solicitous tone in your voice when you knocked—."

We circled warily about for several minutes, not knowing whether to beat or comfort each other. Finally we sat close by, perched on the edge of the davenport, and confessed the sordid details. The anatomical delights exported from Lesbos had, till that moment, been a thorough mystery to me, one that excited little of my curiosity because, no doubt, I feared the lure of its male counterpart. Insistence that the permissible bounds of human love should be confined to heterosexuality, Ruth said with a directness I could not shy from, was brutal and indefensible in a person of my sensibility. "Human feelings are diverse," she said, "and range as widely and may be plucked as delicately—and rewardingly—as a fine violin." I had less mellow chords to sound in praise of adultery. One's desire for a dash of variety in one's partners at lovemaking could be therapeutic as well as disruptive, I offered, adding that monogamy was no doubt a vile invention of the Pharisees and lacked original biblical sanction. Smiling, Ruth agreed and proposed we now each pursue the route the other of us had taken, but not, please, with the same partner.

What had threatened to become a searing disaster for us, then, turned into a binding moment of revelation and understanding. We have replayed it at odd and lengthy intervals in the years that have followed, marveling at our mutual blindness. The first flash of anger yielded almost at once to a joint bemusement, for there had been no wounded party, or, rather, two mutually wounded ones. Toward Mandy, who had equally used and been used by both of us to the gratification of all three, there grew in us an abiding distaste, however unjustifiable. For both affairs had been sustained by the shared partner's exclusive knowledge of them, by the daring of so perilous and perverse a manipulation.

Since the prospect of a *ménage à trois* was unthinkable to any of us, it was plain that from the moment of their disclosure, both arrangements were at an end. No announcement to that effect was necessary. Ruth gave up her teaching position at the school. And while I did not reduce my activities on behalf of the product Mandy had invented on a sunny day when all of us were friends and lovers, they became more purely than ever a business to me, without the emotional overtones they had retained over time. Aside from having a small but quite black and unmistakable crucifix added onto the painted sign that hung in front of her school and thereby designating it an academy exclusively for Christian youth, Mandy remained cordial enough to the two of us on those rare occasions when we would meet all three, or paired as we had been in secret. I cannot recall that Ruth or I ever bemoaned our simultaneous submission to her as an index of our own bad taste, for Amanda Baxter was beyond question a creature who sponged up devotion how and when and where she wished, and left many a helpless heart discarded along her duplicitous course. I never hated her afterwards, just trusted all the world less, save for Ruth Adler.

IV

Of graver consequence than my second parting of the heart from Amanda Baxter was the growing rift between her brother and her uncle. Their relationship deteriorated in inverse ratio to the fortunes of the company.

It was almost as if Gus Griffin could not bear the prospect that his pleasant but wastrel nephew might some day soon, on a tidal

wave of nearly worthless sugar-water, win a fortune a good deal
larger than his own. On the surface, at first, Uncle Gus displayed
nothing but satisfaction over Jubilee's early triumphs. Indeed, he
wished to contribute to them beyond the mere investment of a
founder's equity and the encouragement that implied. He
dropped by the factory every week and mingled with the personnel, took a proprietary interest in the thickening sheaf of sales
figures, and usually had a helpful suggestion or two for Bax about
what markets were ripe for invasion or the effectiveness of the advertising. "Your women need more luster in the eye," he scolded
Happy Hazard on inspecting one demure layout, "and heft in the
bosom. And their gloves are out of style." But these token inter-
ventions could not satisfy a restless magnate who no longer had a
business of his own to fuss over yet who continued to exercise a
strong voice in the back rooms of Georgia politics. He remained
the most feared figure in the state between Macon and the sea,
and no slate of state candidates was assembled or important piece
of legislation put through at Atlanta without reference to him.
Because he had no selfish ends beyond the perpetuation of his
sway, he had sought few favors over the years—only granted
them. Now, in the name of the public good but the interest of
private advantage, he drew upon the accumulated obligation of
his debtors.

Bax was at a loss to understand when, in the spring of 1895, the
managers of several of the mill towns from which the Jubilee
wagons had been expelled by force a few months earlier approached him anew with a most attractive proposition. Jubilee,
having proven exceedingly popular with the mill hands, could
henceforth be sold in the company stores; moreover, it would be
the only carbonated beverage offered. All the companies asked in
return for this exclusive franchise was a slightly higher than usual
discount based on volume. Bax readily agreed, and partly on the
strength of that captive-market bonanza, Jubilee sales in Georgia
shot upward by a full twenty percent within a month.

How this turn of events had occurred was not apparent until
the state legislature next convened. Reformers had been agitating
with great fervor for a child-labor code to curb the seventy-two-
hour work week and other health-shattering abuses that Tom
Watson and like-minded Georgians had denounced for years.

Even citizens little inclined toward egalitarianism were helping build a fire under the drive to modify this cruelest-known form of industrial exploitation. It was with some astonishment, then, that I read an item in the *Constitution* reporting on the proceedings at a Democratic powwow at the capital in which Z. Augustus Griffin, "a downstate party chieftain," expressed strong opposition to the reform bill. "The most beautiful sight that we can see," he was quoted as declaring, "is the child at labor. And the earlier he might get at labor, the more beautiful—and the more useful does his life get to be." Bax was beside himself when I flagged him on the article. And when the legislators narrowly turned down the child-labor proposal shortly thereafter, he was so angry he would not speak to his uncle for a month. I was on hand in Bax's office when the two were reunited, if the word may be used for that tempestuous interview.

"There is no excuse for this despicable business," Bax said. "I can't believe you would descend to this sort of errand-running for the mill owners. They crush the life from these helpless children, Gus, and there's no point pretending otherwise."

"My part in it was small," said Gus, unaccustomedly subdued before Bax's fury. "*Vox populi vicet.*"

"Bilge!" Bax shouted. "You bought those votes with mill money—."

"It's called horse-trading in refined circles—."

"It's a crime against humanity, whatever you call it!"

"Hush up your asshole, son," Gus cried. "A bargain's a bargain. I don't like it no better than you, but that was the price. How do you think I felt when these operators sicked their pugs on your soda wagons? I wanted to crack all their skulls open—."

That Gus had engineered so evil a political swap out of an excess of partisanship did not excuse it in Bax's eyes, although he did not yet doubt his uncle's sincerity as an avowed if misguided promoter of Jubilee. Their differences grew the following year when the company's most famous stockholder stood a fighting chance to become Vice-President of the United States and Gus tried to purge him as a menace to the corporation's future prosperity.

Tom Watson, having narrowly lost his comeback election for Congress in 1894 under polling conditions only slightly less farcical than in the previous race, had the pleasure of watching the national Democratic Party veer sharply leftward and adopt the Populist credo almost *in toto* as its platform for 1896. Free coinage of silver and credit expansion, an income tax, the end of national banks, elimination of high tariffs, control of the runaway railroads—Democrats embraced the whole caboodle of them as well as a messianic young presidential candidate with strong appeal to the fundamentalist outlook of the threadbare South. Still, Watson would not bend to the most earnest entreaties that he lead the Pops into a fusion movement with the Democrats under their standard-bearer, Bryan. Victory over the entrenched plutocracy could be achieved no other way, he was urged. Watson saw it otherwise. The Democrats, he argued, had accepted reform only because of the ceaseless hectoring by the People's Party; to join hands with them now, when national sentiment was beginning to acknowledge the justice of the Populist stand, would be to remove such constructive pressure and free the reactionary elements in the Democratic hierarchy to reassert their ambitions. And once fused with the Democrats, the Populists would be swallowed up forever.

The fusion issue tore apart the Populist convention, and the party was saved only by a compromise in which the Democrat Bryan was named to head the ticket and Watson, at home in Thomson and not eager to yield his principles, was nominated for Vice-President. Rumor swept over the nation for a time that the Democrats, in concession, would scuttle their own vice-presidential candidate and accept the Populist Watson in his place on a true fusion ticket. But the change was never accomplished, Bryan all but ignored his radical Populist supporters in an effort to win the more respectable members of the electorate, and Watson campaigned across the prairies and through the South as the lonely and forlorn voice of a movement likely to achieve its ends now only by self-immolation. Yet he would not yield, even when assured of a primary position in the high councils of the Democratic Party.

I heard him speak in public for the last time that year at a rally in Savannah. He had never been better—a painfully lean, tragically earnest scold whose parchment-skin face looked twenty years of age when he showed his small, widely set teeth in a smile and then suddenly seemed sixty as he drew his brows down fiercely, set his mouth hard, tore up his angry words by their roots and flung them, soil still clinging to the bottom, at the nattering fates. Arms swirling, body swaying, head tossing red locks every which way, he cried out with the rasp of a hawk on the wing against the tormentors of the people.

"A frantic, rabid animal," Gus Griffin called him the following week at the Jubilee stockholders' meeting, from which the candidate had absented himself. So disturbed was Gus by the radical swing of the Democrats—prompted, he said, "by the ravings of Watson and his crew"—that he abandoned his Confederate gray wardrobe, let it be known throughout the county that he was voting the Republican ticket, and slyly flashed at intimates the little gold bug he wore on the inside of his lapel—the symbol of McKinleyism and a rebuke to the free-silver crowd. Bax, on the other hand, contributed generously to Watson's campaign, even when many of the most diehard Pops called his continuing candidacy a divisive force that threatened to hand the state's electoral votes to McKinley. Thus, the meeting of Jubilee stockholders in my office took a spirited turn when Gus introduced a motion to drum Tom Watson out of the corporation by buying his stock. "His association with the company puts us in a mighty sordid light," he said. "Anyone who's for sound money and human decency is gonna boycott our splendid beverage if word gets out he's behind it."

"Word isn't going to get out unless you leak it, Gus," said Bax. "Tom's told me he can't afford to be identified with any sort of corporation—even a down-home outfit like ours. So I'd say that's a stand-off, even by your ungenerous lights—."

"Ungenerous? Who's ungenerous? We've got a goddamned communist cuckoo in our midst, and you're calling me ungenerous? Generosity don't have anything to do with it. Tom Watson's a head-strong lunk—even his worshippers are sayin' that now, save one or two equally pea-brained backers. He's a menace to America and the future prosperity of this fine corporation of ours which is off and runnin' so good—."

"You're out of order, Gus," Bax said firmly.

"You're the one out of order, son," Gus fired back. "I jus' hope we can repair the damage before things get out o' hand. Now I made a motion a while back—."

"Your motion's out of order."

Gus appealed to me as the company parliamentarian. I said there was no way I knew to separate Tom Watson from his stock without due process of law, which of course would mean bringing the controversy before the public. Mandy suggested that Gus simply offer to buy Watson out at a profit if he was so exercised. Bax said no, that would give Gus twice as much voting power as any other stockholder. I said the corporation itself might offer to buy out Watson and then parcel his shares equally among the other holders. "I won't do that to him," said Bax. "He's certain to take it as a slap—which is just what Gus intends. The man put his money in here in good faith, and unless there's provocation, I say he's entitled to keep it in."

Gus insisted nevertheless on putting my casual suggestion to a vote, much to my uneasiness. There were ten votes in all, and Gus held five of them—his own, the widow Venable's proxy, and those of the three Savannah nabobs he had got to invest in the enterprise. Mandy had her own vote and her mother's proxy; Bax had his own and Watson's proxy. And I voted for the Lazarus trust, which Ruth's mother had created for our family. Gus of course cast his five votes to have the company tender for Watson's stock; Mandy voted with Bax. That left it five to four and the decision in my hands, since a tie meant Bax as chairman would rule. I voted against Gus without comment. The very closeness of the vote, however, was chilling confirmation of the growing breach within the family.

That Uncle Gus had been reading the political tea leaves astutely and not merely nursing a private vendetta against radicalism was evidenced the spring following when Democratic regulars raised their battle-axes to smite the miscreants across the state. Watson had attracted something over two hundred thousand votes for Vice-President in seventeen states—an inglorious distance behind the nearly six and a half million for the Democratic candidate and the more than seven million garnered by the victorious Republican. Watson had managed to win twenty-seven electoral votes in the West and South, but none from his native Georgia, where, in disrepute and self-exile, he had turned now to a career of writing books and running a small Populist magazine he had purchased a few years earlier. If there seemed little point in raining fresh blows upon the shattered Watson, vengeance against his allies was swift and harsh. Conservative forces were ascendant throughout the state, reformers stripped of their rank, Populists and poor-white sympathizers shorn of the vote, and the negro legally segregated on trains and in other public places and driven from politics on the ground he was always for purchase and served merely to divide the white population. Curious bills of an unmistakably punitive nature, moreover, were handed up to the state legislature. One of them called for a sales tax of a penny per bottle on all soft drinks manufactured within the state—a kind of tariff-in-reverse.

"They're trying to crucify us," said Bax with dismay.

"Not us," said Gus. "You."

Turning the other cheek, even for a man of lofty principle, is not a promising response to the threat of crucifixion. Bax appealed reluctantly to the only ally he knew who might help him repulse the menace.

"This is going to cost plenty," Gus said knowingly. "Don't say you weren't warned."

"I was warned," Bax said. "How much is it going to cost?"

"How much business would the tax cost you?"

"About a quarter—maybe even a third—of our Georgia sales, for a while at least. And if the tax is collectable, every state in the South will slap it on."

"Then that's the price," said Gus. "Can you pay it?"

Bax's throat constricted. "In cash?"

"Unless you think they'd take rock candy," said Gus with a cackle that suggested he was not entirely unhappy at the development.

"You know we don't have that kind of money in our hands. It's in and out—it'd take a couple of years to put that much aside—."

Gus raised a hand to calm him. "Money isn't everything, son—I believe I've heard you offer that sage opinion from time to time. I'll see what I can do with bear grease."

The gratitude on Bax's face would not have lasted long if he had learned of what wiles his uncle was capable. Gus promoted his intrigue with me. Had I perhaps now shifted my views on the wisdom of ousting Watson from the company? "The wisdom, yes," I said. "The fairness, no." Gus then went to work on his sister, who turned for advice to her daughter, who turned for advice to me. I repeated to Mandy what I had told Gus, and they held fast against him. He asked me to raise the matter anew directly with Bax, who he said was far more likely to listen to me under the circumstances. "To talk straight," Gus said out of the side of his mouth, "my contacts in Atlanta say the growing success of the company is well known—and they want Watson's stock certificate in ashes before it's worth a fortune." I suggested they were vindictive, sadistic, and a few other unlovely things. "They're politicians," said Gus. "They honor the victors and feed on the vanquished."

Bax stopped me before I got two sentences into Gus's overture. "Tom Watson is a saint," he said. "You don't shit on saints."

Gus Griffin asked me to do just that. "As the corporation counsel, you have that responsibility," he said. "More than personal loyalty is involved here. The company could be ruined—."

With the utmost regret, I went to Thomson to do Gus Griffin's sordid bidding. Tom Watson may have been staunchly for the masses, but he was decidedly not of them, I saw upon arrival at Hickory Hill, his gewgawed manse set upon a heavily treed knoll. The fluted columns with their plaster capitals gleamed a dead white in the mid-day sun as he extended a polite welcome and led me off under the balustraded veranda. He was more distracted than morose, and the purpose of my visit was of only the most marginal interest to him. I explained over dinner that I had no enthusiasm for my mission, that Bax knew nothing of it and was opposed to its object, but that Gus Griffin was convinced there was no other way to fend off the potentially ruinous sales tax on our drink.

"If I were yet an active politician," Watson said after absorbing the situation, "I would put out a feeler or two to learn who's really behind this scheme. The answer might surprise you. It wouldn't me—."

The moment he said it, I understood—and was certain he was right. Yet I was without the resources to determine it for sure and, even more, without the stomach. "But they're flesh and blood," was what I said.

"Dying kings can be powerfully venomous," Watson said.

I shook my head sadly. "And he can get the bill killed by just saying the word?"

"Does a dog have fleas?" Watson sipped the last of his wine and said I would have his stock certificate in the mail before the week was over. "My loyal Billy deserves to be spared the intrigues of his kinfolk. I will write him to the effect that I prefer to add to my holdings in land if he doesn't mind—."

Under the circumstances, Bax did not mind, for I of course withheld word of my visit and Watson's suspicions. Gus proved less tactful. He took generous credit for the subsequent death in committee of the proposed soda-pop tax and could not restrain himself from reminding Bax at least once a month of his magnanimous boon.

And soon Gus became incorrigible. What had been playful goading of his nephew with an instructive purpose in view now devolved into mean and petty fault-finding at every turn. Nor could his abrasive, taunting conduct merely be brushed aside as the work of an aging and bitter man, resentful over the achievements of his sister's issue. For with the distribution of Tom Watson's stock among the other holders of Jubilee equity, Gus Griffin emerged as spokesman for 56 percent of the total and held effective voting control of the corporation.

The tempo of his intrusions rose steadily. Gus's weekly visits to the factory became semi-weekly inspection tours, with whole afternoons passed in sifting over the books and sales sheets. There were occasional phone calls from his hotel to Bax's office in between visits and then no day passed without a call or a visit. Wouldn't Richmond be a better spot for the new plant than Memphis? Wasn't the North Carolina market much too soft last month? Hadn't Clint Graves shown he wasn't up to selling all of Alabama? Time to get him help or replace him. Had Bax given any more thought to test-marketing Jubilee-flavored gum? Or cigars? And hadn't Happy Hazard about outlived his usefulness, what with Snuffy Bean barely batting .300 this season and running the bases as if he had a case or two of Jubilee chained to his behind . . . ?

It was plain that if the Jubilation Plantation Corporation was to survive into the twentieth century, Bax was going to have to bar his uncle from the premises. Presented with such an ultimatum, Gus was as likely, in Bax's view, to exercise his voting strength and pick a new president as to obey his upstart nephew. A showdown was therefore avoided while the situation deteriorated month by month. I considered volunteering as an intermediary, but Gus's personal regard for me had never risen much above the tolerable level for years now and his manner left no room to doubt that I would be retained as corporation counsel only so long as I did not cross him. And taking Bax's side in the internecine battle for dominance inside the company would be swift purchase of a one-way ticket out the door. Only Bax himself could face down Gus, whose pride of family would tolerate no intruders or onlookers. And the scepter would have to be wrenched from Gus's grasp; he would not yield it for the asking. But once the struggle was begun and Gus measured his nephew's mettle, I was sure that it would not last long.

The more private and like a recreation the engagement, the more likely it was to end in reconciliation, I estimated. The ideal occasion I thought would be a hunt. Gus, bad leg and all, still loved to shoot and went out a few times every season, never failing to bag his limit. Bax always managed his share of outings, although he had far less time in those early Jubilee years. I myself had become neither proficient in marksmanship nor knowledgeable about game with the passing seasons but I did know one end of the rifle from the other and fired off a few rounds with a semblance of conviction every autumn. To complete our party and serve as *de facto* chaperone, I enlisted my admirer—and one of Gus Griffin's devoted retainers—Weyland Yates, who had become Savannah's chief of police partially on the strength of his reputation as a hunter: a man who could sniff a coon a thousand yards off, a deer at a mile, and a brown bear at a league was a fair bet to track down any human varmint on the loose. We would travel in pairs—Weyland and I up front, Bax and his uncle to the rear in light of Gus's necessarily slower gait. There would be time for the two of them to talk through their differences and a setting to encourage the process. To assure maximum opportunity, I devised a week-long expedition. In the third week of October in 1899, then, the four of us took the train to Waycross and a coach down through the piney woods to a landing Chief Yates knew, where we rented punts to penetrate the lush solitude of the Okefenokee Swamp.

It was not my natural habitat. And Weyland Yates was not my usual company. But being there with him made the throbbing mystery of the place bearable and took my mind off the combustible negotiations between our companions to the rear.

Overhead, the trees pushed back the glinting sky with their crowns of gray, ragged moss; below, the low-hanging canopies of loopy vine made the narrow, clotted streams seem dark and lifeless. In places the foliage was so thick it had to be hacked open, and now and then we came upon a tunnel burrowed by the alligators and infested with wasps. But along the lakes and open waters, where the sunlight flooded down unimpeded, the coloration was of a heightened splendor—the small purple blossoms of water-shield, the delicate blue of the hyacinth, the snow white of the water lily and bright yellow bonnets of the golden-heart, all set warmly against the hosting emerald leaf-pads that seemed to pave the waters wherever the eye roamed. Between the streams and islands stretched the treacherous swamp prairies, great green seas of undulating grass that covered a landscape of muck too fluid to support more than an occasional clump of deformed and shriveled trees. Upon the gnarled limbs of one bald cypress I saw a flock of cranes swoop down and crowd the perch into so grotesque a silhouette that it was a wonder it did not snap. Within the forest depths, other winged creatures sang sweetly—the wren and warbler and flycatcher—and the low-humming surface of a pond was broken now and again by the splash of a big trout lunging with deadly accuracy for a little black-banded sunfish or a green killy. It was like some endless amphitheater, tier upon tier of enchanted sights and smells and sounds that quite engulfed me in their collective spell. I had beheld nothing remotely like it since the boat that brought me from New York turned into the mouth of the Savannah River at Tybee more than twenty-two years before.

Raccoon and possum and skunk thrived there in such profusion that they scooted about in the open, but it took the trained ear of Weyland Yates to detect their rustle in time to gauge their swift course. He picked them off like clay pigeons at a target gallery and soon the boat was reeking from them; I tactfully urged him to save some room for other kill. "Hell, man," the chief said, "we jus' push these little shitbags overboard if'n we need the space. Meantime I got to unrusty my eye and oil my trigger finger." And so he kept blasting away whenever we tied up and sometimes from the boat. Once we came upon a big buck deer drinking at the edge of a stream, and he looked us in the eye so directly and so long that the chief seemed hypnotized. When the buck finally sprang for cover, the best Weyland could manage was to nick him in the hindquarters. The chief cursed his luck for the next two hours, especially regretting that we had not brought deerhounds with us. "That is the finest huntin' animal alive," he said wistfully. "He runs and runs until he drops, an' then he runs some mo'—until the cushions on his feet is worn and shredded and bleeding off o' him. That's an animal after mah heart."

It was late in the afternoon of what was to have been our next-to-last day out there that our adventure turned into nightmare. The chief was pulling perch and jackfish out of the water for supper when I heard the report of a shotgun well behind us, followed in a few moments by Bax's sharp hallooing. Even at first, I thought there was a panicky sound to it. We hollered back that we were coming. It took about half an hour of rowing against that thick current. When we got there, Bax was on the shore, slumped against a huge cypress; Gus was crumpled up in the boat, the left side of his chest cavity shot away and the remains of his thorax a mass of raw pulp. The insects had already begun to gather upon his glistening vitals.

"A panther—," Bax managed, struggling for coherence. "We had tied up. I went in after some game. When I came back, he stood up, waved hello, and began to take a leak. Then—." He pointed above his head. "A goddamned spotted panther leaped on him from up there—right for his throat. He let out a scream. I shot—without thinking almost—."

There was no way to bring that corpse out of the Okefenokee for a decent burial without attracting every manner of pest and vermin and beast of prey en route. None of us might have made it. Instead, we weighted down Gus's boots and each said a prayer in our own way and committed his remains to the boggy deep.

Over supper we each picked at the food and were alone with our thoughts. The chief had spoken of panthers on the trip out there, I remembered. They were relatively rare now, he had said, but a few were reported every year, and once in a great while someone bagged one. We had seen no signs of them, indeed scarcely considered the possibility, although we were actively on the lookout for bear. Weyland fed Bax consoling whiskey to stop his shakes and put a big paw around his shoulder in sympathy. I had not witnessed the quality of tenderness before in that man-mountain. "I'm sorry as Christ to have to ask you this, Billy," the chief said over the campfire, "but you didn't kill your uncle Gus, now, did you? You see why I'm askin' you, don't you, Billy—on accounta the circumstances and my bein' on hand an' Gus's prominence in the community an' all. You can see my position, can't you, Billy—?"

Bax closed his eyes and nodded a few times. Then he sat still for so long that the chief started to get anxious. Finally, Bax looked him straight in the eye. "It was like I said, Weyland."

"A panther?"

"It was an accident, Weyland."

"Why, you loved yo' Uncle Gus a whole lot, didn't you, Billy? I mean aside from the usual family tiffs we all got, you held him in very great respect—ain't that right, Billy?"

"That's right, Weyland. Gus Griffin is—was—a very great man. The greatest in our part of the state."

"An' he took care of folks he cared about, Billy, lemme tell you—."

Bax shook his head. "I know, Weyland. He had a heart of gold."

It occurred to me on the slow sad trip home that, if one wished to be bloodthirsty about it, I had accomplished what we had gone for in the first place. We encountered no more panthers the rest of the way.

SEVEN

The twentieth century!

Nothing had changed but a single leaf on the calendar, yet everything had changed. The rite of passage must have worked its spell on every thinking soul on earth. I supposed and wondered how many of them had endured the entire span of the nineteenth century—one of every million breathing bodies, at a guess—and how many alive this first day of the new one would survive to see the arrival of the twenty-first century. It was an idle conjecture, as vapid as the thought that obsessed me all that day of a resurrected Napoleon, armed now with the telephone, the electric light, the (heaven help us) automobile, and, of course, the grisly Gatling gun. He might have taken the whole world with such marvels at his disposal instead of selling off the American inland empire to Thomas Jefferson and winding up manacled on a small island. The sage of Monticello, on the other hand, might have consigned those technological wonders to the scrap heap and pursued less jarring amenities. My God, the pace of it all! Men were now capable of moving over the surface of the planet at better than a mile per minute. How much of a seer did one need be to conjure them traveling aloft at a multiple of that velocity a century hence? And in five centuries would the Moon be more than an easy bound beyond the gravitational pull?

Heady thoughts for a man who devoted much of each waking day to the unexalted affairs of a soda-water manufacturer. It was not much of a monument to leave behind. Prone as I was to trivialize it, however, our Jubilee had become an enterprise hardly less vigorous, with a future no more limitable, than America herself on the brink of global grandeur. The word and the drink itself were on every pair of lips in the Southland, it seemed, and the task of bringing it to cooler climes and the open spaces across the Mississippi was a fit challenge for our lusty infant, which soon began to outstrip even the high expectations we carried for it into the year 1900.

As his uncle's principal heir, W. Doak Baxter became the largest stockholder of the Jubilation Plantation Corporation, and functioning in harmony with his mother, sister, and attorney, he took control of the corporation absolutely. And not unwisely. He brought in technically proficient managers at the production end, acted himself as spearhead to the ever-expanding sales force, and placed Happy Hazard's bumptious ballyhooing under the constraint of one of the new advertising agencies in New York. For a spell, the operation seemed to advance frictionlessly. I found the half a day I would set aside for Jubilee more than enough and could turn now to new clients. My maladroitness with the shotgun notwithstanding, I was invited to membership in the Yamacraw Club, the first person of my faith so honored, and Ruth was asked to serve on the city school committee. My income was approaching fifteen thousand a year, and the death of her mother left my wife an heiress of considerable means. The Lazarus house had become at last the Adler house and its eight occupants (four in the family, four in help, and a cat I do not count due to our massive indifference toward each other) as evidently well regarded a household as any in Savannah. There was a supposition, even, that our daughter Judith would be permitted to come out at a cotillion at the De Soto a few years hence, provided she did not in the interim take to keening the *Kol Nidre* from the roof of the Cotton Exchange.

When the impact of the full-color Jubilee advertisements in *The Ladies' Home Journal* began to register in markets beyond the South, demand for the drink soon outraced the supply, and a crisis was at hand. An embarrassment of riches is an embarrassment nonetheless. It was plain that if we did not move decisively to capitalize on this swift breakthrough, our product would soon be nudged from the consuming public's consciousness by the likes of Moxie, Nehi, or ten other brands of bubbling sugar water. It was the American way: grow or die. But to put up the factories and man them in sufficient numbers to satisfy the sales Jubilee was generating required more working capital than could be extracted from the regular flow of company income. New venture capital was required, and in view of its profitability to date, the drink was likely to attract nearly as many investors as it had consumers. That, however, would spread the ownership of the corporation far and wide and leave the Baxter interests answerable to a constituency they would sooner or later be unable to resist. "You're the brains of the outfit," Bax said to me. "Figure a way for us to raise the money without yielding the reins." The reins, I told him, were not the problem; it was how to feed the horse.

Amanda Baxter's formula for Jubilee syrup, rejiggered only a bit since that Sunday she first brewed it, provided the basis for overcoming the formidable legal problem Bax had ordered me to shoulder. The solution I proposed was a model of simplicity and exploitation. The Jubilation Plantation Corporation, also known as "the party of the first part" in my ironclad devise, would henceforth limit its sale of the bottled drink to its home state of Georgia; its principal business would then become the manufacture of the one and only Jubilee syrup, which it would continue to distribute to soda-fountain outlets everywhere. But the far more costly and unwieldy sale of the bottled drink would be undertaken by "the party of the second part," a franchise holder who would be licensed to sell Jubilee within a rigidly defined territory that was his exclusively. Each franchised bottler was obliged, of course, to provide the capital for his factory, for bottles by the thousands and tens of thousands, for the delivery wagons and crates, and naturally for the personnel required. Jubilee, for its part, was obliged only to sell the syrup to its bottlers at the fixed price per gallon of $1.10 and to provide the national advertising for the drink. The bottlers, naturally, were constrained from substituting any other for the one and only Jubilee syrup and were expected to keep their territories generously supplied with the drink or suffer the loss of the franchise. The territory was granted for a period of five years and renewable for another five at the unilateral discretion of the parent company in Savannah. Any bottler who failed to maintain the quality of the product was liable to the immediate loss of his franchise. The arrangement was a truly bilateral one in the same sense as a mutual-aid pact between the Roman Empire at its height, let us say, and the island of Malta.

"But we've got them by the short hairs," Bax astutely noted upon a quick reading of the model agreement I had drafted. "They put up all the money and work and risk, and we just sell 'em the juice. It seems lopsided." He thought more. "Also inspired."

There was no shortage of takers. The product was a proven one. Within six months, nineteen bottlers were pumping out the Jubilee at minimal cost to—but a splendid rise in profits for—the parent company. Each bottler was given exclusive rights to at least one entire state, and a few, like the Los Angeles operation, were granted hegemony over several. Sales grew so well that by the expiration of the first five-year licensing period, it became desirable from the parent company's standpoint to subdivide the territories into two or three smaller units, thereby multiplying the family of bottlers, diluting the profits of any one of them, but assuring a steadily more intensifying sales effort in every community. Or so we said. Those bottlers who did not like having their wings clipped were shot down altogether and replaced by others eager to grow rich on our potion.

Financiers everywhere hailed the Jubilee franchise arrangement as the quintessence of enlightened management. By combining decentralization of function with centralization of policymaking, the parent company won maximum return on its own invested capital while spreading profits as well among a vast network of subcontractors who pushed the product hard everywhere without need of excessive prodding. No extraordinary personnel were needed at the top. The system came with its incentives built in. Each sales territory was a self-contained unit where the franchiser prospered or languished on his own. And those who languished were swiftly put out of their misery. Our Savannah headquarters thus kept its hold on the reins yet could boast now of rank upon rank of snorting stallions out there in front of us doing the heavy work. The board of directors voted to double my annual retainer. On the proviso that I might maintain my private practice, I accepted with gratitude.

The franchising system was well launched when tragedy touched both the nation and the company. Bax had gone as corporate ambassador to the Pan-American Exposition in Buffalo, where the Jubilee pavilion was dispensing drinks and trinkets by the tens of thousands and the President of the United States was in attendance. Moments after Mr. McKinley had obligingly swallowed a few sips of the soda and pronounced it a splendid American innovation, Bax looked on with horror as a young fanatic pumped bullets into the President's broad chest and massive belly. From the former cavity, physicians working in semi-light were able to extract the metal, but so vast was his girth and so poor the operating conditions that they were forced to leave the second bullet festering in the presidential entrails. Death followed within the week.

Bax returned from Buffalo badly shaken. His grief ran far deeper than that for a fallen popular President. Bax had, after all, scorned McKinley's politics for the most part. My own reading of his profound response to the assassination was that Mr. McKinley, that doughty champion of hard money and unfettered capitalism, and Uncle Gus were indissolubly linked in Bax's mind, and the manner of both their deaths, witnessed at such close range, proved a double blow he was incapable of sustaining. He went quite to pieces at the end of 1901.

"He's raving," Mandy said, rushing into my office one morning. "After supper last night, he blurted to Cissy and me he had murdered Gus in cold blood and made up the panther. And now, he said, the President has suffered a similar fate, and soon he himself will as well." She struggled for composure. "My God, Seth, you were down in that hateful swamp with him—what in Christ's name happened?"

"I was nowhere near when it happened," I said.

"But you saw him—you saw how he behaved—."

"So did the chief of police. Ask him."

"I'm asking *you*, Seth—."

"Why did you wait so long?"

"Because," she said, "I was afraid to."

"Because," I said, "you knew."

She gave a little nod.

"And because you would have done it yourself before long—?"

"Probably," she said. "Gus had turned monstrous. It was he—or us."

"I see."

"You don't see at all."

"Murder is murder."

"Not when it is provoked by a hate-filled ogre."

"There are other ways to combat a problem besides killing it."

"None more effective," she said and then broke down in great heaving spasms of hot tears. I held her as I had not in years. A long moment expired before she extricated herself from our embrace. "He's guzzling liquor by the gallon," she said. "Something has to be done."

Utmost discretion was required under the circumstances. Any public display of Bax's psychic infirmity would have been both bad business and dubious therapy, and the scandal from it quite conceivably could have resulted in a prison term. He and Cissy were bundled off by steamer to the south of France and the Greek isles for six months during which Mandy occupied his office and I took a smaller desk across the hall. Cissy's long-distance dispatches were not overly encouraging, and although the company's headquarters contingent was competent to keep operations spinning for the time being, a clearheaded and commanding chief officer would have to succeed to the helm at the earliest opportunity if the enterprise was to sustain its forward thrust. Mandy and I took lunch one day in the spring of 1902 to determine the sort of chap most desirable. "Someone like you, I should think," she said before I was even finished with my melon.

"I'm a lawyer," I said. "I like being a lawyer."

"What's to prevent a lawyer from running a corporation?"

"Lawyers have better things to do."

"Oh, my," she said. "Suing widows and orphans, I suppose?"

"Also legless survivors of Gettysburg."

"You would become very rich, Seth."

"And then I could buy happiness."

"Are you pretending you don't care about money?"

"I care up to a point."

"Which is?"

"Which is not enough to give myself over entirely to running any soda-pop company on earth."

"Do it for three years, Seth, and you'll have a million. I promise you. You'll be secure for the rest of your life."

"I'm already secure."

"By virtue of Ruth's inheritance."

"By virtue of my practice."

"Clients can be fickle."

"You mean Gentile clients of Jewish lawyers."

"Did I say that? How *gauche*—and beastly—and true."

I stirred my consommé and thought a moment. "Why three years? I think a pledge of five is the minimum the company ought to consider. A strong man will be needed when the bottlers' first licenses expire and the lame must be culled from the flock."

"Five years it is, then."

"And you really think I'm your man?"

"It would be marvelous for all concerned."

"And Bax—have you broached the idea to him?"

"Well—to Cissy, actually. That seemed wisest under the circumstances. She says he is favorably inclined provided he retained the title of chairman and a larger office than yours."

"But there can be only one boss."

"I believe that point has been established." She pushed her soup to the side and folded her hands in front of her. "There is one other thing, though, and you know I'm not one to pussy-foot—."

She was indeed the most businesslike of women when not at play. "I hear the soft tread of Gulliver approaching through the swamp grass," I said.

"I have read with great interest and not a little sympathy Mr. Herzl's *Judenstaat*. Billy Doak writes that Herzl has half persuaded the Sultan to charter a Jewish homeland in the area of Palestine—everyone at the eastern end of the Mediterranean speaks of nothing else these days—."

"And Billy is all in favor—?"

"Billy is all indifferent. It's what you favor that he cares about."

"Ahh. He wants to know if I am a Zionist—."

"Yes."

"—And will lead the Jews of America across the oceans in single file—and the waves shall part before me as in our ancestral past and close again to engulf our tormentors—."

"Don't be an ass, Seth. We've been through all this—."

"But Billy still thinks that beneath it all I'm a different species. You do, too."

"Neither of us thinks anything of the sort." She touched me lightly on the wrist. "Seth, we love you. We have loved you from the day you came here, as I remember. In different ways and varying degrees, perhaps, but with an undeniable constancy that behooves you not to play the persecuted Jew whenever the subject arises. The question is a straightforward one—."

"It's your question—isn't it?—not Billy's. He's never heard of Herzl."

"What's the difference who brought up the subject? The Jews of the tsarist lands are flooding in upon us now and their patriotism is naturally in doubt. If they can relocate here so readily, why not in Palestine as well?"

"You mean the Jew is really a man without a country."

"I mean I fear that."

"And I, being the most convenient Jew to put the question to—."

She lighted a cigarette. It was said that only two other women in all of Savannah smoked in public at that time, and they were courtesans. "You do not make simple discussion easy for one, Seth Adler," she said.

"We are a somber people." I slid my luncheon plate out of the way. "As it happens, I favor Herzl's scheme—."

Mandy's eyes dropped. "No," she said.

"Yes," I said, "for those who wish it. But not for me. For me there is only one nation, and that is not Palestine. America is dedicated to the separation of the church from the state, and I pray it shall always be. You should pray likewise. So long as that separation is honored, I am an American. No other loyalty interferes. My nation is the United States. My race is the Caucasian. My faith is Judaism. My profession is the law. My eyes are brown. My sexual preferences are well known to you—."

"Other Jews feel otherwise," she said coldly.

"Other Christian ladies do not smoke beyond the boudoir door."

"I want no schoolboy debates, Seth. I'm serious. I read that many Jews are embracing this Zionist proposal."

"Because America can close the door to the tsar's victims tomorrow, and then where should they go? It is an old, old story, and very ugly. The Jews here already have been blessed, but they fear their blessings will end if too many bedraggled followers of the faith arrive to share in them. That may not be admirable but it is understandable. Thus, some American Jews endorse Herzl's scheme without themselves wishing to participate. And those that do—in my view they have despaired of succeeding here and hope for greener pastures in the Holy Land." I took her hand. "For me, Mandy Beth, this is the holy land—until they deny to me what they grant to you—at which point it will no longer be worth my loyalty, or yours." I released her fingers. "And now, let us consider a new president for the company. It must be no one whose loyalties you will feel put upon to explain."

II

My third priceless contribution to the seeding stage of the Jubilation Plantation Corporation was the ivory hunt culminating in the discovery and capture of Amory Gladstone Austin, Jr., a veritable dwarf, to assume charge of it. What he lacked in stature —he stood (and still stands) a shade over five feet, as near as I can estimate—he made up for in austere single-mindedness. I found him in Camden, New Jersey, where he had recently sold off his family's ball-bearing business at a reputedly handsome profit to the Hyatt Works in Newark and was looking now for new worlds to conquer. A dark-haired, whippet-like man in his early forties who came from Maryland's Eastern Shore, he took at once to the idea of relocating in the Deep South. All my inquiries into his financial acumen produced exultations of praise. He was said to be able to confront a sheet full of items and numbers for five seconds, recall it in its entirety for months, and detect the sole error thereon at once. A wizard is the least anyone called him.

"To be honest, though," he said to me, "I don't know any more about soda pop than a dog knows about Sunday."

"But chances are," I said, "you'll pick it up faster than the dog." He thought for a moment and said he had to agree with that. I brought him to Savannah for Mandy's inspection.

"Very alert," she said after their audience, "very gracious, very intelligent, and quite vigorous. But something of a small package, don't you think?"

"No one told me to fetch Gargantua. He's not here to chop trees."

"But one wants a commanding presence," she said.

"One can command from behind a desk, you know, not only astride General Lee's Traveller."

"We should have to arrange for a sawed-off desk, I'm afraid," she giggled, "or only the top of his scalp will be seen."

I suggested that a Sears catalogue or two installed discreetly on his chair would do as well. His Lilliputian size, moreover, had the added advantage of not threatening her brother, who wished to retain titular leadership of the company. Mandy confessed she had not considered that.

The transition came off painlessly. Rehabilitated to all appearances, Bax entered upon a career of public philanthropies and private idiosyncrasies, of which a passionate involvement with the automobile was the most consuming. The gnomish Amory Austin he let run the company with hardly more than a courteous inquiry or two of the bantam executive at the quarterly meeting of the board of directors. Thus freed of meddling from above, Austin at once took control of the corporation by the graceful application of his icy intelligence. Personal considerations did not affect his judgment. He made every man who entered his office believe that their interview was the highlight of both their days, and so extracted the best thinking and supreme effort from his underlings. I never knew him to have a creative thought, but he recognized one when he heard it from others. He listened better than anyone I ever met, save perhaps the late Eugene M. Venable, but Austin was not so dour or forbidding. His littleness invited an initial intimacy to every exchange with his subordinates, but those attendants were soon reminded there was nothing diminutive about his mind. He instituted comprehensive weekly sales and production cost reports that reduced trouble spots to a minimum by early detection. He visited every bottler in the field at least once a year. And he announced, for internal consumption only, the towering goal he had set for the company product: its virtual replacement of water as the universal beverage.

My own relations with Amory Austin were never less than cordial. My value to the corporation was attested to in his eyes when, soon after I had urged the company to end every vestige of medical claims for the drink in our ads, the Congress enacted the Pure Food and Drug Law that ensnared many of our competitors, including the Coca-Cola crowd, who pleaded to the federal inspectors that their product featured neither coca leaves nor cola nuts yet was not misnamed. My voice was rarely raised within the Jubilee sanctum, but Amory Austin listened when it was.

In the nature of things, my long-standing ties with Billy Doak Baxter frayed. It was inevitable, I suppose, from the moment and manner of Gus Griffin's death. There was a quality of disapproval that I no doubt failed to filter from my look each time we met. Such reproach, even unspoken and broadcast by the merest non-flicker of an eye, was more than he could bear. The rest of the world, after all, had exonerated him and deeply commiserated over the loss of so vital and beloved an uncle. My dark glances, however darting and quickly quenched, were the solitary form of recrimination visited upon him, and so naturally he chose to avoid them. Yet he could not risk my enmity. Our friendship merely atrophied by mutual assent.

But Bax seemed to flee from more than me. Assured that the corporation was in deft hands and his fortune secure, he appeared at the office no more often than every second week and then did little beyond exchanging pleasantries. His energies were invested instead in a variety of civic, social, and recreational ventures that bordered upon but never quite entered the realm of the crackpot. He lavished high enthusiasm, for example, upon an effort to establish a state zoo on the outskirts of Atlanta and personally contributed funds for the acquisition of a baboon he insisted be named Ruby Juby. He donated other money for the restoration of churches throughout Georgia, dividing his allocation equally between the evangelical and establishment sects and requiring the pastor and elders of each would-be recipient to set aside a portion of the graveyard for paupers and simpletons. He acquired ownership of the Savannah Buccaneers, the local entry in the professional Peach State League and as sorry a conglomeration of athletic misfits as played the sport. "The next Ty Cobb," he would tell the sportswriter covering the day's game at Oglethorpe Park, "will walk in here next week and knock the good red clay of Georgia from his spikes, y' hear?" And then Bax would settle back in his private rocker beside the dugout, alternate puffs on his cigar with swigs from his rum-laced bottle of Jubilee, and cheer on his ineffectual minions in vicarious replay of his own adolescence. Of supposedly higher civic purpose was the support he lent to the new magazine launched by Tom Watson, freshly hatched from nearly a decade of self-exile and sloughing off the pitiable showing he had made as the Populists' *pro forma* presidential candidate in 1904. Even the openly anti-capitalist Eugene Debs had attracted twice as many votes. Watson henceforth restricted his political bailiwick to Georgia, where lost causes and sidetracked spellbinders have a way of winning endearment from multitudes well after they ought to have been decently buried.

It was Bax's uncontainable fascination with the automobile, however, that reduced all his other activities to the merest of armchair pastimes. Goggled and determined behind the wheel of the cantankerous new horseless buggies, he was his old free-spirited self, bent on outracing the shade of Uncle Gus that I was sure pursued him his every waking hour.

This mechanical obsession was not lost upon the ever-resourceful Happy Hazard, promoter *par excellence*, who deeply regretted Bax's premature withdrawal from the daily affairs of the company and his replacement by the masterful but hardly playful Amory G. Austin. Happy conceived a scheme over the summer of 1905 that would lend heroic posture to the chairman of the board and serve the product nobly. He proposed that Bax undertake a marathon drive, in a car with the company trademark emblazoned on both sides, from Savannah to New York, where he would ceremoniously debark in Herald Square and throw the switch on a big electric sign the company had erected there, with the slogan "Have a Jubilee—and make thirst a pleasure" in ten-foot-high neon. Bax, with not a whole lot better to occupy himself, counterproposed a more spectacular escapade, one that would expose the product in a vaster territory. He and Plato would make a triangular journey of three approximately equal legs—from Savannah to Chicago, Chicago to New York, and New York back to Savannah—and try to complete the 2,500-mile trip within a month. The undertaking would be presented to the public as a tribute by the nation's foremost refreshment to the infant autocar industry, a way of saying that America was growing closer together, and better, all the time. Win or lose the race against the clock, Bax's adventure was sure to attract nationwide attention to Jubilee.

Indian summer was the chosen time. A Locomobile, a forty-four-horsepower dreadnought that cost a cool $7,500 and was advertised as "Easily the best built car in America," was selected for the ordeal. Its solidity was apparent when it arrived in crates from Bridgeport, Connecticut. "See," said Bax, tumescent with anticipation as he supervised its assembly at the old Adelphi warehouse, "they use forgings instead of castings for every part. You could drive this baby over gopher holes from now till hell freezes over and you wouldn't get a rattle." Gopher holes proved the least of their problems, but he and Plato were not unprepared. They had fitted the Loco out in the rear with a special box that held almost enough tools and spare parts to build a new car. You would have thought they had bought out every hardware store in Savannah, the way they piled in the wrenches and pliers and chisels and files. There were special gadgets for removing wheels and gears, a vulcanizing kit to apply patches to tire punctures, and a pump to reinflate the tubes. There was wire and twine and a short length of wood for rigging up a block and tackle, and enough towline to get them to the nearest machine shop by hoof-power when all else failed. Happy's only instructions to Bax were that he find a telephone somewhere once a day and call back reports of his progress; short of that, a wire would do. "And if you discover the world really is flat all over," Happy insisted, "don't break the story in Paducah."

"We don't hit Paducah," Bax said, "it's too far west. How about Owensboro?"

"Owensboro's fine," said Happy, "but you better tell 'em we got two 'e's' in Jubilee—they can't spell for shit in Owensboro."

They left the eighteenth of September at sunup and wired back the first night from Twin City, Georgia: "HAVE FOUND ACCOMMODATIONS IN ABANDONED CHICKEN COOP. LOCO OKAY. WORLD STILL ROUND." They made Macon the next day and Atlanta the next, and as Happy started pumping out the stories, local officials began turning out at every way-stop to greet the Jubymobile, as the headline writers tagged it. Happy picked up the cue and started calling it that in his own bulletins, although company policy remained fixed against formal use of the name "Juby" for the product; Amory Austin thought it demeaning—due, it was said, to his own wee-ness.

The more people who turned out along the way, the better the publicity—and the slower the progress. Happy urged that they keep driving an hour or two after nightfall where the roads permitted. But their feeble acetylene headlights failed to detect craters in the roadway at the northwest corner of the state, and so they dragged into Chattanooga with a broken axle, two popped gaskets, and three or four other severe handicaps. Happy called them "a minor setback" but fidgeted mightily until getting word a whole day later that the journey had been resumed. In Tennessee they busted springs and experienced repeated ignition trouble. In Kentucky they suffered through three tire punctures, a gummed-up feed line, and a night in jail for violating one mountain burg's eight-mile-an-hour speed limit and then refusing to pay the fine. In Indiana the rains came, and would not stop, and the plucky Locomobile was bogged in ooze up to its running boards. Worse yet, the Jubilee sign got so badly splattered they had to borrow a hose from the local fire department each night for cleaning off the muck. As they strained to get out of one mudhole, sections of teeth sheered off from the driving gear, and the best blacksmith in Kokomo labored late into the night to improvise substitutes. Crossing a shallow stretch of the Wabash, the ferryboat carrying them sank and the car with it. By the time the parts were recovered and disassembled and dried off and refitted, the journey was hopelessly behind schedule: Chicago was reached on the sixteenth day.

The local Jubilee bottler provided a small brass band that preceded the Jubymobile down La Salle Street, but the local press was apathetic. The trip east went much faster, over better roads, including the towpath along the Erie Canal. Overtaken mules sluggishly yielded the right-of-way while ship captains bellowed their objections from the middle of the waterway. Bax drove on unhearing. They made New York on the twenty-seventh day and won a hero's welcome. The sign-lighting ceremony made Bax an overnight celebrity in the big town, where he gave endless interviews, was introduced to the financial community, and drank himself blind for three days. The homeward leg, by which time the allotted month had already expired, was a leisurely, raucous trip— "It's downhill all the way," Bax assured Happy on one of the few occasions when he bothered to call in. A tire puncture a day was expected now. They mowed down fifty chickens in Virginia, had the car impounded for scaring a brood mare in North Carolina, drove off the road three times in South Carolina (nearly overturning outside of Orangeburg), and sputtered back into Savannah on the forty-fourth day. The whole factory stopped operating to welcome Bax, who had grown a beard on the southward run, and Plato, from whom the axle grease and other insignia of his travail would take a month of scrubbing to remove. "The world is not flat," Bax confided to Happy, "but larger than I had expected." Then he fell asleep for the better part of a week.

Bax turned from endurance to speed after that and played a central part in the creation of the race course at Thunderbolt, where he himself was a regular participant. The best families of Savannah flocked to the grandstand at the corner of Victory and Waters, bringing along large lunches in wicker hampers for the day-long events. The Savannah Grand Prix and Vanderbilt Cup races drew the likes of Barney Oldfield, Ralph De Palma, and Louis Chevrolet among the entrants, and the more familiar American makes were joined by Fiat, Mercedes, Lancia, and Benz in international spectacles of raw courage and massive bloodthirstiness. His racing days had the salutary effect, at least, of keeping Bax away from shotguns.

He achieved his zenith as a competitive speedster in the 1907 Dixie Double-Century, a two-hundred-mile race limited, more out of prudence than xenophobia, to American drivers and American makes. Often having placed but never having won a major race, Bax entered in a stripped-down Valveless Two-Cycle Elmore, considered the technological sensation of the season. Plato tuned it to within a hairbreadth of operating perfection, as smooth and swift a vehicle as had ever graced the local speedway. On the last lap, only Teddy "Mad Dog" Rivers of Charleston, in a flying Cadillac, was between Bax and a first-place finish. On the back straightaway he called on the Elmore for every grain of energy and thrust of torque it possessed; the vehicle bore down on Mad Dog, who held the inside position and would not yield an inch. When Bax tried to edge past to the left, Mad Dog pulled over and blocked him. The same thing happened when Bax tried to pass on the right. Behind the angry surge of his motor, he looked for a moment as if he were about to drive directly over the Cadillac. In desperation and amid a momentary swirl of dust, Bax bore down right behind Mad Dog, held the wheel with one hand, rose up, and hurled a giant wrench that hit the Cadillac's gas tank with a mighty *thwong*. Mad Dog, fearful the next piece of metal would tear his head off, yielded the inside to Bax, who breezed home the winner.

That hip-high loving cup and the growing local adulation he received did not slake what those few who knew him well took to be Bax's suicidal tendencies. That proneness to risk his neck subsided a few months later after he and Plato went to the Florida beaches to see how high they could push the speed of a Stanley Steamer over a short run on packed sand. They had got it up over one-thirty when their three-year string of luck ran out. The Steamer suffered brake lock at the end and went careening out of control into a dune, where it flipped over and dashed its occupants violently to the earth. They were brought back by train from Jacksonville on litters. Bax recovered more or less in one piece. Plato, suffering damage to his spine, was bed-ridden for six months and emerged a bent figure of shattered vigor who has spent his days ever since under assault of pain. His career behind a wheel was at an end.

I visited Bax once during his convalescence and came away more hurt than he. His burns thickly bandaged, he looked rather like a mummy, but his face was unscathed and his arms functional, so he was passing the endless days by reading up on Tom Watson's *Jeffersonian Magazine*, in which he was a minor investor. Impressionable as ever when it came to Watson's gritty polemics, Bax failed to detect the frustration and self-interest that had begun to shrivel our feisty rebel's feel for humanity. Both of them had become rich, very rich, even while embracing the cause of the downtrodden: Bax was chief stockholder of the South's second largest indigenous manufacturing company (after Buck Duke's American Tobacco giant); Watson had accumulated some ten thousand acres of cotton land, a mountaintop retreat in Virginia, and an island off Florida in addition to the baronial elegance of Hickory Hill, with its woods and trails that he wended on horseback in lonely, brooding contemplation. Their joint accession to great wealth had plainly blinded them to their abandonment of social justice as a consuming life force. Watson's case was the more pathetic because he had begun to turn toxic as well as bitter. With the demise of Populism, he stood four-square now for the rehabilitation of the Lost Cause of the Confederacy, with an ardor that would have made Jeff Davis flinch.

"His language is as powerful as ever," Bax said to me, leafing through a stack of *Jeffersonians* and reading me selected snatches. National literature, for the most part, was an infamous conspiracy "to put our section upon the stool of repentance" and to keep the South on "the mourner's bench" in a posture of abject apology for its former career as rebel and traitor. "He says we are as much a colony of the North as India is of Britain," Bax noted approvingly.

"Horsefeathers," I said. "He's living in the past."

"No," said Bax. "You're still thinking like a Yankee."

"Bax—he's turning more sour than Ben Tillman or Vardaman."

"I don't see that. Tom's thick as thieves with Hoke Smith, and Georgia's never had a more progressive governor—."

Bax saw only what he wanted to. Smith, it is true, had started out as an anti-corporation lawyer with whom Watson had joined in an impassioned plea for child-labor laws in the opening years of the century. And once in the governor's chair, with the backing of Watson and the remnants of his ragtag rural loyalists, he pushed for more democratic government and began imposing controls on the extortionate rates and criminal negligence of the railroads. This modest reform movement, however, was built on the insistent and total degradation of Tom Watson's former comrade-in-arms—the negro. Watson turned racist with a viciousness that seemed to label all his former compassion a hoax. This monstrous transformation grew, undoubtedly, from a misplaced blame of the benighted darkeys whom the Democratic Party machinery had manipulated so facilely—and terrorized so openly—to defeat Tom Watson again and again. Their total disenfranchisement was the sole solution, Watson now averred, and he echoed the Atlanta newspapers in picturing the typical colored man as a lawless brute growing more impudent by the day. The severing of his testicles and other atrocities not excluding lynching were daily events in the peak season of hatred during the 1906 gubernatorial campaign, and Tom Watson, a man of the law, wrote that there were circumstances that justified hanging by mob rule as therapeutic and manly. He drew no distinction between good niggers and bad; he concluded an editorial attacking Booker T. Washington this way:

> What does Civilization owe to the negro?
> Nothing!
> *Nothing!!*
> NOTHING!!!

And what was right by Tom Watson was right by W. Doak Baxter. With disbelief, I heard him abuse the dedicated Plato and blame him for carelessness that he said caused the accident in Florida. "They simply cannot be relied on like white men," said Bax. "They are children all their lives, as untroubled and irresponsible—"

"Except for their insatiable lust," I taunted.

It was lost on him. "Except for that," he agreed. "The other colored races are no better—only more devious. I've been reading an alarming book on the subject—." He turned the spine toward me of *The Passing of the Great Race* by Madison Grant. "Very stimulating. Grant, you know, is a prominent socialite. We met in New York. He has some money, I believe, in our bottler's business up there. A great friend of T.R., too, they say—."

And any friend of Teddy Roosevelt was a friend of Billy Baxter nowadays, so markedly had his social values and political preferences gyrated. A decade earlier, Bax had viewed Roosevelt as more callous than McKinley—it was New York police chief Teddy, after all, who had said the best way to cope with the Tom Watsons and other mangy agitators was to line some of them up against a wall and shoot them—and his rough-riding jingoism as twice as pernicious. In the White House, T.R. had not proven notably more humane or less mischievous, but Bax had seized upon the President's loudly trumpeted anti-trust activities, limited as they were, and conservationist efforts to pronounce him the greatest social reformer in the nation's history. "He understands the uses of courage," said Bax. "He's not the usual pussyfooting politico. And for a Yank, he well understands the ennobling quality of white blood. No doubt he's read his friend Grant's book with warm approval. Here, I was just reading along about the evils of interbreeding." And he began to recite a brief passage:

". . . Whether we like to admit it or not, the result of the mixture of two races, in the long run, gives us a race reverting to the more ancient, generalized, and lower type. The cross between a white man and an Indian is an Indian; the cross between a white man and a negro is a negro; and the cross between any three of the European races and—"

His face suddenly dropped and he halted in mid-sentence. "Well," he said, hoping, I suppose, that I had not noticed, "you get the idea."

"You must go on," I said. "It's entirely fascinating."

"I'm tired, Seth. This thing drains me—."

I drew the book out of his hand and found the conclusion of the passage he had been reading: ". . . and the cross between any three of the European races and a Jew is a Jew." I mulled that for a moment without looking at him. Then I asked, "How is it, if the highest order of mankind is so hardy and vigorous, its bloodstream is so easily polluted? I should think only a fragile and cloistered race would be so readily diminished by humble Jewish sperm—."

He said nothing while I searched through the book for further revelatory passages. They burst from every page like demonic pustules. I waited till I found one of the riper sort and then read aloud:

> ". . . The man of the old stock is being crowded out of many country districts by these foreigners, just as he is today being literally driven off the streets of New York City by the swarms of Polish Jews. These immigrants adopt the language of the native American; they wear his clothes; they steal his name, and they are beginning to take his women, but they seldom adopt his religion or understand his ideals. . . . We shall have a similar experience with the Polish Jew, whose dwarf stature, peculiar mentality, and ruthless concentration on self-interest are being engrafted upon the stock of the nation."

I closed the book with a snap. "Highly illuminating," I said. "The President, no doubt, will soon consider mass murder to stem the ruthless tide. He is very fond of firearms, one gathers—."

"He said Polish Jews!" Bax said sharply. "You have no reason to take such offense. They are a breed apart from you—."

"Not according to your Mr. Grant."

"You're of German stock—and well named. Adler the Eagle—who lets no prey, bed-ridden or otherwise, escape his talons—."

"Forgive me," I said. "I meant only to stimulate your circulation."

"See," he said, trying to smile now, "your cruelty confirms the German element in you—."

I smiled back. "I thought you were suggesting the German element was the better part of my nature." He shrugged and then winced from the movement. I felt my talons retract. But I could not leave him quite yet; I believed, as I had so many times in the past, that there was a basic sweetness of soul worth reclaiming periodically in this fiberless son of the South. "The physical and national distinctions between the Polish Jews and the Russian Jews are inconsequential," I said, "just as they are between the two of them and the German Jews and the English Jews and the Moroccan Jews. It is the degree of persecution imposed or freedom of opportunity permitted that chiefly distinguishes them—not anything in the blood. If the Jews of Poland are small in size, it is because they have been shut up in their quarter and stifled. That they survive at all is what is remarkable. It's the same with our blacks—only it is their intellect that has been stifled, not their bodies. Your Mr. Madison Grant, friend of Mr. Teddy Roosevelt, is every bit as much a gunslinger as the President but with none of his redeeming qualities, from what I read on these shameful pages." I dropped the book at the foot of his bed. "The country is big enough to absorb all these tormented Jews from the east of Europe, Bax. They bring pride and industry as well as gratitude to America. All they ask is what I did when I came to Savannah—to be treated as anyone else."

I had been having that approximate conversation with Billy and Mandy on and off for thirty years now, I thought as I drove my sturdy Buick out of the Baxter plantation, and still they saw Jews as, at best, deviant members of the white race. That I was evidently excepted from that assigned subordination did not lighten my failure, which I grimly took to be irreversible.

III

Shortly after that troubling interview with Bax, the young man whose current plight has prompted this memoir first arrived in Savannah. Given such a time sequence, I am tempted to assign his coming hither to supernatural forces—whether as a reward or penalty, and to whom and for whom and why, I should not care to say, pending the outcome of his trial. If I could tell ahead of time, what need would I have of prayer, except to counter the overactive piety of my scheming opponents?

His name, when my brother Benny first wrote to me about him, was Noah Berkowitz, and he came from that stock of Polish-Russian Jewry whom the defenders of Nordic purity found so deformed and loathsome. Noah, no doubt a mutant, stood tall enough and straight when he appeared in our midst and was judged nice-looking if a trifle severe in mien.

He was first cousin to Benny's wife Sonia, and I had received periodic bulletins of his family's notable progress since emigrating from the vicinity of Lodz and resettling in the vicinity of Orchard Street. Sonia had taken Benny to visit Noah's family out of fear the small damp rooms of their crowded flat, with its constant smell of potato soup and salami, used clothing, and excrement, were an invitation to pestilence. Benny recommended more ventilation, especially in the summer, when the steam press went all day long and into the night while the flat turned into a garment shop as the family drudged to turn out ten dozen greatcoats for fifteen dollars a week. Noah and his two older brothers were allowed to sleep on the rooftop in summer, which was naturally the busiest time for manufacturing greatcoats; at season's end, if the work had gone well, the company for whom the family subcontracted awarded it a pair of coats as a gift just before announcing that there would be no more work for four months. And so Noah's father and uncle and older brother and older sister would take turns strapping the family sewing machine on their backs and going from factory to factory looking for a job or piecework to take home. Sonia's family, which had arrived in America ten years earlier than Noah's, helped out with gifts of food and cloth from time to time, but the Orchard Street Berkowitzes were mortified instead of grateful. But they took nevertheless, promising the day would come when they would repay such charity to the penny.

It arrived far sooner than anyone would have supposed. Noah's father had found work in a shirt shop just when white collars had come into fashion and much time had to be devoted to sewing on neckbands, each individually cut, to which the collars were buttoned. At the end of work one day, as the factory fell behind its quota, the boss gave Mr. Berkowitz a chance to make neckbands at home as night work. On the third night, it dawned on the family that a living was perhaps to be made in turning out nothing but neckbands for every shirtmaker in the city. So serious a snag had the bands proven in the production cycle that the orders poured in from the moment Mr. Berkowitz announced the service. For a year they had the field to themselves, and by the time competition arrived in earnest, the Berkowitz neckband factory was thriving.

The wealth materialized early enough to spare Noah, the second-youngest of the five Berkowitz children, a life in the sweatshops. Something of a prodigy, he entered his teens with a preference for Euclid and Spinoza to Shakespeare and Maimonides, and everyone said he was destined for a career as a fine accountant or perhaps even a professor of mathematics (there being enough brothers to run the family factory). But Noah settled instead on engineering, in spite of Benny's avuncular warning that that profession was no more hospitable to Jews than medicine. Shortly after Noah had made that decision on his career, he happened to be standing outside his father's factory one afternoon when a group of Gentile workers from a nearby mill began hurling nuts and bolts and still larger pieces of metal at members of a Jewish funeral procession that was crossing the Williamsburg Bridge. That sight—of Jews screaming in pain and cringing for cover—coupled with the warning Benny had given him convinced Noah Berkowitz that his life might be easier if he changed his last name to the less ethnically provocative Berg before beginning his studies at Cornell University. Rather than opposing him, the whole family followed suit.

He did superior work at the university and found a position as draftsman with a firm in Lynn, Massachusetts, for a time until loneliness and niggardly wages sent him back to New York, where he caught on with a meter company in Brooklyn. But advancement was not offered, and Noah Berg believed the Irish proprietors did not favor men of his faith, however well trained or deserving. It was then that Benny wrote me to say that Noah thought the South, with its relatively few Jews, might offer him a more promising future and to ask if I knew of any prospects. "He is a polite, well-groomed, highly intelligent young fellow of twenty-five," Benny advised, "whose sole drawback, so far as I can tell, is a quality of intensity unrelieved by delight in life's antic moments. The South, as deficient in industriousness as it is gifted at pleasure-taking, would no doubt provide the perfect antidote for his overly starched soul. I hope you will forgive my asking you to use your good offices to seek a place for this deserving youth."

The original Jubilee plant on Longstreth Way, as it happened,

215

was just then very much on the lookout for technically trained men of Noah's sort. A reformist commission appointed by President Roosevelt had included ours among a list of soda companies in which it claimed that the syrup was brewed "in pots standing in the cellar of some low building, or even a stable, where the ceiling is covered with dust, cobwebs, and dirt of all descriptions, and the floor littered with filth." Jubilee syrup had in fact been brewed on the first floor of the factory—the cellar had never been used for anything but storage and, one had heard with blithe disbelief, an occasional immoral act—but the sanitary conditions had retrogressed to the point where protest over our inclusion among the malefactors would have been disingenuous. Amory Austin ruled instead that the entire syrup-making operation be transferred to new, larger, gleaming facilities in Atlanta, where rail connections were far superior to those in Savannah and would thereby save the company an estimated two cents on every gallon sold. The more he thought about it, the more Austin preferred the convenience of bustling Atlanta as the site for company headquarters to our petite city hard by the sea. The directors approved the transfer with understandable reluctance, but the business sense behind the move was incontestable. The old Savannah factory would be refurbished for use solely as a bottling plant for the southern Georgia market and the work force and supervisory staff revamped accordingly. Loath as I was to seek jobs for relatives of relatives, I thought that Noah Berg could be of use to the company, and after a day of interviews, he was engaged to serve as assistant superintendent of the run-down Savannah plant.

"It's not much to look at," he said, coming by my office to tender thanks for my intervention in his behalf, "but the renovation is to begin soon and—well, it's a beginning. Besides, the rest of the city is very beautiful—if one discounts the heat."

"Even with it," I said. "You get not to notice it after twenty or thirty years."

He smiled at that and then his alert eyes narrowed behind their wire-frame glasses. "I would like your advice if you have a moment," he said and then disclosed a fear that had evidently been lurking within him. "I think I would probably be better received in this community if I adopted an alternate spelling of my last name. I think Burke—as in Edmund Burke—would be more pleasing than Berg, yet phonetically only a slight departure. Do you see any disadvantage?"

I told him I saw none either way, but if he were more comfortable with the anglicized variant, he should use it. "I would not dwell on the matter," I said. "I'm sure you don't intend to mask your faith—."

"Surely not."

"Such matters are common knowledge, at any rate. This is not a large community."

"Religion has not hampered your career, from what I have gathered," he said. It was plain he was asking a question, not offering a surmise.

"Nor helped it," I said. "One just goes about one's business and tries to deal honorably with all comers. We are free men, like any others pursuing free enterprise."

"I understand," he said.

I heard no more from him about altering his name, although there was ample opportunity, for he stayed at our home for several weeks before finding quarters of his own. He was a fellow of disciplined emotion, and minimal jest, given to soft but precise speech, and courteous in the extreme; there was about him a faint but palpable and not displeasing aroma of lye, as if he had scrubbed every pore on his body an hour earlier and polished away all the rough places with a pumice stone. His eyes bespoke a kinetic intelligence that seemed to crouch in wait for the right moment to be activated. Ruth and I introduced him to our circle of friends, upon whom he made a mildly pleasing impression. It was in Jeremiah Weisz, our vigorous new rabbi only five or six years his senior, that Noah found a particularly kindred spirit. Yet I cannot say their friendship has been especially beneficial to Noah, or that the rabbi's ways, popular as they seem to be, have worked to the long-term advantage of our regional Jewry. More than likely, I am reflecting my age, for the reform measures that I encountered upon first attending Mickve Israel long ago—the churchly structure, the stained-glass windows, the organ music, the orderly service, the English prayers—were hardly less radical than our new rabbi's departures. But his have struck me as purposeless beyond the obliteration, almost for its own sake, of all ceremonial distinctions between the Jewish and Christian form of worship, save for the deification of Jesus. Rabbi Weisz has proscribed the lighting of Sabbath candles, the opening of the ark during the adoration, the teaching of Hebrew in the temple school, and the singing of *Hatikva*, the Jewish anthem of hope. Zionism he has denounced from the pulpit as an encrustation of anti-Americanism and thoroughly unwelcome among his congregants. My attendance record, previously spotty at best, became yet less regular in the wake of such mindless anti-traditionalism. "Maybe Weisz studied Talmud with the Klan," I said to Ruth.

"He's a modernist," she said. "They favor the Americanization of worship."

"I know what they favor—and I say they're prompted by ignoble motives they either don't recognize or won't admit to."

Noah Berg did not agree. He found this new bland form of Jewishness comforting in its low visibility and total absence of gutturals. "I am less conscious of being a stranger than I would have dreamed possible," he said. I remember our having a discussion that first autumn he was in Savannah on the contention Rabbi Weisz had voiced to him in private that the great solicitude Jews exhibited toward the blind and the aged and the infirm —those enfeebled sorts whom the Greeks and Romans put outside their city gates as not worthy of succor—did not necessarily bespeak a soaring humanitarianism in the Judaic ethic. "He says it may be seen as just the opposite," Noah reported to me with what seemed a frankly perverse excitement. "He says the Jews have been so fearful in their souls for so long that they identify more with the physically crippled and spiritually tremulous than the able-bodied and potent. He says we must rejoice in our strength and ardor and relish them no less than charity and altruism."

"A stimulating proposition," I said, "worthy of the hairiest caveman. You might ask the rabbi how he reconciles his notion with Herbert Spencer's stylish theory of the survival of the fittest. I would suggest that the durability of the meek Jew is not unrelated to his understanding of the limitations of his physical strength and the regenerative value of his spiritual sources. Few of us are as nimble as David with the sling."

Whether it was offensive or defensive Judaism he practiced, I would not care to say, but Noah Berg did not run from his faith, at least not from the neuterized version of it our rabbi sought to enshrine. The spring of her final year at Radcliffe, I recall, Noah accompanied my daughter Judith to the Purim dance sponsored by the local B'nai B'rith, of which Noah was a charter member. They made an attractive couple, Ruth remarked to me upon their leaving our house. "He was ever so much more interested in the tenderness of the *hamantashen* than anything I had to say," Judith reported the following morning.

"He's probably just a little shy and nervous with girls," said Ruth.

"I hope he overcomes it before he's fifty," said Judith, a touch cruelly, I thought at the time.

"Perhaps you've seen too many ladies' men in Boston, my dear," Ruth persisted.

"Enough to know them from the other sort," said my brazen daughter.

"Surely you're not suggesting that Mr. Berg is an effeminate man?" Ruth asked.

"Surely not," said Judith. "It is a temporary glandular deficiency, no doubt."

At work, by contrast, Noah Berg proved a thoroughgoing tiger. He read up first on the entire history of glassmaking from its origins in the eighteenth dynasty of Egypt. He studied the whole development of carbonated beverages with special attention to the landmark contributions of Priestley, Schweppes, and Lavoisier. Then he turned that same application of diligence upon the human factor in the production process. He quickly got to know the names and faces of the workers. Overnight he picked up the jargon of the factory floor—a "bum" was a reusable but seedy-looking bottle, a "scuffie" was a yet more disheveled bum, and a "crock" was a bum with a chipped bottom. Most helpful of all, he learned to tell the conscientious workers from the malingerers and to lament that the differential in wages between the two types was not greater (and in many cases did not apply at all). Yet he understood the potential viciousness of the piecework system and the vulnerability of unorganized workers to the vagaries of the economic cycle and the not so tender mercies of employers.

"Still and all," I heard him remark after his first few weeks on the job, "a union would cut our production in half if it stripped us of the power to fire incompetent workers at will. Why, they don't need a union so much as a pat on the back every once in a while instead of a kick in the behind." After a bit more time on the job, however, he sang a different song. Even the more kindly treated and amply rewarded of his charges were likely to pick up and move on to other jobs without an apparent second thought. "Loyalty is beyond their conception," he complained to me during one of our occasional exchanges at the plant. "Money is all they're in it for." I suggested that it was naïve for him to view labor, in the final analysis, as more than a commodity like any other and that to do so was to lose sight of the motivating impulse of capitalism and, in the process, reduce his own chief value to management. He accosted me at once for lack of humanity.

"I didn't say to become a sadist," I answered. "But do not expect gratitude from people for permitting them to perform drudgery a dozen hours a day at peon's pay."

Having demonstrated his worth as a diligent overseer within a very few months of his coming to the Jubilee factory, Noah was soon straining to perform a more dynamic and useful part. He tried to hide his ambition from me the first few times I asked how his job was progressing. "Very educational" is how he put it with the merest hint of tedium in his voice. A little later he let on that he had some ideas he was turning over that he wanted to try out on me if I would oblige him. The opportunity arose when we had him to our home for *Seder* at Passover of 1909. Well after the *afikomen* had been recovered intact by the smallest of Ruth's nieces in attendance, Noah bearded me in my study, where we took a cigar together.

"It has occurred to me that the company would benefit if every bottle of Jubilee it sold across the country were identical with every other one," he said, choosing his words with care. "Why, after all, should a bottle sold in Georgia *look* any different from one sold in Texas—any more than it should *taste* different? Only the bottlers' convenience is served by this multiplicity of styles and colors, which of course makes imitation quite easy. Suppose, moreover, that in place of the uninteresting shape of most Jubilee bottles the company substituted a unique shape, at once distinctive and appealing to both the eye and the hand. And suppose the company mandated this shape in every sales territory. And suppose this shape—and color, the color must be universal as well—were so sufficiently distinctive that it was identifiable even without a label on it as a bottle of Jubilee. Suppose you could pick up that bottle in the dark and be sure from its very feel what it was.

Suppose you could see even shards of it and know what they came from. Imagine the advantages! A container befitting the product itself, and so singular that it produced instantaneous identification. Each bottle would be both commodity and advertisement. Imitators would abandon their efforts unless they were willing to invest heavily in new equipment. And greater cost controls could be achieved by the franchise bottlers through standardization."

It did not rank quite with the Newtonian apple or the invention of the incandescent lamp, but I thought the idea meritorious and told Noah so. He beamed and asked how he might best propose it to the company. "Casually," I told him, "and up the chain of command—unless you want to risk a substantial dose of resentment."

A few months later, he joined me and my son Elihu at the ball park to watch Bax's local outfit oppose the Macon Travellers, the only team in the league that performed regularly with more ineptness than our brave but arthritic Buccaneers. The fine points of the contest, including a squeeze play that ended with the catcher's thigh turned to hamburger, were lost upon Noah, who was far more concerned with how well the Jubilee was selling in the stands and the flight pattern the bottles described when lofted toward the playing field by irate fans. "See how the label gets soft and soggy and can be rubbed off easily in hot weather?" he demonstrated to me as the Bucs loaded the bases and threatened to reduce their ten-run deficit in the fifth inning. I told him to take off his jacket before he dissolved in heat. "You could save a lot of time and money," he continued after unburdening himself, "by blowing the Jubilee name and trademark right into the glass itself." Above the din that greeted the bases-full home run, I told him that I had always found the pliable quality of the paper label an attractive feature and that my children preferred mushing the label off the bottle to drinking the soda inside it. No longer on humor than he was on baseball, Noah merely nodded and revealed that he had incorporated his no-label idea in a memorial he had written on the efficacy of a standardized and distinctive Jubilee bottle. "I typed it up a month ago and gave it to Halliday, as you suggested—."

"Do I know Halliday? I don't recall mentioning—."

"He's the superintendent—my immediate superior. You urged me to abide by the chain of command. Halliday's an able enough sort but not very strong on imagination. He's never responded to my memorial—."

"You've no doubt intimidated him unintentionally," I said. "I believe I urged a more casual approach."

"I had hoped he would pass my views on up the line—and rather than trust to his paraphrasing them, I thought it best—."

"You'd be wiser now to have a word with Halliday directly, perhaps inviting him to join you in the proposal if he concurs, or merely to pass it along as the random thoughts of an underling. I would not build it into the Magna Carta."

Noah telephoned a week later to say Halliday had thrown his memorial into the garbage directly upon reading it and declared that assistant superintendents had no business telling the company how to run its affairs when they had not been on the premises for even a year as yet. "He's jealous of my initiative," Noah concluded.

"To be sure," I said. "He also has a point. Your ideas will no doubt receive a more considered hearing six months from now."

He was peeved at my caution. Somebody else was sure to make a similar proposal in the interim, he said. I told him I doubted it but even if that proved to be the case, he would be prudent to wait; he would have other ideas to offer the company.

Six months later—to the day, I suspect—he re-presented his ideas to Halliday and invited the superintendent's views. These were limited to the swift conclusion that Noah was "a pushy kike" and followed by his shredding anew of the three-page memorial. Apprised of this outcome, I agreed that animosity had now entered the picture and Noah should not hesitate to offer his thoughts to the general manager of the factory, J. A. Dettwiler, one of its pioneer employées and the man who had hired him.

Dettwiler, at least, did not destroy the memo, of which Noah by now had made several copies. He sat on it for a month before summoning his assistant superintendent, announcing that factory people were properly concerned with production and not policy, and returning Noah's sheet of suggestions to him without further comment. Noah steamed for a month, during which Halliday did not exchange so much as a word with him and Dettwiler was not notably more communicative. Then he shipped off his memorial and a covering letter to Amory G. Austin in the president's office at Atlanta.

A cool, correct letter in reply came within a week. Noah was thanked for his "stimulating thoughts" and urged to take them up directly with his superiors at Savannah. "If, however, you develop any specific conception of what our standardized bottle ought to look like, I hope you will be kind enough to share it with me," Austin wrote.

He needed no more encouragement. Noah Berg was nothing if not persistent. He carefully laid out his draftsman's tools and spent every night for the next two months designing the perfect Jubilee bottle. He drew short ones and tall ones, fat ones and lean ones, round ones and square ones and triangular ones, concave and convex ones and some that were both. He narrowed the lot of them down to a batch of twelve and invited my preference. I chose one in the shape of a modified hourglass that I thought elegant and alluring. He made a clay model of it, adding a series of deeply etched ridges to the narrow midriff—"It builds in a whole set of unslippable handholds no matter which side you grasp it from," he explained. The Jubilee name was worked right into the surface of the bottom half of the bottle, which he had painted in an aqua tint. I found the thing so fetching that I urged him to seek an appointment with my fellow company director and the inventor of the beverage, taking pains first to mention to her my name as his sponsor and his relationship to Benny. Mandy adored Noah's bottle at first glance and telephoned Amory Austin on the instant; the model was en route to Atlanta in an excelsior-cushioned barrel before the day was out.

All was silence for a month. Then Noah himself was summoned upstate to the presidential suite and confronted by a dozen executives headed by the company's diminutive chief. The idea of a standard Jubilee bottle had been discussed among them for several years, Austin said, and so Noah's basic premise coincided with their own thinking. His particular design, while most attractive, presented them with several problems, however. To accommodate the Jubilee name and the distinctive handhold ridges Noah had proposed, for example, would require a good deal thicker, and therefore more expensive, bottle than was in current use. That would mean either reduced profits or passing on the higher production cost to the public, an impossibility in view of the intensive competition in the soda-pop market. Did Mr. Berg have any ideas to meet this particular problem?

"I thought fast," Noah said in recounting the memorable interview to me the next day, "and suggested that the extra cost might be made up by reducing the amount of soda in every bottle from ten ounces to eight or nine—that's surely enough to quench the thirst of ninety-nine percent of our customers. And if it wasn't, they could always buy another bottle. My God, you should have seen the look on their faces! You'd have thought I called Jesus a *goniff* or something. I was shown the door not long afterward. I suspect that will be the end of it."

Certain unaesthetic modifications were required in the design to make it compatible with the bottle-making equipment in general use by the company's franchisers, but even if a bit stumpier and less lovely than his original model, it was still essentially Noah's bottle that was approved for nationwide use. It was to weigh fourteen ounces and hold eight and a half of soda. The Savannah plant was to develop the prototype before it went into general production, and Noah was to oversee the process. For his design, he was awarded a bonus of one thousand dollars. For having hired Noah, Savannah General Manager J. A. Dettwiler received a bonus of five hundred dollars and a letter of commendation. Dettwiler thereupon fired Superintendent Halliday, whose absentee record had reached the infamous stage, and replaced him with Noah Berg, whom he told, "You have a fine future with us, but you must learn a little patience."

IV

I do not see—and have never seen, mind you—young Noah Berg as my own second coming to the Southland. Our common faith and origins elsewhere might suggest as much, but that is very similar to an Occidental who concludes all Chinamen look alike, especially those from Shanghai.

Noah had advantages of wealth and education that I did not suffer. These perhaps have contributed to my impression of his essential discomfort in these surroundings, of his transient dwelling among us and latent wish to be on his way at the first fertile moment. He has come to harvest what he can here, and that is surely no sin. It is different, however, from my own course. Having less to begin with, I came here perhaps seeking less than he and found, to my pleasure, far more than I ever could have hoped—

warm sun, bright sky, sparkling river and sea, lush leaf and blossom and greensward, sweet smells and soft voices, and enough kindness to match the adversity. It is too much to say I arrived eager to put down roots and am content now to live out my days seeing to it that they be nourished and strengthened. I do not believe much in the efficacy of rootedness: roots are too readily torn up, and men who cling to them are too easily dashed to pieces. I say merely that I have been blessed to find a pleasing place to abide, and have lived as contented and as serene a life as one has any right to ask. Until Noah came.

There has been nothing sordid revealed in his character or even hinted at until now, unless one were to note a certain excess of purposefulness in Noah Berg. In the South, especially, this is not a totally commendable trait, and Noah has had to learn to temper the zeal of his labors and find some mild sedative in social intercourse outside the factory gate. He did this within a small circle that had Rabbi Weisz at its center and the membership of the B'nai B'rith as its perimeter; in between he located the comely Miss Naomi Klein, whom he took to wife in June of 1910, and her family, long-time Savannah dry-goods merchants, with whom they decided to live until they could afford a stately home of their own. Noah and Naomi—friends thought it adorable how the combination fell trippingly from the tongue—were comfortable within the narrow social confines of local Jewry, and he saw no dividend accruing by commingling with Gentiles beyond the very long hours of his work week. It was as if to say that he demonstrated his worth to them by incessant effort on the job and that was how they must judge him, not on his easefulness of manner or how well he put away their alcohol or fried food.

He did not rest on his laurels at the factory. After his bottle had gone into production, he turned his attention to the sealer. The old Hutchinson-type stoppers had been cheap—about a penny and a half each for the initial manufacture and then thirty or forty re-usages—but hard to clean and at any rate not suitable to the new bottle design. Noah proposed a pull-wire cork of the best quality with the Jubilee name burned into the top; the cost was fractionally higher but he argued that whereas customers had to return the bottles, they kept the corks, each of which functioned as a tiny advertisement. And for a year, the pull-corks were in use until the industry-wide adoption of the cork-lined metal crown. Having exhausted the possibilities of the package he was in charge of, Noah next considered the production process itself. He was no little aided in that pursuit by the appearance in book form in 1911 of an essay entitled *The Principles of Scientific Management* by Frederick Winslow Taylor. A former mill laborer who promoted himself by astuteness into the chief engineer's post at the Midvale Steel Corporation, Taylor developed what he called "the task system," a product of intensive study of the use of workers' time and the pattern of their motion. Noah all but memorized Taylor's book and saw at once its applicability to his own factory.

The very foundation of Taylor's time and motion principles was the assertion that employer and employée had the same basic interest in the prosperity of their company but that the owner could not hope to sustain that prosperity through a long term of years unless his workers shared in it. That conception so startled General Manager Joe Dettwiler that he dismissed Noah's introduction of the subject with a brisk wave of the hand. "Dettwiler is typical, according to Taylor," Noah said, coming to me, his guardian angel, "of employers whose attitude toward their workers is that of merely trying to get the largest amount of work out of them for the smallest amount of wages." I suggested that Dettwiler stood in heavy company in that attitude, however antediluvian Noah found it, and that it would be best, perhaps, to play down the philosophy and stress the practical benefits of the Taylor system.

Accordingly, Noah bought another copy of Taylor's book and underscored those passages he felt would most deeply impress his superior, beginning with the sentence "For every individual who is overworked, there are a hundred who intentionally underwork —greatly underwork—every day of their lives, and who for this reason deliberately aid in establishing those conditions which in the end inevitably result in low wages." The solution, Taylor said a few pages later, was to keep careful record of each worker's efficiency and raise his or her wages as productivity increased, "and those who fail to rise to a certain standard are discharged and a fresh supply of carefully selected men are given work in their places." Dettwiler agreed with that in theory but thought it would be difficult as a practical matter. How could they improve worker productivity and where could they find enough skilled girls to fill jobs at a bottling establishment?

The answer to both problems was in Taylor, Noah said. The way to achieve higher output per man-hour was to train each worker properly from the outset, no matter how menial the task at hand, and to establish rigid regulations during work periods and impose brief, mandatory interludes of relaxation. The book was full of graphic examples. But of greatest relevance to the Jubilee factory was the upsurge in productivity that Taylor reported from his studies of girls who worked as inspectors at a ball-bearing company. About two dozen of the hundred-odd girls at the Longstreth Way factory were employed at inspecting returned bottles to make sure they were safe for refilling. It was monotonous, low-paying work, and the turnover was high and wasteful. Noah therefore followed closely when he read of how the work at Taylor's ball-bearing factory required steady concentration by the girls looking for defects—bearings that were chipped, dented, scratched, or fire-cracked—of a kind very similar to those his bottle inspectors searched for. Carried out under strong light, the uninterrupted inspection of ball bearings caused an expenditure of nervous tension that resulted in high fatigue and reduced output. Taylor's study recommended a ten-minute work break for the girls after every seventy-five minutes; during the break they were encouraged to get up, walk around, and talk to one another, but once they resumed working, they were placed far enough apart to make conversation inconvenient if not impossible. Then the workday was cut from ten and a half to eight and a half hours, yet total output rose rather than diminished, largely because the company kept only those girls who were especially adept at the task and paid them a substantially better wage. Taylor noted that "unfortunately this involved laying off many of the most intelligent, hardest-working, and most trustworthy girls merely because they did not possess the quality of quick perception followed by quick action" mandatory in the job. The overall result was far higher output per dollar paid. The process worked, reported Taylor, because "each girl was made to feel that she was the object of especial care and interest on the part of the management." A further example of management solicitude that Noah noted was Taylor's recommendation that "all young women should be given two consecutive days of rest (with pay) each month, to be taken whenever they may choose."

By stages, Noah introduced just such a regimen among his bottle inspectors and added a few touches appropriate to the nature of their specific work task. On extended investigation, for example, he concluded that an inspector's eyes should ideally be twenty-four inches from the bottles as they pass in review and at a level one and a half inches below the top of the bottle; Noah had the chairs bolted to the floor at that distance from the conveyor belt but had the height of each seat made adjustable to the stature of each inspector. The better pay, shorter hours, work breaks, reduced fatigue, and increased attention to their training by management were of course warmly received by the girls. There was only muffled objection to the martinet's way that Noah imposed stringent standards of punctuality (two instances of tardiness, for any cause, in a single month were ground for immediate dismissal), hygiene (every girl had to scrub her hands before starting work and after lunch; dirty hands could also get you fired on the spot), and morality (no fraternizing was permitted with male operatives on the premises and no flirting out the cloak-room window with passersby). To Noah's surprise, only the paid two-day menstrual holiday—"a bleedin' shame," Dettwiler called it with a lewd chuckle when he told me of it with disbelief and disapproval but acquiesced nevertheless—was not a popular innovation. Many of the girls and women declined to accept time off, partly out of reluctance to acknowledge feminine frailty, partly out of displeasure at the thought that male overseers should be privy to so intimate a matter. In time, however, shyness on this score abated, and the only real source of rancor over the remarkable improvement in productivity that Noah had wrought at the factory was the outrage of girls who were let go for failure to make the grade or for violation of the rules. Ex-employées being perforce a notoriously disgruntled group, Noah saw no great harm in the growing ranks of these young women whom he and his assistant superintendent were obliged to dismiss during the eighteen or so months consumed by the changeover in work regulations and personnel. It is this miscalculation—or indifference, if you will—that I suspect is the bottom of the troubles that besiege him in this grave hour. Simon Legree, and those so perceived (justly or not), has ever drawn hisses from the gallery.

That Noah Berg did not in fact become a totally heartless overseer but merely an unusually thorough one I can testify to by personal knowledge of at least one instance of his charitableness. His detractors would no doubt say it was a momentary lapse in an otherwise unbroken pattern of petty tyranny that he practiced toward those under his command.

At the beginning of this year of their Lord 1913, I was paid a visit in my office by the enfeebled figure of Plato Layne. Time and a flying automobile had reduced him to a bent remnant of his once robust form, and the liquor with which Bax so generously plied him out of guilt to ease the pain had taken its toll as well. I recalled our first meeting at the quayside half a lifetime before and the sight of what had become of this decent, dutiful, and by no means unintelligent being rendered me all but inarticulate. I gestured to him to have a seat and offered him a smoke. He preferred to remain standing, he said and then seemed to hesitate to state his business, as if gathering strength for the ordeal. I managed to ask after his health. He said, "Some days good, some days bad, boss." And then he said he wanted to leave Bax's employment and wondered if I might be able to fix him up with a job somewhere because he could still do some things and hated being idle.

"But I thought you and Mr. Baxter always got on famously—."

"Not since de crack-up," Plato said. "He blame me fo' dat—say I didn't check de brakes sufficient—which he know ain't so. He show me his belly burns sometimes when he get mean drunk and say, 'Thank you very much for dis pretty gift, Mr. Chocolate Bar,' and words like dat. An' he reads me out loud from Mr. Watson's magazine sayin' how colored is de scum o' de earth—which I know ain't what Mr. Watson write. Why, he was de only white man I ever heerd give a speech favorin' colored."

I did not wish to protract his discomfort. I said I would ask around to see if there was any work and that he must do the same. "I done it, boss," he said. "Nobody want nigger cripples, even ones what can write—." I called Noah Berg, among others, for a situation with restricted activity that might suit Plato's needs. About the first of April, Noah rang me to say they needed a night watchman at the factory and did I think Plato was up to it, especially since the job involved climbing up and down a trapdoor ladder to the basement twice an hour to check for fire. I said only he and Plato could judge that and I would have him come around. Next day Plato stopped by my office all smiles and said he was due to start at the factory that night and he was in my debt once more. We talked a bit about his daddy, living out his years in a shack at McAllister and surviving on three Jubilees a day, and then he tipped his cap and hobbled away.

Hearing no more from or about him, I assumed Plato had adapted well to his new job and dismissed him from my thoughts. It was with disbelief, therefore, that I was called on the telephone the third Sunday following by Joe Dettwiler, the factory general manager, and told that the police were holding Plato Layne for the murder of a fourteen-year-old white girl named Jean Dugan, whose strangled and bloody body the negro said he found in the basement in the middle of the night while making his watchman's rounds. The only open question, said Dettwiler, was whether he had raped her as well. Miss Dugan, he added, had been a bottle inspector at the factory for the past two years and was well liked by all.

V

Jean Dugan had also been a pretty, well-developed, presumptively chaste, and God-fearing maiden, and the brutal manner of her death awoke immediate fury across the city and the county and the state. Reporters hurried into town from all directions, and the Savannah *Morning Pilot* was on the streets with an extra by Sunday noon, in time to greet returnees from church. Miss Dugan, everyone read, had put on a yellow frock, straw bonnet with a white ribbon, and tennis slippers and taken a streetcar over to the Jubilee factory at about noontime Saturday to collect her pay for the three days she had worked earlier in the week. She had taken off Thursday and Friday under the menstrual-leave program, and the plant had not operated that Saturday because it was Confederate Memorial Day. But she apparently knew that supervisory personnel would be on hand, for she arrived at ten or fifteen minutes after twelve and was paid off the six dollars and sixty cents she was owed by Superintendent Berg, who was attending to managerial paperwork as was his wont on Saturdays. No one reported seeing her between the time Noah Berg said she left his office and when Plato Layne said he found her lifeless body in the cellar about fifteen hours later.

The evidence against Plato was at first purely circumstantial and then so obviously implicating as to suggest it had been fabricated. The girl's dead hand clutched a sheet of notepaper with the words "Big old negro did this" awkwardly printed on it in pencil. That was more than enough to get Plato locked up. And although his time card for that night showed, when Noah reviewed it Sunday morning, that he had punched in regularly every half hour as required, re-examination of it on Monday morning revealed several skips during the night when something apparently prevented him from making, or at any rate from recording, his rounds. A search of his room at the boardinghouse he had moved to when he began the job at the factory produced a bloody shirt of Plato's buried in the middle of a mound of soiled clothing. The gallows loomed. But Plato would not confess.

I telephoned Chief Weyland Yates at police headquarters on Monday afternoon and said I knew they were anxious to close out the case but I had known Plato Layne a good many years and it seemed unthinkable that he could have committed such a crime.

"I know him, too, Seth, but facts're facts. An' old Billy Doak says he become a mighty ornery nigger these past six months, up 'n' leavin' the way he done. This killin' fits in—if you look at it close. He's bein' stubborn as shit, though, 'bout admittin' anythin'—."

"The boys in the back room are helping refresh his memory, I take it—?"

"They been kickin' his ass pretty good, and he ain't budgin'— the dumb lyin' coon!"

I took it upon myself to visit police headquarters the next morning, knowing that Plato was almost certainly not represented by counsel. As I arrived, Noah Berg, looking pale from the encounter, was emerging from the interview room where he had met in private with Plato at the request of the police to see if he could get anything out of the negro. "He denies everything," Noah said, wiping his brow with a kerchief, "but whether he did it or not, I think he knows more than he's let on. The punch clock doesn't lie." I told him I thought I had read in the newspaper that he had checked out Plato's time card himself and found it in order. "I must have read it too hastily," he said, "or maybe it was the wrong card—." I asked him what he had done with the card. "The detectives took it," he said. "They must have put it back in the wall rack afterward—though I find that awfully shoddy work on their part." Then he said he badly wanted a cup of coffee and excused himself.

Given the more sedate nature of my practice in later years, I had been seen only rarely within the inner chambers of the police, but Chief Yates greeted me as the old familiar I was—until it began to appear that my presence might complicate his life. I asked him if I might have five minutes with the prisoner, and he reluctantly agreed. Plato's eyes were puffy with sleeplessness and his abdomen, he said, bore the bruises of police sticks. "They ain't let me be hardly a minute, Mr. Adler," he said. "They keep askin' me the same thing ovah 'n' ovah and makin' me sweat terrible— and nevah give me no water excep' maybe a spoonful." He said he knew nothing about the murder but that it surely looked as if someone was trying to put the guilt on him.

I joined Yates and Al "Doodles" Stone, his head detective, in the chief's office, said I tended to believe Plato, and urged them not to act too swiftly in pinning the charge on him. When they emitted truculent sounds at that, I asked to see the evidence, which they had put in a paper bag and locked in the chief's safe. After a moment or two of hesitation, Doodles displayed it one piece at a time, starting with the note. I examined the rumpled paper carefully without touching it. "If Plato killed her," I said, "why didn't he destroy the note before your men arrived?"

"Probably because he didn't see it bunched in her hand," Doodles said. "She must've wrote it with her dyin' breath after he dragged her to the coal bin." He showed me the little pencil found beside the body.

"Where'd this come from?" I asked.

"From the cellar floor," Doodles said.

"You mean she just found it lying there conveniently with a piece of notepaper nearby—?"

"I don't know," Doodles said. "She must've had it on her—in a purse, probably."

"Did you find a purse?"

He paused a moment before saying no.

"Did she have one on her when she left home that morning?"

He nodded slowly. "So her mother says."

"Well," I said, "there's your first problem."

Doodles looked over at Chief Yates with chagrin.

I turned to the bloody shirt next. Plato had acknowledged it was his and a chemist in the coroner's office had confirmed that the stains were blood. "Is this just the way you found it?" I asked.

"Sandy Phelps—Detective Phelps—found it, not me," Doodles said.

"Did he button up the buttons?"

Doodles shrugged. "Not that I heard of. He's not supposed to—."

"It looks as if it had just been laundered," I said. "It's clean except for the bloodstains—as if it hadn't been worn—."

"What do you mean?" said Doodles, dander rising.

"I mean if the theory is that Plato went home to change his shirt so he wouldn't be found with blood on him—and that's why he didn't punch the time clock a couple of times—this wasn't the shirt he had on. It would be at least a little grimy—this one smells from soap, not sweat—and why in the world would he have taken the trouble to button it back up? I'd say that someone stole it out of his room from the fresh laundry, smeared blood on it, and shoved it back in the soiled heap."

"You sayin' someone planted it on him?"

"No doubt you've had the same suspicion—." Then I studied the time card and saw that several of the punches had been skipped. "Is this the first card or the second card?" I asked.

"There's only one card," Doodles said, "and you're lookin' at it."

"Berg says there's something fishy about it."

"Berg was practically jumpin' out of his skin when we brought him in to the factory Sunday morning. No wonder he read the card wrong, the way his hand was shaking. I felt sorry for the guy—."

"He says he gave you the card afterward."

"He says wrong. He may *think* that's what he did but he wasn't thinkin' too straight right then, take it from me. I told him to hang on to the card till we went over the whole place later in the morning. I think maybe he stuck it right back in the nigger's slot on the board—."

"And you forgot to pick it up—?"

Doodles pressed his lips together and shook his head grimly. "Okay," he said, "I forgot—till the next morning."

"By which time Berg was calmer and read it over and found the skips?"

"Right."

"Meanwhile, though, someone could have put a doctored card in Layne's slot."

Chief Yates was holding his head in his palms by this point. "Didn't I tell you," he said to Doodles, "this here's the smartest son of a bitch on two legs south of Rabun Gap?"

The telephone rang a moment or two later, and the chief listened to his caller glumly. "They just found what looks like bloodstains in the cloakroom on the second floor at the factory," he said after hanging up.

"Why," I asked, "would a black night watchman drag a young white woman up to the second floor of an empty factory to do his nasty work? Or do you suppose his charms were so manifest that she went with him willingly? And where was she between midday and the time the night watchman supposedly did her in?"

"And if the note and the shirt and the time card are plants," said Doodles, the light glimmering on across his long, lean face, "how do we know the bloodstains aren't, too?"

The chief expelled a mighty sigh. "All right," he said, "tell Sandy to leave off on the nigger for a time. We got more work to do, it looks as if—."

Amory Austin had been trying to rouse me on the telephone at my office. Disturbed about the murder and the ensuing seamy publicity that extended to our product, he wanted my advice on engaging the Pinkerton Agency to investigate the crime in the company's behalf so that the air might be cleared as soon as possible. I confessed to no lost love for the Pinkertons but granted the wisdom of the proposal. I rang up Joe Dettwiler at the factory and told him to follow through on orders from the top. Within hours, Pinkerton Arthur Cavaretta, a square-shouldered, fast-talking operative who wore his hat down nearly to his eyebrows, was on the case. We asked him to give us the courtesy of hearing about any evidence he uncovered before he brought it to the police. "I can't do that," he said. "We work with the police hand in glove." I suggested that it was not the police who were paying him. "No, but they won't have us muscling in on their game," he said. "You're either with them or agin 'em."

The point seemed academic the next day when Dettwiler called to say the police had arrested, thanks to the services of Art Cavaretta, a former Jubilee employée named Vernon Pike, who had stopped by the factory around six o'clock on the Saturday afternoon of the murder allegedly to pick up some work boots he had left behind when Noah Berg fired him two weeks earlier. Pike, a long-legged, fair-haired white man of twenty-eight or -nine, had worked in the superintendent's office as paymaster and shipping clerk until Noah found the payroll account coming up short a few weeks running and Pike denied any knowledge of the reason. Pike, moreover, hailed from Wilkinson County outside of Macon, had known Jean Dugan and her folks when they lived there, and had come by the Dugan house to visit a few times after starting work at the factory the previous fall and discovering the Dugans' whereabouts. Pike, according to reports, had come by the factory for his boots just as Noah Berg was leaving for the day and Plato Layne was coming on duty. According to Plato, however, Pike stayed in the plant only a short time, found his boots, and left. Nowhere to be found in Savannah or its environs after the murder, he was located in Macon on the Thursday following the crime and brought back for intensive examination by Doodles Stone and his fellow virtuosos in the third degree. But Pike claimed dozens of witnesses to vouch that he had spent all Saturday afternoon at a tavern a few blocks from the factory where he nursed three or four mugs of beer and stood out front every now and then to watch the passing Memorial Day pageant. He said he had his suitcase with him later when he stopped by the factory to get his boots just before taking the night train north to Macon, where he had decided to look for work. His story was readily corroborated, and Jean Dugan's mother, furthermore, said Vern Pike was a kind and wholesome young man of good folks and very like a member of the family.

After Pike's release, no word reached me on the progress of the investigation until Saturday night. Rabbi Weisz called me at home around nine to say Naomi Berg had telephoned a moment earlier and reported with terror that the police had just taken Noah down to headquarters and were charging him with the murder of Jean Dugan. "It's a pogrom," the rabbi said. "The man wouldn't hurt a fly."

I went at once to see Chief Yates, but the door was barred to me. I told the officer on duty at the front desk that I was the attorney for the company that employed the accused man and was entitled to see him. Word filtered back an hour later that the chief would see me in the morning and not before.

It was necessary to battle my way through a melee of reporters to get in then, and in the process I heard the words "Jew boss" jump through the undertow of speculation on Noah's arrest. It had a savage sound.

The chief was clearly haggard when I was admitted to see him. He was flanked by Doodles Stone and our Pinkerton, Cavaretta. The three of them sat there with eyes averted looking like a star-chamber panel ready to drop the scaffold door without bother of a trial. "I know how you feel, Seth," said the chief, "his bein' one of your boys an' all, but the evidence has been pilin' up—thanks in part to Arthur here and your company's civic concern—."

It was not clear whether he meant by "one of your boys" a company official or a fellow Jew or both, and there seemed no point in pressing him for a clarification. But I needed to know the nature of the evidence, and with that they were forthcoming. Doodles read off the incriminating items from a long legal pad in approximately chronological order. "On Friday, the day before the murder and the regular payday," he began dolefully, "one of Jean Dugan's girl friends at the factory asked for Jean's pay envelope and said she would drop it by her house. She says Noah Berg refused to give it to her and said that Jean would probably be by for it herself the next day.

"Second, Berg says he was in his office steadily from noon to twelve-thirty on the Saturday of the murder—the time when Jean allegedly came by for her pay and then left—but another girl who came by for her pay a few minutes after twelve said no one was in the superintendent's office when she arrived, and after waiting in the hall outside for five or ten minutes, she left.

"Third, the husband of the cook at the Klein residence, where Mr. and Mrs. Berg live, says his wife told him that Mr. Berg didn't touch his food when he came home for dinner a little after one on Saturday, even though the main dish was chicken dumplings, one of Berg's favorites.

"Fourth, Plato Layne says that Berg told him to report to work on Saturday at four in the afternoon instead of six, the usual hour, because it was a holiday, but when he got there, Berg sent him away for two hours. And when he got there both times, the front door of the factory was locked, which had not been the case the previous Saturdays when Layne came to work.

"Fifth, Vernon Pike said that when he came by to pick up his boots, Berg seemed startled by his arrival and greatly upset. Furthermore, Berg objected during Pike's employment at the factory when he would stop by her chair and say hello for a moment or two to Jean, even though their families were old friends.

"Sixth, the paper on which the note found in the girl's hand was written matches the note pads regularly used in the superintendent's office.

"Seventh, the light in the cellar was much dimmer than usual, says Plato, suggesting that it had been turned down. If he hadn't heard what he thought was a kind of clattering around the coal chute a little after three, he might not have found the body.

"Eighth, when Sandy Phelps—Detective Phelps—telephoned Berg around seven Sunday morning to say there had been a tragedy at the factory, Berg didn't ask right away what the matter was but waited till our car came to pick him up.

"Ninth, Berg was extremely nervous and trembling when we reached him and has been that way, more or less, through much of our investigation. Even Art here will testify to that—"

Cavaretta nodded. "He's been jumpy as an alley cat since I first laid eyes on him—mopping his face or tapping his toe or pacing around like he was gettin' set to bust apart but always managing to collect himself."

"Tenth," Doodles went on grimly, "on the ride to the factory Berg said he wasn't sure if Jean was one of his employées, although she had worked there for two years, on the same floor as Berg's office, and he is known to have played a major part in laying down the new working conditions affecting the girls in the bottle-inspecting department.

"Eleventh, at the undertaker's parlor, Berg scarcely glanced at the dead girl's body yet he identified her as Jean Dugan and said he remembered then that she had come by just that noon on Saturday for her pay envelope.

"Twelfth, bloodstains were found in the cloakroom, which is just around the corner from the superintendent's office on the second floor. And the cloakroom contains plenty of coat hooks, which could well have inflicted the sort of scalp wound the dead girl suffered, and plenty of wire hangers, of the sort that was found unwound and tied around the strangled child's throat.

"Thirteenth, a number of past and present female employées say that Berg would look into the cloakroom from time to time when the girls were disrobing.

"Fourteenth, Berg as superintendent had the key to the punch clock and could easily have counterfeited a time card that incriminated his night watchman, just as he might have written the incriminating note found in the dead girl's hand—"

"—And planted the bloody shirt in the watchman's room at the boardinghouse," I broke in.

"Or arranged for it to be done," Doodles said with a nod.

"And the purse," I asked, "what about the girl's purse?"

Cavaretta rubbed his chin. "We haven't got that part of it yet," he said, "but we're working on it."

I sat there thinking about that roster of circumstantial clues, no single one of which was damning but which in aggregate threw a sharp beam of suspicion on Noah Berg. "So," I said, "this mild, bespectacled, highly able businessman allowed himself to be consumed by passion at his place of work, drew a young employée who weighed only twenty or so pounds less than he into the cloakroom against her will, subdued her by banging her head against a coat hook or some such metal object, ravished her—"

"That part's not clear yet, either," said Doodles.

"Whatever he did," I said, "and then he choked her to death with a wire hanger lest she recover and disclose his bestial conduct. Then he disposed of her in the cellar, taking pains to try to incriminate the night watchman—." My voice trailed off in questioning scorn.

"Yup," said Weyland Yates, "that's how it looks to us."

"And don't you think," I said, "Berg is smart enough to have figured out a better alibi for himself if everything you say is true? All he had to do was tell you he never saw the girl at the factory on Saturday. You've got no one else who saw her there then—."

"But he didn't know that when we questioned him," said Doodles. "For all he knew, five people saw her come in and go upstairs—."

"You people are foxy as shit," said the chief, "but you don't know everything."

I looked at him and saw the fixed hardness in his eyes. "I didn't hear that, Chief," I said.

He rubbed his nose and said, "Suit yourself, Mr. Defense Attorney. You got your hands full."

Noah Berg, whom I expected to be fidgety as a Mexican jumping bean from what the police had told me, was relatively calm when they let me see him in his cell later that afternoon. I put to him as many of the items of circumstantial evidence as I could remember, and in every case he responded with plausible explanations. I told him that was encouraging and he should rest as easy as possible. Always a studious sort, Berg said he was struck by the similarity between his case and the one of Mendel Beilis, the Jewish manager of a brick factory in Kiev, who had been charged with committing a ritual murder of a Russian boy in 1911 and, after a massive international outcry over his innocence, had been just lately acquitted by the tsar's court. "And that was Russia," I said, by way of trying to cheer him further, "not here."

"You mean America," he said, "land where we free men pursue free enterprise, whatever our church—."

I could not blame him for that mocking of me just then. It was he, after all, who was behind bars.

Noah was bound over to the grand jury early the next week. It was not at all certain, from the evidence I had heard, that an indictment would be returned. My hopes rose with news that the police had arrested a colored janitor named Mo Easter, who had worked at the Jubilee factory for the past few years and whose curious conduct at the plant since the day of the murder had led to his being questioned and a search of his premises, where the dead girl's purse was found inside the mattress. Known as a shiftless and unreliable rogue, Mo insisted at first that he had found the purse in a vacant lot not far from the factory. Later, he was said to have found it in a corner of the first-floor coatroom. Finally, Art Cavaretta came by with a withering advisory.

"Mo Easter's made a full confession," said the Pinkerton. "Berg called him to his office, he says, and told him he'd killed the girl on Saturday when she rejected his advances. Then he asked Mo to help him get rid of the body. He says he did because Berg was his boss and had been good to him and promised to reward him—and if he hadn't helped him, he was sure Berg would have told the cops that he had done it instead."

"I don't believe it," I said. "I think Doodles and the boys fed him the whole story."

"Maybe," Cavaretta said, "but since when did everyone around there start lovin' niggers better than Jews?"

II

Judith's Book

EIGHT

Poughkeepsie, July 27, 1945

Even across this chasm of years and miles, I would venture to say
in only the most speculative fashion that my father must have
believed deep within himself that he was defending, in addition
to Noah Berg's hide (a tissue of debatable worth), Dreyfus and
Beilis and Moses in the bargain and everything he himself stood
for in life.

Often enough in my pampered girlhood, father dear had said to
me, taking me upon his angular yet never discomforting lap
(where I performed irreparable damage to the knife-like crease in
his trousers) or seizing my small, sticky hand for a turn around
our yard, that we Jews belonged to America no less than the rest
and had prospered on these shores according to our merits and
our enterprise. Only the slackers and swindlers and mediocrities
blamed religious persecution for their low estate. The sole odd aspect of that otherwise unexceptionable bit of sermonizing, as I
think back, was that it had never been prompted by any inquiry
or fretting on my part. Father, at those quite widely interspersed
moments, was simply taken by an impulse to unburden himself,
and he would do so with a vehemence that left my braids rattling
if the soliloquy had been rendered in the drawing room or, if out
of doors, our giant hydrangea, a formidable growth, bowing in
agreement with his conviction as we passed.

It seems evident to me now that he was bent not so much on
arming a darling daughter to war with life's vicissitudes (which I
felt menaced my small personage in nonsectarian fashion) as
fending off the great doubt and fear of his own life. His well-

243

justified esteem in the community to the contrary notwithstanding, he appeared to be stricken periodically by the receipt of an ancestral telegram that reached him through the stars or some other unmonitored station. The message was a reminder, or so it seems to me now, not to forget that in every land, however wide or green, however freshly or anciently peopled by whatever diversity of human stock, however great its bounty or wise its ruler, the Jew is destined to dwell there a perpetual stranger among the common run of folk. For the Lord had indeed chosen him to wander the earth and everywhere bear witness to its peoples of their departure from righteousness, of their betrayal of justice, of their gluttony and their frailty, and to prophesize their richly deserved downfall from among the mighty unless they swiftly check their vileness. A nasty sort of job, that one, not likely to endear thee to thine neighbors. Indeed, that divinely ordained assignment as history's nag served to assure the Jew he would be tolerated only so long as he stood by dutifully as victim for the next outburst of savagery among the people whose decay he had so astutely forecast. And if he were not victimized in this year, or decade, or generation, or century, he would be the next. To all of which, I believe, father kept drafting a reply telegram which he would rehearse to me in those talks and walks of his initiating: America is different.

It is this contention that animates me now as I review the foregoing pages, drafted thirty-two years ago to the day by father and which I have decided to carry forward as a collaborative memoir. A dubious enterprise, perhaps, but one that seems suddenly urgent to me even when his pages have idled in a family vault these many years. The reason for this transformation is not hard to unpuzzle. All this spring the newsreels have been relaying ghastly confirmation of the reports as we had heard for so long of the massive mutilation of European Jewry. A demonic monument to Teutonic methodology. No Caesar, no sultan, no tsar, no frenzied priest bearing faggots to the pyre, no pack of mad dogs or famished tigers ever perpetrated a more grisly slaughter. The glimpse for but an instant of those endless ditches, heaped with shards of bone and putrefying flesh like so much despicable effluvia, is needed to bear testimony to the enormity of the crime. And where on earth had civilized man risen higher than in Germany? It is impossible just now to be a Jew here and not ask if America is so different. And if the answer for the moment is yes, for how long will it remain yes?

That is the question that must have haunted father on the eve of Noah Berg's trial for the murder of the Dugan girl. For even before the jury had been selected, the state was aswarm with low-life muttering, "Hang the Juby Jew!" (as Noah had come to be called after the soda whose manufacture he superintended for a living). We thought it odd, and not the happiest omen, that father, an infrequent worshipper in public, had attended services at Mickve Israel on the Friday before the trial. It was odder still that he closeted himself the weekend long to do what he called "some scribbling"—of what, he would not say. Not to mother, at any rate. But on the way to the courtroom Monday morning, to which I drove him while he glanced over some notes, he disclosed to me the nature of his frenetic labors: a private memoir of his own times past. Writing it, he said, had served to clear his mind and empty him of passion that might otherwise have worked only to disrupt his performance in court. He said the confidential writing was not fit for disclosure to any living soul—a revelation that, I must say, piqued my curiosity nearly to the bursting point—but that some day, if he did not dispose of it in the interim, as was most likely, it would come into my possession for whatever interest I might find in it or use make of it. Meanwhile, I might serve him well, he said, if I could keep a diary or some form of intimate record of the trial proceedings. He did not say why he wanted me to do it or why this trial was so different from any other in which he had participated, and I did not need, or think, to ask. The graduate study in which I was then engaged in the field of cultural anthropology at Columbia University, where I was a doctoral candidate under the supervision of the genius (no other word will do) Boas, qualified me in father's view as an astute observer of primates in their habitats. Having no other pressing business that torpid summer, I took up the task he proposed and made extensive notes of the unfolding ordeal. On these I now draw.

At no point during that whole trying time did I consciously cast myself as the ravishing Rebecca, ministering with filial devotion to the *tsuris* of Isaac of York. For one thing, I was only half so

245

pretty as she and not nearly the sly puss of a healer; father, more-over, genuflected to no man, and was no more to be confused with Isaac than Louis *Quatorze* with Harry Truman. But it is true that, like Rebecca, I wanted badly to be of comfort to my father through those troubles. My concern for the object of his efforts—Noah Berg—was, by contrast, almost strictly of a clinical sort. What little association I had had with him when he arrived in Savannah, as father's memoir accurately recounts, established him in my thoughts (briefly) as a limp spirit, bright enough but curiously vacant inside, as if there were no tallow to him, only wick and a lusterless flame. It was with some surprise that I learned he had proven a most proficient bumblebee about the fac-tory, humming with great energy and ideas. My suspicion that the female of the species set off few vibrations within his body chem-istry, however, was confirmed in my view when he married the harmless and marginally feminine Naomi Klein, a girl my own age with whom I had taken some schooling and exchanged perhaps three dozen words *in toto,* none of them memorable. She neither sang nor played an instrument nor rode a horse nor danced be-yond a sort of flounce she managed on those rare occasions she found herself forcefully projected onto the floor. It was said of her, in fairness, that she showed promise as a *petit-pointilliste,* but I recall seeing none of her handiwork nor asking for a display. She was far more to be pitied than despised, yet I think I nurtured a dislike for her from the day I learned her family made part of its considerable living by selling bed sheets throughout the state to the membership of the Ku Klux Klan. It did not matter to me that such trade could have constituted only an infinitesimal por-tion of Klein's Dry Goods' annual sales; the very idea filled me with loathing, and poor Naomi as a result suffered my intense scorn. Her marriage to Noah Berg occurred while I was studying in New York; mother, I believe, mentioned it in passing in one of her weekly letters. That she was a fit and dutiful wife, no one much doubted or speculated upon. That Noah Berg might be a Jekyll-Hyde capable of slaying a husky young wench whose charms he had been denied was beyond my wildest imagining—or that of anyone who knew him.

There were good reasons why father should never have defended Noah, and they were forcefully advanced at a high council in our drawing room the day following the grand jury indictment. Present besides father, mother, and me (my brother Eli was off at law school in Cambridge) were Naomi Berg, her father Sigmund Klein, Rabbi Jeremiah Weisz from Mickve Israel, the factory manager Joe Dettwiler, the fabled Amanda Lizabeth Baxter herself, and the corporate overseer of her fabulously successful invention—the gnomish Amory G. Austin. Noah himself was being held without bail in a private cell at the county jail to await his trial. Missing was the chairman of the board of the Jubilation Plantation Corporation—W. Doak Baxter, who was said to be off seeing about the possible purchase of a panda bear for the Atlanta Zoo, one of his more deserving philanthropies.

Naomi, predictably, was a puddle of tears throughout the day-long deliberations, but Noah's father-in-law and Rabbi Weisz stood up firmly for the accused man's interests. There was never much doubt whose interest the natty Mr. Austin was there to protect. "I know you are remotely related to Mr. Berg," he said to father, "and that you intervened in his behalf when he obtained his position with our company. I gather, furthermore, that you have acted as something of the man's patron during his hitherto exemplary career with us. But you owe us, as chief corporation counsel, a higher loyalty and duty than you do Mr. Berg, who can be represented ably by any of a number of distinguished attorneys. Mr. Klein, with whom I have conferred on the telephone, advises me that between his own family and Mr. Berg's there are sufficient funds to meet the fees of the finest practitioners in the nation. Therefore, I cannot see the need or the wisdom of your active participation in the case, Mr. Adler. It links the company and our product intimately with the interests of an accused murderer —hardly the most glorious advertisement of our brand, I think you must admit. And should the young man eventually be found guilty, a tragic outcome I pray shall be averted, the damage to our product is likely to be, I daresay, irreparable. The company is grateful to Mr. Berg for his past services, has recompensed him for them, and has stood ready to advance him to posts of high responsibility once he gathered a bit more seasoning. But at this moment, the company must divorce itself from Mr. Berg's unfortunate plight, and as its chief executive officer I am firmly opposed to our deeper involvement in his defense, especially since we are assured that a more than adequate one can be obtained for him in some other fashion. I would suggest we try to get Darrow or, if he is unwilling, Louis Marshall of New York."

It came out so neat and reasonable, so well parsed and pleasantly modulated, that a moment was required to realize that father was being ordered to withdraw from the case. And father did not relish taking orders.

After a terrifyingly protracted silence, Rabbi Weisz spoke, no louder than Austin. "Noah has conveyed to me his wish," he said, smoothing down his already finely barbered mustache, "that Mr. Adler direct whatever effort is mustered in his defense. He has complete and total faith in Mr. Adler's abilities and knows that he is well regarded in the community by citizens of all faiths—."

"It is not merely the Savannah community that is involved here, sir," Austin intervened. "All of Georgia is overwrought by this crime—and much of the South and the rest of the nation as well. Mr. Adler's sterling abilities are not at issue here, nor his place in the eyes of men of good will who know him or of him. All I am saying is that there is no need to jeopardize further the interests of the company that Mr. Adler and so many of us have worked so hard and so long to promote by his participation in Berg's defense. Other hands can carry on that task."

"Are you not also implying, sir," asked the rabbi, "that should it become general knowledge that your chief corporation counsel is of the Hebrew faith, your product will suffer?"

"Our product, perhaps; the defendant, most assuredly."

"Does it not seem apparent to you, Reverend Weisz," asked Amanda Baxter, enthroned in a wing chair and manipulating a ruffled parasol as if it were no larger than a pencil, "that a Jew defending a Jew smacks of special pleading? I believe Mr. Berg is a gifted young man who has made precocious contributions to our company. We undeniably owe him a measure of gratitude and loyalty in this crisis, but we cannot be expected to sacrifice our entire enterprise in his cause, especially when we are not fully certain—and do forgive me, Mrs. Berg, but we must speak with brutal candor in this room—of his innocence. Our collective wisdom, however—such as it is—is at his disposal just now, and I think it not untoward to note that the identity of Mr. Berg's faith is well known and, given the unfortunate nature of things at this moment, not a factor working to his advantage. He compounds that factor by asking Mr. Adler to defend him, a request that no doubt summons Mr. Adler's highest sense of professional duty but runs directly counter to the interests of his principal retainer. A man of compassion to match his integrity, he is unlikely to abandon a co-religionist whose very life is at stake even when impartial heads may counsel that the accused is misguided in his request of Mr. Adler."

I thought her quite the cleverest and most commanding woman of the South I had ever known. My mother, knowing of her then what I came to know only years afterward, was uncowed. "Beautifully uttered," she said, "but what precisely is it you are saying, Amanda? Do you share Mr. Austin's position or merely sympathize with it—?"

"With it and Seth's dilemma as well."

"Well," said mother, "I'm not sure that advances the discussion any, but your appreciation of Mr. Adler's problem is reassuring—."

"Thank you, Mrs. Adler," said father, speaking for the first time, "and thank you, Miss Baxter. All this solicitude over my awkward position threatens to overcome me with dyspepsia." A small ripple of laughter circled the room, driving off a wave of tension that had begun to pulse from egg to dart upon the very woodwork. "I seem to be at the call of several masters at once," he continued, "when in fact I have striven to arrange my professional life in a way that requires me to be answerable only for the conscientious rendering of services paid for." He turned to Mr. Austin. "From the start of my association with Miss Baxter's delicious beverage, which I need hardly remind you antedates yours by a good decade, I have insisted on not going on the corporate payroll in order to maintain my identity as a private practitioner. Yet my dedication to the company's welfare needs no documentation, I think, at this point. So let us establish at the outset, sir, that my participation in Mr. Berg's defense is a matter for me to decide, and not the company."

"I do not contest that, Mr. Adler," said Austin. "I was mainly outlining our mutual vested interests."

"The young man in jail, too, has a vested interest," offered Sig

Klein in his son-in-law's behalf. "Let us, please, not lose sight of the human heart in all this, ladies and gentlemen."

"May I respectfully make a suggestion in view of the overall problem?" asked the rabbi. "Could we not assemble a team of defense counselors of which Mr. Adler was a member but not the titular head, although he would play the presiding role in private? His association with the case would be entirely separated from his services to the corporation, which would in no way recompense him for his time on the case. The other member or members of the defense team would have to be mutually agreeable to the corporation and of course Mr. Adler and Mr. Berg."

It seemed an entirely reasonable solution, and father gave a tentative nod of approval.

"It is an intelligent proposal, sir," said Austin, crossing his legs opposite from the way they had been and taking care to preserve the crease in his trousers by lifting the fabric ever so slightly at the knee, "but it does not obviate the problem from the corporation's standpoint. I cannot, of course, direct Mr. Adler's actions, but as its chief operating official, I am obliged to say without pussyfooting that his involvement in the Berg defense in any overt fashion will embarrass the corporation and leave us no choice but to call upon his services no longer."

"And I," said Amanda Baxter, giving her parasol a quite sharp swivel, "as the corporation's largest stockholder in collaboration with my brother, am obliged to say without pussyfooting that Mr. Adler must be free to proceed as he chooses without threat of reprisal from the company in whose success he has played no little part. Mr. Austin has said, I think, what he must, and within his range of vision, he is right. But there are other points of view also to be taken into account. I have taken the liberty of discussing the situation in advance of this meeting with my brother, and he has a proposal that I think oddly interesting and not inconsistent with Reverend Weisz's. He suggests that Mr. Adler be joined as cocounsel not by an outlander of merit such as Mr. Darrow but by a prominent native Georgian of Christian persuasion who is well known for his skills as a defense attorney and a champion of the oppressed. He means Mr. Tom Watson, whose power in the high councils of this state, one gathers, has never been greater."

A thin shriek of astonishment escaped my throat. Tom Watson! The epitome of manifest venality—and his weekly printed compilations of hatemongering! Was ever a more ludicrous thought conceived? Long had I heard, to be sure, of Watson's splendid exploits as a courageous young idealist, suffering constant defeat even while advancing the course of social justice. That my father and the Baxters had been much taken with him during those years of thankless tribulation was as understandable as Watson's bitter struggles were commendable. But he had not been content to retire as a wounded prophet, taking balm in his writings and ever greater fortune as a planter. Self-resurrected, he sought political power at any price, and the price was plain to any who were not slavishly devoted to the man: he simply surrendered all his principles. Not all at once, perhaps, but the depletion went on rapidly as anyone could tell who followed his *Jeffersonian Magazine*, to which father had subscribed at the behest of Mr. Baxter, whose allegiance to Watson seemed to have grown in inverse ratio to the man's warranting it.

Watson's betrayal of the negroes, who had been his staunchest supporters in the early years, meant nothing so long as it won him sway over our reformist governor Hoke Smith, behind whose banner he rallied the dirt farmers and the urban depressed. Their chronically losing fight against an exploitive industrial economy made them hungrier than ever for any semi-presentable champion and any promise of relief. Barring the latter, they at least wanted someone to hate worse than themselves. Governor Smith in fact brought a margin of relief by curbing the power of the railroad and liquor interests, but when the economic decline of 1907 produced a vicious anti-labor sentiment, Smith was imperiled and then sunk by the desertion of Watson over an issue of purely private concern. The governor had declined to commute the death sentence of a devoted former Watson henchman, whose guilt in a murder case was never in doubt; when Smith proved unresponsive to Watson's earnest and thoroughly unjustifiable request, the latter moved heaven and earth to drive him from office. Watson backed a conservative, bitter enemy of organized labor and got him elected. Soon thereafter, the onetime Populist rebel announced his formal return to the Democratic Party, in which he was now not only an honored ornament but a major force, thanks to his ready access to the governor. But it was at best a covert kind of power he exercised, spent on negating the efforts of his erstwhile reformer colleagues.

Watson cried out now against taming the railroads because of the harm it would do to the widows, orphans, hospitals, colleges, church groups, and (I would not be far mistaken) bide-a-wee homes for aged schnauzers, all of which were allegedly dependent upon railroad stocks for their continued well-being. His magazine he employed as the full vessel of his venom, which he splashed about him in all directions. He was against everything and everybody. He became a fiercer sectionalist than John Calhoun had ever been. All business enterprise of note was run by "Yankee capitalists." Those who would comfort the workingman were worse scoundrels yet: socialists were Huns and Goths, and anyone who would take from the rich to relieve the poor was scum because "whatever I earn is mine and not to feed some lazy lout." He trusted majority rule no more than Jefferson, preferring some sort of idealized Greek democracy made up of the landed gentry but excluding, of course, that half of the farming community composed of black men, who he thought had best adjust to their natural-born destiny as a perpetual peasantry. Women, being the inferior sex, he wanted not to mix into politics and they were plainly addled in their campaign to seek the franchise. Catholicism he took to denouncing as a "jackassical faith," the Roman clergy as a bunch of lewd and lusty perverts masquerading in black skirts, and the Pope as "a fat old dago." Having mined his anti-Roman vein to exhaustion, he had turned lately upon the White House, whose first Southern-born occupant since the departure of Andrew Johnson he had taken to calling "Woodpile" Wilson. And this hydrophobic monster was to function in league with my father! I could not contain myself at the very mention of the prospect by the throaty Miss Baxter.

"Judith!" my mother admonished in a tone that said children, even in their middle twenties, are to be seen and not heard in such a setting.

"Forgive me," I said softly, "but it seems so extraordinary a notion."

"Quite," said Amanda Baxter. "But whatever its obvious drawbacks, it deserves serious reflection. My brother says that Mr. Watson was a remarkably potent courtroom advocate in his day—

a judgment in which I suspect Mr. Adler will concur. His influence among the luminaries of the party, which I take to extend to the judiciary, is at its zenith. And those economically depressed citizens who still make up the core of his followers are precisely the roughhewn and roughneck sort who are least sympathetic to Mr. Berg's case. Mr. Watson's participation in his defense would perhaps substantially neutralize their enmity, inside the courtroom and out."

Lord, she was a formidable woman. Part Cleopatra, part Metternich. I wished to cry out against the foulness of Watson's writings and the inconstancy of his principles, but she had made these seem as mere irrelevancies. The rabbi was not so easily blinded to the moral issue at stake. "With all due respect, madam," he said, "the man publishes the most detestable sort of rot in his paper. Every Catholic on the jury would take offense at his presence at our counsel table."

"I am not versed in these matters beyond a certain minimal point, learned reverend," she said, "but I should suspect our eminent lawyers would be at as great pains to prevent a Catholic from being impaneled in the jury box as the prosecution would be in excluding any Jewish juror. Mr. Watson's excesses in print, moreover, could be made to work to Mr. Berg's advantage. It is all a bit perverse, I rather agree, but I think the feeling might be that if even Tom Watson thinks Mr. Berg is innocent, why, then so he must be."

Sig Klein thought the scheme clever, although adding he had never had much use for Watson. Joe Dettwiler, who had come to Savannah from an upriver rural county in Watson's old Congressional district, called it a fine idea, certain to help the company and Noah's case with the workingman. Amory Austin acknowledged the shrewdness behind the suggestion but expressed uncertainty whether it would help or hurt the company more. "I'd rather a safer choice," he said, "but I would not stand in the way of the consensus."

That brought it down to father. He sat with his chin in his hand for a moment, considering all that had been said. "I loved the man for what he once was," he announced slowly. "He was plain and simply an inspiration to me, although he was and is very few years my senior. But I am saddened by what he has become and why. A glance at a column or two of his journal discloses a pathetic misanthrope, up to as much mischief as he can stir. It is inconceivable to me that he will share in the defense of Noah Berg."

"But if he would agree—?" asked Amanda Baxter.

"It could spare Noah's life."

"Then we must ask him," said Amanda.

"*You* must ask him," said father. "There is a telephone in my study. You will be undisturbed."

To my surprise, the commanding Miss Baxter did as she was told. Sherry and sponge cake were produced to keep our gums occupied during the anxious spell before Amanda re-appeared. My head, nevertheless, ached over father's apparent acquiescence in so shameful a scheme. Was Noah Berg's plight all that dire? Were Watson's oratorical gifts all that glorious yet or had he not some time ago devolved into a pathological windbag? I wanted to appeal to Rabbi Weisz to intercede in the name of simple decency, but he had already won one point on the day as an honest broker and could not be expected to risk escalating the stakes for fear of losing all. He would say we must take the bad with the good in this life, I had no doubt, and so I waited with mounting perturbation.

Amanda Baxter returned within a quarter of an hour. She was holding her parasol tightly around the middle, as if choking its life out: the outcome of her mission was plain, thank the Lord.

"I could not get through to him directly," she told the roomful of us. "One must deal with that coarse Lytle woman who apparently directs the entire establishment. Whether she be his paramour, as I have heard, or merely plies him with excessive quantities of alcohol, as I have also heard, or works her wiles by both means, the effect is of a total blockade. She insisted on knowing the nature of my business. I insisted that Mr. Watson would hear it soon enough from my lips. She said her instructions from Mr. Watson were quite explicit. I said our family was well known to him, at which point she agreed to relay my message to him while I stayed on the line. Whether she did, I cannot say. There was an appropriate pause, at any rate, during which a piano I heard being played in the background ceased. Her message, a few moments later—by which time the piano was again sounding—was that Mr.

Watson had given up his active law practice some time ago and if he were to resume it at this time, it would not be to defend a lecherous Yankee Jew against the charge of murdering an Aryan girl of spotless virtue. She said also to tell his old acquaintance, my brother Billy, that Mr. Watson was disappointed that a Southern enterprise such as ours continued to exploit the labor of children like the dead girl in a manner no more admirable than that of Northern capitalists." She turned to Amory Austin with that piece of intelligence. "So you see, sir, that Mr. Watson, whatever toxins fill him, remains a reformer still in some remote part of his soul."

"We pay slightly more on average than the competition," said Austin, "and those girls who excel at Mr. Dettwiler's factory, thanks to his and Mr. Berg's innovations, do a good deal better— a program we hope to put into general usage. Mr. Watson has not let the facts stand in his way for some years now—a trait that is perhaps useful in a defense lawyer but dubious in a social reformer with any pretensions to seriousness." Without shifting his tone of voice, he concluded, "And now, unless anyone objects, I shall place a call to Archibald Ruskin in Atlanta. I know him. Archie is crotchety and fat and a bit abrasive when he does not get his way, but I am told he is the finest defense attorney south of Baltimore and utterly fearless of judge or jury. I have, through indirect channels, asked if he might be available for Mr. Berg's defense. I am told he said that no wiser choice could be made— which I take to be an affirmative sign. To protect the company's position, I propose to call him for the sole purpose of introducing Mr. Klein here, who would be the appropriate party to enlist his participation and discuss fees."

"I've seen him work," said father. "He applies the vitriol a bit lavishly at times but I doubt it's ever cost him a case. He'll do fine."

Archie Ruskin arrived the next day, a top-heavy bear of a man in a homburg that he wore in all weather. Word of his participation in the case had preceded him, and the rail depot was astir with clamoring newsmen and photographers, all of whom the burly lawyer brushed aside with a mahogany cane whose handle, one hawk-eyed reporter noted, was carved in the shape of a judge's gavel. "I argue my cases in court," he said gruffly but with a saving wink upon being invited to make a comment. When the camera boys asked him to pause for a quick shot, he marched faster still into the car in which father and I were awaiting him.

After the briefest of amenities, he asked us, "Did Berg do it?"

Father and I looked at each other. It was a question that seemed at once absurd yet undeniably pregnant. "I doubt it," father said. "Nothing I have known about him the five years he has been in Savannah suggests it."

Ruskin grunted. "And you, young lady—have you formed an opinion?"

"I have not thought hard about it," I said.

"Odd," he said. "And why is that?"

"I have never been very fond of Noah Berg—."

"And his living or dying now is a matter of no interest to you—?"

I must have flushed. "Well, I would scarcely put it so heartlessly."

"Then enlighten me if you will."

"Father knows him far better than I."

"Your father has already given his opinion."

Inside barely a moment, he had demonstrated to me the validity of his reputation. I should have hated to be in the witness chair while he stalked his prey. "I—I have never been convinced of Noah Berg's flawless character," I said. "There is some substance lacking in him—I cannot define it. But I would not suggest for a moment that he could commit premeditated murder."

"How about the unpremeditated garden variety?"

"I—could not say. I should be very much surprised, however—."

He asked to be dropped off at police headquarters for a moment's visit with Chief Weyland Yates, with whom he turned out to have become well acquainted during the Spanish-American conflict. Ruskin preferred us to stay in the car if we did not mind; he came out a few minutes later shaking his head somewhat cryptically. "He's put on a bit of weight" is all that portly sage would say just then, but back at our house, where the council of the previous day—minus Amory Austin—reconvened, he disclosed the purpose of his visit with Chief Yates. "You-all know this splendid community far better than I," he said, "and can perhaps better tell its temper. But I for one would oppose our seeking a change of venue for Mr. Berg's trial."

Father had confided to me that very morning that he felt there was a disturbing mood in the air—he had heard the epithet "degenerate Jew" directed at Noah Berg enough times since the arrest to suspect the linkage of the two words was more than that of proper noun and invidious modifier. Here was racial stereotyping of the most prejudicial sort circulating among all walks of local society. It was not a phenomenon he had encountered before in Savannah, or anywhere in Georgia, for that matter, and if unchecked, he thought, was the likely harbinger of mob justice once the trial began. Only once in my own life—when the De Soto had declined to book us a room for my introduction to polite society (in company with half a dozen other of southern Georgia's most radiant Jewesses)—had I been confronted with a comparable display of bias. But that incident, while it firmed my budding conviction that I must not long remain in a place that could be so mean and narrow toward those who stepped out of their assigned rank, was a mere slap. What father sensed brewing now was a crusade—and crusades require plump infidels to sustain them.

Archie Ruskin had detected the same sort of glandular unrest even way up in Atlanta, for without father's even having to verbalize his concern, the other lawyer at once confronted the first decision the pair of them would have to make. "Everyone in Georgia who can read has read every word about the case already," he said. "Even if you moved the trial to Atlanta, you won't keep the rednecks locked in a closet. They'll come in off o' the fields and out from the hills up there just the same as down this way when the crops're rising in the summer sun and they ain't got nothin' better to do than jab a pitchfork in someone's tail end. They want some critter to hate—they always have—it's one of the few pleasures of their miserable lives. And lookee here now what they got in this Noah Berg—one of them rich carpetbag Jews come down here to steal our bread and mess with out little lily-white girlchildren—why, there's only one way to deal with a *be*-spectacled *de*-generate like that, and us boys all know what that is—." He shook his head. "No, sir, Mr. Adler—you move your case out of Chatham County, about as genteel a corner as there be in all o' Georgia, for fear you can't get your man a fair-minded jury, why, then, you better keep movin' him right on out of the state and head for the Canadian border—."

Father looked out the window saying nothing for a few minutes while we all waited. "The only reason I'd trust this case in the hands of Roland Vickery," he said finally in referring to Chatham County's gift to semi-sober jurisprudence, "is that he's the one shot in all Savannah who's worse than me. The judge once missed a quail drowsing on a stewpot not ten feet away—and claimed humanitarian reasons."

Trial was set at the Savannah courthouse for July 28. It was hoped that Judge Vickery would not, in the interim, turn blood-thirsty toward roosting quail or sitting ducks.

II

That Fourth of July, while excitement mounted over the impending trial and every Jew in Savannah seemed to fill with trepidation that he or she was in the dock no less than Noah Berg, our rabbi, the youngish and devoted proponent of ultra-reform Judaism, Jeremiah Weisz, delivered a most extraordinary sermon. It was addressed to the community at large more than to his own congregants, and although the *Pilot* ran the full text of the sermon, which I have preserved under glass, it is doubtful that more than a handful of Christians read it, and those almost surely of the enlightened sort to begin with. But if Rabbi Weisz's words did not precisely alter the emotional and intellectual climate, they rehabilitated in this inconstant parishioner a joy in the faith that has never left me. No doubt the outcome of the trial and its aftermath contributed greatly to that result as well as the fact that the rabbi drew upon a number of exchanges he and I had had in the preceding weeks as grist for his memorable message.

Father's objection to Rabbi Weisz's more-American-than-thou brand of Judaism seemed to have turned our family into quondam Jews, to judge by the frequency of our attendance at temple. Father and mother carried on a running debate whether the fault lay more with the rabbi or our own fuddy-duddyism. "I don't wish to be assigned to a ghetto," mother would say. "And I don't wish to pretend my forebears arrived on the *Mayflower*," father would say. My brother Eli had been *bar-mitzvah* in a service in which the *Sh'ma* made up about the only prayer spoken in Hebrew and he turned almost entirely from spiritual to corporeal thoughts before the ravages of puberty. And I meanwhile had fallen heavily under the influence of one of the half-dozen globally acclaimed geniuses of Jewish extraction reared in the nineteenth century (my other five candidates being, beyond much dispute, Beaconsfield, Marx, Freud, Proust, and Einstein) and turned into a steadily more bewildered agnostic.

"Papa Franz" Boas, as the Eskimos and Indians he worked among (and we students behind his back) called him, became a naturalized American in his twenty-ninth year, leaving the German academy that resented the unorthodoxy of his methods and the gathering clinical evidence of his opposition to flourishing Teutonic racism. It resented even more his refusal to declare his religious affiliation, which he deemed immaterial to his scientific investigations into tribal customs, among other subjects. His parents had been Jews who renounced their faith and had thereby, Boas later said, "broken through the shackles of dogma." The family retained a certain emotional affection for the Jewish ceremonial, but that could not be permitted to tether his intellectual freedom, which he prized as the highest form of human enterprise. That break with his heritage, he found, was more easily intended than accomplished, for when I first saw him directing anthropological studies in native American Indian languages at Columbia, he bore deep scars on his cheeks that he would say had been inflicted by polar-bear clawings during his field work in Baffin Land, but intimates among his circle knew were dueling wounds inflicted at Kiel and Bonn and Heidelberg in swordplay prompted by anti-semitic slurs.

His early work in anthropometry in America did not endear him much to nativist-racist pseudo-scholars who propounded the natural superiority of the so-called Nordic stock and of whom Theodore Roosevelt's friend Madison Grant (cf. *The Passing of the Great Race*) was the most stylish if not quite the most iniquitous. Boas directed a monumental study that measured some 17,000 American immigrants and their children and found that the younger generation did not necessarily replicate the cranial and other features of their elders when growing up in a different environment. He assailed the view that every people was a more or less exotic culture representing a stage of progression either higher or lower on a single scale favored by the observer. Racial inheritance, moreover, mattered a good deal less in assessing the worth or potential of a human being than such factors as malnutrition, poor hygiene, and low exposure to learning. Environment and not substandard racial stock was the core of pathogenesis. The fashionable racist slogan of the age—"Nurture cannot overcome nature"—was at least beginning to be seen for what it was: a defense mechanism nervously pumped by early-American offspring fearful of the challenge by fresh waves of strangers with odd names, peculiar cadences to their speech, and perhaps differently pigmented skin.

None of this intensifying debate was lost upon our new rabbi, who kept up, much to my pleasure upon discovering it, with the latest literature on the subject. He had digested Dr. Boas's *The Mind of Primitive Man* just a few weeks before I returned from New York that summer of Noah Berg's trial and, learning that I was a disciple of the great professor, invited me to his study to discuss those path-breaking conceptions. Rabbi Weisz had been much depressed by the appearance of Madison Grant's book and any number of other still more blatantly hateful tracts that charged pollution of America's racial stock to the inrushing waves of Eastern European Jewry. Noah Berg was one of the few such specimens to arrive in Savannah during the rabbi's first years in the pulpit, and the two men openly discussed the subject. In New York, the giant portal through which most of the Jewish immigrants came, the great social schism between the established German Jewish and Sephardic community and the disreputable hordes of poor and unwashed masses fleeing the tsardom reduced such exchanges to the level of charity toward desperate and very distant *landsmen*. But between Rabbi Weisz and Noah Berg there grew a bond—the German Jew and the *Litvak*, authenticating by their spirited intercourse the emergent theories of Franz Boas and branding for what it was the hateful offal about biological degeneracy spread by the Madison Grants of their time. Plainly, the Jews were neither debauching America nor turning it into a land of dwarfs. Jews of Polish ancestry grew larger than their parents here—Noah Berg was living evidence of the fact—and so did those of every stock. Nor was there any such thing as a racially pure people anywhere on earth, Dr. Boas had written and Rabbi Weisz noted and Noah Berg was quick to grasp. In every land there were racial overlappings and migrations and gradations. And where a people largely succeeded in driving out disparate elements from their midst, as the Spaniards had done to the Jews and the Moors centuries earlier, the result was genetic stagnation and a precipitous decline in national stamina. America's ethnic variety was her greatest resource, Boas taught, not her gravest peril. Georgia, 99 percent Anglo-Saxon, thought otherwise—when it thought at all.

"No doubt the number of deviants in our nation will grow," Rabbi Weisz declaimed from the pulpit at Mickve Israel on that Friday before Independence Day, "if one chooses to enumerate them in terms of strictly negative divergence from normality. Thus, crime, delinquency, insanity, those on poor relief—all will grow as we continue to receive upon our shores these battered, helpless refugees from foreign parts. It is easy to measure these clear signs of social disease. But this great scientist of ours—this Boas at Columbia—this son of Jews who renounced the faith—he asks: what of the great riches these thousands upon thousands of immigrants will bring to us? What of the geniuses who will spring from their midst? What of the good work and lovingkindness that will be their mark? We have this vastness of a continent to people and to develop, and our standards of excellence and intelligence are steadily on the rise, and our wealth multiplies. These are not the signs of a degenerate people. You cannot measure the overall quality of a people by dwelling only on its most pitiable element, our Boas tells us. There are no humble races, no peoples doomed by heredity in this land of freedom, where honest enterprise rarely goes unrewarded. And that enterprise may be of a commercial sort, the type being pursued with such vigor by our imprisoned Noah Berg—to whom all hearts here go out this day—before his liberty was denied him by public authorities eager to claim solution to a ghastly crime. Or it may be an enterprise of purely mental exertion, the freedom of the mind which our great Boas came to this land to win."

Everything he said pleased me except that palpably sardonic

"our" before he mentioned Boas each time. I could not fathom his purpose until his final remarks reminded me how, in our talks, it galled him that the Boas family had renounced Judaism for its "dogma." "I cannot end this tribute to a great American and a great thinker," said the rabbi from the pulpit, "without a moment's regret at his announced departure from this, our faith. For never in all man's history has a faith been less fiercely addicted to dogma and to doctrine." He stood tall in his place. "I have been called down by some of you—as my predecessor was in his time— for departing too radically from dogma, from doctrine, from ritual —and yet I hold myself no less a Jew than any within earshot. Our rituals blind us. They do not define us. Understanding—of life, of death, of God, of ourselves and the world we inhabit—this is the supreme goal of our faith. And there is no understanding without knowledge, the possession prized above all others by the faithful Jew. And there is no knowledge without inquiry. The faiths of Christ, in their many forms, are by no means altogether opposed to inquiry into these profound subjects, but their very essence is derived from their separate doctrines and dogma, as set down by their founders and disciples, and he who strays from them is marked an unbeliever. In that sense, of course, Jews are unbelievers. They are forever on a quest. Theirs is the free enterprise of the soul—of the human mind—and in misconstruing that interrogative spirit at the core of our faith, Franz Boas and his family denied what Judaism offered to them as its greatest gift: the liberty to ponder all existence and seek their own answers to its mighty puzzle. But, as if to compensate, Boas came to America to carry on that quest by which he validates the beat of each human heart and says that all men are, if not equal, capable of contributing in their fashion to any society that will give them the chance to do so. That is what freedom is about. That is what America is about. That is what Judaism is about."

It was all very stirring—and a rather cheap intellectual trick. Jeremiah Weisz was not the first clergyman to practice distortion to drive home his point. The rabbi, whose otherwise admirable lionization of my mentor pleased me greatly, knew perfectly well that Boas had not spurned Judaism for some other faith offering greater temporal grace or more promising of eternal salvation. It was, rather, that his objectivity as a scientist would have been fatally compromised, he felt, by commitment to a single creed, however much it exalted human reason. For Judaism, no less than other faiths, was honeycombed with rules and canon that had long since lost even their talismanic value—I had once heard there were 623 rituals required of the pious Jew in *Leviticus* and *Deuteronomy* alone—and I asked the rabbi why I, any more than Boas, ought to believe that God had parted the Red Sea out of consideration for the fleeing Hebrews and yet doubt the miracle of the loaves and fishes.

"Because Jesus was not God," said the rabbi. "We have only his disciples' word for that—and they had a vested interest in the claim. The Jew need not believe that God created the universe in seven days or rained on earth for forty or parted the Red Sea. The Jew understands that the Bible deals in parable, that he is being given moral precepts and not literal history. It is not the seven days and nights in which the heavens and the earth were created that are important to the Jew—it is God's immanence. But the Christian cannot cope with such abstractions. He must have certitude. He must have his Jesus, his God in the form of man, and he must believe literally in the miracles of Jesus or he is an infidel, for Jesus without the miracles was merely a gifted rabbi—not the lowest form of mankind, I like to think, but human nonetheless. If God is indwelling, therefore, in all of life, He has no need to shape Himself into a man to teach and test us—."

"Unless He so chose," I said.

"Well," said the rabbi, "I suppose."

"You just do not happen to believe it—and that is your privilege. Boas wanted to be free of the impulse to pass value judgments on this or that belief—to conjecture where objectivity leaves off and subjectivity begins. He cannot be faulted for that. As a Jew, however, you take his position as a personal insult."

"I believe he had motives of convenience as well as conscience," the rabbi said, and that ended our exchange until I heard, to my amazement, that Fourth of July sermon. But when my anger ebbed, I saw the rabbi's larger point and purpose. He had titled his sermon "Free Enterprise" and I was full of admiration for how sinuously he had linked faith and nation. And as I thought more on it, as my father had in his generation, the more characteristic of America did I conceive Judaism to be. Did not the Torah and the Ten Commandments glow with the selfsame high-mindedness and promise of justice as the Declaration of Independence and the Bill of Rights? Were not Jews and Americans in general remarkably akin—proud and pragmatic and disputatious, boisterous yet contemplative, disorderly yet businesslike, self-serving yet generous to a fault? The mingling of these impulses was more than chance; for Jews, America was native soil of the soul.

And then, in that hot summer when not much else was going on, all of Georgia seemed to descend on Savannah and started salivating at the thought of tying a rope around a Jew neck for what had been done to a white flower of Jesus-craving girlhood.

III

That the dead girl might not have been quite so virginal as reflexively described in the press was a possibility that I called to my father's attention as the trial neared.

I had been assigned the task of interviewing as many of the young ladies from the Jubilee factory as were willing to take the afternoon off (with pay) to come to father's office and chat with an unmenacing female not many years their senior. After speaking with two dozen or so of them, I was able to offer up several general findings: First, nobody much liked Noah Berg because he was something of a slavedriver but almost all the girls thought he was fair and very competent at his job. None of them so much as hinted that he might be a womanizer. Second, everybody more or less liked Jean Dugan, although she was not an especially sparkling or warm person. She was neat, polite, and went to church each Sunday—sang in the choir, even. Many of the girls thought she was on the gloomy side, perhaps because of a not very happy home life; there were vague allusions to a hard-drinking stepfather. Then, too, Jean Dugan's good looks and precociously developing body were commented upon by many of her acquaintances, yet she seemed shy about boys and never flirted from the cloakroom window with men passersby as many of the others did for laughs. One girl speculated that Jean may have been molested by her stepfather—perhaps it had been no more than a pawed breast, perhaps something worse. Another girl said she thought she had heard that Jean went out with older men from time to time—and many of them said that Vernon Pike, the fired paymaster who had come from Jean's home county, had paid her a good deal of attention, even during working hours, and that was strictly forbidden under Mr. Berg's code. They thought that, and not his alleged pilfering, might have been the cause of Pike's discharge.

Father and Archie Ruskin clucked over my suspicions and tried to tie them to something concrete. Meanwhile, I was dispatched to spy out the moral purity of the defendant by pretending to commiserate with his wife. I took Naomi Berg to luncheon and dropped by for tea at the Kleins' a few times, all in an apparent effort to cheer her up. And an effort it was, for she was a sadly spiritless and self-pitying creature. She had visited Noah only once at the jail and was mortified by the conditions and the abuse she suffered from the reporters and the onlookers who seemed to have no other business but to loll in the sunshine and curse Noah Berg. "Get the Jew out of Juby!" was the slur that stuck in her mind, and when she was unable to contain her tears upon confronting Noah, he ordered her to stay away until the trial. And she did. I thought it a serious mistake, sure to be seized upon by the press and public as the sign of a loveless wife, thereby lending credence to the charge against him. But she would dwindle into a near-swoon any time I mentioned the prospect of further visits to the jailhouse. Rabbi Weisz had counseled her to stay away, she said, and promised to convey her heartful of love and prayer when he paid his daily visit to the prisoner.

I could extract from her no hint of infidelity on his part or of any perverse proclivities, beyond perhaps an obsession with cleanliness and a compulsive absorption with his work for the company, which left scant time for recreation. He would attend a baseball game one or two times a season, she a sewing or quilting bee, and otherwise they were at home with the Kleins of an evening, reading or playing cards; copulation must have seemed far too ungainly and unsanitary, not to mention audible, an exercise to manage. Their life together thus appeared to be thoroughly devoid of that delight in sensual pleasures—the very physicality of the place and all the warm charms it holds for the eye and ear and nostril and palate—that my father discovered in coming to the South and that has always set it apart from the rest of

America. Noah Berg shunned it, seemed to fear it, preferring to wall himself, ghetto-fashion, into that factory and that shrub-hidden home of his in-laws. No doubt my report on the spotless nature of the Bergs' domestic tranquillity cheered father and Archie Ruskin as much as it fed my contempt for it and determination to seek a far more vigorous style of life in a far less drowsy sort of place.

Reassured of their client's apparent innocence, father and Archie fretted most, as July turned on its heat, about the tactics they could expect from their saber-toothed adversary, the state's solicitor. Vincent Tunney was nearly twenty years younger than father, ambitious as Caesar, and certain that this case would serve as his Rubicon. Dapper was the word for him if one were kindly disposed; slick, if not. He had a head of gleaming black hair pasted close to the scalp, the sort of oiled thatch that the antimacassar had been invented to absorb, and pinpoint eyes that did terrible damage to his quarry in the courtroom. His record for success as a prosecutor was spectacular, enhanced no doubt, said father, by his preference for trying only sure things and making certain they did not slip through his noose. Tunney's zeal in prosecuting Noah Berg—the press ran almost daily reports on his chipper predictions of victory—was therefore all the more puzzling; father and Archie put it down to psychological warfare and the prosecutor's yen for a diadem in Georgia politics. Victory here would catapult him far along toward the statehouse. He was therefore likely to practice little or no restraint in hammering together his case and breathing fire down the necks of Chief Yates, "Doodles" Stone, and the rest of the constabulary to get them to hound down every clue or whiff of one. "We're hoping," said father, "they'll over-reach themselves. Most predators eventually do."

The newspapers were naturally busy trying the case well in advance of the trial. Their consensual wisdom was that the defense would move for a change of venue, possibly to Atlanta, where a more sophisticated and open-minded jury might be enlisted and Archie Ruskin knew the territory inside out. The defense counsel's sole statement that "our client fears no jury" was discounted as a pretrial decoy. Even those Georgia newspapers with a reputation for integrity of a sort disclosed the growing tendency to convict Noah Berg of murder before the first word of testimony was spoken. Some, even while taking pains to advise the public it must not prejudge the case, did just that. The Atlanta *Constitution*, for example, which had six reporters in town to cover the case, wrote in a large, heavily illustrated feature story on the Sunday before the trial opened:

> . . . In the eyes of the law, Berg is an innocent man, as innocent as is the soul of little Jeannie Dugan, and before the law he will remain so until a jury of twelve men shall have heard all the evidence presented and then agreed unanimously that he is guilty.

That it might reach a different conclusion was nowhere suggested.

Archie said the hot weather more than the papers put the rabble in a hanging mood, and he and father considered seeking a postponement of the trial. But that would have left Noah melting in jail all the while and given State Solicitor Tunney yet more time to strengthen his case. And so we drove into Wright Square that Monday morning late in July to find it nearly unpassable with humanity of every sort, like a huge country fair transported to town and milling within a space half as large as it needed to breathe. By noontime, they would be hugging the hot walls of the buildings like lethargic leeches and occupying every blade of grass in the square like an overpopulated colony of ants. The chamber composing the criminal branch of Superior Court was built to hold, at most, a few hundred people. But fifty members of the press corps alone commanded a goodly portion of the space available, and well before court convened at ten o'clock, every seat was taken and the room fringed with standees and the aisles clogged with still others hopeful of spotting a space among the spectator benches. The pressed-tin ceiling of pale green seemed to buckle from the crowd that backed up out the door and down the long stairway to the ground floor and formed a disorderly clot about the courthouse steps, from where it spread out every which way. Four large fans suspended from the courtroom ceiling, plainly inadequate to their assignment, revolved lazily overhead; at best, they stirred a few flies about the muggy upper reaches of the polished-oak chamber; below, the hubbub was steady and the swelter unabating as the day lengthened.

A hush and then a sudden spurt of babble attended the arrival in court of the defendant, who had not been seen in public for the better part of three months. Noah glanced quickly around the thronged hall, unable to take in with a single sweep that the searching eyes and faces straining to catch his expression had been summoned there by something short of brotherly love. If there was compassion in that room, I could not detect it; if there was contrition in the accused, the crowd could not find it. A nervous little smile came over his face. His eyes were partly obscured behind the thick, slightly darkened glasses he wore but his appearance was otherwise pleasing enough. He was slim and clean-shaven, with smallish and rather even features—nicer-looking than I had recalled him and apparently none too haggard from having remained prison-bound for so long. It was said in the papers that he was a pampered prisoner, who had been given a large, private cell and because of his family and employer, would be the beneficiary of a well-financed defense. Father had been obliged to issue a statement thoroughly dissociating his participation in the defense from his duties as general counsel to the corporation, from which he had taken temporary leave. But in the public mind, Noah and father were linked as Jews, I suspect; the company, for its part, referred all inquiries made of it in connection with the case to Archie Ruskin, a *bona fide* Gentile. Both father and Archie offered firm handshakes and good wishes to Noah as they met in court and made reassuring sounds to Naomi and to Noah's mother Sophie, who had come South to be with her son during his ordeal. The family had been allowed to breakfast together in an anteroom.

"Too many people in here," Archie murmured to father, who nodded and sought out the sheriff to urge that the aisles be cleared and the standees evacuated. The sheriff told him that the latter process would probably require the introduction of the state militia, father said that would not be a great peril to the public safety and might in fact prove salutary. The sheriff snorted and then attended to the unglutting of the aisles.

And so the trial began with a courtroom bursting its capacity and a steady hum from the massed legions of the curious down on the streets seeping in through the windows. All rose with the appearance of the honorable Judge Roland Vickery, white-maned and a trifle wall-eyed—an ex-railroad lawyer and Democratic Party operative-in-good-standing who, according to father, was a cut and a half above the average pillar of the Southern judiciary. That he had once been heard over highballs at the Yamacraw Club to refer to Noah Berg's father-in-law as "that clothing-goods kike" was perhaps mere rumor, and father himself had established a cordial if not ardent acquaintance with his honor. "He has read some law," father told Archie, "but not a burdensome amount. He tends to leniency in what goes into the record—except when he does not. Consistency is not a Vickery hallmark. But then he rarely naps when court is in session, so there is generally a modicum of control over events—."

To the apparent surprise of the press, the defense moved for neither a postponement nor a change of venue, and the jury selection process began at once. Father and Archie had settled beforehand on their ideal juror, a man in his middle to younger years, with as much education as possible, who worked at a white-collar job, had no blood in his eye, and did not believe all Jews should pay penance till kingdom come for not embracing Christ. The first man summoned was a building contractor aged forty-three who had lived nearly all his life in Savannah and the vicinity. Solicitor Tunney, whose voice had the same fluidity as his unctuous tonsure, put a few routine questions to the man and then asked if he had any scruples against sending a fellow human being to the gallows for the crime of murder. "No, sir," said the contractor, "if that's what's comin' to him."

Archie Ruskin moved in for the defense. His largeness was awesome. But he did not bluster. He saved that weight and force of being for critical moments. With the prospective juror he was more offhand, even, than Tunney, chatting about the contracting business in general and confessing concern that the fellow's enterprise might suffer if the trial dragged on too long. "We orators tend to get a little windy at times," he said, and the man smiled and said his business affairs were well in hand. "You a churchgoer?" Archie asked, tossing the question over his shoulder as if it were of no grave concern. The man said he was. "Pretty dedicated about it, are you?" The man said he didn't get Archie's drift. "Go every week, do you?" Archie asked. The man paused a moment. "Well," he said, "I miss a Sunday now and then. The missus don't like it, but we work long hours sometimes, including all day Saturday—not half a day like some—so, you know, a man'll take his slumber on the Lord's day every once and again." Archie said he guessed the Lord understood that, and the man said he hoped so. Both sides accepted him.

The whole process, in fact, was accomplished with surprising speed. The defense used up just three of its allotted twenty challenges, and the state just one of its quota of ten—excusing a high-school history teacher whom father very much wanted on the panel. The approved twelve good men and true were composed of, besides the contractor: the head salesman for the southern Georgia region of a buggy company, a real-estate agent, a shipping clerk, a pressman at a print shop, a postal carrier, an optician, an agent for an electrical manufacturer, a bank teller, a claim agent for the Georgia Central Railroad, a cashier at a hardware company, and a farmer who worked yams and peanuts besides cotton and said he read the newspaper every day and the Bible Sundays only. "The good book don't change none," he explained. "It just gets better and better—which is more'n I can say for the papers." Twelve men: the oldest forty-six (the railroad claim agent), the youngest twenty-three (the bank teller), the average thirty-three. All were married, save the hardware-store cashier, who volunteered that he had prospects after Archie had commended him on his emancipated state. All, of course, were white; none, of course, was a Jew. I wished there were a woman in the lot. I wished men would admit women to the human race before I died.

The jury impaneled, father moved at once to have the court honor the defense's *duces tecum*, requiring the solicitor to hand over all statements and affidavits made by Mo Easter, the negro floorsweep at the factory whose alleged confession to the police as an accomplice after the fact was the incriminating keystone to the state's entire case against Noah. Cavaretta, the Pinkerton, while apparently rendering more devoted service to the police than the corporation that hired him, had confided to father and Archie that the black man had been given a great deal of time and attention, if not kicks in the testicles, in the interrogation chambers at police headquarters and his story kept changing accordingly. "He must have finally understood what they wanted," Cavaretta surmised, "and given it to them." The court granted father's motion. He gave me a wink. I thought things were off on the right track.

At recess shortly after noon, the sidewalk crowd constricted unwillingly as we made our way through it to the car for a quick bite of lunch at home. By human wireless, word circulated out of doors of every development within the courtroom. Each exiting seat-holder was buttonholed for information, and each new nugget passed quickly out in ripples to the perimeter of the throng. The people were not so much festive or unruly as they were expectant. Any news was welcome and busily chewed over. And amid the chewing, tobacco juice flew every which way. One unsightly quid caught the hem of my dress, turning me into a quick-change artist at home and prompting the suggestion that our party, not likely to prove the people's choice, enter and leave the courthouse from then on by a little-used rear door.

At two-fifteen on the torpid afternoon of July 28, court reconvened and the state called its first witness, Josephine Dugan, the mother of the murdered girl.

IV

I have the yellowed and flaking newspaper reports of the trial before me now, and they crumble at too harsh a touch, but it is all down in black and white—exhaustive accounts of the courtroom proceedings with extensive segments of the verbatim testimony filling column upon column of every journal of any size in the state. I kept a careful sampling of the clippings on a day-to-day basis along with my personal notes. Even now, though, at a distance of thirty-two years, I can summon up without such documentary aids the pain and anguish of that pudgy woman as she took the stand in her black mourning dress and black hat and laboriously pulled back the heavy veil that kept her grief from the world. It was written upon her every expression and carried with every word she uttered.

The state solicitor was at his most solicitous. He put the mandatory questions to the woman in a voice lubricated with official sympathy. She answered but so softly at times that the whole room seemed to lean forward and cup its collective ear. What surprised me was the refinement of her voice; it had none of the coarseness I had assumed would characterize the speech of families that sent their daughters, at the first bloom of womanliness, to toil in factories.

Q. And how old was your daughter, Mrs. Dugan?

A. She was—nearly fourteen. Her birthday would have been June the first.

Q. So Jean was just thirteen—?

A. She looked older, though, the way she'd sprouted that last year. She was tall for her age, taller than I am by several inches, and well developed. Folks took her for sixteen, seventeen. I'd forget myself sometimes, looking at her—.

She fought back the tears. I glanced over at Noah Berg, flanked by his wife and mother. He could manage no more than a sideways glance at the witness.

Q. And was she a good girl, Mrs. Dugan?

A. Oh, very good.

Q. Could you tell us what Jean did that morning—that last morning?

A. It was a holiday, so she slept late. Normal Saturdays she'd be up at seven for the eight-to-twelve shift at the factory. That day she didn't get up till eleven or so. I called her Lazy Bones when she came in the parlor and helped me finish the dusting.

Q. Did she have something to eat?

A. Yes, at about half past eleven. She ate some cabbage and some bread. She always liked the way I fixed cabbage. We would joke that that was what had made her grow so—.

Q. Did she eat anything else?

A. No, sir—nothing I know of, except a little bread and water.

Q. What else did she do that morning?

A. Just primp and dress. She told me she was going to the factory to get her pay—Friday was normal payday but she'd been out the two days previous on account of it being her female time of the month and she got paid time-off. And then she was going to watch the Memorial parade and make the final payment on the dress—she still owed fifty cents—if the store was open, and a few other small errands.

Q. What time did she leave your home, Mrs. Dugan?

A. A few minutes before noon.

Q. Could you tell us what Miss Jeannie was wearing that morning when she left home for the last time?

A. Yes, It was her new daffodil frock—she'd just got it the day before. She'd saved up for it, and I'd helped out with the price—and a bonnet with a white ribbon—.

Her voice caught and cracked. A moment later, an aide from the solicitor's office spread out on the floor between the jury and witness boxes the clothes in which the girl was found dead. There were rusty smudges of what everyone in the room understood to be dried blood on the right shoulder and sleeve. Mrs. Dugan had been covering her eyes with her hand from the rays of the sun which strafed cruelly across the witness stand for a few minutes at that time of day and were unblocked by any window shade. When she removed her shielding hand and saw what was on display before her, all the woman's restraints gave way to a great shudder and then a burst of tears that held us all breathless. Finally the solicitor asked the obligatory question, and Mrs. Dugan indicated by a renewed sob and dropping of her jaw that those were indeed the garments her daughter had worn the last day of her life.

Archie Ruskin respectfully recommended that court recess for five minutes—a gesture of decency all sides honored. Mrs. Dugan seemed to have regained her composure sufficiently in the interim for Archie, ever so delicately, to go about his business. That little Jeannie, in her daffodil finery, might have been a bit of a hoyden or perhaps a fledgling strumpet could scarcely have been suggested in that courtroom without souring the jury at once upon the defense's efforts. Only the merest of hints could be dropped.

"Why," Archie began his cross-examination, "did a pretty and refined young lady like Miss Jean perform common labor at the soda factory starting in her twelfth year, Mrs. Dugan?"

A. Why—for the wages, of course. We kept a decent home, but we was never—were never well-off people.

Q. Did not Jean's father provide well enough for your family?

A. Well, Mr. Dugan—first off, Mr. Dugan was not Jean's father. That poor man died some years ago when we lived in the country, up Macon way. I married Mr. Dugan four years back. To please him, I had her take his name.

Q. Was he a drinking man, Mrs. Dugan?

A. I don't know what you mean.

Q. Was he given to drinking alcoholic beverages?

SOLICITOR TUNNEY: Immaterial, your honor.

MR. RUSKIN: I believe I can show materiality, your honor.

THE COURT: Well, try it for a moment. [To the witness:] You may answer the question, Mrs. Dugan.

A. Now and then he takes a drink—yes.

Q. Isn't it more than now and then? And hasn't that eaten up your family's earnings, requiring your daughter to toil at an early age—?

A. He's been curbing it. It's not like you say—.

SOLICITOR TUNNEY: Objection! The murdered child's stepfather is not on trial here—.

THE COURT: Sustained.

But Archie had made his point. He waited a moment for the buzzing in the room to cease under the judge's gavel.

Q. How did you feel about Miss Jean's going out to work at a tender age?

A. Not happy. But it was necessary, and she was able and willing—.

Q. Were you particular about the sort of job she took?

A. Oh, yes. I wanted her to be with a nice class of girls and not in any sweatshop.

Q. Then you thought the Jubilee factory a decent sort of workplace?

A. Well, yes. We had heard something about it from Mr. Dettwiler, the manager. He lived up the street a ways, and we went to the same church. I asked him about a job for Jeannie and he said for her to come by. He said they paid according to skill and were strict about certain things—.

Q. What kinds of things?

A. Oh, like cleanliness. That meant something to me.

Q. And when she got there, did Miss Jean have complaints about the work or the factory?

A. Just that they were strict and worked her hard. But they gave her one advance in salary after a time and seemed to show an interest in her progress. She liked that.

Q. Did she ever complain about any of the men who worked at the factory being too familiar with her?

A. No.

The solicitor seemed displeased that Archie had done so well. He chose to re-examine.

Q. Mrs. Dugan, did your daughter and husband get along?

A. Pretty well. She was at that age when children are apt to be a little headstrong, so they would have words now and again.

Q. Were they real spats—with real anger?

A. Oh, no, sir. Mr. Dugan wouldn't have permitted that. He'd just call her down for showing a bit of sass, now that she was a working girl and a provider and growing so big—.

Q. Yours was not an angry household, was it, Mrs. Dugan?

A. No, sir.

Q. Did Miss Jeannie ever say anything to you about the superintendent at the factory—one way or the other?

A. Only that he was very hard-working and kept after the girls not to dawdle or gossip when they were

supposed to be working. And once or twice he had
stopped by her chair and watched her work—and
that had made her a little nervous, his examining her
that way—.

SOLICITOR TUNNEY: Thank you, Mrs. Dugan.

The poor woman was about to leave the stand when father rose
up slowly to indicate there would be a re-cross-examination. A
low, disapproving murmur swept the room: the witness had had
enough for one day. I felt my stomach contract as father advanced upon the woman in black.

Q. I'll detain you only another moment, madam.

A. Thank you.

Q. When your daughter failed to return home later that
same afternoon, were you alarmed?

A. No. She was a big girl. I guessed she must have had a
good reason. Perhaps she had met a friend and they
had gone to a show—.

Q. Was she in the habit of doing that?

A. Once in a great while. We have no phone, so it was
difficult for her to get a message home.

Q. What sort of friend did she join on these occasions?

SOLICITOR TUNNEY: Objection. Immaterial—.

THE COURT: We'll hear that.

A. I don't really know. Girl friends from the factory, I
suppose—.

Q. Might they have been boy friends?

SOLICITOR TUNNEY: Objection.

A. Not that I know of—.

SOLICITOR TUNNEY: Will the court kindly instruct
the witness not to answer when the state has objected to a question.

THE WITNESS: I'm very sorry.

THE COURT: Objection sustained.

Q. As the evening wore on and your daughter did not
come home, were you not increasingly alarmed?

A. Not overly. As I remember, I fell asleep early that
evening—about nine or so. Mr. Dugan had been

bed-ridden all day and I was a bit tuckered from nursing him.

Q. So it was not all that extraordinary for your daughter to be out on her own on a Saturday night without your knowing her whereabouts?

A. It was unusual, yes, sir—but she always had a good reason, so I dropped off that night not fretting overly. I trusted her.

Father had walked the tightrope. He did not sully the dead girl's honor; he merely fertilized the suspicion that she might have known a bit more of life's seamier side than her mother imagined or, at any rate, would admit.

A streetcar ticket-taker on the Avon Avenue line took the stand and testified that Jean Dugan had come aboard his run that Saturday morning at a few minutes to noon—the schedule never varied by more than a minute or two, and he remembered her gay yellow dress and cheery greeting. He was followed to the stand by a twelve-year-old newsboy who testified that he had known Jean Dugan from the neighborhood for several years, had boarded the streetcar at mid-day and shared the seat with her on the fatal Saturday, and watched her get off a few minutes past noon at the stop nearest the factory where she worked. She promised to try to find him later in the crowd near a well-known pharmacy, where he planned to hawk his papers to the parade-watchers. "Only she never came," the lad said.

The state next brought on Sanford Phelps, the police detective who headed up the team of three officers and a newspaper reporter who responded to the telephone call from Plato Layne, then working as the night watchman at the factory, saying that he had found a body in the cellar and it looked quite thoroughly dead. They arrived at about three-twenty that Sunday morning, said Sergeant Phelps, and found the girl face down at the edge of the coal bin at the end of the cellar farthest from the elevator.

"There was some blood on the back of her head," he recounted, "and it was dry and matted on the outside but moist near the skull where I placed my hand." A chill ran through me as he spoke in his flat, clinical way. "A wire hanger had been unbraided and tied tightly around her neck, apparently to choke her. It had cut deeply into the flesh. I turned the body over and brushed coal dust and dirt from the floor off her face and saw that it was a white girl. She had a bruised eye and many scratches on her face. The body was cold and rigid. The hands were folded across the breast. In one of them I saw a crumpled piece of notepaper. I removed it carefully and read it aloud. It said in pencil, 'Big old negro did this.' The night watchman said, 'They can't mean me, boss', and got very upset."

Q. Did you assume the killing had occurred in that spot?

A. There were tracks across the earth floor indicating the body may have been dragged quite a distance.

Q. How far did the tracks go?

A. It was a little hard to tell since a number of us had to walk over the same route, but it looked as if they began at the bottom of the elevator shaft at the other end.

Q. And how far was that?

A. About one hundred and fifty feet.

Archie looked a mite miffed as he took over. He began by asking the policeman how he had reached the basement.

A. Down a ladder leading from a trap-door on the first floor—it's behind the staircase.

Q. Is there any other way down to the cellar besides the trap-door and the elevator?

A. None that I know of.

Q. Since you made it down the ladder, couldn't the dead girl's body have been lowered the same way?

A. I doubt it. It's a tight squeeze for a normal-sized man. You couldn't very well carry a body down through that opening.

Q. But you could drop it through, probably, couldn't you?

A. I suppose so.

Q. Of course the deceased might have climbed down the ladder under her own power and been killed in the basement?

A. I suppose so. But the tracks I found and the dirt on the girl's face made me believe she had been dragged across the floor, so I would think she was dead before her body reached the basement.

Q. But that is merely conjecture on your part, is it not?

A. Well—I suppose so.

Q. Now about those tracks, or partial tracks, you say you saw—you told us something this afternoon different from what you told the coroner's jury shortly after the crime. I am quoting from your testimony before that panel. "I could not tell exactly where the tracks began—there were marks in the surface running to the elevator shaft but they could have been made by almost anything."

A. Yes—well, that's true. But I think they were made by the girl's body. The tracks looked similar.

Q. Then you have changed your mind in the interim?

A. I have thought more about it.

Q. Could the tracks have in fact begun at the base of the ladder—under the trap-door?

A. That's possible. But it is not my impression.

Q. Did you find any items belonging to the girl in that basement?

A. Her hat was near the body.

Q. Anything else?

A. One of her slippers—it was in the middle of the cellar, a little off to one side.

Q. Not far from the foot of the ladder, isn't that so?

A. Yes, that's right. It must have fallen off while she was being dragged across the floor.

Q. Or it might have come off if her body had been dropped through the trap-door?

A. I suppose it might have.

The embalmer from the funeral home to which the corpse was shortly removed added a few ghastly details. The coagulated state of the girl's blood, when he first began removing it at about four o'clock Sunday morning, led him to place the time of death at ten to fifteen hours earlier—some time during the previous afternoon.

Her body yielded about a gallon of blood, he said, which was replaced with embalming fluid. There was blood on her undergarments, he added, and a hose supporter had been ripped loose from her corset. The strong possibility of sexual assault was thus introduced. The ladies in the room, who comprised more than half the spectators, murmured heavily as the embalmer left the stand.

The county coroner, a Dr. Mayhew, who lacked only tusks in his close resemblance to the walrus, described the gore with medical precision. The crowd that had come in quest of the messy details hung on his testimony. He had examined the slain girl at the undertaking establishment at about nine o'clock Sunday morning. "There was a scalp wound on the left side of the head toward the rear that was about two and a half inches long," he said. "It had penetrated the skin and left a small part of the skull exposed. The right eye was black and contused. There were minor scratches on the cheek and a slight contusion on the forehead, but the skin was not broken there. The tongue protruded about two inches from the mouth. A wire hanger was still around her neck and so deeply did it dig into the skin that it seemed apparent that death was due to strangulation. The congested blood in the face and hands also supported that conclusion, as did the protruding tongue."

Q. Is it possible that death had been caused by the head wound?

A. That seems out of the question. It was not severe enough to produce even noticeable pressure. It seems to have been made by some sort of hard instrument —jagged yet not overly sharp—perhaps by a protrusion of some sort. The blow appears to have been delivered from below upward.

Q. Would it have been sufficient to produce unconsciousness?

A. More than likely.

Q. You say the right eye was blackened?

A. Black and blue—contused—but the skin not broken.

Q. Does that indicate that it was done before or after death?

A. Before, certainly, or it would not have become contused.

Q. What sort of an instrument could have caused that
effect?

A. A soft instrument.

Q. A human fist, for example?

A. Yes, quite possibly.

Q. Might a blow with a fist, driving the girl against a
protruding metal object—a coat hook, for example,
or something of that sort—have produced these bodily signs?

A. Very possibly.

Q. Were there other bruises or scratches about the face?

A. Yes, a good many of both—around and above the
cheeks and on the forehead.

Q. Is it your opinion these were inflicted before or after
the death?

A. Some time after. I did not see any blood, sir, that
went through the dermis.

Q. Were there wounds elsewhere on the body?

A. Yes, sir. There was a wound on the left leg, about
two inches above the knee. There was a similar contusion on the right leg, but slightly higher.

Q. Did you examine the female organs, sir, to determine
whether violence had been done to them?

A. Yes, sir.

Q. And what conclusion did you reach?

A. It is possible that the girl had been sexually violated.

Q. What evidence did you find to that effect?

A. The epithelium was detached from the vaginal walls.
The blood vessels in the vicinity were congested.
There was no sign of the hymen—.

Every palm-leaf fan in the courtroom seemed to be fluttering
frantically in front of the female spectators, as if they wished to
hide their faces from but not close their ears to the sordid minu-
tiae of the crime. Father, having consulted at length with Uncle
Benny ahead of time, cross-examined the coroner without flinch-
ing from the explicitly sexual aspects of the testimony.

Q. Dr. Mayhew, did you find any evidence of spermatozoa in the vagina or uterus of the deceased?

A. I did not.

Q. That, and that alone, would have been conclusive evidence of sexual assault, is that not correct, sir?

A. Yes, sir, but its absence does not signify that no attack occurred. The law does not require ejaculation by the male intruder to qualify the incident as rape.

Q. Would you briefly describe the clinical procedures you used in examining the female organs of the deceased?

A. I observed them externally. Then I performed a digital examination to determine if the hymen was intact or if I could find other evidence of assault. Finally, I thought it best to remove the organs from the body for dissection and microscopic examination for semen.

Q. Let us, sir, take these possible indicators of sexual assault one at a time. Does the absence of the hymen tell us when—or if—the young woman had performed intercourse?

A. No, sir. It could have happened well before the time of her death. Or been broken by other than sexual contact.

Q. Isn't it likely that some membranes or remnant of the hymen would have still been present when you examined the body if she had been violated for the first time on that day?

A. Not necessarily. Their presence, I'll grant you, would tend to suggest a virginal woman till that time.

Q. As to the congested blood vessels in the female organs, might death by strangulation also have caused a dilation of the vessels in that area?

A. Well—that is possible.

Q. And would not the fact that the girl's menstrual period had just ended or was about to end also help explain any engorged vascular condition in and around the uterus?

A. Probably—if the girl had in fact just had her period.

It was impossible to determine that. If it had ended, say, a day earlier, the vessels would have about returned to normal.

Q. But that is another mitigating factor you cannot be certain of?

A. Not certain, no.

Q. And the fact that the epithelium had been detached from the uterine walls—might that not have been accounted for by the digital examination you yourself made?

A. That is dubious, sir. I am a man of science, not a butcher.

Q. I do not suggest the latter, sir. I ask only if it is not entirely possible that such an examination, conducted after death, could have caused that detachment, no matter how delicately the process was undertaken.

A. Many things are possible, sir, but highly unlikely.

Q. Is it possible, sir—if you will address yourself to that question and not take it as a slur on your great gifts, since none is intended—?

A. Yes, it is possible.

Court adjourned at 4:53, I wrote in my notebook, adding, "Not a bad start, all in all. In that room I am in love with father and Archie about equally."

At home that night, I suggested that our side held its own very well, even during that formative stage of the trial. Father saw the first day's proceedings as scant cause for celebration. "A stand-off is not good enough," he said. "It won't do to match the state point for point, as if this were a schoolboy debate. The presumption in those jurors' minds is that Noah Berg murdered that girl—or else why would we all be in there, perspiring profusely instead of going off fishing somewhere?" I said that I had thought an accused criminal was innocent until proven guilty. "In the first place," said father, taking a glass of sherry, "that is hooey. The state has set its sight upon this target. It is never an equal contest. Grand rhetoric, that, but it does not change the fact that we must paddle upstream. If we merely hold our own against it, we are not progressing, because we will tire before the stream does. In the second place, the accused is a Jew—and not a terribly genial one. In the third place, there is a mob out there, and their presence infiltrates the courtroom. It is hard for justice to prevail under such circumstances."

I thought he had perhaps overstated the matter. Then around midnight, someone hurled an empty bottle of Jubilee through the fan window above the front door of our home. It made a frightful mess.

V

Plato Layne was not only a particular negro to my father—the colored man he had met first and known the longest during his years in Savannah—but also the universal one. Plato had been young and strong and willing during the early years father knew him, and the possessor of a demonstrable intelligence and certain cunning. But time had ground all that off, time and fate and enmity, and when he took the stand as the state's first witness on the second day of the trial of Noah Berg, Plato was a humpbacked, bleary-eyed, lardish old man with a gimp. He had never, so far as father knew, performed a mean or unkind act in his life. Victim of a social process that had gone on essentially unchanged for a dozen generations, he stood there in court swearing to tell the whole truth while no doubt calculating the fat lot of good that practice had ever earned him.

Because the police had arrested and held him for several days as a prime suspect, Plato could be expected to cooperate fully with the state solicitor, father had predicted, out of gratitude that they had stopped mauling him and decided to pin the crime on someone else. Father was not wrong. Plato testified that although Noah Berg had told him the previous day to report to work at four in the afternoon on Saturday on account of the holiday, the door was locked when he arrived to begin his watch and the superintendent seemed surprised at his arrival. "He say he was sorry he had tole me to come in so early. He say he had got behind in his work so I could go off and have a good time till six, it bein' a holiday an' all," the black man said. But all he wanted to do, Plato went on, was to curl up somewhere on the premises and nap because a friend had come by his room at two o'clock and roused him to go watch the parade and have a holiday drink. "Mr. Berg, though, he seemed to want me away from the factory till later—." Archie objected promptly, but the damage was done.

When he returned to the factory just before six, the black watchman continued, the front door was still locked, but this time the superintendent was far more agreeable upon opening it. "He say he sure glad I come back then 'cause he was fixin' to leave," said Plato, "an' he went up to fetch his things." While Berg was collecting himself, his former assistant, Vernon Pike, appeared at the factory door with a valise in hand, explained to Plato that he was leaving town on the night train to look for work in Macon, and asked if he might look around the place for a pair of work shoes he said he had left behind. "I weren't s'posed to let no one in," Plato recounted, "but Mr. Berg, he come along just then, all ready to leave, an' when he look up and see who's dere wif me, he gives a kinder jump of surprise." Pike promptly stated his business, and Berg said he thought the floorsweep had thrown out a pair of boots a little while back, but Pike said he would just as soon look around for them if the superintendent had no objections. Flashing Plato a look that the negro said he understood to mean he ought to keep a close eye on the tall intruder, Berg went home.

Q. What did Mr. Pike do then?
A. He go off to the coatroom and get his boots. He couldn't have stayed but five minutes all together.
Q. Did Mr. Berg call you that night?
A. Yes, sir, he call me maybe seven o'clock. He axe if everythin' is all right and if Mr. Pike was gone. I tole him yes, and that was all he wanted.
Q. Had he ever called you before at the factory—on any previous evening?
A. No, sir.

Things were quiet after that until a little past three, just after he had made his half-hourly punch on the time clock on the second floor. It was then, Plato said, that he heard a noise in the cellar—"kinder like someone messin' with the coal chute." The watchman headed at once for the cellar, squeezed through the trap-door on the ground floor, and found the body. "I got up the ladder fast as I knows how," he said, "and called the police. They come fast."

Q. Had you been down to the cellar before that during the evening? Wasn't that part of your rounds?

A. Yes, sir—only Mr. Berg tole me never to get too close to the coal-bin area wif my lantern. So mostly I just climbed down the ladder, and peer around to see if there was any fire happenin' down there.

Q. Did you have anything at all to do with that girl's death, Plato—on your oath on the Bible?

A. No, sir, I did not. I swear to heaven!

Q. Had you ever seen the girl before?

A. I didn't even know for sure it was no girl till the police made me go back down to the cellar wif them when they come to investigate. I never seen that chile before then.

Next morning, when the police brought him back to confront Noah Berg and the plant manager, Joe Dettwiler, Plato said he watched them check over his time slip and pronounce it all in order. "They say I couldn't have nothin' to do wif de killin'," he said and added that he was dumbstruck the following day when the police searched his rooming house and found a bloody shirt of his in the midst of a pile of soiled linen. "I told 'em it must be like wif de note—whoever wrote that must have took the shirt from my room and got it bloody and stuck it back—it ain't no hard trick to sneak through my window on de groun' floor rear 'cause de lock's so flimsy I sometimes forgets to bolt it tight."

Q. On Tuesday, I believe, the police brought Mr. Berg in to meet with you in private at the jail, is that right?

A. Yes, sir.

Q. Can you tell us what was said during that conversation?

A. Well, they put me in a room by myself, handcuffed to a chair. Then they bring in Mr. Berg. He looked at me and sort of dropped his head. He said, "I

don't think you did do it, Plato—I know you is
honest and hired you on the recommendation of
Mr. Adler, who is a very fine gentleman. But I think
maybe you know something more than you are lettin' on." I said no-sir. I didn't know a thing but what
I have tole the police. I only discover the body. He
say, "Yes, and you keep that up and we'll both go to
hell." I say what does he mean, and he say the police
was starting to investigate him, too. Well, I didn't
say nothin' to that, so we just sat quiet for a minute
or two till they come and fetched him away.

I believed every word he said. There seemed a goodness about
that large, sad, black face. That he should be framed for the girl's
death was entirely consistent with the hand fate had dealt him:
his whole life had been a frame-up.

Having known him, father thought it best that he take Plato
through the cross-examination. It was a tender grilling.

Q. Now, Plato, you say that the door was locked when
   you got to the factory that Saturday.
A. Yes, sir.
Q. Did you also work Sunday evenings, generally, as the
   night watchman?
A. Yes, sir—the two Sundays before that.
Q. And was the door locked when you arrived on those
   Sundays?
A. Yes, sir. I lock it myself and took the key home wif
   me Sunday morning so as to let myself back in Sun-
   day night.
Q. In other words, the factory was locked up on Sunday
   because Sunday is a holiday.
A. Yes, sir.
Q. But Saturday was also a holiday that week, wasn't it?
A. Well—yes, sir.
Q. Wouldn't you think it natural for Mr. Berg if he
   were the only one working in the place then, to lock
   up that Saturday afternoon, it being a holiday?
A. Well, now—I don't remember thinkin' that.
Q. Suppose you start now?

287

A. Well—that could be what he done.

Q. Now, then, you said that Mr. Berg wanted you to go off and have a good time for the next couple of hours when all you really wanted to do was curl up and have a nap in some quiet corner of the factory till you were ready to go on duty.

A. Yes, sir, Mr. Adler, that's about it.

Q. Did you tell Mr. Berg you wanted to do that—to have a nap right there?

A. Well—I don't exactly recall sayin' that. I was mostly thinkin' that. Mr. Berg, he'd probably figure I'd punch in and go take my nap, and he'd have to pay me overtime for doing nothin'—I guess that's what I thought he'd think.

Q. But you didn't ask him and he didn't tell you no, you couldn't nap there at the factory?

A. No, not in them words.

Father then got Plato to acknowledge that he had gone to punch in on the time clock outside the superintendent's office while Vernon Pike was still in the building on his errand.

A. Yes, sir. I tole him I be right back.

Q. And when you came back down, did you go with Mr. Pike to the coatroom to look for his shoes?

A. Well, no, sir, he already been. See, the coatroom is just inside the main workroom there on the first floor. He went and got his things while I was punchin' in.

Q. How do you know he got them?

A. He tole me. He sorter give his carrying bag a pat and say they just fit in and he was lucky they was still there and nobody done walked off wif 'em—or in 'em.

Q. So then you didn't actually see Mr. Pike's shoes?

A. Well—I don't rightly recall seein' them. It was just the way he patted that bag o' his.

Q. Isn't it true, Plato, that you don't really know what Mr. Pike did in your absence—and that you only think he did what he told you he did?

A. I guess I couldn't be sure, seein' I wasn't there.

Q. Now you say you went down to the cellar every hour to look for fire?

A. Yes, sir.

Q. But didn't Mr. Berg instruct you to go down there every half hour—not just every hour?

A. Well, yes, sir—that's true. But that's a mighty small hole to scuttle down and a hard ladder to climb back up. I kinder opened the trap-door on the half hour and gave a big sniff for any smoke.

Q. When Mr. Berg walked you around the factory the first time, didn't he take you pretty far toward each end of the basement, and didn't he explain he wanted you to have a good look but not come too close to the coal bin at the north end?

A. Well—yes, sir, he done that.

Q. Wasn't there a light down in that basement that they left burning all the time?

A. A real little one. You couldn' hardly see nothin' by it, though, excep' it were right nearby. I tole the police after it look t' me like de light was even lower than usual that night, as if maybe someone didn' want me to see nothin' down there.

Q. Now, Plato, can you tell us one more thing? Did you see what Mr. Berg did with your time slip when he finished reading it on Sunday morning?

A. He handed it to somebody—I can't rightly recall who. I figure they was goin' to keep it to show I wairn't the killer.

Q. The next day, however, your card seemed to show some skips when Mr. Berg and the police examined it again.

A. That's what they said. I couldn't figure how that could be, if it was fine when they first seen it.

Q. Did you tell the police that you thought the time slip that seemed to involve you in the crime was just like the note in the dead girl's hand and the bloody shirt?

A. That's what I tole them. I say someone else must be tryin' to lay it off on me.

The state solicitor now began to establish his direct case against Noah Berg. Tunney put on Detective Joseph Reilly, popularly known in town as "Running Board" Reilly for his swashbuckling manner of arrival at the scene of a crime. He banged the first nails into Noah's coffin.

Reilly, a member of the police party that responded to Plato's summons, recounted how he had telephoned the superintendent at about six o'clock in the morning and told him he would have to come directly to the factory, where there was a problem that needed his attention. "He said he hadn't had breakfast yet," Reilly testified. "I said I was afraid that would have to wait and that I would be coming to pick him up in a police car in a few minutes. He asked if the night watchman was there, and I said yes."

Q. Did you tell him what had happened at the factory?
A. No—and he didn't ask.
Q. Why didn't you tell him?
A. Standard procedure. We often obtain important clues or accidental admissions from suspects who have not been told the nature of the crime—or incriminating statements of one kind or another.
Q. Can you describe Mr. Berg's manner when you arrived at his residence?
A. Yes, he seemed exceedingly nervous. He talked in the tones of a refined lady but rapidly and was rubbing his hands a great deal. He put a lot of questions to me in quick succession, but I said he would see everything for himself. His excitement was evident. His hands began to tremble, and he had trouble putting on his tie and collar. He must have asked for a minute to have a cup of coffee two or three times. His voice became kind of wobbly.
Q. What was said in the car ride to the factory?
A. Well, before I had gone to get Mr. Berg, Chief Detective Stone had telephoned Mr. Dettwiler, the factory manager—they're old friends—and asked him to come to the undertaker's parlor to see if he could identify the girl. Mr. Dettwiler agreed, and he told

us right away who she was and that he had known the girl and her family from church. He cried when he saw her. He said she was a nice girl and he had helped get her her job at the factory. Then he said he had been out of the office for a couple of weeks due to illness and that Mr. Berg was running things in his absence and that he was the one we ought to see. I asked Mr. Berg on the ride if he knew a girl at the factory named Jean Dugan and told him she had been found murdered. He said he didn't know the name for sure but he would look it up on the payroll right away.

Q. Did he ask you for any details about the murder?

A. No.

Q. Did he seem more nervous after that?

A. About the same.

Q. What happened at the factory when you got there?

A. Mr. Berg went right up to his office, opened the safe, and took out the payroll book. He said Jean Dugan worked at the factory and had been paid off six dollars and sixty cents the previous day for her work that week. He said, "My stenographer left yesterday exactly at noon—I remember hearing the noon whistles—and the office boy left right after. Miss Dugan came a few minutes after that to collect her envelope. I didn't pay her much attention—I was proofreading some letters just then. She took her pay envelope and left."

Q. What were Mr. Berg's manner and deportment then?

A. He was still nervous. He stepped quickly about, almost like he was dancing, and his words were sharp and fast. When I suggested we go down to the basement to look over the situation, he got out the key from his desk and turned on the elevator motor. But when we got into the car and started down, it went a little ways and hung there, so he called down in kind of a hoarse voice to Mr. Dettwiler to come up and fix it. Mr. Dettwiler is an older man, and he was puffing when he got up there and made some little adjustment or other. He joked that he couldn't turn over the reins of the factory to a superintendent who didn't know every machine inside out. He said something about "these college engineers," meaning Mr. Berg, but Mr. Berg didn't seem to think it was very funny.

Archie could get nothing out of him on the cross-examination other than the concession that people in responsible positions sometimes exhibit nervousness when a crime has been committed on the premises of which they are in charge.

Chief Detective "Doodles" Stone followed with similar testimony on Noah's nervousness, especially at the undertaker's, where the police took him to identify the body. "He barely looked at her," said Detective Stone, "and hurried out of the viewing room. He said he recognized her from the dress as the young woman he had paid off the previous day. He seemed to grow queasy after that and asked for some coffee. We finally got him some and then went back to the factory."

Q. Is that when Mr. Berg checked out the night watchman's time slip?

A. Yes, sir. He glanced over it—I was sort of looking over his shoulder but not all that closely at it—and said it seemed all right and that there were no skips on the card.

Q. What did he do with the slip?

A. I'm not certain. He may have returned it to the big rack next to the punch clock or put it into the safe in his office.

Q. Is it possible that he handed it to you or one of the other detectives?

A. I have no recollection of that.

Q. Did Mr. Berg make any further discoveries regarding the night watchman's time slip?

A. Yes, he telephoned me the next morning—Monday —and said he had found another slip—or that maybe he had been mistaken on Sunday in his upset condition and read it wrong—but now the slip

showed skips at ten o'clock and eleven-thirty and—
one other time I can't remember for certain, so that
the watchman had had time to do some mischief
and that perhaps his home ought to be inspected.
On that advice, we went to Plato Layne's room,
where we found the bloody shirt. But the fact that
the shirt was buttoned and had not been worn led us
to believe it had been planted there to implicate the
darkey.

Q. In the course of your lengthy investigation, Detective
Stone, was or was not Mr. Berg the last person who
admitted to seeing Jean Dugan alive?

MR. RUSKIN: Objection. "Admits" is a prejudicial
word.

SOLICITOR TUNNEY: All right, make it "remembers"—did anyone else remember seeing her
after the time Mr. Berg says she came to his office
for her pay envelope?

A. No, sir.

Q. Was other evidence uncovered that week that caused
you to intensify your investigation of Superintendent
Berg?

A. Yes. On the Wednesday following the crime, when
bottling operations resumed, we discovered spots
that looked like they might be blood in the second-
floor cloakroom, where the girls changed their outer
garments. Some white powder or cleanser had been
spread over the area to cover up the stains. We took
chips of the wood and had them chemically an-
alyzed. The report said it was hard to tell because of
the bleach, but it may well have been blood.

Q. How far from the superintendent's office is the cloakroom?

A. It's right next to it. We felt a pattern was emerging
and had Mr. Berg brought in for extensive questioning.

Q. When was that?

A. Toward the end of the week. He was most coopera-
tive and less nervous than he had been. He suggested

that we search his home as we had the night watchman's. He also took off his shirt and showed us that he had no scratches or other marks on him and that if a man his size had assaulted a large and strong young woman of Miss Dugan's size, a struggle would assuredly have ensued.

Q. Did he bear any marks?

A. No.

Q. What did you think about that?

A. That he was protesting too much—volunteering more than we had asked. He kept saying he felt the darky and Vernon Pike knew a lot more than they were letting on about the murder, since they were still in the building when he left the factory on Saturday. But Pike's story was checked out—we found many witnesses who testified that he'd been around a tavern almost all day, sipping beer and watching the parade, before he took the night train to Macon.

Q. Did you find wire hangers, like the one Jean Dugan was strangled with, in Mr. Berg's private coat closet in his office?

A. Yes, sir.

Q. Did you also find in Mr. Berg's office memorandum pads with paper of the same size and texture as those on which the note in the dead girl's hand was written?

A. Yes, sir, quite a number of pads.

This time Archie managed some counterpunches. At once he got the chief detective to admit that wire hangers were to be found all over the factory—in the second-floor cloakroom, where the girls put their outer garments; in the first-floor coatroom, where the male workers put theirs; and in half a dozen other private offices. Identical memo pads, too, were to be found on almost every desk in the place. Detective Stone granted, furthermore, that the blood spots had not been found when the police searched the factory from top to bottom on Sunday, so there was no certain way of knowing when they fell—or were placed—there. Grudgingly, he acknowledged as well that the night watchman's time slip should have been seized as evidence on Sunday and not left, as the detective claimed, on the factory premises. Then Archie gambited, a bit desperately and unnecessarily, I thought.

Q. Detective Stone, doesn't your sister-in-law work at the Jubilee factory?

A. Yes, she does.

Q. Is she happy in her work there?

SOLICITOR TUNNEY: Objection. The question is extraneous.

MR. RUSKIN: I ask the court's indulgence for a moment.

THE COURT: Well, try it and we'll see. The witness will answer.

A. Happy enough, I guess.

Q. Was she not reprimanded on several occasions for arriving late and her pay docked?

SOLICITOR TUNNEY: Objection. Immaterial and extraneous.

Q. And was she not similarly docked for reporting to work with unclean hands?

SOLICITOR TUNNEY: Objection! Lieutenant Stone's sister-in-law is not on trial here.

THE COURT: Well, let's see it through and get on with it. The witness will answer.

A. I don't know about any of that.

Tunney, snapping like a terrier, came back for a re-direct, "Lieutenant Stone," he asked, "do you bear any grudge or harsh feelings personally toward the defendant?" The detective shrugged and said he had never met the man before his investigation of the Dugan girl's murder. "Thank you," said Tunney and whirled around toward the jury before dismissing the witness.

Father's face was growing longer by the minute. It was not going to be a good day for our side. Just how bad it would prove was mercifully withheld from us until the state's final witness that afternoon—a surprise the solicitor had confected to inflict instant misery in our camp. The witness was Dr. Harris Paternoster, a onetime practicing physician and more lately professor of chemistry at the Atlanta College of Medicine and director of laboratory for the state board of health since its creation five years previous. His specialty, said the professor, was human digestion, about which he had written one large book and many papers. Dr. Paternoster, it seemed, had performed an autopsy upon the dead girl a week after her burial at the request of the chief of police and the solicitor.

Q. And why was this procedure, requiring disinterment, undergone?
A. Because you and the chief felt it would be helpful to attempt to determine the time of the girl's death as accurately as possible.
Q. Did you dissect the girl's stomach?
A. Yes.
Q. What did you find?
A. One hundred sixty-six cubic centimeters of masticated cabbage and biscuits.
Q. Was this substance digested?
A. No. This vial, which the state has asked me to bring into court and which I now hand to you, contains some of the material I removed from the girl's stomach.
Q. How long do you estimate this substance was in her stomach before death?
A. The girl was either killed or received the blow upon her head that rendered her unconscious—and thereby interrupted the digestive process—forty to fifty minutes after she ate the meal.
Q. Her mother says she ate at about eleven-thirty. That would place the time of death, or at least the blow that rendered her unconscious, at about twelve-fifteen.
A. That is correct.

The courtroom ignited over the astonishing disclosure. Father's eyes fell to the floor. The judge pounded for order while a squad of newspapermen dashed for the door. There was still an undertow of excitement in the chamber as Tunney moved to take full advantage of the witness's expertise.

Q. Dr. Paternoster, how can you be so sure of your calculations?

A. I have done a good deal of experimentation with cabbage, as it happens. Its fibrous quality makes it uniquely useful in testing the capabilities of the human digestive tract. The stomach generally frees itself quickly of cabbage. Other foods remain in the stomach far longer, where the digestive juices can have at them. But I found in Jean Dugan's case that none of the cabbage had entered the smaller intestines. Also, the amount of gastric juice present was less than would have normally occurred in an hour. Hydrochloric acid forms at certain periods of digestion. I found no free hydrochloric acid but thirty-two degrees of combined hydrochloric acid—or about the amount that might be expected to be found after about three quarters of an hour from the beginning of the digestive process.

Given the lateness of the hour, the technical nature of the doctor's testimony, and our state of shock and dejection, Archie Ruskin asked that the cross-examination be held over until the next day and court adjourned. A night even longer than the day we had just been through lay in store for us.

NINE

If my father suffered a single serious deficiency in the way he faced the world, it was his seeming want of self-disclosure. From all available evidence, it was not a disabling affliction, for on the surface, at least, he functioned well and popularly. Yet he was so thoroughly circumspect in his speech, so damnably judicious in his dealings, that I wondered how anyone of his obvious spirit and feeling could control his responses to the daily episodes of life without periodically blowing a gasket or two.

I never asked him about it in so many words for fear he would take it as grave criticism. My studied surmise now is that being demonstrative was a luxury he could not afford or so he must have felt. But it is facile to conclude therefore that he was insecure beneath that mask of impassivity. He did not, after all, have a father to lean on, as I did, or anyone or anything else beyond his own intellectual and emotional resources. True, my mother was a support, but a strut, not a pillar; he would not burden her with his anxieties. He retreated inward, where he found ample capacity to play them out and prevail. No day passed, I suspect, in which he did not remind himself he was a Jew in a menacingly un-Jewish world and that unless he conducted himself with ultimate decorum, he would be denied the professional and social acceptance he enjoyed. That it was a limited acceptance and, beneath the courtesies and civilities of the region, a precarious one, he did not doubt. And while he never felt stigmatized by his differentness, he insisted, he was incapable of ever putting it out of mind altogether. He treated it instead as a given condition of his life—one of several—and got on with his living and the law. On the night after the second day of the trial of Noah Berg, however, I saw an unraveling in father, a sudden display of partisanship that was entirely out of character. I think he saw the Gentiles building a scaffold plank by circumstantial plank, and they meant to hang the Jewish defendant no matter how wobbly the structure. And if one Jew unjustifiably, why not another? The specter left father momentarily beside himself.

Every piece of medical information any of us could gather that night contributed to the conviction that the state was playing with loaded dice. Dr. Paternoster's surprise testimony establishing the Dugan girl's time of death at a few minutes after her arrival at the factory drew incredulous responses from a widely varying group of doctors and chemists we canvassed by telephone up and down the eastern seaboard that evening. A dozen top authorities agreed to come to Savannah as rebuttal witnesses if need be later in the trial, but meanwhile we were faced with the cruel weight of Paternoster's testimony and how to undermine it before it made an ineradicable impression upon the jury's thinking. To accept his testimony as scientific fact instead of convenient theorizing would leave the defense with the burden of proving Noah's innocence instead of requiring the state to prove his guilt. Weary but combative after a post-midnight session of long-distance coaching by Uncle Benny, father handled the cross-examination when court reconvened next morning.

Paternoster proved a most elusive prey. Father argued that the removal of the dead girl's blood and its replacement by a gallon of what was essentially formaldehyde at the time of her embalming and burial necessarily worked significant chemical changes on the body during the ten days before she was disinterred and that therefore the doctor's analysis lacked validity. The doctor argued back that the preservative chemicals arrested decay in the corpse and made his investigation possible. "But does not the active ingredient in embalming fluid affect the presence and quantity of digestive juices one might expect to find in a stomach ten days after it has ceased to function?" father demanded. "The pancreatic juices, for example, had they in fact been operating on the cabbage at the time of the girl's death—say, at two o'clock in the afternoon—would no longer have been present or observable at the time of your explorations, isn't that so, doctor? Similarly, with the amount of hydrochloric acid one might expect to find in the stomach in view of the fact that that substance is so highly volatile and soluble—isn't that so, doctor?" But Paternoster insisted that he had taken such factors into consideration in estimating the time of death. Father kept driving at him, getting his rebuttal points on the record even though the witness fended them off skillfully. Yes, the doctor acknowledged, the digestive process might have been slowed by a large unchewed piece of cabbage obstructing the passageway from the stomach into the intestines, "but I found no such piece of food during my examination." Well, yes, such a piece might have been present in that position and crumbled during the interval since the girl died, "but I find that a highly unlikely possibility," the doctor added.

Q. Just one more thing, doctor. Where is the dead girl's stomach now?

A. I don't understand.

Q. Where did you put the girl's dissected stomach? Did you replace it in her exhumed body?

A. I—no, I believe it was disposed of.

Q. How?

A. By a laboratory assistant.

Q. How—in the garbage?

A. I'm not sure.

Q. Did any other chemist or doctor work with you during your analysis of the girl's stomach?

A. No. But I had the sanction of the coroner and, of course, the approval of the solicitor, who authorized the examination.

Q. Did you not think to preserve the stomach so that your findings might be validated by showing them to the court or to the defendant and his counsel?

A. I did not.

Q. And the cabbage itself, do you have that?

A. Just the vial I presented to the court.

Q. So you gave the solicitor the testimony he asked for and destroyed the evidence itself?

SOLICITOR TUNNEY: I strongly object. Dr. Paternoster acted in a totally professional manner—.

MR. ADLER: Your honor, Mr. Tunney may not protect his witness from valid cross-examination. Here is
a case of a chemist who is hired by the solicitor and
takes the specimens into his own back room and,
after he has finished with them, destroys them. He
gives our side no opportunity to examine the evidence or to enlist other experts to corroborate or
take exception to his findings. I am suggesting, based
on the advice I have received from any number of
specialists in forensic medicine, that this witness has
acted in an unethical and unprecendented manner.

SOLICITOR TUNNEY: Defense counsel's slurs are irrelevant in every respect and cannot be permitted.

MR. ADLER: And I suggest the witness's testimony is
invalid on its face, given the length of time that
passed between death and his examination, and that
his disposition of the evidence violates orderly judicial procedure.

The judge hushed them both and told father to bring in his
own experts if he wished to discredit the doctor and not expect
the court to do it for him. Dr. Paternoster's testimony had been
shaken but not toppled. The solicitor, recognizing he had been
under heavy assault, proceeded as if his witness had repulsed it ad-
equately. From then on, he assumed that the time of the murderous attack on the girl had been fixed as fact in the jury's mind. He
put on a string of witnesses now to describe activities at the
factory within the time frame thus established, however arguably.

Cavaretta, the Pinkerton double-agent, was designated a hostile
witness by the solicitor, who then deftly used him to present
Noah Berg's account of his movements on and after that tragic
day. When he was hired by the soda company, said Cavaretta, he
made a point of interviewing everyone who acknowledged being
in the factory on the Saturday of the murder. Only Mr. Berg and
Morris "Mo" Easter, the floor-sweeper, admitted working on the
two floors the dead girl was believed to have visited that day—the

superintendent on the second and the black custodian on the first
—at the time she was believed to have been there. "I intensified
my investigation of those two," he said.

Given permission by the judge to consult the notes he had
made at the time, the Pinkerton studiously reconstructed Noah
Berg's Saturday timetable for the court. The superintendent had
reported to work as usual at eight in the morning—"He said thirst
takes no holidays, so neither could soda companies," Cavaretta
noted—and planned to catch up on his correspondence, compile
his weekly production cost report, and try to catch the Buccaneers' game at the ball grounds in the afternoon. But his assistant,
Bryce Woodcock, telephoned in sick and said he would be by
later in the morning with the completed tabulations that Berg
needed to compile his production data for the week. The superintendent did what he could in the meanwhile, sent his stenographer and office boy home at noon, and then started sifting
through the work sheets that Woodcock had dropped off. The
Dugan girl appeared in his office a few minutes later "but Berg
said he did not pay much attention to her since he had just begun
to work over the production figures in earnest," Cavaretta reported. "He got out her pay envelope for her, keeping in mind
her employment number but hardly noticing the girl herself. She
thanked him and left, and that was the last he saw of her that
day, he told me."

Q. Can you describe the superintendent's office for us?
A. Well, there is an outer office, where Mr. Berg's stenographer and the office boy work and where he interviews people, and there is an inner office, where
   the safe is and Mr. Berg does his harder work at a
   desk. There is a door in between with a large glass
   panel in it. It also has a shade.
Q. A shade?
A. Yes. Mr. Berg says both the outer and inner office
   doors were open that morning.
Q. Did he say what direction Miss Dugan took when
   and if, as he claims, she left his office?
A. He said he didn't know, since he was working in the
   inner office. He said he thought he heard some

voices out in the hall or down the stairway when she
left, but he couldn't tell whose.

Berg kept working till half past twelve or a quarter to one, the
Pinkerton said Noah had told him, and then went up to the third
floor, where Gomer Camp, the mechanical foreman, and his assistant were refitting some leaky pipes and tightening belts.
Camp's wife had come by a little before noon to take his lunch
up to him but had not re-appeared. "He said he asked if the repair
work was about done, and when they said no, he told Mrs. Camp
he was going home to dinner in a few minutes and would lock the
men in while he was gone since there was no watchman on duty,
and if she wanted to leave, she had better head downstairs in another minute or two. Waiting for her, he proofread a few of the
letters his stenographer had typed up that morning. Then he went
home to dinner—he had given up on the ball game by that time
—came back around three after watching the parade for a bit, and
worked till six. He spent the evening at home with his wife,
in-laws, and friends who came over to play cards."

Q. Did Mr. Berg say that he saw Mo Easter, the floorsweep, at the factory that Saturday?
A. He said he did not see him there that day.
Q. Did you tell him that Mo's time card showed he had
punched in and out that day?
A. Yes. Mr. Berg said that was possible since Mo may
have worked just on the first floor that morning. He
said Mo liked to sleep on the job and the packing
room on the first floor was a good place for that sort
of loafing. But if he was at the factory, the police
ought to check him very carefully because Mo had a
record of arrests and also because Mo knew how to
read and write and could have written the note
found in the dead girl's hand.
Q. What did you learn from your questioning of Mo
Easter?
A. He said he was working on the first floor all morning.
I asked him if he remembered who had come in and
gone out. He gave me most of the same names as
Mr. Berg had. I asked him if he had seen Miss

303

Dugan go in. He said yes, he saw her go upstairs but he never saw her come down.

Q. Wasn't it possible that his work duties had caused him to miss seeing her come down?

A. He said that was possible. But since he was sweeping up around the front doorway about then, he doubted that he could have missed her.

Q. What conclusion did you reach?

A. It seemed clear that either Berg or Mo was lying about the girl. I reported my suspicions to the police.

Q. Did it occur to you that both of them could have been lying?

A. No—not then.

Some hostile witness. Archie dealt briefly in the cross with so dangerous a friend.

Q. Did you ask Mr. Berg how well he knew Miss Dugan, or if he knew her at all?

A. Yes. He said he knew her by face, certainly, but not by name. There are nearly three hundred workers at the factory, and he could hardly know each of them. His assistant, Mr. Woodcock, did most of the hiring, though he himself took a brief hand in the training of each new worker.

Q. But he had seen Miss Dugan the day of the murder, and she must have identified herself to him by name when she came in for her pay envelope. Why, then, when he was picked up early Sunday morning, did Mr. Berg tell the police, in the person of Officer Reilly, that he wasn't sure if Miss Dugan worked at the plant?

A. He said he was just being cautious and not trying to get the company involved more than necessary. Since Detective Reilly had held back the details of the tragedy at the factory from him till that point, Mr. Berg thought he ought to be similarly careful. Besides, Dugan is a common enough name, and he had not paid much attention to the girl when she came by that noontime.

Q. I have just one other question. Subsequent to your interviews with them, did you learn from the police that Mo Easter began changing his story, a little more each day, while Mr. Berg's account never varied?

A. Yes.

Q. Did that suggest to you which of them might be telling the truth?

A. It certainly suggested that the nigger had been lying—or at least holding back. But it did not mean to me that Berg was necessarily more truthful—just smarter.

The stenographer and office boy testified briefly in corroboration of Noah's account of the morning as rendered by the Pinkerton. Both left at the crack of noon; neither remembered a whistle, just the bongs of the clock in the superintendent's outer office. Bryce Woodcock, Noah's handsome assistant, then came on to say he had gone straight home to his apartment and back to bed after delivering his production work sheets to the office late that morning. Archie asked him if he had seen any sign of Mo Easter on the first floor. Woodcock said he had not. Then he was asked what sort of a boss Noah Berg was to work for.

A. Quite good. And very instructive. He was always detecting the soft spots in the production system and thinking of ways to improve them—or remove them.

Q. You mean he did not hesitate to fire people who did not work out?

A. No—although I actually did most of the hiring and firing under his guidance. He acted more or less as a monitor of each worker's performance.

Q. Did you know most of the girls by name?

A. I usually gave them their pay envelopes each Friday, so I pretty much knew what name went with which face.

Q. Did you know Jean Dugan?

A. Yes.

Q. What kind of worker was she?

A. Conscientious and quiet.

Q. Did Mr. Berg know her?

A. I don't know. By face, surely. He often made the rounds, checking for problem areas—girls chatting when they should have been working, girls fumbling their task, girls with dirty hands. I did more of that, though, than he. I had recommended Miss Dugan for a merit raise a few months before her death, and he approved it, so he may have known who she was.

Q. Did he pay Miss Dugan any special attention?

A. Certainly none that I know of.

Q. Did he pay any of the female workers special attention?

A. Not that I ever saw. He said that was my department.

Q. What did he mean by that?

A. Well, that I was to be the principal taskmaster—and ogre—in the eyes of the girls. He was also making a joking reference, I suppose, to my being a bachelor.

Q. And did you ever go out with any of the girls from the factory, Mr. Woodcock?

A. Mr. Berg frowned on that. And I had other friends.

Q. When Mr. Berg was engaged in his work at the factory, wasn't he very intent on it?

A. Yes, very. He seemed more interested in the work itself, in a way, than the people performing it. That was perhaps his only weakness, in my opinion.

Q. Have you ever seen Mr. Berg get excited when things went wrong?

A. Oh, yes. Never a day went by without his getting excited. I've seen him rub his hands together in excitement or worry a thousand times. One day when Joe Dettwiler—he's the factory manager but he's been in poor health for some time now and around the place less and less—one day Mr. Dettwiler raised cain over something—a machine that had overheated because it hadn't been oiled, I think—and Mr. Berg became terribly excited and began trembling.

Q. When he got excited and worried, he would call on you for help, wouldn't he?

A. Yes, a lot.

Q. Did he also drink coffee to calm himself?

A. Yes, he would send the office boy out for cups for both of us. Usually he hated having food and dirt around the office. He thought it set a bad example. But he took coffee to calm himself.

Q. In your judgment, was Mr. Berg the sort of man capable of assaulting and murdering a young girl—?

SOLICITOR TUNNEY: Objection. The question is improper. No one has introduced evidence regarding Mr. Berg's character. This witness may answer only with regard to the defendant's work habits, not the sterling quality of his character—or the lack thereof.

THE COURT: I'll sustain the objection.

Now Tunney began closing in. He put on a sixteen-year-old girl named Heather Ferguson, who had worked near Jean Dugan in the factory and been a close friend. She testified that she had asked for Jean's pay envelope at the close of work on Friday evening, the day before the murder, and been refused by Noah Berg. "He said that I couldn't get it," she said, "but that Jean would be in Saturday and could get it then herself, all right." The solicitor asked whether the girl had ever picked up Miss Dugan's pay envelope for her before. "Yes, twice," she said.

Those menacing murmurs around the room began again. The grim possibility that Noah Berg might have been crouching, with malice aforethought, in wait for the Dugan girl that Saturday morning was thus introduced. Archie moved to squelch the very idea.

Q. Miss Ferguson, who generally paid off the workers on Friday night? It wasn't Mr. Berg, was it?

A. No. Usually the paymaster did it. Like Mr. Pike would do it until he left a few weeks before—before Jean's death. Then Mr. Woodcock took over.

Q. Then why are you sure, Miss Ferguson, that Mr. Berg and not Mr. Woodcock spoke to you in the superintendent's outer office that Friday and are you sure that whoever it was didn't say, "Miss Dugan can come in tomorrow and pick up the envelope herself, all right" and not that she *was* coming by, as you testified?

A. Both Mr. Berg and Mr. Woodcock were there, but I know one from the other well enough. And I know what Mr. Berg said.

Q. Weren't there a lot of people in the area and a good deal of jostling, with everyone anxious to be gone for the holiday weekend? Wasn't it possible you misunderstood or thought one person was talking to you when it was another?

A. It was kind of noisy, but not so bad I couldn't hear straight.

Q. Miss Ferguson, how long have you worked at the Jubilee factory?

A. About two years—a little longer than Jeannie had.

Q. Were you earning the same pay as she?

A. No.

Q. Who earned more?

A. She did, by a dollar twenty.

Q. Why was that?

A. I don't know. I guess they thought she was a better worker.

Q. Who's they?

A. Well—the superintendent and his assistant.

Q. Were you angry that she was getting more?

A. I didn't think all that much about it.

Q. Did you think the superintendent was partial to Miss Dugan?

A. I don't understand.

Q. Did he favor her?

A. I suppose—if they paid her more.

Q. Did he know who she was? Did he call her by name?

A. Not that I heard.

Q. Or you?

A. No.

Q. Did she ever say anything to you about Mr. Berg?

A. No. She was a quiet person that way.

The climate in that hotbox grew warmer still when Tunney put on a dainty little girl named Mary Ellen Stiles, who worked in the bottle-capping department and had come by Saturday, as Jean

Dugan had, to get paid. She had been out on Friday with a cough, and her mother feared it was the beginning of a recurrence of the croup that had stricken her the previous winter. In a soft voice, Miss Stiles said she came to the factory on the day of the murder at five minutes after noon; the first thing she did on entering the building was to look up at the clock in the entranceway out of concern that she had come too late to be paid. She then went directly up to the superintendent's office but found no one there, she continued. She went out into the hall and sat on the bench for a few minutes, but when no one came and the only sound she heard was some banging on machinery upstairs, she decided to leave. Coming downstairs to the first floor, she noticed the time again—twelve-ten, or perhaps a minute later, she could not tell exactly from that angle. She said she saw no one she knew while either entering or leaving the building.

Father used his kid-glove approach on the frail young woman.

Q. Miss Stiles, how did you know that the factory would be open at all for paying off that Saturday? You knew it was a holiday, didn't you?

A. Oh, yes, sir. They had posted a notice at the beginning of the week that there would be no work Saturday. But it said some supervisory personnel would be on hand in the morning and would pay off then to help that was absent Friday.

Q. That was posted where any of the girls could see it?

A. Yes, sir.

Q. You say you went up to Mr. Berg's office to get paid. Which office did you go into—the outer one or the inner one?

A. The outer one. But the door to the inner one was open, and I didn't see anyone in there or hear any movement.

Q. Could you see every part of that inner office?

A. Well, not entirely, but enough to see no one was there.

Q. But you didn't enter that room and look around it?

A. No, sir, I wouldn't have done that. But it was awfully still.

Q. Did you notice the safe in that inner office?

A. No, sir.

Q. Did you notice a wardrobe in which men's clothes were put?

A. No, sir.

Q. You seem to be a very courteous young lady. Isn't it possible that Mr. Berg was working hard over some figures at his desk—at a corner of his desk obscured from your view—and since that is not a form of work that creates any noise, you did not hear him? And isn't it possible—?

SOLICITOR TUNNEY: Objection. The witness need not answer hypothetical questions.

MR. ADLER: What were you wearing on your feet that day, Miss Stiles?

A. Tennis slippers.

Q. They are not very noisy, are they?

A. No, sir. That's one reason I like them. You sort of just glide along in them.

Q. So if there was someone in Mr. Berg's office, it is possible, is it not, that he would not have been aware of your gentle arrival?

SOLICITOR TUNNEY: Objection. The question is argumentative and not answerable by the witness.

THE COURT: Re-word your question, counselor.

Q. Miss Stiles, did you say "Hello" or anything like that or perhaps clear your throat gently as a lady might to attract attention from anyone who could have been in that inner office?

A. I—don't think so. I may have.

Q. But you're not certain?

A. No, sir.

Father had done well in mitigating the girl's testimony, but as with the cabbage-digestion theory of Dr. Paternoster, the essential point could not be warded off readily. Each new thread in the thickening web of suspicion that the state solicitor was weaving added its portion of strength.

Tunney closed out the day by producing a prelude witness to

his *pièce de résistance*. Mrs. Maggie Camp told how she arrived at the factory that morning at about eleven-fifty to see whether her husband had progressed far enough in his repair work to join her for a trip to a furniture store. She stopped by in Noah Berg's office first to find out exactly where her husband was working in the building. "My father and brother work there as well," she said, "and he commented on the family resemblance." The superintendent seemed perfectly cordial and relaxed, she added in answer to the solicitor's question. Mr. Berg sent his office boy to fetch Mr. Camp, who talked with his wife in the hall for several minutes; she promised to bring him back some ham on a roll at around half past twelve, and he would see if the work was far enough along to join her then or soon after.

Q. What time did you come back?
A. About twelve-thirty.
Q. Why do you say "about" twelve-thirty?
A. I more or less glanced at the clock coming in.
Q. Did you see Mr. Berg on that second visit?
A. Yes, I wanted to let him know I was going straight upstairs with my husband's lunch unless he minded.
Q. What did he say?
A. He jumped when I went into his office and spoke to him.
Q. Had you taken him by surprise?
A. I don't think so. He was working at his desk. I approached him directly.
Q. What did you ask Mr. Berg after he jumped?
A. Whether my husband had gone back up to work and if I might go up to see him.
Q. What did Berg say?
A. He asked me to repeat the question.
Q. Did he seem distracted?
A. A bit.
Q. Did you see Mr. Berg any more after that?
A. Yes, he came up about ten or fifteen minutes later and said that if I wanted to leave the building before

three o'clock, I had better go now as he was going out to lunch and had to lock up.

Q. Did there seem to be some urgency in his words?

A. Well—just the idea that I had better get a move on pretty soon.

Q. When did you leave?

A. About ten minutes later.

Q. Did you see Mr. Berg on your way out?

A. Yes. I saw him sitting at a table in his outer office.

Q. Did he have his hat and coat on, as if he were waiting for you to come down?

A. No. He was just sitting there. I waved goodbye.

Q. Did you see anyone else on your way out?

A. Yes. I saw a negro behind some boxes in the main room as I came down the stairs.

Q. When was that?

A. Just a little before one.

Q. Can you describe the negro in any detail?

A. Just that he was of medium size and seemed on the young side—maybe in his twenties. He was sort of lurking there. He seemed to scoot when I came along. But I've got mighty good eyes. I saw him, all right.

Our side skipped the cross, seeing no profit in it, but Tunney briefly brought back Cavaretta, the Pinkerton, to ask him if he had put to Noah Mrs. Camp's version of her comings and goings. "I did," he said, "since Mr. Berg seemed a bit confused about it and had not mentioned her second appearance in his office. He said he was concentrating on his production figures just then and probably did not notice her the second time—he just more or less waved her upstairs. He had no recollection of jumping at the sound of her voice. I told him to search his memory to make certain he had forgotten nothing else."

II

We were drawing a most unwholesome assortment of spectators to the trial. Their pressing in on the chamber in steadily rising numbers was a felt presence as the week went on. Father and Archie were uneasy about the crowds and urged the sheriff to do his best to weed out the most undesirable element from those gorging the entranceway each morning and at the mid-day break. He obliged to the extent of turning aside known derelicts and some wool-hat boys with liquor on their breath and the vein jumping at their temple. But no attempt was or could be made to bar professional loafers tricked out in a fresh straw boater or other items new from the haberdashery. I told father I thought half the beachcombers at Tybee had decamped and come to the courthouse for their mid-summer entertainment.

It was the women, though, who were the most palpably vivid and sternly attentive part of the crowd. They made up no fewer than half the spectators in the courtroom, and they fought their way, often with children in hand, for a place on the jammed benches no less vehemently than the male contenders. It looked like the opening of the Cherokee Strip when the deputies let the cordon down at the beginning of each session. And the women were of every sort: teen-agers and grandmothers sat side by side; women with painted cheeks and hollow eyes bearing the unmistakable look and stain of crimson; here and there a graceful matron in a wide-brim hat with flowing plume that, when removed out of courtesy to those behind, revealed a wealth of auburn hair crowning a face of porcelain features. Most of them, however, were more ordinary. Housewives, I should say, on hand ostensibly in protest at the outrage perpetrated against all Georgia womanhood, and insistent that retribution be taken. Under that moralistic veil, it was plain that they had come as common thrill-seekers, eager above all for a break in the tedium of their stay-at-home lives. No doubt many of their husbands did not know they had come. Those who brought youngsters, presumably because there was nowhere else to park them, sat them on their knee and hushed them fiercely lest an escaping wail cause the parent to be ejected by a bailiff. They came early and stayed all day, some of them, eyes drilled forward, cauterizing the defendant, testing every witness, consuming each gruesome piece of evidence, sometimes half-standing to see and having to be yanked down by the sheriff's men. They were more than morbidly curious; they were famished for excitement.

It came at the beginning of the fourth day of the trial as Solicitor Tunney, his dark eyes and pomaded hair gleaming, called out, "Bring in Mo Easter!" So great a charge of anticipation shot through the room that some of the women spectators clapped momentarily at the mention of the negro floor-sweeper's name.

The black man was an unlikely star. He came into court unmanacled but flanked by our bulky police chief and one of his brawnier patrolmen. There was a lithe, definite feline quality about the man's movements to the witness chair. He was slender and neat-looking in a pair of fresh Levi's and a good grade of work shirt. His hair was short and freshly barbered, his cheekbones high, his skin of an amber tincture, and his eyes a study in directness. He never let his look wander from the counselor addressing him. "They've scrubbed him up nice," Archie whispered to me. I glanced back and saw Noah Berg staring at the witness with what could only be deep foreboding; his look radiated ill tidings.

Mo Easter was not what local whites called a cornfield nigger. He was a good-for-nothing and desperate city black. He had kicked around the urban jungles of Georgia all his twenty-seven years, his early testimony established—an unschooled, unskilled, unmotivated, and unprincipled drifter who drowned his misfortune in liquor and the laps of what dusky wenches would have him (there seemed to be no shortage, he implied slyly, enjoying his moment in the sun and pleased to have the world know he was quite a ladies' man). He took work when the spirit, and hunger, moved him, but he was an inconstant employée and sooner or later got into a scrape, usually over his borrowings to buy hooch, and wound up in jail on a disorderly-conduct charge. Twice he made the chain gang. But an evident native charm landed him on his feet and he would start over each time, full of good intentions, and so it was that he had been hired at the Jubilee factory two years before.

Q. What kind of work did you do around the factory, Mo?

A. I worked on the elevator until last Christmas and then they took me off and put me to cleaning up the building.

Q. How much did they pay you?

A. I ain't proud of that. Do I have to tell?

Q. Yes, Mo.

A. Six dollars and five cents—not much for a growed man.

Q. Was there some way you had of earning extra?

A. Yes, sir. That's how I got in this fix.

Q. I'd like you to tell us about it.

A. Well, Mr. Berg—he sometimes paid me extra—.

Q. Excuse me, Mo. I wonder if you could identify Mr. Berg for the court.

A. Yes, sir—that's him right over there [pointing to the defendant].

Q. Go ahead, now.

A. Well, sometimes Mr. Berg had me do special work for him.

Q. What kind of work?

A. Watchin' work.

Q. What do you mean?

A. Watchin' the door whilst he had ladies in for a chat.

Just exactly there, Archie or father could have objected and almost certainly would have been sustained. The rules were quite explicit, father had explained to me the night before, against the introduction of testimony on a defendant's moral conduct prior to the crime with which he was charged—unless or until the defendant's character was introduced into the case by the defense and cited as evidence of his likely innocence. But so blatant were Mo Easter's accusations against Noah Berg, and so vital to the state's case, that father and Archie had decided to give the negro enough rope to perjure himself, if not worse. Then, by a pounding cross-examination, at which Archie was so expert, they would tear his testimony to pieces and reveal the whole case against Noah as a conspiracy in which the police were willing participants and perhaps even instigators. Father had the gravest misgivings about such strategy, but Archie's gritty confidence and superb reputation convinced him that it was a risk worth taking.

Tunney went ahead unchallenged:

Q. When was the last time you watched for Mr. Berg?

A. Well, sir, he come up to me on that Friday—the one before the girl died—.

Q. Friday, April twenty-fifth?

A. Yes, sir. At about three o'clock that day Mr. Berg come up to where I was at work and told me to come in on Saturday even if it was a holiday because he had some work for me to do.

Q. Did he say what sort of work?

A. Not just then. He just say to be there and come to his office 'round noontime when the others had left. I come in nex' morning maybe nine o'clock and did some sweepin' and fixin' downstairs.

Q. Did anyone see you there? Did you greet anyone?

A. No, sir. I was more or less layin' low, out of sight, keepin' track of who come into the building and who was left.

Q. Why was that?

A. Well, I knew the kind of work Mr. Berg had in mind.

The solicitor had him recite the comings and goings of everyone at the factory that morning, and the black witness replied flawlessly. After Berg's stenographer and office boy had departed, he said, he went straight to the superintendent's office. "He say he wanted me to watch the door for him as he was expecting a young lady," said Easter. "He say to do it like we had the other times I watched for him. He would stamp on the floor over my head when he wanted me to close up the front door. If anyone rang to get in, I'd rattle the elevator door first to make sure Mr. Berg had heard and could leave off his chattin'. If no one come along whilst I was watchin', then I'd stay there till he give me the signal by a whistle that it was all right to open up the front door again."

Q. How many times had you watched the door that way for Mr. Berg?

A. I can't remember 'zactly how many times, but it was lots o' times I done it. Holidays an' Saturday afternoons mostly.

316

Q. Why did you do it?

A. He was my boss. I make him happy, he make me happy. Sometimes he give me a quarter, sometimes half a dollar, oncet even a dollar afterwards.

Q. Tell us some particular time that you'd watched the door before.

A. Well, I remembers watchin' the door last Thanksgiving Day for him. Dere was a big handsome lady up dere, and another man and another lady, too. They all stayed up in the factory whilze I watched the door.

Q. Go back now to that Saturday, April twenty-sixth. Tell us what happened after Mr. Berg told you to go down and keep watch.

A. Well, I didn't have long to wait that time. Way I figured, only some lady who I learn later was Mr. Camp's missus, she's still up there by the elevator talkin' to him when I come outa Mr. Berg's office and make myself scarce. Soon she come downstairs and go out, and I hear hammerin' again all the way up on the third floor. Dat's all who's left in the building. Well, den along comes dis Miss Stiles walkin' real soft-like on up the stairs, and I'm wonderin' if she's de young lady Mr. Berg was expectin'. But I don't hear the stampin' of his foot overhead, and then down she come in fi' minutes or so. But right after she leave, de other lady comes on in and goes up.

Q. What other lady, Mo?

A. De lady what's dead.

Q. What was her name?

A. Miss Jean—Miss Jeannie Duggins, I allus called her.

Q. Go on.

A. Well, soon I gets the signal from Mr. Berg's foot an' I close the door like I'm spozed. Everythin' was quiet for a time. But den I hear footsteps and think two people was coming from Mr. Berg's office and headin' down the steps. But them steps pass on back

from dere more toward the rear part, and then it was
all quiet again for a little while. Next I heard someone walkin' around like on dey tiptoes and den I
hear the elevator door give a rattle, which was another signal me 'n' Mr. Berg got meanin' I was to go
on up to see him. So I did that.

Q. Did you see Berg then?

A. Yes, sir, I seed him. He was standin' there in his
office jes' ashiverin' and rubbin' his hands together.

Q. Did you look at his eyes?

A. Yes, sir.

Q. How did they look?

A. Dey was large and he looked funny outa them.

Q. How did his face look?

A. His face was all red like.

Q. What did he say?

A. Well, sir, Mr. Berg asked me ef I'd seed a girl come
up, and I told him I'd seed two of 'em come up and
seed one of 'em go back down, but I hadn't seed the
other go back down yet. Then he said I never would
see that other one go back down. He said the girl
had gone into the cloakroom to get her smock to
launder an' he went in there, too, 'cause o' his want-
in' to be with her. But when he come in, she tried
to stop him and he say he guessed he hit her too
hard. He say he knock her by mistake against one o'
dem clothes hooks what cut her head open. "Mo,"
he says to me, "you know I ain't made like other
men."

Q. Have you ever seen that he was not made like other
men?

A. Yes, sir.

Q. When?

A. Well, like last Thanksgiving, for instance, I seed him
with a lady up there. I thought I hear him rattle the
elevator door, so I went on up. From the hall I could
see de lady was sittin' in a chair in his office, kinder
sprawled out, and he was kneelin' on de floor in
front o' her.

The courtroom could not contain itself. The noise overflowed, and several women among the spectators rushed from the room, hiding their faces behind a newspaper or fan. The judge, himself stunned, required a moment or two to pull his robes together and pound for order. I leaned over to ask father whether Noah had in fact worked at the factory on Thanksgiving. Archie had already put the question to Noah, who said yes but that the rest was a monstrous lie, as was the negro's entire testimony.

Tunney exploited the sensation to the hilt:

Q. Had you seen this often?

A. Several times.

Q. At the Jubilee factory?

A. Yes, sir.

Q. What did Mr. Berg say to you then that Saturday— April twenty-sixth?

A. He told me to go get the girl and bring her to the basement. So I went on back o' his office to the cloakroom an' found de girl lyin' there with her hands kinder stretched out above her head and one o' dem wire hangers wrung tight aroun' her neck. Her eyes was open horrible-like and her tongue floppin' outa her mouth. I sees blood on de floor oozin' from her head. Dere wairn't no doubt she was dead. I went back an' told Mr. Berg she was a goner an' say he didn't tell me he strangulated her. He look at me funny and say was I sure she is dead and he didn't remember nothin' about strangulatin' her. He say maybe someone else do it—maybe me. I say, "No, sir, you know I jus' come up. You musta done it outa bein' nervous an' excited." He say, "That must be it, Mo." Den he ask me to get some baggin' like what de soap come in for cleanin' out de soda bottles—they got bags like that in the supply room on dat floor—and put the girl in it and carry her downstairs to the cellar an' put her in de furthest corner whilze he cleaned up the mess in the cloak-room. I done that—.

Q. Why did you do that, Mo? Didn't you know what he had done was a terrible crime?

A. Yes, sir, I knowed that. But he was my boss an' friend an' he tole me to. If'n I didn't, see, I was in de soup anyway, bein' around him like I was. He coulda blame me for it all, and people gonna believe a smart, fancy white man, not some no-'count nigger floorsweep.

Q. So you felt you had no choice but to help him?

A. No, sir, not much.

Q. How did you get the girl to the basement?

A. I put her inside de sack an' her hat, too, an' tied her up just like a washerwoman does clothes in dem from the white folks' home to wash 'em. I picked her up but she was so heavy I dropped her on the floor. When she fell that scared me so dat I went an' got Mr. Berg and tell him to please help me carry her. He say we better take her down d' elevator an' he come runnin' back dere on his tiptoes an' he was tremblin' awful-like, but we got her onto d' elevator an' started on down, only it got hung up at the first floor and he says, "Jesus Christ!" Finally he got it started again and took me down all de way. I dragged de sack a far way to the dust heap and dumped out de poor girl. Then I fold up de sack and stick it in de furnace.

Q. Where was Berg at the time?

A. Oh, he take d' elevator right on back up and unlock de front door so no one'd be suspectin' anything, and then he go back to his desk.

Q. What did you do after that?

A. I went to his office, too. He was dryin' off his hands from cleanin' up de mess next door.

Q. Was his face red, then?

A. Yes, sir, and his eyes was lookin' like diamonds.

The meticulously rehearsed character of the negro's testimony was so transparent that I thought the jury would be shifting around in disbelief. But they appeared to be swallowing every word. There was just enough embellishment in the man's narrative to make it all sound plausible—an artistic effect that I did not doubt had been painfully achieved.

320

Easter went on to describe how he had had to hide in the clothes wardrobe in Berg's office when Mrs. Camp made her reappearance. After that, he said, the superintendent had hit upon the scheme of writing a note to pin the blame on someone else. "He gave me a cigarette to smoke," said Easter, "which was against de rules o' de factory, but he bein' in charge, I knowed it was all right. Den he sat there in his chair squirmin' and thinkin' away till he say, 'Mo, you can write some, can't you?' and I say yes. He say he got an idear to save us both, an' he has me print off de note on a piece o' paper. When I get all done, he slap me on de shoulder and say dat's fine an' he take out a roll o' greenbacks and hand me two fi'-dolla' bills. He say dere'll be more o' dem later so long as I keep my mouth shut. 'Mo,' he say, 'I've got lots of money what I've saved up. Dat fat wife o' mine want to buy an automobile, but I wouldn't do it, no, sir. I've saved my money, an' my folks up north got money, too—why should I hang?' Dat's what he say." Mo said he took the note obediently down to the basement and crumpled it up into the dead girl's hand. On the way back to Berg's office, he punched out his time slip (all business, that darkey) and reported back to the superintendent that he wanted to get something to eat. "I really meant somethin' t' drink," said Mo. "Mr. Berg ask me to come back a little after three o'clock to help him burn the body. I say yes, but the idear didn't 'peal to me none. As I was readyin' to leave, I sees he's got the girl's purse a-sittin' inside de open safe across from his desk. He say it got tossed into a corner of de cloakroom an' he just discover it. I say maybe he better throw it away. He ask me ef'n I'd do it for him—maybe put it near her body on my way out. I took it, all right, but I jus' didn't feel like goin' back down dat scuttle-hole and seein' dat little girl's dead body no mo'. I stuck de purse inside my belt and hung around de first floor a few minutes an' then I went to a near-beer saloon and had me a double-header and some sandwiches. When I got home, I gave my woman de money Mr. Berg hand me and tole her to pay some rent. Then I stuck de purse inside my mattress an' went to sleep. Time I get up, it was dark."

I slumped back as Tunney turned triumphantly to our table and said, "Your witness." Less true words were never spoken.

Archie tried everything. Every trick in his book. He cross-examined Mo Easter the rest of that day and all the next. He sweet-talked to him first, sympathized with him, played up to his vanity, mocked his ignorance, strove mightily to confuse and confound him—and that dumb, lying, pathetic, low-life of a nigger (as he called himself) bested Archie Ruskin every time.

In fact, all Archie succeeded in doing was to intensify the effectiveness of Easter's meticulously coached testimony. It did not become clear to us how thoroughly the negro had been drilled until Archie began to pump him on Noah's alleged prior instances of lecherousness.

Q. You say you watched for Mr. Berg on many occasions?

A. Yes, sir.

Q. When was the first time?

A. Some time last July.

Q. What did Mr. Berg say at that time?

A. He just come out and called me into his office and said what he wanted me to do.

Q. Was a lady with him?

A. Yes—Miss Flora Hopkins.

Q. How did you know her name?

A. She worked at the factory a few months. So I knowed who she was.

Q. Was anyone else there?

A. Yes, sir—a Mr. Dawson or somethin'. I had never seed him before.

Q. What happened?

A. Well, I went down to watch the door like Mr. Berg say, and after maybe fifteen minutes, de man an' woman come down and he say Mr. Berg say it was all right to open de trap-door and let 'em go down to the basement.

Q. How long till they came up?

A. It was after a while.

Q. But Mr. Berg wasn't with the woman alone, so far as you know?

A. Not then. It was two weeks later when dat happened.

Q. What day and time?

A. Saturday, after dinner—maybe three o'clock. I was workin' around the third floor, an' Mr. Berg come up to me an' say, "Remember what you did the other Saturday, Mo?" an' I say I did, so he say he want me to do the same thing now. So I went downstairs and Miss Hopkins come on up into his office.

Q. How long did you stand by the door?

A. 'Bout half an hour. Den the lady come down and went out, an' Mr. Berg gave me half a dollar.

The deeper Archie got into it, the more the black man made it sound as if Noah were running a den of iniquity. The "Dawson" man was said to have come to the factory on several occasions and been given access to the dubious comforts of its grimy cellar. And Noah was said to have had any number of lady guests; Easter remembered one in particular who wore a green dress and had hair colored "jus' like yours" (he told Archie) and visited one Saturday in August the year before. But it was the Thanksgiving Day lady visitor—the one before whose jewels Noah was said to have knelt—whom the negro remembered best. "She was a big, handsome lady," he said, "who wore a kinder fancy white hat. When she and him come down from his office, she ask if I was the nigger he'd talked of, an' he said, 'Yes, that's the best nigger in the world.' She ask him if I talk much, an' he say I didn't talk at all." It was precisely the sort of plausible detail that added weight to the negro's testimony—and precisely the sort that could have been totally invented; it was neither provable nor disprovable, and it left the listener the choice of believing Easter entirely or not at all.

Archie dwelled for a time on the three different statements Mo had given the police after they had taken him into custody. Our side had had copies of the affidavits and studied them carefully; we could afford no more surprises from the witness.

Q. Now, Mo, you first told the detectives that you were at the factory that morning and watching the door and saw Miss Dugan go upstairs but never come down. That was the extent of your statement, wasn't it?

A. That's about it.

Q. You lied, then, didn't you?

323

A. Well, I held back, like.

Q. And you said you found the girl's purse in a vacant lot?

A. Yes, sir. That was wrong.

Q. You looked the police straight in the face—just like you're looking at me—and you lied to them, didn't you?

A. No, sir—I hung my head whenever I told them a lie, an' I looked them right in the eye when I told de truth. I thought I'd tell just a little bit o' the truth, so Mr. Berg would get scared an' send somebody to come get me outa trouble.

That, too, was plausible. And the way the police eked out the full tale of horror from him piece by piece. Archie asked if he hadn't been questioned for endless hours by the police and deprived of sleep and threatened with brutality if he did not incriminate Noah. Mo said no, that wasn't the case. "What dey said was, 'Mo, if'n you don't 'fess up, we're gonna start believin' you had a lot more to do with all this than you been lettin' on.' So I come clean."

Hour after hour, Archie tried to punch holes in the black man's story. He went to elaborate lengths to show that Mo couldn't spell worth a damn and thus could hardly have written the note found in the dead girl's hand. "You spell 'cat' with a 'k,' don't you, Mo?" he asked, and the colored man said, "Yes, sir." and the whole court laughed. But when Archie asked him how he could expect anyone to believe he had written that note when he couldn't spell the simplest words in the language, Mo just said, "I didn't claim to be no good speller—I can write good, is all I said. Mr. Berg spelled out each one o' dem words an' I jus' write it down like he say."

Parried, Archie gambled. "I want to ask you about that black-and-white sack you put the dead girl in to take her down to the cellar," he began. "I didn't say nothin' about no black-an'-white sack," said Mo. "It was just a regular ol' sack." Archie asked him if, during the first days after Noah's arrest, he hadn't told various workers at the factory that the superintendent was "innocent as an angel" of the crime. We had a handful of witnesses ready to

324

testify to that. "No, sir, I don't remember sayin' it like that," Mo answered. "I meant that he couldn'ta done such a thing as they said."

Q. But you've told us you knew that wasn't true.
A. Yes, sir. I was tryin' to protec' Mr. Berg.
Q. By lying?
A. Sorter.
Q. You lie whenever it suits you, don't you, Mo?
A. No, sir. I was jus' trying to help my boss.

Most remarkable about the black man's two-day performance in that courtroom was the fixity of his posture. He was a Rodin in ebony. His back was straight, head up and never turning, eyes fastened to his questioner. He never used a handkerchief, never mopped a hand across his brow, never twiddled his fingers or folded his arms or crossed his legs. His feet were planted on the floor as if they had grown there. There seemed nary a nerve, not even an isolated twitch, in his body. His sustained act of massive self-control, of course, lent substance to his answers. How rewarding the police must have found it to mold this dark clay, rehabilitating him for this memorable occasion, running him over and over his lines, and steeling him against any outbreak of emotion. And how easy. All it required, no doubt, to win and hold his unstinting cooperation was the threat of mutilation and slow death.

Mo Easter's two days on the witness stand had been a catastrophe for our side. Without his testimony, the case against Noah Berg as unfolded by the state was largely if not entirely circumstantial. By implicating himself in the disposal of the body, Mo had dramatically re-aligned the balance pans. Our job in that courtroom had plainly been to limit his testimony as drastically as possible and to impeach whatever he said as thoroughly as possible. Having failed in both purposes, Archie argued in recess now that we had no choice but to move to strike all of the negro's testimony pertaining to events prior to the crime. Father said that would be a confession of the damage that Mo had done us, and Tunney would chew us up. "Let him chew," Archie said. "We've got to be thinking about the record—if and when we appeal." It was the first clear sign that the magisterial Archibald Ruskin saw his chief hope for salvation residing in a higher court. Father uneasily acknowledged the point. "Your honor," Archie said upon releasing Mo from the stand, "we ask the court to rule out this witness's entire testimony pertaining to his having allegedly watched for the defendant on occasions before the day the girl was killed. The defense proposes to withdraw from the record all cross-examination on this point."

Tunney came out snarling. The man was in conniptions of righteous rage. "It is too late now, your honor, for this sort of barefaced maneuver," he foamed. "As an original proposition, it might have had some merit. But is it just, as a matter of plain common sense, to let these able counsel give this negro a grueling cross-examination for nearly a dozen hours and after they have failed utterly to shake his rendition, let it be expunged from the record? We expect to introduce testimony that will sustain Mo Easter's words, and if they are removed now, after the fact, our case will be done inestimable damage. There isn't a lawyer or layman who cannot see that these defense counsel should have made a timely plea and not one so absurd and insulting as this. They are reeling, after two days of cross-examination, from the terrific force of this testimony, and I sympathize with their plight. But fair is fair. The people of this state are entitled to be protected. The laws of Georgia govern this case, and they state unequivocally that an objection of this sort must be made at the time the testimony is introduced and the question of its admissibility propounded. The court may withhold its response till the testimony is taken, but that is not what we have here. Here the defense decided, upon the most careful calculation, to hold back and see if it could not trap this witness. Having failed, it chooses an unlawful maneuver—to erase the damning testimony from the record, even though nothing can erase it from all our minds."

Archie let the smoke settle for a moment before climbing to his feet like a listless pachyderm. "The learned solicitor has some more learning to do," he said. "As a practical matter, the defense could not move to strike something it did not know and does not believe until it heard the whole, sleazy presentation. As a matter of law, the twenty-eighth Georgia states that illegal testimony is always subject to withdrawal. If the evidence is illegal, a move can be made at any time to withdraw it, whether it has been permitted as an experiment or otherwise. The time for withdrawal always exists. There is nothing unjust or unfair about the defense motion."

You could practically hear the walls hiss as we made our way out of court. The judge, wanting the weekend to ponder, promised to rule on the motion at the beginning of the next week of the trial. But Tunney's point was undeniable. Whatever the record would show, Mo Easter had testified fully and damningly. The defense was on its knees, whether or not Noah Berg had been on the Thanksgiving prior.

III

Gloom was so impenetrable within father's office that weekend that it had grown a crust by mid-day Sunday. Dinner at our home did little to dissipate the discouragement. Archie reported that Tunney had supped at the De Soto the previous night and been interrupted by so many admirers and well-wishers coming to his table that our best hope may have become the solicitor's developing a sudden case of malnutrition. That was about the prevailing quality of wit inside our camp—sodden and self-pitying. Then providence sent us a visitor.

Plato Layne hobbled down the driveway to the rear door of our place and knocked gently. The colored help, not knowing who he was, was ready to offer him a morsel or two and send him off before mother or father could catch sight of him. When father came to the pantry and greeted Plato warmly, their puzzlement was mighty. And when the disheveled old colored man was ushered into the drawing room like an honored guest, they must have concluded that Elijah was black.

He had read every word of Mo Easter's testimony in court, Plato told our whole assemblage, "an' it ain't exactly like he say." Father and Archie exchanged glances and then looked up at heaven in unison. They told Plato to take his time and say whatever he wanted. "I want to help you, Mr. Adler," he said. He had been convinced, he told us, that Noah Berg—or somebody in authority at the factory—was trying to blame the murder on him, and so naturally he was angry and ill disposed to come forward with any information that might reduce the likelihood of the superintendent's conviction for the crime. Father said that was understandable. Then he said that it looked to us now as if someone was trying to put the blame on Noah Berg, just as they had on him. Plato nodded and said that was what he had concluded, too.

He had testified in court, Plato reminded us, that he reported to work on the groggy side on the Saturday of the murder because an acquaintance had come to his room and awakened him, urging that they go and have a drink to celebrate the holiday before he had to report to work. That acquaintance, Plato now revealed to us, was Mo Easter.

"He weren't no friend o' mine before then," the black man said. "Fac' is, I only seed him once or twice when I punch in to work and he's gettin' ready to leave." Mo jollied him out of bed around quarter past two and said he wanted to talk to Plato about something and would like to buy him a mug of near-beer. Mo hung around his room while Plato got dressed, chattering away amiably and trying to win his confidence. "At the nigger saloon is where he had dat double-header he tole about in court, and that's the truth—he gulped his down so fast before I even had a sip, I figure maybe they's givin' it away on accounta the holiday. So he have another and wait till I get goin' on mine, and then he tell me about this scheme o' his. He say he was makin' good money for a time when Mr. Vernon Pike was in the employ of the factory. He say after the noon whistle at the end o' work on Saturdays, Mr. Pike invited some o' his drinkin' friends to come to the factory an' he'd sneak 'em down into the cellar—not all at once, 'course, but one by one, takin' turns through the afternoon—where for them to enjoy the favors of the girls he got to go down there. The girls take turns, too, he say. He say they put some kinder cot or two down there so dey don't lie on the ground. Mo says his job was to watch de door for the men customers comin' and also listen for Mr. Berg so he don't catch on to what's happenin' downstairs. See, from his office up on the second floor, he couldn't see no front door, so anyone could slip in an' out. Mo laugh when he tell me one of the jobs Mr. Berg give him on Saturdays was watchin' the door—it was like he say in court, only he didn't 'zactly say who and what he was really watchin' fo'."

There was sudden and brilliant suffusion of light in that drawing room. Father and Archie were on the edge of their seats,

328

bursting with questions, but they forbore as Plato added to his disclosure. "Mo say he make three, four, maybe more dollars every Saturday from Mr. Pike for watchin' out good and keepin' his face shut. But ever since Mr. Pike get fired by Mr. Berg, Mo say that Saturday business all dry up. An' since Mr. Pike was leavin' town now, there weren't no likelihood it'd start up again. So Mo say, 'Why don't you an' me run the business for black folk down in that cellar? Mr. Pike done took out his cots but we get our own ones and put 'em down there and then we get customers—at night, too, see, when no one's around and it's easy. Mr. Pike, he got all his friends and acquaintances from the saloon he patronize —we do the same from nigger saloons. We make a fortune, Plato, you an' me, and do a good service fo' everybody.' That's what he say to me."

"So," said Archie, cracking his knuckles with glee, "he made you a sporting proposition, did he?"

"Yes, sir," Plato said and smiled slowly.

"What did you say back?"

"Nothin' much. I say I want to think it over. It weren't nothin' I'd ever cotton to, but he was buyin' the beer an' it didn't cost me nothin' to listen. Mo say to take my time and he get back to me the nex' week."

"The girls," father said, as excited as I had ever seen him, "did Mo tell you who the girls were that Pike got to go down into the cellar? Were they girls from the factory?"

"He didn' say," said Plato, "an' I didn' ask. But it wouldn' surprise me none. They don't get much pay, some of them girls."

Pieces of the puzzle began now to fall into place for us. Of course it was Pike. Pike admittedly knew Jean Dugan. Pike was admittedly at the factory the day of the murder, albeit late in the afternoon so far as we knew for certain—returning to the scene of his crime, no doubt. Pike had admittedly had a falling out with Noah, who deprived the lanky white man, if Mo was telling Plato the truth, of his legitimate and illegitimate sources of income. It would have been hard to remain in the procurement business from outside the factory where he lacked access to the tender flesh of all those destitute young women. So his animus toward Noah must have been considerable. Who better to blame for Jean Dugan's death? And in view of all the loyal customers he had supplied from among the clientele at the saloon he habituated, Pike naturally had no trouble producing countless witnesses to his presence at the tavern throughout that Saturday. Many of them were doubtless married men, whose philandering they did not wish to have advertised—and whose procurement agent, having the goods on them, they would doubtless go to any reasonable length to protect. Nor, of course, would any girl involved in that flesh-peddling enterprise come forward to testify to Vernon Pike's bad character for fear her own name would be irreparably tarnished. Our problem was to place Pike in the factory that Saturday at a time that coincided with the estimated moment of the girl's murder.

"If Mo Easter had been telling the truth in the courtroom," Archie speculated out loud, "then he came to Plato's room that afternoon already knowing that the Dugan girl's body was in that basement. And he must have known that when she was found, that basement would not be a very promising place to operate a prostitution business. So either he never helped Noah dispose of the body, as he swore to under oath, or he must have had some other purpose in coming to Plato's place."

I said that Mo might have thought that Noah had disposed of the body in the furnace by himself. "Yes," Archie said, "but that would mean what he testified to in court was true and what he told Plato about Pike and his basement business was a lie." Unless, I said, Pike was running his operation downstairs while Noah was partaking upstairs, and Mo was guardian of the door for both activities—kind of Janus the Janitor.

"I have a simpler explanation of Easter's visit to Plato's room," said father, "and one more suitable to our needs. Easter came to steal a piece of Plato's clothing and see the layout of his quarters, so he'd have no trouble smuggling the garment back in once he'd got it good and bloody." He turned to Plato. "Were you out of the room at all while he was there—to go to the water-closet, for instance?"

Plato nodded. "That's the way it happen—and that's why I come over here. I reckon Mo Easter's in this thing deep as his eyeballs, only Mr. Berg got nothin' to do with it—or with tryin' to trap me for the killin'."

Father and Archie decided to brazen it out with Pike directly and not take their chances with him in the courtroom as they had with Mo Easter and lost so badly.

They found him at dusk rocking on the porch of the rooming house where the state was putting him up till his turn in the witness box the next week. Pike had clearly been imbibing—"This here ain't nothin' but a pitcher o' warm spit," he said out of deference to the Sunday blue laws—but was still wary of the two lawyers whose visit he knew could scarcely be to his interest. He declined at first to come with them to father's office, but Archie decided the moment was right to throw his weight into the encounter. He scooped up the glass from which Pike was drinking and, as he recounted it, "took a deep whiff of whatever rotgut he had got hold of. 'My,' I said, 'I'd hate to have to call Chief Yates tomorrow morning and tell him one of the state's star witnesses is an illegal boozer whose word in court ain't worth diddly-squat.' Ol' Vernon, he came along right gentle after that."

I was stationed behind a partition in father's office, surreptitiously taking notes on the interview with that reluctant country boy. Archie did most of the baiting. "The way we figure it," he said, hoping to produce the maximum shock value, "Jeannie Dugan was on to that den of vice you were operating in the factory basement and either threatened to tell Noah Berg about it—and maybe she did, which is why you really got fired—or you tried to enlist her as one of your lovely young temptresses and she refused. Either way, you had a grudge against the girl as well as the superintendent. What's more, what you were up to in that basement makes you, and not our client, the prime candidate for Jean Dugan's murderer, and we expect the jury'll see it the same way when we finish with our case."

There was quiet for a moment. Then Pike said softly, "Is that a fact?"

"We asked you by here, son," Archie said, "to let you know what we know and to give you the chance to come clean, so things won't go so hard on you when the full story comes out."

"Why, that's very kindly of you gentlemen," said Pike. "But lemme tell you somethin'." His voice was low and hard. "I'm nobody's fool, least of all Noah Berg's. I read the papers—everybody in Georgia knows what Mo Easter testified in that court last week—and the way I figure it, the jury's about ready to measure your boy Berg's smart yid neck for a rope tie."

"Don't you count on it, Vernon," Archie said.

"Don't you flimflam me, Mr. Defense Attorney, 'cause I know a con when I see it. Now you just hear me out. First off, I loved that little Jeannie Dugan and wouldn't never have touched her. Why, even her mother said as much in court the first day. Second of all, Jean didn't have nothin' to do with anything goin' on in the cellar—." He caught himself up at once. "Third of all, nothin' at all was happening in the cellar, so I don't know what you're talkin' about. Fourth of all, I got dozens of witnesses to my where'bouts all that day, an' you-all know it. So who you tryin' to fool?"

"What would you say," Archie said, "if I told you we got five girls who'll testify what your game was in the factory?"

"I'd say you're a liar. I'd also say Tunney would never let that kind o' shit get testified to—hell, I ain't the one on trial—."

"Not yet."

"Not never."

But he was beginning to perspire. Father offered to get him a cool drink, and he accepted. His tone of voice became noticeably less truculent thereafter. They all had some cider in silence for a while to let Pike think over the situation.

"I'll tell you something," he said finally. "Last Thanksgiving, after I'd been working for Noah Berg for a while, I came in to the office to catch up on a little work. I don't rightly know whether he forgot I had a key or he just didn't expect nobody else would come in to work on the holiday, but I come in, nice an' quiet probably, and open up the door to the outer office—see, I worked close by him and did the payroll in those days. I look on over and the shade is half pulled down—maybe it was three quarters pulled. Now I never seen that shade pulled before, so I squint in through the open part, and what did I see? I'll tell you what I saw. It's like what nigger Mo Easter said in court, only it was me who seen him and the woman—she was his stenographer, an' it wasn't him who was on his knees but her. An' o' course his drawers was dropped—."

The silence was on our side now. "You're lying to save your butt," Archie said after a while.

"You just go ask your client about it. I backed on out the door quiet that day, but I let him know what I knew. He got rid of the stenographer right fast. An' we had ourselves a kinda agreement—I wouldn't ever say nothin' about his little dirty business an' he'd keep his nose out o' mine. I told him about the basement, all right, and he said he didn't want to hear or know anythin' about it, just so long as I did my regular job fine—."

"Did he know you were using girls from the factory?" father asked.

"He never asked," said Pike.

"Then why'd he fire you?" Archie asked.

"What he said was the payroll account come up a little short two weeks runnin' an' he thought I was stealin' on him. Shit, I was makin' twice my salary out o' the basement business, so why'd I mess that up by stealin' a few bucks from payroll? But, see, it gave him an excuse to throw me out on my ass. He said if I ever tried to tell about Thanksgiving, he'd say I was a liar and thief jus' trying to get back at him with some filthy story. That was more gumption that I thought he had."

"So he outfoxed you," said Archie, "and you hated him for it?"

"He's a pimply-ass little pervert," said Pike.

"And what's that make you?" said Archie.

"It don't make me no murderer, that's what it don't. And if you try to bring out any of this hound-shit in that courtroom, I'm gonna tell just what I told you now. See, the shoe's on the other foot now, ain't it, genul'men?"

It was midnight before father got back home. He and Archie had let Pike off at his rooming house and then driven straight to the police station, where both men used all their wiles on Chief Yates to get an after-hours session with their client. "We laid it all out for him," father said, his face slack from exhaustion. "I said I was sure Plato would testify for us—and we'd do our damnedest to get what Easter told him about Pike into the record. But he's afraid Pike will get the Thanksgiving story into the testimony again, and he can't bear that." Noah admitted to father that Pike's version of that sexual episode was true—"but he says the woman took the initiative, and he suspects that Pike put her up to it."

It was astonishing to me that a man accused of murder, whose trial was not going very well, would not risk admitting to a non-lethal act of carnality if it held the strong promise of diverting blame for the capital crime to another man. The only thing wrong with that, father pointed out, was that the particular sexual act in question was categorized under Georgia law as sodomy—and that, too, was a capital offense.

"They've never strung up a white man for it," Archie had said when father noted as much to him. "Of course they've probably never had a Jew they could convict for it before."

The real problem with the day's astonishing revelations was that even if we were able to establish in court that Vernon Pike was a whoremaster—and witnesses might well come forward to verify as much—that was the sort of social addiction society brushed aside; it did not make Pike a killer. And in the exchange of testimony, assuming Pike would keep his word and tar Noah as promised, the defendant would emerge undeniably as a sexual deviant. If that were so, could murder be far beyond his dark thoughts?

IV

As we had expected, Judge Vickery ruled on Monday morning that the challenged portion of Mo Easter's testimony regarding Noah's alleged sexual adventures prior to the crime could remain in the record. The defense, he said, had mistimed its motion, and the interests of justice and equity had been served by the extensive cross-examination in which the court had allowed defense counsel the widest latitude. What we did not expect was the reaction to the judge's ruling.

It began with a single sharp handclap, like the report of a cap pistol, and then exploded in a giant wave of applause that seemed to roll up from every side of the courtroom. It was so massive a sound that at first it stunned us all—the lawyers, the officers of the court, the judge himself, whose eyes seemed to swim in disbelief at so impermissible a display of partisanship. It could not have lasted more than twenty seconds, but that was enough: I remember feeling as if the earth had opened up and we were all about to be sucked down into the crevasse. The common loathing of Noah Berg was thus made manifest in our ears, and even as the clapping stilled and the judge's gavel sounded urgently above it, a great spume of exultation from the masses outside in the square came in through the windows and drenched us further.

Father put his finger in the dike. "I will ask for a mistrial if such a demonstration occurs again," he declared into the hush that fell as suddenly as the outbreak preceding it had arisen. "I will ask that the court be cleared if it continues in even a modulated form. Your honor is obliged, along with other officers of the court, to prevent such disgraceful exhibitions and perversions of the judicial process."

"The court knows its business, counselor," said the judge, who then offered a perfunctory lecture to the assemblage and ordered the bailiffs to remove forthwith any violators of courtroom decorum. He did not say he would hold them in contempt and see that they were clapped in irons. It was about as limp an admonishment as could have been rendered under the circumstances. The damage was done. The dramatic impact on the jury of that show of community sentiment could have been no less than Mo Easter's testimony itself.

Tunney moved confidently now to wind up his case. He recalled Mrs. Camp to the stand and had Mo Easter brought back into the courtroom. "Was this the negro you saw lurking about on the first floor that Saturday as you came down the stairway shortly before one o'clock?" he asked.

She looked at him carefully. "He seems to be about the same size and physique," she said, "but I cannot be absolutely certain. This one's hair is shorter. But there is a definite resemblance."

The solicitor recalled Mo just long enough to bring out that the negro had had his hair cut the previous week and normally wore it a good deal more full and woolly than at present. Then Tunney brought on his key corroborative witness, Orville Oliver Dalton, who said he had worked on and off as a railroad carpenter for the past ten years. He had a large, square face with recessed eyes and beetling brows and wore a tie of clamorous pattern that contrasted incongruously with his dark suit.

Q. Were you ever employed at the Jubilee soda bottling factory on Longstreth Way?
A. No, sir.

335

Q. Did you ever go there?
A. Yes, sir.
Q. Under what circumstances?
A. I was invited there by a lady friend.
Q. What was her name?
A. Flora Hopkins. She worked there.
Q. How many times did you go there with her?
A. Two or three times.
Q. Did you ever go into Noah Berg's office with her?
A. Yes, sir—on several occasions.
Q. When were they?
A. Last summer and fall.
Q. Can you be more precise?
A. Not really. My memory isn't very good at that sort of thing.
Q. Was there anyone in the office with Berg when you got there?
A. Yes, sir—a woman.
Q. Do you know who she was or what she was doing there?
A. No, sir.
Q. Was this after regular working hours?
A. Yes, sir—I would come on Saturday afternoons.
Q. Were you ever in the basement of the factory?
A. Yes, sir.
Q. How did you get there?
A. Down that ladder.
Q. Was Miss Hopkins with you?
A. Yes.
Q. Did Berg know you two were down in the basement?
A. I'm not sure. He certainly knew we were in the building.
Q. When you were in Berg's office, did you see any drinks on his desk?
A. Yes, sir.
Q. What kind of drinks?
A. I'm not sure. They were iced, is all I remember.

Archie, revived, riddled him on the cross:

Q. How do you know Mr. Berg knew you and your friend were in the building after you left his office?

A. He said, "You-all go have a good time now."

Q. Wasn't it possible he meant have a good time doing whatever you were doing wherever you were doing it?

A. It didn't sound like that.

Q. Did you see the nigger Easter watching at the door when you came in and went out?

A. Yes. He helped us down the ladder.

Q. Is it possible that you assumed Mr. Berg knew what you were up to because Mo Easter seemed to have been assigned to being a lookout for your—activities?

A. Maybe. I don't think so, though.

Q. Did you pay Mr. Berg anything for the use of the basement or give him any other sign of your appreciation?

A. Miss Hopkins assured me she had taken care of that.

Q. The woman who was in Mr. Berg's office when you arrived—was that on one occasion, by the way, or several?

A. I don't remember for certain. More than once, I think.

Q. Couldn't she have been his stenographer?

A. I—no. She didn't look much like a stenographer, though.

Q. Was she in a state of undress?

A. I don't remember.

Q. Are you in the habit of meeting strange women in a state of undress in someone else's office?

A. No.

Q. Then you probably would have remembered if she were not fully dressed, wouldn't you?

A. I don't know—yes, probably.

Q. You say the woman didn't look like a stenographer. What does a stenographer look like? Do they have pencils in place of fingers—or some other distinctive physical traits?

A. It's hard to say.

Q. Then why did you say it?
A. She seemed too young and pretty to be a stenographer.
Q. You will have all the young and pretty stenographers in America among your detractors, Mr. Dalton. I have one such in my office. Now tell us about these drinks in Mr. Berg's office—what color were they?
A. I don't remember.
Q. Might they have been dark?
A. They might have.
Q. Were they alcoholic?
A. I don't know.
Q. Then you didn't have any?
A. No.
Q. So you can't tell us if the drink Mr. Berg was evidently enjoying was in fact a glass of cold Jubilee —the very product bottled in that factory?
A. It didn't look like that.
Q. I thought you said a minute ago you didn't remember what it looked like?
A. You've got me confused.

With his next-to-last witness, the state solicitor nearly overstepped himself.

He put on Melba Swann, the black cook at the Klein residence, where the Bergs lived, who testified that Noah had eaten only one of the three chicken dumplings she served him for dinner at about one-thirty on the afternoon of the murder. She remembered because that was his favorite dish and he apologized to her for leaving over most of it, saying it was fine but he just wasn't very hungry that day. But hadn't she told her husband, who was in the kitchen at the time, that Berg seemed nervous and upset, the solicitor asked icily, and had she not signed a statement for the police to that effect?

The black woman sighed hugely. "Well," she said, "that weren't how it happen'. They had my husband Robert in jail then for bein' drunk and disorderly and he naturally want to get out, so he tells 'em that's what I done told him about Mr. Berg."

Tunney fumed. He shoved the woman's affidavit under her

nose and demanded, "Did you sign this or didn't you, Melba? You're under oath now, just like you were when you signed this."

She looked him in the eye. "The police wrote it down and put it under my nose, just like yo' doin'," she said evenly, "and they say if I want my husband back I better sign it. I said it weren't de truf, so they say that mus' mean Robert's lyin' so they gonna hold him even longer. So I sign it."

We skipped a cross-examination. The cook's testimony seemed to speak volumes of the conspiratorial nature of the police work dedicated to getting Noah Berg convicted. Tunney, lucky not to have had his case more badly hurt by Mrs. Swann's testimony, turned finally to Vernon Pike.

He was dressed to the nines, for a country boy; he had clearly learned city ways since abandoning his rural origins. Tall and raw-boned, he towered above the clerk who administered him the oath. He chose his words with care, knowing as he did that the defense would pounce on any opening he provided. He said that he had worked at the Jubilee factory from the middle of the previous September to the beginning of April as shipping clerk and paymaster and that he performed the latter function in Noah Berg's outer office. He was discharged, he said, when one of the office boys reported a two-dollar shortage in his pay envelope.

"Didn't it seem strange to you that Mr. Berg would dismiss you for such an offense, especially when there was no proof that you were the culprit?" the solicitor asked. Pike said yes and that he was upset by his firing, especially since Berg had commended him several times for the quality of his work and entrusted him with the keys to the factory, the combination to the safe, and all the cash that flowed through the office. Tunney then asked if he had known Jean Dugan. "Yes, sir," Pike answered, "I knew her as a little girl when both our families lived up in Wilkinson County." He said she was a fine young lady and he was pleased to renew her acquaintance when he came to work at the factory.

Q. Did Mr. Berg know Jean Dugan?
A. He did.
Q. How do you know that?
A. It was his business to know everyone and how well they worked. He didn't permit slackers to stay long.

339

Q. How else do you know that he knew her?

A. One Friday she come by during work because I had a question in going over her time slip. After she left, Berg come by and said, "You seem to know Jean pretty well."

Q. Did he seem annoyed when he said that?

A. That's hard to say.

Q. Did he speak with Miss Dugan often?

A. He would speak with most of the girls every now and again.

Q. With her more than any of the rest?

A. Maybe a little more. She worked nearer our office.

He wound up telling how Noah had jumped at the sight of him late the Saturday afternoon of the murder when he came by to pick up his work shoes. Archie let him stew for a bit before beginning the cross.

Q. How much did Mr. Berg jump when he saw you that day?

A. How much?

Q. Yes—how far? A foot, a yard, a rail post, a furlong—or what?

A. It wasn't like that. He just seemed startled.

Q. Don't you think he had some reason to be startled?

A. Not that I know of.

Q. Didn't you tell us that he had dismissed you for what he thought was an act of dishonesty?

A. Yes.

Q. And did you have any business on those premises—any legitimate business—after that?

A. Well, I came to get my work shoes.

Q. But he couldn't have known that when he first saw you and, as you say, jumped, could he have?

A. Well—no, I suppose not. But I gave him no cause.

Q. Don't you think coming by the factory three weeks after you were let go and at a time it was closed constituted suspicious behavior?

A. I was taking the train to Macon that night.

Q. But Mr. Berg didn't know that at first, did he?

A. I guess not.

Q. Let me ask you, Mr. Pike, whether you like people who act unfairly toward you.

A. I don't understand your question.

Q. Do you like people who are unfair to you?

A. I suppose not.

Q. Did Mr. Berg act fairly in dismissing you, a trusted and able worker, for so minor a matter as a disputed two-dollar shortage in a pay envelope?

A. I don't think he did, no.

Q. Did you tell him that?

A. I think so. Yes, I must have.

Q. What did he say to that?

A. Something about not being able to tolerate even the slightest doubt about the honesty of his paymaster.

Q. Would it be fair to say, then, that you resented Mr. Berg's precipitous action and bore a dislike toward him? Even a strong dislike?

A. Not strong. But anyone would get riled over being fired like that.

Q. Exactly—and might well want to get even.

SOLICITOR TUNNEY: Objection!

THE COURT: Counsel will rephrase the question.

Q. Didn't you want to get back at Mr. Berg for firing you?

A. I had better things to do.

Q. In your capacity as a trusted assistant, didn't Mr. Berg teach you how to work the punch clock?

A. Yes.

Q. How to fix it and set it?

A. Yes. As paymaster, I was constantly working with the time slips. Sometimes the workers tried to fool with the clock and jammed it.

Q. So you knew how the time clock worked inside out?

A. Pretty much.

Q. Did you have a key to it?

A. Yes.

Q. Did you ever use that key to fix up the time slips of workers you favored?

A. I did not.

Q. But you could have if you had wanted to?

A. So could Berg and Woodcock and three or four other people who knew how it worked.

Q. Just answer the question, Mr. Pike.

A. Yes, I suppose I could have if I'd wanted to.

Q. As his trusted assistant, did you know where Mr. Berg kept a spare set of keys to the doors and the clock?

A. I had my own set of keys.

Q. That isn't what I was asking. The question is: did you know where Mr. Berg kept his spare keys?

A. He may have said something about their being in a part of the safe, but I never saw them there.

Q. But since you knew the combination, you could easily have looked for them in an emergency?

A. I suppose. It never came up.

Q. Now these work shoes you claim to have left at the factory—why hadn't you taken them with you when you were dismissed?

A. I guess I thought Berg would rehire me.

Q. Why did a clerk like you need a pair of work shoes?

A. I didn't want to get my dress shoes dirty, and there's a lot of dirt around a factory.

Q. Why didn't you just wear your work shoes to work instead of changing at the factory?

A. I like to dress nice, and sometimes I'd stop by at a tavern on the way from work or meet a lady friend.

Q. Do you have a lot of lady friends, Mr. Pike?

A. I have my share.

Q. Was Jean Dugan part of that share?

SOLICITOR TUNNEY: Objection. Counsel is abusing the witness.

MR. RUSKIN: I did no such thing, your honor. I asked a straightforward question.

THE COURT: Try it again in different words.

Q. Did you ever see Jean Dugan away from the factory?

A. I walked her home from work a few times. We liked to talk about the old days in the country. And then I'd pay my respects to Miss Jean's mother—she's a fine woman.

Q. Do you know Mr. O. O. Dalton?

A. Slightly.

Q. How do you know him?

A. I think we met at the saloon—the Eye of the Storm, it's called.

Q. Do you know Flora Hopkins?

A. Not socially.

Q. How then?

A. I've seen her around town. She is well known.

Q. Did you ever use the basement of the factory for immoral purposes?

A. No, sir.

Q. Did you have any knowledge that the basement was used for such purposes?

A. I did not.

Q. May I remind you that you are under oath, Mr. Pike?

SOLICITOR TUNNEY: Objection! The witness answered the question. Moreover, the question is improper and entirely irrelevant.

THE COURT: I will sustain the objection.

And that was as close as we came to labeling that long drink of foul water as the moral derelict he assuredly was.

After a ten-minute recess toward the end of testimony on Tuesday afternoon of that second week of the trial, Judge Vickery came wheeling out of his chambers into the courtroom in a fashion that brought a gawk of horror from father, Archie, and the men of the press. Under his arm, the judge had tucked a sheaf of documents, and clearly visible on the top of the bunch was a copy of the afternoon paper bearing a banner headline in big red letters you could see in the next county, "STATE ADDS KEY LINKS TO CASE." He might as well have sequestered the jury in the state solicitor's drawing room and invited Tunney to pass around his bonded bourbon.

The sight was too much for Noah's mother, who till that time had reserved the principal part of her energy for glaring at the solicitor and praying his tongue should turn to molten lead before its next hateful utterance. She began to sob now at this gross instance of official misfeasance, her formidable bosom heaving out of control for several moments as the court paid its reverence to motherhood—even the mothers of accused murderers, even the mothers of Yankee Jews—by its perfect stillness. Maternal tears had been shed now by both sides, watering the floor of that hard arena without notably cleansing it for longer than an instant. Archie then rose to say the defense wished to make a statement without the jury present. The judge, eyes spinning out of synchronization in his distress over such a dreadful gaffe, readily obliged.

"No doubt your honor forgot himself in bringing such unsanctionable reading matter with him into this room just now," Archie said as solemnly yet gently as he knew how, "for I know that your honor would do nothing to jeopardize this case. We all know you and your distinguished reputation as a jurist. Yet we are faced with the fact that the jury have had the opportunity to read an inflammatory headline that even an infirm jackrabbit could see five fields away. The headline itself is open to dispute—I, for one, dispute it—and the jury will have no opportunity now to read the article beneath it and any mitigating details. We are not going to ask a mistrial, but we do request that the jury be told not to be influenced by what it has just seen."

Chastened, the judge called the jurors back in and, without explicitly confessing his own blunder, warned the panel that it must decide the case solely on the basis of evidence "regularly and legally admitted before the court." Nothing they had seen or might see in the newspapers could be permitted to sway them in any way.

"He should rot in hell!" Sophie Berg exclaimed between sobs as court adjourned. Her tearful voice was hardly less audible than the scarlet headline had been visible throughout the chamber.

TEN

Father and Archie Ruskin launched their counter-assault in the middle of the second week of the trial. During the ensuing fortnight, they summoned one hundred eighty-seven witnesses in massive support of the defendant's innocence. Nevertheless, I found myself speculating intermittently, even as the defense team built its case with artful and compelling skill (father supplied the art, Archie the compulsion), on Noah Berg's innocence. Wasn't it possible that he had duped us? Wasn't it possible that he was a vulpine monster beneath that bland exterior of compulsive conscientiousness? Perhaps he had corked up so many of his ignoble impulses that they tore apart their container from time to time in displays of violent licentiousness. If Jews were as good as anybody else in the world, why could they also not be as vile? Had we organized a cartel on virtue? Could that black slickster Mo Easter, a sad and liquored-up ignoramus, turn suddenly into so masterful a dissembler—or was the truth, or an approximation thereof, on his lips during those long hours in that courtroom?

Yes, the negro could very well have invented the whole thing, said father when I asked, "especially if the alternative was to have had his back stripped raw and his gonads crushed by our dedicated law-enforcement hooligans. More than likely, they would have charged him with the murder—what's one worthless darkey subtracted from the general population?"

I had not, before then, ever heard father refer to the gonads, even in passing. Could there have been a surer sign of his engagement, at the most elemental level of his very proper being, in that torrid contest? I confessed to him my doubts, feckless though they were, about Noah. He said they were traceable directly to my having found him an unstimulating young man; others had detected gifts where I sensed only vacancies. Perhaps, I said, but there remained an elusive quality about him that no amount of researches had disclosed. Father replied that I had perhaps been looking too hard. "Where ignorance is bliss, you mean, 'tis folly to be wise?" I asked. He took that more kindly than I deserved. "Surely no Jew ever acceded to that tripe," he said. "That's not Shakespeare, is it?" Thomas Gray, I told him—*On a Distant Prospect of Eton College*. "I am glad everyone in this family is not illiterate," he said in self-reproof and then gently hinted that I was in danger of becoming overwrought by the trial.

No doubt he was right. Despite myself, I identified increasingly with Noah Berg's plight. I paid more attention now to how closely he followed the proceedings, how easily he took his wife's or mother's hand, how alertly he scribbled a note to himself from time to time and whispered a few illuminating words to his lawyers. I could find nothing furtive about him; he may not have been the most appealing creature on earth, but how could I doubt his innocence and be taken in even for a moment by this onslaught of the *goyim*?

I began to study the jury for a clue to its response to the diametrically opposing stories that had emerged from the testimony. If the bias of the spectators in and out of the courtroom was plain, what chance was there that these twelve men might rise above the mentality of the mob? Did the mere fact of their impanelment infuse them with a higher vision of justice, a nobler sense of duty? Father said yes. So I searched their faces keenly for a glimmer of warmth and understanding. They were a study in lassitude, their features as animated as a dozen wilted pecan pies in two orderly rows. They never smiled, they never snickered, they never sighed, they never frowned. All they did was watch. Every once in a long while, one of them would let his gaze go wandering to the wallpaper or the lethargically turning fans overhead and the little knot of flies that were ever holding a caucus around the middle chandelier on the ceiling. As the trial ground on and fatigue and boredom took their inevitable toll, their characteristic immobility began to yield to a tendency to squirm about furtively in the hard, straight-backed juror's chairs in an effort to remain comfortable and still look dignified.

I found some solace in the newspaper stories about the jury's ordeal and how its members were weathering it with manly fortitude. They had all become chums, though you would never know it from their courtroom decorum, and passed the weekends in cheery enough quarantine. One juror was a sufficiently skillful pianist to inspire the sheriff to have a spinet hauled in to keep the men's spirits high with barbershop singing (and, no doubt, an occasional off-color verse). They sang together, took short walks together under the watchful eye of a pair of deputies, read from the Bible together on Sunday mornings, played cards together every night, fretted together over the troubled health of an infant belonging to one of their number, and celebrated together when the portliest juror's wife smuggled in a round of cup custards and a lemon pie. From these strands I convinced myself that father was right: twelve such men, plucked at random from their natural lives, in fact assume an exalted sense of mission about their grim collective chore and are no longer the common run of humanity but a higher, more reflective, and therefore more compassionate species.

I was brought down from this wishful sortie by Archie, who said it was bunk, and by a squib one of the newspapers ran about midway through the trial. They asked a veteran court-watcher named Charlie Riddlemoser, who was said not to have missed a major trial at Chatham County courthouse for thirty years, which way he thought the jury was leaning. "You know," he said, "there's three things that Providence Himself don't happen to know—namely, how to argue with a woman, where your wife's goin' to whet her knife when she cuts meat, and just 'zactly what's on the minds of the Berg jury." I only hoped that Providence had arranged to keep those minds open.

Father began the defense effort with Joe Dettwiler, Noah's titular superior at the factory. He had been out with bronchitis for the two weeks preceding the murder but had had no fear, he said, that production would fall off under Noah and his underlings. "He's a crackerjack worker," old Joe said of Noah, and his moral character, so far as the manager could tell over the past five years, was of the best quality. He had not the slightest indication that

Noah ever did, or ever would, take advantage of any of the many young ladies who worked at the factory. "He cared about one thing," Dettwiler said, "and that was getting the job done right at the lowest possible cost."

Q. Was Mr. Berg popular with his fellow workers?
A. He got on well enough with them, if that's what you mean.
Q. But he was a stickler for work quotas and regulations and matters of that sort, wasn't he?
A. He surely was.
Q. Didn't that cause a good deal of resentment toward him among the help?
A. I see what you mean—and that's true. Them that he felt weren't up to the standard, we had to let go. There was always a lot of bodies coming and going.
Q. Would you ever hear complaints from the help that Mr. Berg was a slavedriver?
A. Not in so many words. Just a little grumbling now and then, maybe.

Tunney was a cautious cross-examiner, rather as if he were continually mulling how much he could get away with. He dealt briefly with the aging plant chief.

Q. It wasn't likely, was it, that a young lady who was discharged for alleged inefficiency would come running to your office to complain? That wasn't your function at the factory, was it, Mr. Dettwiler? You left that to the younger fellows.
A. To Berg and Woodcock, yes. They managed the day-to-day affairs of the work force.
Q. So far as you know, the high rate of turnover at the factory might just as well have been due to the fact that Noah Berg was not only a stickler for work rules but a quite industrious womanizer as well?
MR. ADLER: Objection. The solicitor's question is argumentative and inflammatory.
THE COURT: Try it a little differently, Mr. Tunney.
Q. Mr. Dettwiler, because you were remote—by your own admission—from the day-to-day problems of the

work force at the factory, isn't it possible that the real reason for the high turnover of employées was different from the one you assumed?

A. "Remote" is your word, not mine. I never said I didn't know generally what was going on there. Your suggestion is most ungentlemanly—.

Q. And is murder gentlemanly, sir? That's all, thank you.

Encouraged by Bryce Woodcock's crisp testimony as a prosecution witness, father recalled the bright, good-looking assistant superintendent and banked on him to repudiate a number of the more troubling circumstantial points in the state's case. He had large, wide-set eyes and curly hair the color of corn; how the young ladies must have preferred his open, outdoor face to Noah's pinched and ascetic features! At first, Woodcock proved an ideal witness under father's drill. He described the office suite that he and Noah shared. No, he said, there was no sofa or armchair in either office of the sort suitable for gamy pastimes; indeed, there was none such in the entire factory, so far as he knew. No, he said, he had never seen any girls in the office except during work hours and on official business. He explained that Noah generally left the door to the safe open in his interior office on Saturdays because the superintendent had to make constant reference to the various record books kept in it as well as to dig out an occasional pay envelope for a worker who hadn't been on hand to collect it the previous afternoon at closing time. When that safe door was open, anyone outside of the office would have trouble looking into it unless he or she came up very close. Nor, he said, could a girl the size of Mary Ellen Stiles see over that safe door. The factory elevator was a very noisy contraption, he added, and when it was in use, everyone in the place could tell—even when the production machinery was operating at full steam. "It kind of moaned and groaned when it moved even a little, like it had arthritis real bad," Bryce said, eliciting small smiles here and there around the room. As to the events preceding the murder, he testified that he, and not Noah, had paid off the help on Friday at the close of the day. "There's a little pass-through window in the front office opening out into the hallway, and I'd hand out the envelopes through that," he said. "Mr. Berg usually remained in his office at

payoff time. Now that's kind of an itty-bitty window, and sometimes maybe it's hard to tell exactly who's on either side of it."

Q. Do you know Heather Ferguson?
A. Yes, sir. She works at the factory.
Q. Did you pay her off that Friday?
A. I believe I did.
Q. Did she—or anyone—ask for Jean Dugan's pay enve-
lope that afternoon?
A. Not to my recollection—at least not by Miss Dugan's
name. Someone could have asked for it by her em-
ployée number, though, and that would not have
registered in my memory, I'm afraid.
Q. Do you know Mo Easter?
A. Yes, sir.
Q. What is your opinion of him?
A. There's not much to him.
Q. What was his character?
A. It was bad.
Q. Would you believe him on oath?
A. No, I would not.
Q. Did Mr. Berg ever use to jolly with Mo Easter?
A. Not that I know of. He'd exchange a few words now
and then when Mo came by to sweep up.
Q. Did you ever jolly with Mo Easter?
A. No, sir. I used to kick him whenever I caught him
loafing, which was frequently.

Tunney spotted an opening and moved in at once. If Mo
Easter was such a rotten egg, he asked, why did the factory keep
him employed? "It was not a job that required great skill or paid
very much," said Woodcock. Nevertheless, the solicitor persisted,
the factory was not in the habit of retaining workers of bad character and marked indolence, was it? Woodcock conceded that it
was not, and when asked if he had ever recommended the negro's
dismissal, he said that he had "on more than one occasion. But
Mr. Berg said it was not worth worrying about."

Q. What did you tell the coroner's jury when you were
asked your opinion of Mr. Berg's character?
A. I said it was good.

Q. Did you tell of any instances of its being less than good?

A. Not that I recall.

Q. Didn't you tell them that an office boy once said Mr. Berg had made improper advances toward him?

A. Well, yes.

Q. That's all.

A. But I also said that I did not believe the boy—.

Q. You may step down.

A. I haven't finished answering your question, sir.

Q. I beg your pardon.

A. I also said that the boy was somewhat slovenly and had earned Mr. Berg's disapproval.

Q. Didn't the boy claim Mr. Berg had touched his body?

A. Yes. But I thought he was lying and trying to get back at Mr. Berg. The boy was let go the week following.

Q. Not compliant enough, eh?

MR. ADLER: Objection—to the solicitor's unpardonable comment and the entire line of hearsay testimony.

Father was sustained, but the damaging concession by the witness had been aired. Why, he wondered, had Woodcock volunteered his unwholesome piece of testimony to the coroner's jury if he had held the office boy in such low regard? Why not spare Noah that added whiff of suspicion? Ah, the wages of blond, blue-eyed forthrightness. On balance, I could not say whether his closest and presumably most devoted co-worker had helped or hurt Noah's case the more.

Father countered with a pearl I had discovered during my pretrial interviewing among the help—a wan slip of a girl named Prudence Jordan, who had worked at the factory for four years.

Q. On April twenty-fifth, did you and Heather Ferguson go together to get your pay envelopes?

A. Yes.

Q. Whom did you get it from?

A. Mr. Woodcock.

Q. Both of you?

A. Yes, sir.

Q. Where were you in relation to Miss Ferguson when you appeared at the pay window?

A. Just behind her.

Q. Did she ask Mr. Berg for Jean Dugan's pay envelope?

A. No—not like that. What happened was that Mr. Woodcock was called away from the window for a minute or two to take a phone call and Mr. Berg passed by on the inside. Heather asked him if she could collect a friend's envelope for her, the way Mr. Pike had allowed, and he said no, anyone who didn't show up in person then could jolly well get it the next day or the Monday following.

Q. What was Miss Ferguson's reaction?

A. She turned to me and called Mr. Berg a vile name under her breath.

Noah's stenographer testified that he had given her quite a large number of letters to type up that Saturday morning and he had not begun work on the production report by the time she left work at noon. But hadn't she sworn at the inquest, Tunney asked, that she had helped Berg make out the production report?

A. Yes, I did. But I thought then they were talking about something else.

Q. What was that?

A. The payroll report. Mr. Berg said we could get started with that while we were waiting for Mr. Woodcock's figures.

Q. And how much time did you spend on the payroll report with him?

A. Neither of us spent more than a few minutes on it.

Q. Didn't you get a raise last week?

A. A small one, yes.

Q. Did you ask for it?

A. More or less. I had been promised one at the beginning of the year.

Q. And this seemed a good time to press your case?

A. I thought I was entitled.

Gomer Camp, the mechanical foreman who had been doing repair work on the third floor on the day of the murder, came on and said that the elevator shook the entire building whenever it started or stopped and that it was most unlikely he would have failed to hear if somebody had operated it that Saturday, as Mo Easter testified he and the superintendent had done to dispose of the body. "Things was very still," he said, "except for me and Lemmie Wilson rootin' around up there." Camp also said he had been the one to discover the bloodstains in the second-floor cloakroom the Wednesday after the murder. "I come in about half an hour before the help to get some of the machines warmed up, on account of they'd been idle since the Friday previous. No one had come in the first two days that week because of the tragedy. I put my head into the cloakroom that morning to see if any of the help had shown up yet—I wanted to make sure the absences wouldn't be permanent. Then's when I saw the stain. I told Mr. Woodcock about it right off, and he called the police." No, the burly machinist said, he had never noticed that Mr. Berg took a fancy to any of the girls, although he would talk to them all as the occasion demanded—"like when they were slacking or they was running a machine wrong or too fast or too slow."

Tunney saw his case starting to fray a bit and fought every point:

Q. What kind of work were you doing on the third floor that Saturday, Mr. Camp?

A. Refitting pipes and re-rigging belts and pulleys.

Q. Did you use any tools in the process?

A. Sure—hammers and wrenches mostly.

Q. You did a lot of hammering, did you?

A. Yes, sir.

Q. On metal?

A. Yes, sir.

Q. Doesn't that make what some people might call quite a racket?

A. Not if you're used to it.

Q. And aren't you used to the noise of that elevator so you might not even notice it? And wasn't the noise you yourselves were making such that it might have

353

drowned out any elevator noise or shuddering or
whatever?

A. Maybe.

Q. Hadn't the elevator been fixed recently?

A. It was always being fixed. You couldn't hardly miss
it in a hurricane.

Q. But you might if you had your ear a few inches from
a hammer that was pounding away at pipes, isn't
that so?

A. Like I say—maybe. But I don't think so.

Noah's mother-in-law, father-in-law, sister-in-law, and half a
dozen other assorted kin and near ones swore to the normality of
his behavior on the Saturday evening of the murder when the
Kleins had a card party at their home. "Sometimes he played,"
said Mr. Klein, "sometimes he didn't. This time, he didn't. He
was off in the hall, answering the door and reading a magazine.
He liked to read. Once that night, maybe around ten o'clock, he
came in to read aloud to us a funny part of a baseball story. I
don't follow baseball too much, but Noah did. He seemed in a
happy mood." The dozen or so people there that night told the
same story. Only Sig Klein's testimony seemed to rise above the
expected defense of a loved one.

Q. Was your son-in-law a wastrel? By that I mean did
he often go out without your daughter—?

A. Never that I heard of.

Q. Did he drink of galavant?

A. I would like to say something about that. Naturally,
my opinion is affected by my closeness to the defendant, but I can hardly believe that I see Noah Berg
here in this courtroom, charged with so dreadful a
crime. Mrs. Klein and I have seen this young man
every day of our lives—we have shared our home
with him—for the past two years, and he is a kind
and gentle person. There is not a trace of scandal
about his conduct—and believe me, in our world any
acting up does not escape notice. He is a devoted
husband to our Naomi. He stays within a limited circle of our family and friends. He gives his time and
dedication to charity work. This past year, he was in

charge of the annual dance to benefit the orphanage
for Jewish children—and the boy can't dance a step.

Father cut him off before the *schmaltz* flowed. I thought the testimony touching. So, too, apparently, did Tunney, who asked just a single question. "The humorous story—the baseball story— that your son-in-law read to the group that Saturday evening, did anybody else think it was especially funny?" Sig Klein said he couldn't remember; besides, he added, Noah had a quite dry wit. Parched, I would have said.

Three former office boys followed and swore, as if a chorus, that Noah's conduct was always proper and pleasant toward them and that they had learned a good deal about punctuality, personal hygiene, and correct speech from him. None had ever seen a woman other than his wife and stenographer in the inner office, and none had ever seen a man named Dalton on the premises. The lad who had worked as office boy on the prior Thanksgiving Day said no one unconnected with the company happened by while he was there but admitted to Tunney he had left work a bit after midday. Father asked him if he had seen Mo Easter anywhere on the premises that day; the boy said he had not. Charged with murder and accused of sodomy, Noah for the moment seemed to have scattered the suspicion of pederasty as well that had been aroused, however obliquely, by his assistant superintendent.

Archie Ruskin came on to rough up the redoubtable O. O. Dalton, that unsavory mastiff who had testified for the state on his rutting expeditions in the basement of the factory and implicated Noah in his tawdry doings. On a tip from one of father's old friends within the police department, we had checked a bit more into the character and veracity of this Dalton and hit a gusher.

Q. Have you ever been in jail, Mr. Dalton?
A. Quite a ways back.
Q. Does that mean yes?
A. Yes.
Q. Didn't you and a cousin and an in-law go on the chain gang in Walton County for stealing?
A. Yes, I did, but I was pardoned before my term was out.
Q. How long did you serve?
A. About eight months.

Q. Did that cure you?

A. Pretty much.

Q. Didn't you plead guilty to three charges in 1884 and go back on the chain gang?

A. No—only to one. My cousin pleaded to the other two.

Q. And you served a second term?

A. Yes—maybe four months.

Q. So, you were making progress, at least, in cutting down on your time of incarceration. But that didn't cure you, either, did it, Mr. Dalton, because you were indicted for stealing cotton in 1899, weren't you?

A. I was indicted for helping steal the cotton.

Q. Oh, pardon me, Mr. Dalton. And you went back to the chain gang, did you?

A. No, I paid a fine of a hundred forty-one dollars and some costs.

Q. Oh, so you paid out?

A. Yes.

Q. Well, that really was progress. Didn't you also do time for stealing corn?

A. No, they didn't find me guilty of that.

Q. Didn't you steal a mechanical hammer once from a shop?

A. I was drunk. I gave it back, and they dropped the charges.

On the cross, Tunney asked Dalton if he had not truly reformed and become a steady workman since his last brush with the law. Dalton said yes and that it had been a dozen years since he had been in trouble and he planned to keep it that way. In addition, he had been reborn in Christ four years back and was a regular churchgoer now. Archie came back at him:

Q. You say you're reformed now, Mr. Dalton?

A. Yes, sir, I do.

Q. Do you consider fornication in the basement of an industrial enterprise conduct befitting a gentleman?

A. No—that's why I give it up.

356

Q. As a matter of fact, aren't you right now under indictment in Bulloch County on four counts for
selling liquor illegally, Mr. Dalton?

A. An indictment don't mean a man is guilty.

Q. That's quite true, Mr. Dalton, but you testified a moment ago that you hadn't been in trouble with the
law in many years. Don't you call a four-count indictment trouble?

A. I've seen worse.

My momentary temptation to gloat over the way our case was
developing was routed after Archie brought on the notorious
Flora Hopkins, whose alleged dalliances with both Dalton and
Berg had been testified to by Mo Easter. Miss Hopkins appeared
peeved at the damage done her character. Someone had told her
to restrain her rouge to half a barrelful, and at first she gave a convincing display of indignation. No, she had had no dealing with
Berg at the factory and had never visited with him, alone or with
anyone else, in his office. She knew Dalton only by sight—"He
was at the house where I stayed once"—but she never came to the
factory with him before, during, or after hours and never introduced him to Noah Berg. Then Tunney mauled her.

Q. What sort of house were you staying in when you
saw Mr. Dalton that time?

A. Just a house.

Q. And what was he doing there?

A. Just visiting, I suppose.

Q. Was he seeking the favors of women?

A. I wouldn't know. I didn't pay him any mind.

Q. But enough to know who he was?

A. Somebody said his name.

Q. Aren't you under a physician's care now, Miss Hopkins?

A. Yes—I am.

Q. For what?

A. A stomach disorder.

Q. You're sure it's not some other sector of the anat-
omy?

A. That's between me and my physician.

357

Q. Yes, you're quite right. Tell me, Miss Hopkins, how many times have you been in jail?

A. I've never been in jail in my life.

Q. Is that a fact?

A. Yes.

Q. Why, that's very odd, Miss Hopkins. Mr. Wade Anderson, one of my deputies, tells me he got you out of jail only recently.

A. No, he never got me out of jail. I never been in jail.

Q. That's Mr. Anderson over there—could you please stand up, Mr. Anderson?—and he's quite positive, so perhaps you'll want to reconsider your answer, Miss Hopkins?

A. No, he never got me out of jail.

Q. Well, who did, then?

A. Mr. Smith.

Q. Who's he?

A. My lawyer—T. W. Smith.

Q. Didn't they take you to jail on a morals charge?

A. People told tales on me and that got me into trouble.

Q. You weren't there for reasons of immorality?

A. That's what people said.

Q. What jail were you in?

A. I don't know. Out in the county somewhere.

Archie took her back, chagrined, but managed to show that she had not been tried on a morals charge and never been convicted. "Is that what you meant when you said you've never been in jail?" he asked, and she said that was right. Her ample expanse of bared bosom, which could not be denied by a demure navy dress that was unfortunately a size or two too small, was graphic testimony, rather, that she had never been caught in the act, not that she did not practice it with abandon and more than likely in subterranean places. The very thought of Noah Berg partaking of her heavily trafficked flesh seemed perfectly ludicrous; he would have had her fumigated, if anything.

Uncle Benny was on hand the next morning when father undertook his counter-assault on Dr. Paternoster's testimony for the state. It was perhaps the weightiest of the links in the chain of circumstances that Tunney had drawn around Noah. If the time frame of the crime could be altered—*i.e.*, widened—the net of suspicion could then be cast far beyond the factory door.

With Uncle Benny's most welcome expertise to guide them, father and Archie winnowed the field of authorities available for rebuttal to three. The lead-off slot was given to one of Uncle Benny's former teachers at Jefferson Medical College who, whatever his rank nationally, was almost certainly the most capable medical scientist in Georgia with regard to the chemistry of human digestion. Dr. George Bache, professor of physiology and chairman of that department at the Atlanta College of Physicians and Surgeons, tugged at his small goatee while listening to father recount Paternoster's theory that, based on the undigested state of the cabbage found in the dead girl's stomach, the time of death or assault could be fixed at about three quarters of an hour after ingestion. "I should call that," said Dr. Bache flatly, "about as wild a guess as I have ever heard."

Working systematically, father had the expert assert that cabbage generally remained in the stomach for four hours or longer before passing into the intestines, where its fibrous resistance was mainly broken down. He said he was surprised that the state's medical expert claimed he could identify any digestive fluids in a discrete and reliably identifiable condition ten days after burial. Tunney put the witness through a grueling cross-examination, dredging up a number of obscure scientific terms, asking Dr. Bache to identify them, and then quibbling with his answers in an effort to discredit his standing as an expert. The solicitor stated that most authorities sided with Dr. Paternoster on the time required for cabbage to be digested, and when Bache disagreed, Tunney asked whether he himself had ever performed experiments with cabbage. No, said Bache. Then how did he know how long it takes to be digested? "I have never been inside a burning building, either, sir," said the doctor coolly, "but I would know enough to leave it quickly if I found myself in that predicament. I have studied human digestion for many years."

Father's other two experts offered reinforcing testimony, the most damaging of which cast doubt upon the ethics of the state's expert for having performed his investigation without corroborating attendants and then discarding the exhumed evidence without showing it to the other side or producing more than a fraction of it in court. Asked if he had any special knowledge on the digestibility of cabbage, the final defense expert offered, "Only that my belly hurts for days after I eat any."

II

Not the slightest hint had been given out that the defense would open the third day of its presentation by calling Sophie Berg, the mother of the defendant. A whisper of surprise spread throughout the courtroom as the leaden-eyed woman, weary from the ordeal of listening to every manner of calumny directed toward her issue, slowly ascended to the witness stand. But there was unexpected strength in her voice when she took the oath, as if she were suddenly buoyed by the chance to lend comfort to her son's uneasy cause.

After some introductory questions, it became clear that she had been called to read the text of a letter that Noah had written to his parents in Brooklyn bearing the date of April 26, 1913—the day of the murder. The solicitor predictably objected. The letter would be immaterial and necessarily self-serving, he said; moreover, there would be no way of telling whether it had been written before or after the likely time of the murder. And, indeed, how could the jury know if the letter was authentic? "How can the jury know," father shot back, "if Dr. Paternoster's findings were authentic? How can it know whether Mo Easter, or any witness, has told us the truth? Testimony is testimony, and in its aggregate the jury may hope to find ultimate truth. This letter, the content of which makes clear when it was written, reflects the frame of mind of its writer and is therefore highly germane to our case." The judge said he would rule on its admissibility after hearing the text.

In a voice that turned quickly hoarse, Mrs. Berg read:

Savannah, April 26, 1913

My Dearest Parents,

Today was Yontif here—the Confederates celebrate their own Memorial Day. It is the fifth year now that I have witnessed this spectacle, but I cannot say yet that my sentiments have been entirely converted to the Southern cause. I have come, however, to understand better why the rebel side thought—and still thinks—it was wronged.

I watched the parade for a few minutes after dinner this afternoon before returning to the factory to finish up the week's work. My emotions were mingled with the drumbeats, just as my fortunes have become wrapped with the fate of North and South together. The thin gray line of veterans, smaller each year, braved the chilly weather to do honor to their fallen comrades. I must say that I am touched by the people's devotion to this memory as well as distressed by their unwillingness to leave the sinful past dead and buried. It is a fester they do not know how to cure, and it keeps infecting them. May I never be bitten.

The work continues well, and the company prospers. We have the usual problems at the factory—lazy and careless help and the need for more modern equipment —but our production is efficient, and I have reason to suspect that I will be transferred to the main headquarters in Atlanta before the year is out. I have not told Naomi that as yet, as it will be a sore wrench for her to leave her family. But the time for candor is fast approaching.

Savannah is lovely as ever in the spring. Tell father the local ball club is not quite so dreadful as the Trolley Dodgers this year. I hope this note finds you and all the dear ones in Brooklyn well. Much love to you both, in which Naomi joins me. The Kleins, too, ask as always to be remembered.

Your devoted son,
Noah

Father asked Mrs. Berg when the letter was received. "I have tried my best to remember exactly," she said, "but I can't say for certain whether it was Tuesday or Wednesday. It was one of them."

Q. By the way, why has your husband not joined you in attending this trial, Mrs. Berg?
A. He is a sick man, Mr. Adler. His heart could not stand it. And there is his diabetes.

Q. Has your son ever behaved in an immoral or illegal manner so far as you know?

A. Not in his whole life, so help me God.

Tunney could not allow that affecting moment to become protracted. He gave the woman a moment of respite and then confronted her with his usual indelicacy.

Q. Your husband is a highly successful businessman, is he not, Mrs. Berg?

A. He worked very hard for every cent.

Q. I don't doubt that. But he accumulated quite a considerable fortune, did he not?

A. Kings have fortunes, not businessmen. He put most of the money back into the business to keep building it. Later there were losses, and he sold out while there was still something to sell. We moved to Brooklyn, which is less costly than the city. We have lived well enough, but I wear no jewels.

Q. Your son is your jewel, is he not, Mrs. Berg?

A. He is.

Q. He is a fine *mensch*—isn't that the Jewish word?

A. Yes, he is a *mensch*. You don't have to say "fine" in front of it. *Mensch* already means he is fine.

Q. Thank you. Could you tell the court, Mrs. Berg, just how rich your family actually is?

MR. ADLER: Objection. There is no excuse for that.

THE COURT: I agree with counsel. Re-phrase it.

Q. Would you mind telling us, Mrs. Berg, your financial situation?

A. Why is that anybody's business?

Q. Because your son is charged with murder and, according to one witness, believes the wealth of his family will allow him to escape without paying the penalty for his actions.

MR. ADLER: I object.

Q. Very well. Let me just ask if you have any money out at interest.

MR. ADLER: I object. That is entirely immaterial.

SOLICITOR TUNNEY: With all due respect to the privileges of motherhood and parenthood, your honor, this woman appears as a character witness for her son, and her own character is not irrelevant.

THE COURT: You may proceed, Mr. Tunney, but you are on mighty thin ice.

MR. ADLER: Let the record show that the defense takes exception to this line of questioning as inflammatory and prejudicial.

THE COURT: The court reporter will so note.

Q. Could you tell us, Mrs. Berg?

A. We have a little money out.

Q. How much is a little?

A. I believe about twenty thousand. But I am not a businesswoman.

Q. What is the rate of interest it earns?

A. Six percent.

Q. Do you think twenty thousand is "a little money"?

A. It is not a fortune, is what I mean. When Mr. Berg sold his shirt business, he was too sick to invest his profit in a business in which he could take an active part. So he put the money out. Is that a crime? Better he should put it in a breadbox? The crime is making money without working for it—and then hoarding it and buying luxuries no one needs.

Q. You are making a speech, Mrs. Berg.

A. You are making an accusation, Mr. Lawyer.

Q. I was asking a question.

A. You were hinting at something sinful in my family's conduct.

Q. Will the court instruct the witness to limit her answers to the questions put to her?

THE COURT: I believe the thin ice just broke, counselor. Move on with your examination.

But Vincent Tunney had nowhere to move. He dangled there, hoist by his own petard, and then gave it up. I felt a surge of elation. The tide had turned, I was sure.

Briskly now, father and Archie marched dozens of employées from the factory to the stand, the older and more senior ones first, to testify to Noah's good character and Mo Easter's bad one. The cumulative effect, while numbing after a time, was of a massive rebuttal to the state's case without touching upon any of the circumstantial aspects that seemed to have conspired against Noah. What any number of the witnesses agreed upon, furthermore, was the highly suspicious behavior of Mo Easter when the factory reopened the week after the murder. Mrs. Vera Appleton, a machine operator in the bottle-capping department for five years, testified, for example, that she had seen the negro reading about the case in the newspapers with intense interest. "I hadn't thought he could read till then," she said.

> Q. Perhaps he had merely picked up a discarded copy of the paper—wouldn't that have been natural in view of the great attention the case had attracted in the press and what with his working right there?
> A. No, it went beyond that. He borrowed money from me to buy the papers with.
> Q. And he looked as if he was really reading them?
> A. Oh, he was reading them, all right. In fact, I don't think he did anything else around the factory.
> Q. Did Mo make any comment to you about the case?
> A. Yes. He said Mr. Berg was as innocent as I was.

Since Mo's credibility was the key to the state's case, Archie and father were disinclined to cut short the parade of factory people who denounced him as a no-good. Occasionally, a witness would leave the inference that his testimony was based more on bias than neutral observation. Asked if he would believe the floorsweeper on oath, one of the veteran male workers in the carbonating section of the plant testified, "I don't believe no niggers—him especially—oath or no oath." Tunney knifed in at that.

> Q. Why do you think Berg kept Mo Easter around the factory if he was such a bad man?
> A. Some of us wondered. See, we knew Mo had been on the chain gang and figure Mr. Berg knew it, too. Only we heard Mo had only been on the city squad for a police case, no big crime, so Mr. Berg was nice enough to give him a chance to go straight. Only you could tell lots o' ways that his character was tricky.
> Q. For example?
> A. Well, I drink a mug of beer every morning about ten-

thirty, see, and one day last summer I sent Mo out to get twenty-five cents' worth of beer, and he drank half of it off himself and filled it back up with water. He came on back and says, "Here's yo' beer, Al," and kind of leered and then hightailed it. I took a swallow or two and figured it out.

Q. What did you do to Mo?

A. Nothin'—but I got my own beer after that.

Perhaps the most convincing of all in this cluster of witnesses was the old black drayman who said he used to work at loading and unloading supplies at the factory on Saturdays after regular closing time.

Q. How long have you worked on Saturday afternoons?

A. For about two years.

Q. How late would you work?

A. Three or four o'clock—sometimes to five.

Q. On any Saturday afternoon did you ever see the front door locked when Mr. Berg was in the building?

A. No, sir.

Q. Ever see Mo Easter around the front door Saturday afternoons?

A. No, sir.

Q. Who would be in the building on Saturday afternoons?

A. Mr. Berg—and Mr. Woodcock sometimes—and Mr. Pike when he was working there.

Q. Did you work that Saturday of the murder?

A. No, sir. I was tired and wanted de holiday.

Q. Would you believe Mo Easter on oath?

A. No, sir.

Q. Did he ever borrow money from you and not repay it?

A. Yes, sir.

Tunney tried to destroy the white-headed negro with a quick blow:

Q. Do you think Mo Easter is the kind of man who gives negroes a bad name with whites?

A. I sure do.

365

Q. You're a high-class nigger, eh?

A. No, sir—but I'm a different grade from him. Him and his family is liars. They got me in trouble by lyin' once—.

Our cup runneth over, a trifle messily, with the appearance of Mrs. Dora Barnes, who proved so ardent in her ratifying of Noah's character that Archie had to hustle her off the stand. A clerk in the shipping department, she said she had worked at the factory for four years and four months and never missed a day or been late. "Noah Berg is one of the best men I or anyone else has ever seen," she said. "He is the soul of honor. He always asks after your health—leastways he does of the people he knows are reliable. I would fight for him and even die for him if that would prove his innocence." Archie thanked her and invited her to step down on the off chance that Tunney had been stunned with disbelief. The solicitor, though, hungry now after mostly slim pickings, came to feast:

Q. You say, Mrs. Barnes, that you would die for Mr. Berg's innocence?

A. That's right.

Q. Would you lie for him?

A. He doesn't need anyone to lie for him.

Q. But would you—if it meant saving him?

A. I—I can't say. I'm not a liar. I just believe that he is innocent. I wish I could get everyone to believe it.

Q. How do you think Mr. Barnes would feel about your dying to save Mr. Berg?

A. There is no Mr. Barnes. I'm a widow eight years.

Q. Do you love Mr. Berg?

A. Not romantically, if that's what you mean.

Q. That's what I mean.

A. No, I just admire him a great deal.

Q. Evidently, if you would die for him. Did you ever see him outside of your work area?

A. I did not.

Q. Never went to his office for a visit?

A. I should say not.

Q. But you would die for him?

A. If it would do any good.

The sad, love-starved little sparrow of a woman represented about the only eddy in the otherwise orderly and growing flow of favorable character witnesses as the trial entered its third week. And even Mrs. Barnes's excessive admiration-from-afar could not readily be turned into something sinister by the state. Tunney got no real break until our side was running through its roster of secondary character witnesses drawn from the factory work force— most of them young women, like the dead girl, whom I had screened and endorsed as safe during the pre-trial lull. Girl after girl came on to say that Noah Berg was a good man and Mo Easter was a bad one. None of them had ever seen Noah behave in an ungentlemanly way, and none had seen him speak with Jean Dugan in a way or for a length of time out of the ordinary when he made his rounds of the factory. Then Archie put on Irene Johnson, who I thought would be a particularly useful young witness since her father worked as an officer for the county police force. It soon became clear that I had made a serious error, or that the young woman had been reached and influenced, for she offered revelations she had concealed from me entirely.

Q. But you know Mr. Berg, even though Mr. Woodcock was the one to hire you?
A. Yes, everyone knew Mr. Berg.
Q. Are you able to testify to his character?
A. It's all right, I suppose.
Q. First, Miss Johnson, you must say whether you know enough about his character to testify about it.
A. I don't know whether I do or not.

Sensing trouble, Archie excused her. Tunney, with a sureness that left little doubt he was prepared for the opportunity, came on directly.

Q. What did you hear the other girls say about Berg?
A. They were afraid of him and didn't have much to say.
Q. They were afraid of him?
A. Yes. Whenever he came around, they would all get to work again right hard.
Q. Were they afraid for any other reason?
A. Yes. They thought he was lecherous.
Q. Oh, really? What did he do to inspire that reputation?

367

A. He liked to look into the girls' dressing room.

Q. You mean when the girls were in there?

A. Yes.

The judge had to pound away for order before the testimony could continue. I looked over at father with panic on my face; he merely stared at the witness as Tunney picked up again.

Q. Is this dressing room the same one in which the murder took place?

A. Yes.

MR. RUSKIN: Objection. The site of the murder has not been established. We have only the testimony of a singularly unreliable witness as to where the murder allegedly occurred, and even he does not claim to have witnessed the killing.

THE COURT: Re-phrase it, counselor.

Q. Is that the same room in which the bloodstains were found on the Wednesday after the murder?

A. Yes.

Q. Were you ever in that room when Mr. Berg looked in or are you just telling us what you heard?

A. Oh, I was in there. He came to the door one morning when Emily Mayfield and myself were in there.

Q. What did he do?

A. He just pushed open the door and looked in and walked away that time.

Q. Were you dressed?

A. Yes.

Q. And Miss Mayfield?

A. She had off her top dress and was holding her old work dress in her hand.

Q. Did he look in any other time when you were there?

A. Yes, he opened the door one day and looked when my sister was lying down in there during a break.

Q. When your sister was lying down?

A. Yes, She had her feet resting on a stool.

Q. And you were there?

A. Yes.

Q. What did he do?

A. He just looked and sort of smiled.

Q. He smiled at your sister?

A. He twisted his face or did something like that and I thought it was meant to be a smile.

Q. Did you ever hear of times that he looked into the girls' dressing room when you weren't there?

A. Yes, I heard them talk about him going in several times.

Q. Did any of the girls object? Did they protest?

A. Some of them spoke to our forelady.

Q. What did she say?

A. She said to pay no mind, he was probably just looking for someone or something. I think she was afraid of him.

Q. Did Berg knock before he came in?

A. No. The door was pushed to, and he just shoved it open and stood in the doorway and stared at us.

Archie had to take her back. The girl's answers to him reflected a quickness of mind and a partisanship to the state.

Q. The time your sister and you were in the dressing room, were you both fully clothed?

A. Yes—but he didn't know that before he pushed on in.

Q. Isn't it possible that what you took for a smile was something else—like a frown—as if he didn't approve of your sister's stretching out that way?

A. Oh, I think he approved.

Q. Isn't it true that some of the girls flirted from that room—flirted out the window?

A. I don't know. I heard something about that.

Q. But of course you never engaged in the custom?

A. Certainly not.

Q. Isn't it possible that Mr. Berg wanted to see if the flirting was going on, and he couldn't very well knock first if he had hoped to catch somebody in the act?

A. He could have sent in the forelady.

All in all, it was the most damaging testimony against Noah since Mo Easter left the stand. Rationally, I knew I could not have prevented the setback; if I had urged father and Archie not to call

369

the girl, the state surely would have as a rebuttal witness. Still, I was glum at the development.

Vincent Tunney was of course emboldened by it. As our side began to run through a series of character witnesses from the community at large, the solicitor's reservoir of venom became uncontainable. Father had questioned a life-insurance agent who had written a standard policy on Noah and said that investigators from his company had thoroughly examined him morally and physically before issuing a policy. "I came down to his office late one Saturday afternoon," he said, "and he introduced me to Mrs. Berg. We had a very pleasant conversation. I believe the couple was going to see the Gilbert and Sullivan show at the theater that evening. Mr. Berg promised to introduce me to other executives with his firm if I wanted to solicit their insurance business."

All that bliss was blown away as Tunney picked up the cross-examination.

Q. I assume, sir, that your investigators did not advise you that Mr. Berg took girls on his lap and caressed them?

MR. ADLER: Your honor, this is outrageous! We are not trying this man on every vile and slanderous lie that has been pronounced against him since April twenty-sixth by crackbrain extremists. Is this a court of law or the Spanish Inquisition?

SOLICITOR TUNNEY: Your honor, I am not four-flushing one bit. I propose to introduce a witness who will testify that this witness was aware of the reports circulated against Berg to which I alluded.

MR. ADLER: We cannot and will not submit to such unethical and disorderly procedure by the state. The solicitor knows that he cannot substantiate such reports and is stooping lower than I would have believed possible to put them on the record and poison the hearts and minds of the jury. If he makes another such statement, we will move for a mistrial.

SOLICITOR TUNNEY: Mr. Adler protests too much, your honor. This is a trial for the murder of an innocent young woman, not cheating at a spelling bee. The defense have chosen to put the defendant's character in evidence and know full well that substantial latitude is thereby afforded to the state to exhibit contrary evidence.

THE COURT: Proceed, Mr. Tunney.

Q. You never heard that Berg went out to the Delilah Falls with a little girl and played with her on his lap?

A. No.

Q. You and your people at the agency have been very active in this case. Didn't you and some others write a letter to the grand jury urging that Mo Easter be indicted for the murder?

A. Yes, we did.

Q. Why did you do that? It wouldn't have had anything to do with the help Berg gave you in landing a number of policies with his associates at the company, would it?

A. No, it did not. We just felt Mr. Berg's character to be exemplary.

Q. Didn't you hear about a year ago that Berg took little girls into his office and played with them?

A. No, sir.

Q. And you are sure you never heard of his taking a girl to the Delilah Falls—?

At which point, in mid-question, Noah Berg's mother arose in her place and with full fury in her throat shrieked at the solicitor, "No, nor did you, either, you dog!"

The room froze in a tableau of incredulity. Then father came around and gently guided the trembling woman out the side door. It was the second time she had stood up to the viperous tactics of the state's attorney. He plainly wanted Noah's neck for a trophy, and it was just as plain that he and the hangman both would have to deal with a mother who would perish before letting her son's life be taken unjustly.

III

With each passing day, the size of the press corps covering the trial grew. But it was not from New York or Chicago or Reuters that the reporters came; it was from Augusta and Macon and Albany and Jesup. Even the weekly newspapers throughout the state began sending correspondents down. It was an all-Georgia morbidity festival, and the more words telegraphed out around the state, the more the psychological climate against Noah Berg heated up, no matter what the course of the testimony in the courtroom.

One of the Atlanta writers came by to see father and Archie to do an interview on the defense strategy. His editors couldn't get enough stories to fill the daily demand for new sensations in the case. "And it's not in the city where the interest is keenest," the fellow told us. "It's in the towns and villages and hamlets. Every crossroads country store has its own jury weighing the case. Why, they send me up into the Blue Ridge each year about this time for feature stories, and a couple of years ago I came upon this fella in the depths of Rabun Gap, and he didn't know William Howard Taft from a side of bacon. I did a piece about some kind o' waterwheel he'd set up there to keep his run-down mill from going broke. I went to see him last week again for the paper and asked him what the news was, figurin' maybe to hear about his daughter's scrap with the measles or some such. But he said, 'I don't know—I thought you'd tell us. What're they goin' to do with this here feller Berg?'"

I wondered why all the obsessive interest. The Atlanta man shoved his hat back and gave his suspenders a few portentous snaps. "Well now, I'll tell ya," he said. "Partly it's because a little white working girl got killed, and that always plucks the heartstrings. And partly it's because the defendant is a Jew and a Yankee, and you couldn't hardly have a more villainous combination. I mean niggers get strung up a dime a dozen for lookin' cross-eyed at a white woman's butt, so there'd be no novelty in that. And a poor-white boy'd be likely to get a lot of sympathy. People'd figure he was just bein' playful or tryin' to spread his oats and the girl became a little too fidgety. But a genuine Jew? Why, that's a twist. Jews are exciting. They're foreign—even if they're not, they seem that way in most of Georgia—and smart and rich and look kinda spooky, like Noah Berg. Everybody knows they're tightfisted and money-crazy, no matter what-all nice things get said about 'em. And o' course his being a Yankee Jew to boot makes him just perfect to hate. On top o' which, most of these people around the state got nothin' to do this time o' year except sit and whittle and watch the crops grow by day and count June bugs by night. It's quiet as a lizard out there, so all they do is talk about the murder of this poor innocent girl-child and how Berg's eyes're gonna pop right out of his skull when the noose is sprung."

It was, in short, the ideal spectacle for armchair sadists, whose ranks were legion. And many did not settle for passive ruminating from afar. The crowds on the streets of Savannah so exceeded anything in memory that you would have thought that William Tecumseh Sherman was the defendant, not an ascetic-looking factory superintendent who would not expectorate on a dung heap let alone do violence to a virgin. Midway through the third week of the trial, the sidewalk and street mobs began to demonstrate their impatience for a verdict by lining the path taken by the jury at the end of the day's court session and shouting at the jurors, "Hang the Jew! Hang the Jew! Hang the Jew!" Happily, we now understood it was nothing personal, just high spirits fed by the miasma in a midsummer's nightmare. Father called the sheriff the first night after it happened and said he was going into court for a writ of mandamus against him unless the mob was dispersed. "They got freedom o' speech and freedom of assembly on their side, or ain't you heard o' them, Seth?" said the sheriff. "But I'll have the boys try to hush 'em up when the jurymen come by." That helped a little, but the predatory mood of the crowds scarcely abated. For the first time in my life, I began to wake up with a knot of fear in my stomach.

Father was convinced that only Noah could save his own life. But Archie, burned by Mo Easter's bravado performance on the stand, greatly feared another such setback. Georgia law provided that the defendant could make an unsworn statement in his own behalf without risk of cross-examination. But father wanted Noah to submit to the solicitor's interrogation on the theory that he had nothing to fear from Tunney except malevolence. "Ain't that enough?" Archie asked. "The bastard tastes blood, and he aims to have some."

Father prevailed, however. Whatever the risks of Noah's appearance, they were greater still if he did not appear. Tunney would surely stress the omission in his summation, whereas the likelihood was that he would disdain cross-examining Noah if his statement proved a strong one.

One more day was devoted to character witnesses—Noah's for-

mer high-school teachers, former college professors, former class-
mates, and his banker and his doctor and his grocer and his spiritual adviser, Rabbi Weisz, who pronounced him "a good and
civilized man, full of kindness and charity." There were dozens of
endorsements of him as a quiet, studious, and clean-living young
man, with no known aberrations and scant penchant for cutting
up. In their zeal to make a saint of him, I feared, father and
Archie had rendered Noah as very much a Goody Two-shoes—
just the sort of velveted Fauntleroy any good old Southern boy
would like to boot in the arse and drop in the mud. Father agreed
and called a halt to the process, especially when Tunney was be-
stirred to start cross-examining to show that many of the witnesses
had not known the defendant all that well in his youth and had
not seen him for many years. Then, on the third Thursday of the
trial, the defense called Noah Berg to the stand.

Word of the defendant's impending appearance had been
rumored for the previous two days, and the press of rabid humanity upon the courtroom door intensified accordingly. Noah had
spurned the offer of help from his counsel in the preparation of
his statement, saying that the simple truth was all he knew and all
he would say. Father and Archie feared that he would say too little or too much, inviting suspicion in the former instance of holding back or opening the door, in the latter instance, to a damaging
examination by the solicitor. Archie argued till the end against
Noah's testifying under oath. Noah said he would do it no other
way.

The courtroom hum turned into a hush of surprise as Archie
told the judge his client's preference. Noah took the oath standing, and remained standing the entire time he spoke. He spoke
with the most extraordinary control imaginable in a man on trial
for his life in a courtroom that was hot and hostile. His suit was
too warm for the day and too big for its wearer, whose slender
shoulders were nevertheless thrust back and perfectly horizontal.
He looked directly at the jury, never away, and he spoke without
using a single note. He did not whine. He did not shout. He did
not mumble or obfuscate.

First he quickly sketched in the essential facts of his biography,
dwelling at some length upon the hospitality with which the people of Savannah had received him into their midst and allowed
him to earn his livelihood and lead a private, quiet life. "I married

a Savannah girl named Naomi Klein," he said. "The major portion of my married life has been spent in the home of my parents-in-law, and while some no doubt would find such intimacy constraining, it has done much to make me feel at ease in this beautiful city far from where I grew up. My married life has been exceptionally happy." And for an instant he let his glance fall upon sad-eyed Naomi.

With meticulous detail he took up the events of his life at the time of the murder. He told how he worked closely with Bryce Woodcock on that Friday, as he always did, in drawing up the payroll and counting out the amounts, to the last penny, that went into every envelope. But the handing out of the pay was a duty specifically assigned to his assistant. "No one came to my office to ask for the envelope of any other employée," he said, delivering the sentence with a shade more precise enunciation than those just before it. "Had anyone done so, I would have recited the established rule that only those who appeared in person got paid. And if someone had asked me that evening for the pay of an absent colleague on the ground that the factory would be closed the next morning because of the holiday, I would no doubt have said that the supervisory staff would be on hand as usual and the worker in question could come collect his or her money then."

He and his wife spent that Friday evening attending religious services at Temple Mickve Israel, he said, and then playing auction bridge at the home of friends. He rose the next morning between seven and seven-thirty, as he was wont, took a modest breakfast, and caught a streetcar that stopped two blocks from his office, where he arrived at about half past eight. The day, so far as he was aware at the time, proved unexceptional, save for the indisposition of his assistant. "I took off my coat and hat, opened my desk and the safe, and removed the various books and files and wire trays containing the papers I would have to refer to during the course of that day." He revealed the compulsive orderliness of his clerkly regimen; he was finicky about the details of his job, he said, for that was what 99 percent of his work came to—details—especially on Saturdays when he totted up the week's endeavors. He had seemed to me, till the moment, what I had always thought him—a fussy, earnest, dedicated, and quite boring man who feared his own shadow. For all that, he was taking on, with every added sentence, a courage and dignity I had not before thought possible. His very act of standing up before that tidal wave of human *dreck* out there was converting him from a displeasing gnat to a hero of Masada. My heart quickened as he held fast.

Noah reviewed the comings and goings of workers that morning, told how he had concentrated on catching up with his correspondence when his assistant superintendent came in late with the preliminary production data, and contended that when he was proofreading a letter that was to bear his signature, he gave it absolute concentration and may thus have appeared startled when Mrs. Camp came by on the way to visiting with her husband. "Indeed, I may have seemed not to be present to anyone who might have been waiting for me in the outer office or in the hallway," he said. "I have no doubt that Miss Stiles appeared when she says, but I cannot see through my safe door, any more than she can, and unless she ventured close to it or made some identifying sound to stir me from my paperwork, I would not have been aware of her presence."

Jean Dugan came in, he said, shortly after noon. "I did not pay her much heed," he said. "She asked for her pay by her employée number. I got my cashbox from the safe, referred to the number, and gave her the envelope. She thanked me and wished me a pleasant holiday. I bid her the same. The last I heard was her footsteps retreating down the hall. A few moments later, I had the impression, a very faint one, of a voice or two down the stairway on the first landing by the entranceway. But there was nothing urgent about it to draw me away from my desk. I did not then recall the girl's name, although I had of course recognized her as one of the young women who worked in a department on the same floor as my office. There are more than two hundred girls employed at our bottling factory at any one time, and it is impossible to know any substantial part of them by name and face. And, given the nature of the work, there is a considerable turnover in our personnel, so that since I first came to the factory, perhaps five or six hundred young women have worked there. In the normal course of the factory routine, I came to know but a small number by their full name. I knew a number by their first name only. One reason for this is that when I would come around the factory to check on the flow of work, I might stop by a given ma-

awakened by the telephone ringing and a man's voice which I afterwards found out belonged to Detective Reilly. He said, "I want you to come down to the factory," and that he was coming to get me in a police vehicle and would fill me in on the details when he arrived.

He came before I had finished dressing. And at this point I differ with Detective Reilly's recollection of our exchange. He says he did not go into any details until after we had left the house and I was with him in his machine. I say it was before we left the house. I asked him at once on his arrival what the matter was. He asked me if I knew who Jean Dugan was, and I either said no or I wasn't sure if I knew her. I wanted at any rate to know what the matter was. He asked me if I hadn't paid off a little girl with long hair down her back the afternoon before, and he described what she was wearing. I said I had, and he told me she had been found dead in the factory basement. He said he wanted me to go with him first to the undertaking establishment—not to the factory, as was indicated by the police—to see if I could identify the body.

We drove there very quickly. Detective Reilly is something of a daredevil behind the wheel. I went into the undertaker's and stood in the doorway. The attendant removed the sheet from the little girl's face and turned the head toward me. His finger was right by the cut on her head. I noticed her nostrils were filled with dirt and cinders, and there were several discolorations on her cheeks and forehead. There was a piece of wire twisted around her neck, and her tongue protruded. I said it seemed to be the girl who had come to the factory for her pay the day before.

He recounted every step of that Sunday morning investigation of the factory on which he accompanied the police. "Everything seemed to be in order," he said. "We saw no blood or stains on the floor or walls—not on the floor of the girls' cloakroom on the second floor or anywhere else, and every inch of the building was gone over in my presence." As to the time slips, he confessed to a slight haziness. "I checked over the night watchman's card, and at

chine and the young woman operating it would not know w
I was about to praise or upbraid her, and so fearing the latt
would tell me only her first name when I began by asking h
she was."

He went on in that cool, informing way. He told how h
upstairs to advise Gomer Camp, his wife, and his assistant
mie Wilson working on the repairs that he had to lock
lunch. He said he saw some of the parade while he was go
and returning from his home that afternoon. He remember
feeling up to his cook's full portion of chicken dumpling
dinnertime—"I was a little edgy because I was behind at tl
tory," he said, "and her dumplings are delicious but very
One is a meal, two are a banquet, three render you immo
believe she served me four."

He recounted, in fatiguing detail, how he prepared the p
tion report for the week during the latter part of that Saturo
ternoon; of how he sent Plato Layne away when he repor
that he might enjoy a few more hours of the holiday since
was no need for him yet; of the letter he wrote to his paren
posted on the way out, along with the production report; a
how Vernon Pike had appeared in the front doorway just
was leaving. "Pike had been discharged from the company s
weeks earlier over a question of his honesty," said Noah, "
had not seen him since. His presence there at that time o
and on a holiday at that, caught me unawares. He had no bu
on the premises, so far as I knew. He stated his errand
straight enough fashion, however, and I gave him permissi
fetch his shoes. He and the night watchman remained behin
left the factory for the day. I was uneasy enough about h
timely appearance to feel obliged to call the watchman aft
arrival at home to see that there had been no disturbance."

His detachment quite amazed me. He resisted every impu
vilify. He pointed no fingers. He explained only his own con
He told how he had spent that Saturday evening at home
his in-laws had guests in for cards. Having played the previou
ning, he did not want to again that night; instead, he and his
read and helped serve the company.

   I retired Saturday night at about midnight, perhaps a
   bit later. Sunday morning about seven o'clock I wa

a quick glance, I did not notice any skips. I handed the slip to one of the detectives—Sergeant Phelps, I believe, but I do not wish to swear to that. He looked at it briefly and asked me if it was in order. I said I thought it was. He may have given it back to me, but that is not my recollection. He may have handed it to Mr. Woodcock, who could have put it back on the rack, with all the other time cards. There was a great deal of turmoil going on around me just then, and I cannot be certain of every last detail. I do recall my surprise the next day, however, when the watchman's time card reappeared and showed several obvious skips on it for Saturday night. Conceivably I had read it too hurriedly on Sunday morning. Other explanations are possible, but they would be sheer speculation on my part."

He paused for a glass of water. He had been speaking for more than two hours; they seemed like minutes, so rapt were I and everyone in that room by the man's unadorned words. He cleared his throat and continued:

A great deal has been made of my nervousness that morning. I readily admit it. I was nervous. In fact, I was completely unstrung. Imagine yourself called from sound slumber in the early hours of the morning, whisked through the chill air without breakfast to an undertaking establishment, and have the light suddenly flashed on a scene like that. To see that little girl on the dawn of womanhood so cruelly murdered—it was a scene that would have melted stone. Is it any wonder I was nervous? She had been found, moreover, at the factory of which I was superintendent, and whatever the circumstances, the event would scandalize our company and redound unfavorably to me as the official in charge.

He went on to tell of his increasingly abrasive dealings with the police as it became clear that their suspicions were coming to focus more and more upon him. "The discovery on Wednesday of what was said to be blood in the cloakroom not far from my office seemed to attract a good deal of their attention," he said, "although I reminded them that no such stain had been glimpsed by any of us on the round we all took on Sunday. Chief Detective Stone insisted, as I recall, that the cloakroom had not been sufficiently lighted on that first inspection. To me it was plain

379

that somebody was trying to locate the scene of the murder on the second floor, and since I was the only person known to have been there after noon, I began to feel that I was well on the way toward becoming a leading suspect." Soon after, he said, he had heard Detective Phelps say to Detective Stone that a man who had committed such a crime would likely be marked up with bruises from the resisting victim. "When I heard that, I took off my shirt and showed them my body. I also urged the detectives to go to my home and examine my clothes for bloodstains, and they did, piece by piece."

The callousness he himself would later experience at the hands of the authorities was foreshadowed, Noah said, by what he saw and heard on Tuesday when the police asked him to meet with Plato Layne, then being held in jail on suspicion. "I heard him shriek and cry out from a room within," he said. "He screamed, 'Lord, God, I don't know a thing!' But they kept after him. When they brought him in to where I was and handcuffed him to a chair, he was sweating and crying and all puffed up in the face. And they wanted me to do their dirty work. I felt sorry for the old man. It was inconceivable to me that he could have had anything to do with the crime."

Toward the close, he addressed himself to specific points that had been raised, in and out of the courtroom, against him and disposed of each without ado.

> Mo Easter's statement in this room is a lie from first to last. I never saw him in the factory that Saturday. The statement that women came into my office for immoral purposes is infamous, and the statement that he saw me in that unspeakable position with one of them is a lie so vicious that I have not the language with which to denounce it.

> The statement of Dalton's about bringing Flora Hopkins into my office is false as well. I cannot tell you what prompts these men to bear false witness against someone who never did them harm, but I am sure they will answer to someone higher some day for this act of monstrous unkindness.

> I never peered into the girls' dressing room, as it has been referred to here and as Irene Johnson testified. It is

more properly called the second-floor cloakroom, and it is where the girls hang their outer garments. I had learned that girls flirted from the window in there and I wanted to break up the practice. I never looked into that room at any time when I had reason to suspect the girls were dressing or undressing. The employées are supposed to have put on their work clothes by seven in the morning.

With regard to the report that I once made improper advances toward an office boy and touched his body, I can tell you that there is an element of truth in that. I slapped the boy across the mouth. He had a habit of spitting onto the floor, and I had warned him several times that it was a vile practice and also an unsanitary one in an establishment devoted to the production of a popular beverage. He nevertheless kept doing it, and I struck him in a last effort at bringing him around, but we had to release him soon afterward.

There is an element of truth, too, if you discount the gross distortion, in the report that I took small children upon my knee and played with them, both at the Delilah's Falls and in my office. The children, without exception, were from the Hebrew Orphan Home, to which I devoted a good deal of time. One of my favorite activities was the annual picnic and outing at the falls, which my wife and I and perhaps three or four other couples supervised. No doubt I could be seen on that occasion with children climbing upon my lap for a game of "Horsey" or some such pleasantry. From time to time as well, children from the home would come to the factory to see how our soda is produced, and at the end of the tour, the group would come to my office and each little boy and girl given a bottle of our product. I would pick one or two children up on these occasions and sit them on my knees, so they could pretend for the moment that they were in charge of the factory. It was an altogether innocent practice, and never in my wildest dreams did I conceive that my efforts to bring a small portion of joy to these unfortunate children would be interpreted as an act of perversion.

Finally, it has been gossiped that my wife has not come to see me in jail because she does not care for me and perhaps suspects my guilt. In fact, my wife did visit me once and is willing to share my cell with me, but I did not wish to subject her to the embarrassment and abuse that would have attended her frequent visits. I wanted to save her from the snap-shotters and the detectives who, despite their presentable appearance in this courtroom, can be something other than gentlemen.

I have told you members of the jury the truth, the whole truth, and nothing but the truth. I ask you not for mercy but justice. Thank you for your close attention.

Only the soft whir of the overhead fans could be heard for a long moment. Tunney then rose and said, "I have no questions of this witness, your honor." Father's gamble, it seemed, had paid off richly.

His mother and wife fell upon Noah's shoulders, weeping unrestrainedly with joy, while the jury filed past, each man in his turn throwing a sidelong glance at the three of them embraced. Friends formed around them and thrust congratulatory handshakes into their midst. It lasted briefly. No doubt to hide his emotion, Noah beckoned the sheriff to take him away from his well-wishers. The reporter from Atlanta who had come by father's office for the interview two nights earlier wrote in his paper: "When the defendant concluded, a hush fell over the courtroom. His statement carried the ring of truth in every sentence. Scores in the room whose minds had not been made up—and perhaps some whose had—left the chamber convinced that Noah Berg is innocent."

I read that aloud at breakfast the next morning. Father nodded and attacked his omelette with unswerving attention. It was more, I noted, than he had taken for breakfast in months.

IV

With fresh resolve, Vincent Tunney took up his pitiless rebuttal attack. He began in decent enough fashion by seeking a ruling from the bench, with the jury out of the room, on just how far he might go in soiling the defendant's character, which "after all has become a central factor in this trial." The solicitor revealed, by way of example, that he planned to call first a young woman who he said had been summoned to Superintendent Berg's office on her second day of employment at the factory and been made an indecent proposal that caused her promptly to quit. Archie insisted such testimony would be intolerable. "You cannot try this man on every harebrained claim made against him," he said to the judge. "The defendant has already shown, in his own statement, how scurrilous and totally ill-founded are the reports that have been directed against him." The solicitor insisted that if the defense had called dozens upon dozens of witnesses to testify to Berg's character, the rules were perfectly plain in allowing him comparable latitude to bring in rebuttal evidence.

The judge ruled that the state could not introduce claims of specific acts of immorality by the defendant prior to the time of the murder. It was free, however, to present general evaluations of his character, to rebut specific testimony already introduced by the defense, and to cite any evidence it might have gathered regarding the defendant's relationship to the dead girl. "Does that mean, your honor," Tunney asked, "that I will not be able to put up a witness who will swear she saw the defendant in an indecent position with a woman in a dark part of the factory?" "That's precisely what it means!" shouted Archie. "I didn't ask you!" the solicitor shot back. The judge rapped for order and told Tunney such a claim would be inadmissible and he had better hew to the line.

Tunney put on a ferret-faced young fellow named Willie Sturgess, who until a few months earlier had worked as a bottle-washer at the factory. He testified that one day in mid-March he had seen Noah Berg talking with Jean Dugan in a deserted corner of the inspection room during the lunchtime break. "I heard her say that she had to go back to work and she backed off from him," the witness said, his voice a mite quavery, "but Berg kept on walking towards her and talking to her. The last words that I heard him say was that he wanted to talk to her—that he was the superintendent of the factory and he wanted to talk to her."

Archie asked that the jury be removed and then insisted that the solicitor had plainly broken the court's ruling on admissibility by this insinuating testimony. "On the contrary," said Tunney. "The state seeks only to show that Berg was familiar with the girl and was displaying his superiority to her—and this was just a short time before the murder. The defendant has claimed he did not know the girl. If this testimony is not material, I don't know what is." The judge ruled for the state. Archie had a word or two with Noah and then went immediately after the boy:

Q. So you're a farmer boy now out in Sandy Springs?
A. Yes, sir.
Q. Factory work get you down, did it?
A. Yes, sir.
Q. Is that why you left Mr. Berg's plant?
A. Mostly.
Q. Didn't you have a little problem moving the bottle bins?
A. Well, yes, sir. He got me nervous.
Q. Who got you nervous?
A. Mr. Berg, sir. He was always watching me.
Q. Didn't he begin watching you after you dropped three or four dozen bottles?
A. I don't know when he began watching. But he watched.
Q. Did you drop any more after that?
A. A few.
Q. Wasn't it a hundred or so, and didn't Mr. Berg in fact dismiss you from the factory for clumsiness?
A. I was fixing to leave anyway.

Archie retreated to the counsel table and let the boy be for a moment. Then he wheeled around and showed his fangs.

Q. Describe Jean Dugan to me.
A. She had light hair—.
Q. Brown or blond?
A. In between, kind of.
Q. Long or short?
A. In between.
Q. No, it was long. Curly or straight?
A. I didn't notice.
Q. How tall was she, what color eyes, what shape face?
A. She had light hair—and—I know her, but I can't

describe her very good. I know her. I know it was her because I heard other boys describing her.

Tunney sent up a new wave of assassins. One was a former bottle inspector who testified that she had seen Noah instructing Jean Dugan on the proper inspecting technique when she came to work at the factory. He had leaned close over her shoulder to point out the various kinds of imperfections that they had to watch out for in the bottles. "He called her Jean," the girl said in answer to the solicitor's question. It seemed harmless enough testimony, and Archie let it go. But when the state summoned Miss Dewey Holland, I flashed father an alert. I had assembled quite a little dossier on Miss Holland. Tunney, a gleam in his eye, must have thought he could get her on and off the stand fast.

Q. Did you know Jean Dugan?
A. I knew her well. I worked near her.
Q. Did you ever see Noah Berg talking with Miss Dugan?
A. Yes.
Q. How often?
A. Three or four times in one day sometimes.
Q. Did he seem friendly when he talked to her, or was it just business?
A. I saw him put his hand on her shoulder.
Q. What did he call her?
A. He called her Jean.
Q. Did he talk so you could hear much?
A. No, he kind of leaned over in her face.
Q. That's all.

Archie thumbed through my sheet of notes about the girl, who was a green-eyed vixen of about sixteen. He decided to waste little time on subtlety.

Q. Miss Holland, didn't you yourself take a fancy to Mr. Berg? Didn't you go to his office uninvited on several occasions on the pretext of discussing working conditions with him? And didn't you once tell him he would be better-looking if he discarded his glasses?
A. That's not how it happened exactly.

Q. But close enough. Can you tell us where you live?
A. In Cincinnati.
Q. Where in Cincinnati?
A. At the Home of the Good Shepherd.
Q. What kind of home is that?
A. For homeless girls.
Q. For delinquent homeless girls. Is it or isn't it true that you have faced charges of larceny and immorality in three different cities?
A. I was let off.
Q. Because of your age, Miss Holland. You may come down.

Nonplussed, the solicitor sent up a pair of former factory girls whose testimony was in effect that Noah was carrying on with Dora Barnes, the little shipping clerk who had said she would die to help him. Archie objected at once as the first girl began to testify. Tunney insisted that Miss Barnes, who had been put on by the defense, had said she was not romantically involved with Berg, and the witness was prepared to offer directly contradictory evidence. The judge ruled for the state, and the damage was considerable:

Q. Did you ever see Miss Dora Barnes go into the girls' dressing room—also called the cloakroom—with Noah Berg?
A. Yes.
Q. How often?
A. Twice.
Q. What time of day was this?
A. About ten o'clock one morning and in the afternoon once.
Q. When did this happen?
A. I don't remember exactly but it was earlier this year.

The second girl said she saw the pair go into the room three or four times during working hours and that they stayed there between fifteen and thirty minutes. Archie showed that the first girl had been dismissed from the factory for chronic tardiness and the other for insubordination; each admitted, too, that there was no lock on the cloakroom door, although Tunney was quick to suggest on re-direct that the door could readily be wedged shut from the inside by a chair under the knob. On re-cross, Archie got on the record that there was no knob on the door.

Tunney kept at it. He put on ten more ex-Jubilee girls who said they thought Noah's character in general was bad. When he asked the first of them what they thought about his character with regard to women, Archie came to his feet in a twinkling and roared his objection to the rafters. "A blatant violation of the court's ruling!" he yelled. Not so, said the solicitor; his question made no reference to any specific acts of immorality. The defendant had been presented to the court as a knight in shining armor; the state was therefore free to challenge his character within the guidelines put down by the judge. To allow implications of wantonness toward women, Archie insisted, was even worse than introducing direct testimony to that effect. Yet to our total bafflement, the judge ruled for the state, and girl after girl marched to the stand to declare that Noah had a lascivious character. Father rose as the last of these little snips retired and said the defense was formally protesting the bench's ruling in the matter and asked that the record show that objection unmistakably.

Tunney wound up with three medical experts who sounded every bit as authoritative as ours and got them to endorse Dr. Paternoster's findings inside the dead girl's stomach as both scientifically and ethically sound. Placing her time of death as precisely as Paternoster had was perhaps arguable but it was surely not wild guessing, they said, as the defense experts had insisted. Archie, in the rebuttal, recalled only the widow Barnes, who vehemently denied that she had habitually retired to the cloakroom with Noah for extended periods of time. "I once took him there," she said, "to show him a dead mouse in the corner and to urge him to have the floor-sweeper get his broom moving instead of laying around in corners drunk." The floor-sweeper she meant, she said, was Mo Easter.

It was the longest trial in Georgia history, the newspapers reported. More than two hundred fifty witnesses had been called. Now, only the summations remained, and then the verdict. Our reporter friend from Atlanta wrote on the front page of the state's best newspaper:

. . . For three weeks and a half, lawyers have fought like soldiers charging or defending a fortress. For over three weeks twelve tried men and true have sat stolidly and viewed the fight. Not one has succumbed to sickness. For nearly a month Noah Berg has sat watching the battle for his life. His face has been as impenetrable as the Sphinx. Something of the stoicism of his people who for centuries have suffered is writ on his features. The trace of a smile has from time to time flickered momentarily and then vanished to give place to his habitual attitude of impersonal interest.

My father, on the other hand, after having displayed three dozen years of the vaunted stoicism of his people, was frazzled and frightened. The judge had been pliant and allowed far too much into the record. "And the mobs should have been dispersed on the first day," he said. "I don't like the smell of it."

V

The rising clamor for blood was reported from various corners of the state. Up in Atlanta, a streetcar motorman was charged with disorderly conduct for announcing over and over to his passengers that Noah Berg was "nothing but a damned Jew" and "guilty as a snake" and if the jury did not convict, he would lead the lynch party himself. When called down for bigotry by a boy, the motorman shouted at the lad, "Are you hired by a Jew?" Over in Americus in the western part of the state, the Klan announced its own verdict and offered to supplement city and county law officers at the execution festivities. A women's temperance group in Augusta voted to ban the migration of non-Christians to the state. And in Savannah, the crowds pelted Vincent Tunney's gleaming locks with rose petals and cheered him as a conquering hero as he came to the courtroom each morning and left it each night—always within view or hearing of the jury.

Father and Archie wrangled till four in the morning over whether and how to confront the bigotry that both were not entirely convinced was at the root of Noah's prosecution. It had been latent throughout the trial but scarcely touched upon in the course of the testimony. The defense's dilemma had been very like trying to row a sinking boat to shore without taking time to fix the leak for fear too much water would get in. Archie insisted they seize this foaming bull by its horns, however deadly the peril, for nothing less would tame the passions that seemed to be astir on all sides. Father, reluctant to the end to grant that hate would best reason in any decently refereed contest between them, wanted to stick to the known facts of the case and show how inadequate they were to convict any man. They resolved their differences the only way possible: each man would take the tack he preferred, Archie confronting the emotional element in the case, father trying to reason with the jury.

I was up at dawn, father an hour later, the fatigue seeming to have hollowed him to a gauntness he had never before evidenced. It was not all that unattractive, that driven look, but it was plainly a condition he had not chosen to cultivate. I kissed his cheek and said he had done just splendidly already and this day in court would be no different from any other. "Worse" was all he said and took his coffee.

The courtroom was vibrant with anticipation of a dogged closing clash, and the biggest crowds of all filled the square outside, where the grass had been stunted by so many trampling brogans. Leading off, Archie seized the moment and blurted out the truth so fast and so unartfully that the effect was stunning in its directness and, it was apparent, its accuracy.

> I am reminded, at this somber moment, of a fellow I ran into up in Milledgeville last year, where they had a killing in a grocery store and three suspected negroes had been hanged for it. This here fellow I ran into, he said he wasn't sure they'd got the ones who did it but he was sure there'd been a bad crime and some niggers ought to have been strung up for it.

> Now have we got anything daintier on our hands right here? I say we've got a shameless lot of people who figure there ought to be a hanging because that innocent little girl was murdered—and who better to hang than this Jew since somebody ought to?

> Gentlemen of the jury, I tell you straight out that if

389

Noah Berg weren't a Jew, there never would have been a prosecution against him. They had a couple of niggers on the rug for a while, and gave 'em the third degree and the fourth degree and maybe a few other degrees, but that didn't work. And they had this poor-white boy Pike in there and tried to get the shoe to fit, but it wouldn't go. So they hit upon a Jew. And Jews make good victims. They've had plenty of practice for centuries.

Why, this case is the biggest frame-up in the history of Georgia—maybe in the history of the whole blamed country. They stuck a few loose facts together and threw in a whole lot of lies and perjurers from the gutter and have tried to make it stick. But it can't stick because it isn't the truth—there isn't a word of truth in the whole state case except that Noah Berg was in that factory that day and saw the girl for a moment. He told them that himself, Noah Berg did, and he didn't have to. If Noah Berg was a murderer, all he had to do was put that little girl's pay envelope back into his office safe, wait till the building cleared out to dispose of the body, and claim he had never seen her that day.

But instead of detective work, instead of real evidence, the police found only a scapegoat. And I am asking you men, as good Christians and Good Americans, to do justice to a Jew—and I am not a Jew myself, but I would rather die than do injustice to a Jew.

Let us, I pray you gentlemen, have no Captain Dreyfus on these shores. We do not persecute in the United States of America. Let Georgia show the way.

Archie professed sympathy with the police in trying to cope with the pressure in the community to find the perpetrator of so bestial a crime. "But that does not excuse the sort of unconscionable twisting of facts and distortion of character reports and monstrous perjury upon which the state has built this case with sticks and stones instead of the planking of solid evidence," he said. Every fragment in the solicitor's case was open to challenge or multiple interpretations.

You take this business of Berg's nervousness. The police couldn't tell you often enough how nervous the man was and how he had to have his coffee or he'd faint dead away. So what if the man was nervous? I'd be nervous too if I ran a factory and a girl had just been found murdered in the basement. Besides, you don't send men to the gallows for being nervous. And so what if he jumped when he saw that long drink of water Vernon Pike lingering in the doorway of the factory at a time he had no business being there. Noah Berg must have thought Pike was there to do him dirt—why wouldn't he jump at the sight of him, a man a head taller and bearing a grudge?

Point by point he tore into the state's case.

If both sides agreed that someone had made a systematic effort to pin the crime on the colored night watchman, said Archie, there was not a shred of hard evidence linking Noah Berg to "that transparent set of tricks."

And how, pray tell, could the stalwart Hawkshaws of the Savannah constabulary have missed finding a blood spot on the floor on Sunday and suddenly discovered it on Wednesday? "I'll tell you how," Archie said. "Somebody put it there, next to Noah Berg's office, to pin the crime on the one person known to have been on that floor at the alleged time of the murder."

And why would the police go to the extraordinary lengths of having the dead body exhumed and hiring an alchemist to do their bidding by claiming the time of death to have been precisely —*precisely*, even though the girl had been long dead and her vital fluids drained or dried up—when Noah Berg was alone in his office? Responsible medical experts have told you that such precision in a matter of this sort is a scientific impossibility, but that has not deterred the state from building its circumstantial case against this good and totally innocent man.

But by far the grossest ingredient in the state's effort to frame Berg, he said, was "the sort of low-life they persuaded to come here and testify against this man. Just compare our witnesses with theirs, and what do you find? The state is dependent on admitted jailbirds—thieves and drunks and fornicators—and a dozen or so disgruntled little girls who had worked at the factory once and for reasons of their own incompetence or shortcomings of character, did not tarry there long. They have been persuaded to come here and take out their grudge on this highly able executive who they have been convinced was their tormentor. They remind me of nothing so much as the hysterical maidens who testified so darkly at the Salem witch trials—those addled children who were encouraged to vent the basest instincts of the community. Why, you could find a dozen people to speak against the good character of the Bishop of Atlanta, or even our distinguished Judge Vickery here, and what would it mean? You must weigh the words of these misguided and bitter young women against the disinterested testimony of many dozens of solid citizens who have said that Noah Berg's character is exemplary." If the factory had been the den of iniquity the state pictures and its superintendent the arch-fiend of lasciviousness, would not these conditions be general knowledge to the police and the laboring community? What respectable young woman would come to work at such a place, or, learning of the polluted moral climate there, remain employed there?

In the end, said Archie, the state's case all boiled down to the testimony of one man. "And what a man."

What followed was not pretty. And it grieved me. But Archie Ruskin was charged with getting Noah Berg off, and he did what he thought he had to—and what father never would have. "Now the state has said that Mo Easter's testimony is so rich and detailed that it is very damning to the defendant," he began. "And they will tell you that no black man could make up such a story. But I tell you gentlemen if there is any one thing that nigger can do it is to lie. He is a habitual liar—everyone at the factory knows it—a liar, a drunkard, a malingerer, a deadbeat. And he is the state's star witness, and you are asked to take his word against Noah Berg's. But why should you? The state asks you to because it suits the state's convenience. But it does not suit the cause of justice."

He reviewed the circumstances of Easter's arrest, his suspicious behavior around the factory after the murder, the discovery of the dead girl's mesh purse in his room, and the various statements he had made to the authorities "before he and they figured out together how this worthless nigger could be of most use." Archie moved closer to the jury box now.

> The police decided he could not be their man because
> there were just too many unanswered questions. What

black man ever commits a crime and leaves a note putting the murder on someone else—especially another nigger? The time slip presented them with another problem, and the bloody shirt—it was all too crafty for a black man to have thought up. But Mo Easter didn't know that's what they decided. All he knew was that he was in jail and they'd just as soon stretch his neck as anybody else's. That purse did him in.

But no! Ol' Mo Easter, as he lay in his cell and read the papers and talked with the detectives, conjured up his wonderful story laying the crime on Noah Berg because the detectives were starting to lay it there and were helping him do the same.

Now I don't know that they told Mo to swear to this and swear to that, but they made the suggestions and Mo knew whom he had to please. He knew that when he pleased the detectives, the rope knot around his neck grew looser. And so his story kept changing to fit the needs of the police. And to make it convincing, they fed him the details of things they knew would be sworn to in court. They would say, "And then you saw Mrs. Camp come in, didn't you, Mo, going up to visit her husband—you know Mrs. Camp, don't you, Mo?" and the poor nigger, understanding and trying to please, said, "Oh, yas, sir, boss, dat's right, I seen Mrs. Camp go on up." And his nimble mind would add flourishes of its own, for every detail that brought Noah Berg closer to the jailhouse meant that Mo's chances of staying alive were improved. And so between them, the police and the detectives and the solicitor—oh, yes, our friend Mr. Tunney joined willingly and knowingly in this hunt—they put the pieces together and told the nigger what would fit, and he played it all back to them and they mended it and embellished it and rehearsed it till they thought it would be enough to convict Noah Berg but keep Easter clear except as an accessory after the fact.

The real fact was, said Archie, that there was considerably more evidence in hand and testimony sworn to for laying the crime on Mo Easter than on Noah Berg. The dead girl's purse alone would be enough to implicate him deeply. His clandestine but confessed presence on the premises that day was another somber circumstance. "Why, gentlemen," he said, "I submit to you that this dirty, filthy, drunken, lying nigger was huddled there in wait like a black spider as the little Dugan girl went up and got her money and came on down the stairs in full innocence. Mo must have crouched there, by the elevator shaft, out of sight, like a great, passionate, lustful animal, full of mean whiskey and wanting money with which to buy more. It would have been the work of but a moment for him to reach out and grab her purse, and when she resisted, to have struck her, and then again behind the stairs, and then dropped her down that scuttle-hole to the basement, like a sack of flour, and finished up his dirty work down there. I do not say to you gentlemen that that is how it happened. I say that is very likely how it happened—or at least far more likely than to believe that a decent white man like Noah Berg could have committed such a crime. That, gentlemen, was no civilized man's crime."

It was not a proud moment for father, I could see, and I loathed Archie for stooping to such blatant bigotry to save a client whose very indictment stemmed, he had argued, from comparable hatred. The irony was no doubt plain to others in that room. It was a card, however, that Archie felt he had to play.

Father showed a different sort of hand.

Quietly, he pulled Mo Easter's testimony to pieces. Under no stretch of the imagination, he declared, would Noah Berg, an intelligent man, have done in Jean Dugan on the second floor of the factory when two able-bodied workmen were making repairs on the floor just above and the colored floor sweeper was allegedly watching for him on the first floor. And he most assuredly would not have taken the body downstairs in an elevator when it was well known that the whole building shook anytime someone operated it. Was it even physically possible for Noah Berg, a slender man, to have subdued the strapping young Dugan girl and not suffered her blows in return? Is it conceivable that he would have been so muddled by the crime that he would have put his victim's purse in the safe in his own office?

Why would Noah Berg, if he were as calculating as the state has painted him, take into his confidence this

Mo Easter, a low type of fellow, and thereby risk his life even further than it would already have been jeopardized? Surely here was a secret he would not have willingly shared with another soul.

There is only one answer to these questions, and that is the one you heard the defendant state to you himself: Easter's testimony is a tissue of falsehood, from first to last.

There were other convincing signs of the defendant's innocence, he added. It is highly unlikely that Noah Berg would have been able to execute the many computations required in the factory production report, which he put into the mail late on Saturday—a claim verified by an affidavit from a company official in Atlanta, where the data had been received late on Monday—if he had had blood on his hands. Berg's letter to his parents, similarly, revealed a man who was composed and reflective. And could a man with a murder on his mind have relaxed and laughed around the hearth that Saturday evening as Noah Berg did—a man who the state said was highly prone to nervousness born of guilt? "Gentlemen," he said, "it is not enough for the state to say that it is possible that Noah Berg killed the girl. It must prove it. It is not good enough for the authorities to say he is more likely to have done it than anyone else they have managed to find."

At the end, he faced them not up close but from the middle of that hushed room where he spoke words that sprang from a conviction he had spent thirty years nourishing. "The American jury, gentlemen, is supreme," he said. "It is sovereign over all our lives. There are times when you can sway it by passion and prejudice, I'm afraid, but no one can make it believe anything as preposterous and foul as the state's case against this man. A jury is not a mob. The attitude of the juror's mind is not that of the man who carelessly walks the streets. You are unprejudiced and know it is your duty to pass on this man's life with no passion and no cruelty but as men purged by your sacred oath. You are to decide from the evidence alone, without fear of a hostile mob or thought of favor to anyone. The name and face and faith and position of this defendant, or any defendant, cannot move you. And for that I thank God, who is the father of us all."

I fought back all but the first rush of tears. Dear father! To have reached his advanced age and still have stars and stripes in his eyes. Upon his return to our table, I reached over and touched him briefly on the wrist; he would have countenanced no more overt show of emotion. I glanced back at my mother, who was mopping her nostrils delicately with a kerchief till she saw me spy her and abruptly ceased. They had both ventilated their feelings in the course of the trial as I had never seen before, but the moment father's public rôle was done, the gates slammed shut and he and mother seemed to take up anew that monotonously decorous bearing they confused with dignity.

So caught up had I been by my father's summation that half a dozen sentences had escaped from Vincent Tunney's slippery throat before I was brought back to earth and the realization that the state would have the last word, as it had had the first, and that word was likely to be as underhanded in manner as it would be lethal in intent. Tunney had been an authentic, unvarying villain, to my eyes, and I had undoubtedly lost the power to assess his work in that courtroom for what it was: the jagged craftsmanship of a professional prosecutor, every bit as conscientious about his labor as was the man he was trying to execute. His adroitness, energy, endurance, and fortitude—he was, after all, pitted against a pair of masterful veteran advocates—were lost upon me. I saw only a clawed Beelzebub, beetle-browed and glowering, in gigantic combat with the Godhead. The solicitor, a future as the darling of the rabble beckoning to him brightly, did not disappoint any of my expectations.

"Prejudice and perjury is the cry of the defense against our case," he was saying when I tuned in. "But do not let this purchased indignation mislead you. These learned counsel were paid to play the part. Gentlemen, can you really believe that we sworn officers of law and order were really controlled by prejudice in this case and against this defendant? Is it likely that we would have passed over two black men whose circumstances suggested they were involved in the crime in order to get at this white citizen? No, the cry of prejudice arose only when Noah Berg was arrested. But have you heard words of racial persecution fall from my lips during this trial? It is the defense, not the state, that introduces the issue at this late hour, and it is a straw man—an obvious device to distract you from your sworn duty. I say the race this man Berg stems from is as good as ours. His forefathers were civilized and living in cities and following laws while ours were roaming at large in forests and painting their faces and still eating human flesh. I say his race is as good as—but no better than—our own."

The snake! The absolutely insidious swine! He patronized us with faint praise for our precocity before the Christian era and in the process labels us a people apart. Our "race" indeed. He persevered:

> Yes, I honor the race that produced Disraeli, the greatest of British statesmen, and Judah Benjamin, as splendid a lawyer as England or America ever saw. I honor the Straus family and the Lehman brothers and the Seligman tribe. I roomed with one of the defendant's race at my college. One of the partners of the law firm I was with before coming to this office was of his race. I serve on the same hospital board with the mother-in-law of this defendant and have shared the courtroom on more than one occasion with his able co-counselor, Mr. Adler, who stems from this same race. Yes, its members rise to heights sublime. But they also sink to the lowest depths of degradation, for they are only human—and we have the defendant's lurid crime to demonstrate this undeniable fact.

God, he was a skillful scroundrel, and for Georgia a subtle one. Having shown his own great liberality to these pariah people (and letting the jury know, in the process, that father was one of them and his words in behalf of a coreligionist therefore discountable), the solicitor set about to dismember the defendant. It mattered not that Noah Berg had a spotless past so far as the law could determine, he said. "For the law says that the claim or proof of previous good character cannot stand in the way of a conviction if the evidence indicates." But the previous character of the defendant was not so sterling as the defense had suggested, regardless of how many endorsements it managed to solicit, he said.

> . . . For if fifty men were asked the character of a certain man, and forty said it was good and ten of them said it was bad, would you conclude it was good or bad?

You would conclude, I suspect, that the ten may well have known something that the forty did not. I ask you whether this man's old schoolmates and family friends and casual acquaintances and spiritual adviser know him in the way that these young girls who worked at his factory knew him—worked there until his conduct became intolerable in their eyes. Oh, yes, there is much evidence that the state could have introduced along this line if it had been permitted to do so—.

Archie objected that this was an improper argument, and the judge sustained him, but the solicitor seemed scarcely to pause.

I hope you noticed, my friends, the tactic used by the defense to try to discredit every witness who spoke out against their client. Oh, yes, he got his money's worth. For they were quick to let you know that everyone who found fault with him was a flawed and perhaps despicable human being, trying merely to even a score against this wholly admirable soul. He alone possessed virtue. His detractors, without exception, were low.

But let me tell you that there is enough on the record to suggest to you the sort of lascivious pervert this man was. We do not say that he tried to paw every innocent young woman who came through the door. He knew, after all, the rules of society and what would be permitted and how to use his authority to seek his foul ends. The preponderance of girls from the factory, therefore, will say naught against him—and if they want to stay on the payroll, they had best not. But enough of these young women have been sufficiently intrepid to come forward to testify against the character of the man.

In this connection, I want to ask you two questions. Do you think it possible that I or the police could have coaxed these girls to come here or coerced them—could have or would have urged them to come before this court and commit perjury? In the second place, I ask you why the defense failed to cross-examine these fifteen or twenty young women who testified against Noah Berg's character. This failure, I submit, is ample proof that the defense had much to fear from them, for if it had not, there is no power on earth that could have discouraged counsel from cross-examining.

Archie renewed his objection, saying the defense had shown in previous cross-examination how ill-founded the reports of Noah's low character had been and the solicitor could not use words that were not spoken as evidence against the defendant. The judge overruled him, and Tunney steamrolled on.

"The girls, this man Dalton, the negro Easter," he said, "they saw the dark side of Berg, who was a dual personality, of that there can be no doubt—a veritable Jekyll and Hyde." The state had shown a pattern of immoral behavior in the defendant well before the crime occurred: what, for example, was he doing looking in that cloakroom? Not to ferret out flirtatious conduct, as he claimed, but more than likely to see if the coast was clear so he might use the room, as he had on other occasions, for his libertine pursuits. And the state had shown beyond peradventure, he said, that Noah Berg had known Jean Dugan, and perhaps quite well— "if not so well as he would have liked"—despite his statement to the police that he was not sure that such a girl worked at his factory.

> . . . Why, you can't tell me that a brilliant man like him could pass her machine every day—several times a day, probably—and not notice her, as attractive and bright and conscientious a little girl as she was. You can't tell me that this man, with the brain he's got, could have helped make out the payroll fifty-two times a year and then claim to be so unfamiliar with her name that he had to look up in the time book to be sure a girl named Jean Dugan worked at his factory. Why, he knew every single thing that went on in that building!

He was midway through his oration when court adjourned for the afternoon. The final day of the trial would belong to the solicitor—and the jury. The prospect was thoroughly unsettling. Our anxiety was not eased when, just two minutes before court was due to reconvene at nine the next morning, a great roar of cheers reached our ears from the outside and announced that Tunney was making his way toward us. The cheering accompanied him on his entire route and picked up inside the courtroom itself. Archie was on his feet calling for the sheriff to restrain the spectators and telling the judge he would move for an immediate mistrial if there was any such outburst once the jury entered the room. But surely the jury had heard that upswell of approval from the throng, and if it could not identify the source, there must have been deputies partisan to the solicitor's cause who tactfully passed the word.

He was the total master of the arena that morning. He preened as he spoke, as if there were no contest at all and his function was merely to make the jury's painful task less disagreeable. "Now it has been suggested," he said, "that circumstantial evidence is somehow tainted evidence—as if the word 'mere' appears before it —and that is not so. There is nothing mysterious about circumstantial evidence and nothing trivial. It means simply that when you've got a fact, you've got it, and while it alone is not conclusive, a great many such facts may very well be. A preponderance of circumstantial evidence counts for a great deal; otherwise, society would be exposed to freedom in the commission of all sorts of the most horrible crimes. It is true that circumstances which justify only a conjecture of guilt are not warranted as the basis for a conviction. But when the circumstantial evidence is consistent with all the facts in the crime, only a conviction can result. If we offered you only the circumstantial evidence—and omitted entirely the testimony of Mo Easter—you would have enough to find Noah Berg guilty of murder most horrible."

The evidence showed that Berg was in the right place at the right time—by his own admission—to have committed the crime, the solicitor thundered. And then, one after another, he recited the circumstances that the defense had in every instance mitigated. "Who else could have doctored that time slip," Tunney demanded, "and written that note and planted that bloody shirt in order to turn the finger of suspicion against a bent and defenseless old darkey?" And didn't those blood spots in the cloakroom fix the site of the murder just around the corner from the superintendent's office? That was something he had failed to cover up well enough, but it had not been for lack of trying, just as he tried to cover himself by that letter, that incredible letter to his parents that was written well after it was claimed. "Now there, if ever there was one, was a contrived piece of work," he declared. "What on earth did Noah Berg care for the thinning gray line of the veterans of the Confederacy? He—a Yankee! He cared only for his position with his company and the opportunity it afforded him to get ahead in a world that his Northern countrymen had tried so hard to destroy."

My ears tingled and my head rang. There was no room for reason or debate in that courtroom. It had become a star chamber. Tunney ended by making a hero of Mo Easter.

> Perhaps, in the last analysis, Mo had no choice but to let it all out. His testimony had been mocked by the defense as a gross perjury, but I ask you to recall the ordeal they put him through on the witness stand in a totally fruitless attempt to break him down. But he did not yield. He did not because it was the truth he finally told in this courtroom. Yes, he had lied earlier to the police, but he knew when the lying had to end. I ask you gentlemen whether any darkey could have invented such a detailed and verifiable story?

Beyond the testimony in the case, he said, his voice quieting now, there was one highly curious omission in the defendant's behavior that could not be ignored. Noah Berg had been portrayed by the defense as a devoted family man and doer of good works in his community, "yet isn't it odd that no words of kindness or commiseration ever fell from his lips—no gesture of solicitude or sign of sorrow was directed by this allegedly charitable and decent man toward the bereaved family of that slain child? Was he so inhuman a creature—or merely too human and unable to face that heartbroken mother who came to this courtroom and wept before us all?"

Tunney departed from the battlefield a self-proclaimed martyr. The defense, he said, had abused him. "And they have abused the detective force. And they have heaped so much calumny on the state that the mother of the defendant was constrained to arise in their presence and denounce me as a dog. Well, there's an old adage, and it's true, that goes, 'When did any thief ever feel the halter draw with any good opinion of the law?'" He looked hard at Noah now and then at our whole table. "I do not want your approval, and I do not seek it. And your good opinion is not worth the having."

He pivoted toward the jury then and said, "Every circumstance in this case proves that this man killed that girl. Extraordinary? Yes, I grant you—but as true as the fact that Jean Dugan lies moldering in the ground this day. She died a noble death, I tell you— a martyr to the virtue she protected till the end from her lust-crazed employer." At the end, he turned to the judge and said, "Your honor, I have done my duty. I have no apologies to make. There will be, I know, but one verdict: guilty—guilty—guilty."

ELEVEN

Father and Archie were summoned to Judge Vickery's chambers during the ten-minute recess before he charged the jury. Threats upon the lives of the defendant and his counsel, in the event the jury voted for acquittal, had been received by the sheriff and Chief of Police Yates, said the judge, and in the view of the commanding colonel of the Third Georgia Regiment, which was standing by in the city, the crowds had reached proportions that would make them very difficult to control if they did not get what they wanted. In the interest of their own safety, therefore, the judge urged the defendant and his attorneys to waive their right to be present in the courtroom when the jury returned its verdict.

The two lawyers met in private with Noah for a few minutes. Archie viewed the request as an outrage and a confession of the court's inability to conduct its business beyond the reach of the mob; he said he was flat against accepting the judge's recommendation. Father, as he explained it to me as soon as the jury retired for its deliberations, agreed with Archie's analysis but reached precisely the opposite conclusion. "It will be very useful if we have to appeal," he said, "whereas no purpose is served by our being stubborn. I told the judge that just as we disapprove of the conditions that prompted it but would reluctantly accept the court's proposal, so our client disapproved but would accept the advice of his counsel to absent himself when the verdict is read." To me it was lynch law, pure and simple, and the judge had yielded to it instead of instructing the sheriff, the police chief, and the Third Georgia to disperse the mobs and impose a curfew if need be to protect the lives of innocent citizens. "No doubt of it," said father, dispatching me and a young associate from his firm to stand vigil in the courtroom while the jury met. Noah was taken to the private cell block that had been allotted to him because of the steady stream of visitors attending him at all hours since the trial began. Archie, grumbling all the while, joined father in his office on Factors' Row, where they would await word from me on the telephone.

The longer the jury remained out, I knew, the brighter our chances; I was not brought up a lawyer's daughter for nothing. Still, the clock seemed to have forgotten its duty as I glanced up at it every five minutes in the hope that another half hour had elapsed since my last furtive look. A few of the newspapermen detected my anxiety and tried to allay it. They had cultivated me as a source for stories on the defense team's efforts—a purpose I usefully served since father was by preference taciturn during the course of a trial and Archie's idea of effective press relations was to shake his mahogany cane under the nose of newsmen and threaten them with a detached scalp if they filed copy friendly to his adversaries. The consensus of the press corps was that even if the jury found Noah Berg guilty, the state of Georgia would never put him to death. "Tunney done it up brown," said the reigning sage of the Atlanta *Constitution,* "but all he's really got is one coon's word for it, and you don't hang a white man for that." He tactfully omitted "even a Jew."

It was a muggy, beastly afternoon, so stifling in that courtroom that I felt myself submerged in a swamp and battling for breath. Only a few palm-leaf fans fluttered sporadically in odd corners. The spectators seemed more drowsy than expectant, but not a seat was yielded. Reporters shuttled in and out the side door to the vestibule, where special telephones had been installed; every newspaper in the South was standing by to rush out an extra as soon as the jury decided.

Just after five o'clock, when I was all but crazed by the chambered density, the judge burst through the door to the side of the bench and, looking a freshly scrubbed pink, took his place. At once the deadly hum of anticipation that I had heard throughout the trial but never accustomed myself to picked up and grew into a menacing drone. The judge reached for his gavel and snuffed out the noise with uncharacteristic vigor. The next moment he ordered the sheriff to clear the courtroom. The crowd was caught by surprise, but it flocked out obediently before the summoning marshals and deputies, for it was evident to us all that the moment of decision had been reached. Something close to a festive air took hold of the exiting throng. Their semi-gaiety acted upon me as a depressant. I vainly sought a crack in the woodwork big enough to hide in.

The jury returned at a quarter past five. They had been out a bit more than three and a half hours—not long enough. The room was eerily quiet. No sound reached it from outside. I looked over at Tunney across the aisle, seated immobile at his table, arms folded and glance riveted upon the floor. I guessed he was praying. I prayed, too. "God, in Your infinite mercy, do not forsake this frail man and all Your people, amen." There was no time, or need, for more. I scanned from Tunney and the pair of pie-faced aides with him to the few others left in the room—the judge, the sheriff, two deputies, the court stenographer, the bailiff, and two dozen reporters, their pencils poised. All of us now turned toward the jurors, whose faces told an unmistakable story. To a man, they looked drawn and grim. I could not tell them apart. Once I knew each man of them by name, occupation, and likely proportion of anti-semitism coursing through his veins. Now they were as one man, with gray pouches beneath a fixed set of coal-black, steel-hard eyes. I shuddered at the sight.

Slowly, with a voice that disclosed no tremble, the foreman stood and read out the verdict: "We find the defendant guilty as charged."

The reporters galloped off in a herd. From them word reached the street below in another instant, and a shout went up. And then another. And another. It became a deep, steady roar soon, and we were all consumed by it. After a few minutes, when it was clear that the cheering would not quickly abate, father's associate stood and said, in a voice just this side of a shout, that he wished the jury to be polled. The judge frowned briefly, then instructed the sheriff to have the crowd stilled, and waited till that great exultant rumble was reduced by half. The polling had not proceeded beyond the third juror when a new wave of thunder came rolling up from the ground, and each subsequent juryman had to shout out his conviction to the bench. It was as gross a travesty of the deliberative process as I suspect anyone in that room had ever witnessed. My only solace was that father was not there to see it.

The judge, straining to make himself heard, thanked the jurors for "your faithful service during this most arduous case." He added, his voice breaking, "I hope you find your families well. I wish you Godspeed." He set the sentencing for the following day and then gave a final short rap of the gavel. It was done. Exhaustively and hideously done. It could not be, I knew: not in this America. I felt nothing, nothing at all, at first.

The sheriff came up behind me to say one of the deputies had already telephoned the news to father and that I had best leave by the side entrance. I thanked him and said no but that I would wait for a minute until the jurymen had gone. You could trace their progress by the volley of cheers that greeted each man as he reached the entrance and made his way through the parting crowd. The last to go before me was Vincent Tunney, who collected his carrying case, glanced back at me over his shoulder with a small, silent nod that I took to be a twitch of commiseration, and went out to be greeted by his constituency, the people. I watched from the doorway.

Men hurled their hats into the air. Women wept with joy and threw kisses toward him. The word "Guilty!" rattled like musketry around the square in an unabating chant. The solicitor reached no farther than the sidewalk. While mounted elements of the Third Georgia rode like Quantrill's Raiders to clear the thoroughfares, three muscular titans slung Vincent Tunney on their shoulders and passed him over the heads of the crowd to his office across the street. He raised his hat in acknowledgment of the adoration. Tears were streaming down his face, the papers said the next day, though all I saw from where I stood was the back of that glittering scalp. The victor was carried up in the elevator and dropped limply into a seat in his office, where his only comment was said to be: "I feel sorry for his wife and mother."

I reached the prison a few moments before Archie and father. The crowd in front consisted mostly of colored people, and its mood was deep blue. Rabbi Weisz, Noah's personal physician, and Sig Klein and his wife waited for us inside, where we climbed to the second floor in gloomy procession.

A group of friends sat surrounding Noah and Naomi on the far side of the cell as our party trailed in, father and the rabbi in the lead. Noah rose to greet them. "I'm glad you came up," he said, a smile on his boyish face.

"Noah," said the rabbi, "the jury has found you guilty."

"I know," he said, nodding quickly, "I've always known."

There was only terror in Naomi's eyes as she gnawed upon the back of her hand and then swooned. Noah's mother carried the girl into a corner. In a moment she had recovered and was weeping bitterly. Noah went to her and stroked her head and pleaded with her to be brave. Her spasmodic wails hardly muted as the Kleins led her away down the corridor to the waiting family car and chauffeur.

Somebody told Noah that there were ten reporters outside waiting for a comment. Archie said he would attend to them, but Noah looked at me and said, "Tell them I am as innocent as I was a year ago. Tell them I could hardly believe it when I was told the jury had convicted me. Tell them I hope to get justice yet." He threw his head back. "Tell them that my devoted and superb lawyers will seek a new trial."

I looked over at father for swift confirmation. "Tell them," he said. "Tell them we say justice in Georgia miscarried this day."

I told them, and it was printed. And they went and sought out Mo Easter in his cell, too, and asked him what he thought of the verdict. He said, "Me, boss? Lawd, I got nothin' to say," and turned his back. Downstairs, Plato Layne was part of the crowd. He came up to father and me as we left and said, "I'se sorry, Mr. Adler—I sho' is sorry." Father took his hand and held it and thanked his oldest friend in Georgia, and then we went home.

II

The hanging was set for October 10, but father's motion for a new trial was scheduled to be heard a week earlier, and that assured a delay in the execution. But the shadow of the noose was suspended over the entire Jewish community of Savannah—of Georgia, of the South, of the whole land, it almost seemed. I had returned to New York and my studies but there was no fleeing that lamentation. My mother wrote that no one was more severely stricken than Rabbi Weisz, who seemed unable to bestir himself to lead the congregation through the High Holy Days with his usual animation of mind and tongue. Men of God were supposed to be immune from such emotional sloughs, I had thought; were they not anointed precisely to comfort the rest of us who are so ignorant of the Lord's capricious ways and fearful of His terrible wrath? Some rabbi.

I found myself in that season dwelling on the concepts of God as love and of the enveloping goodness of the merciful Jesus, and of how I could detect so little manifestation of either sublime force in those adamant Christian hearts that beat all around me and would go on beating whenever they finally placed Noah Berg in the ground. Among those uncharitable souls, none seemed to me less expansive than the one inhabiting Amory G. Austin, the Southland's leading industrialist.

Austin was strong enough to know when to be unprincipled. Loyalty to a devoted employée was one thing; economic suicide was another. One could honestly not expect a profit-seeking corporation to stand by a convicted murderer, regardless of his past contributions to the enterprise. For it was unarguable that Noah Berg had been bad for Jubilee's business—until the jury convicted him, at which point the tacit boycott of the product infecting wide sectors of the market was lifted and sales rose to record levels. Amory Austin celebrated by advising father that so long as he planned to appeal Noah's conviction—a process that might consume months or even years—it would be best for him to make the leave he had taken from the company permanent. Both the Baxters agreed with him, he added. Father would be retained formally on individual matters, of course, and his recompense not materially reduced. Father, as a sizable stockholder in the company, surely understood, did he not, where the line had to be drawn between personal conviction and economic prudence. Father, to my annoyance, said he did.

His motion for a new trial cited one hundred three grounds. The principal complaint was that the entire tribunal functioned under thrall to a street mob whose vocal presence had thoroughly cowed the jury, which ought to have been insulated from it, and thus denied the defendant due process of law. There had been countless instances, inside and outside of the courtroom, of mob domination of the trial. The sustained outbreak of applause by spectators upon the judge's ruling to admit Mo Easter's testimony on the defendant's alleged lascivious acts prior to the murder of Jean Dugan was a flagrant demonstration to the jury of public sentiment and should not have been permitted. There were similar outbreaks when the court allowed the state to put questions to its character witnesses regarding the defendant's behavior toward women, and when the solicitor entered the chamber to complete delivery of his summation. The preference of the street throngs was never in doubt, and its demands for conviction were vociferously directed toward the jurors on their way to and from the courtroom. Its delight with the verdict was ringing in their ears even as the jurors were obliged to state their vote in the final polling by the bench. The court, father charged, scarcely waved a finger at all this unconscionable disorderliness, while the law-enforcement corps of the community likewise declined to mobilize itself and disperse these incendiary elements. There were some three dozen rulings by the bench, moreover, that were both irregular and prejudicial. Most of them dealt with the admissibility of testimony, including large portions of Mo Easter's narrative, Dr. Paternoster's unverified (and unverifiable) report on the time of the murder, the solicitor's inquiries of the defendant's mother on the financial position of her family, his yet lewder questions of the insurance salesman on Noah's alleged child-fondling, and the spiteful derogations of former factory girls whose words lacked all specificity but were nonetheless toxic in their effect. The judge had compounded these errors, unwittingly no doubt, by himself bringing into court a newspaper with its banner headline, complimentary to the state, open to the jury's contemplation. "Justice was not served by this month-long exhibition of judicial capriciousness and civil disorder," father's charges concluded.

To nobody's surprise, Judge Vickery denied the motion for a retrial, and father appealed at once to the Supreme Court of Georgia. "I am hopeful but not overly," he told Noah, who passed the hours now with the nearly numbed disposition of a man who knows his days are numbered. Hope was too precious a commodity for him to partake of it airily. There were, at least, no wails from him about desertion from on high, and, sustained by the steadying presence of Rabbi Weisz, the prisoner embraced a fatalism that could easily have been taken for fortitude. His wife, on the other hand, retreated into dysfunction for long periods of the day. Her mother applied drugs and cosmetics in substantial quantity so that Naomi's dinnertime visit each day would not prove excessively dispiriting to her son-in-law.

Father found encouragement in the request by the state's high court for affidavits from each of the jurors as to the effect on them of the cheering in the streets below at the time the court polled the panel. All of them acknowledged hearing the tumult; none, that he was affected by it. Father, during the oral argument before the court in Atlanta, suggested that the jurors' admission of having heard the noise was the pertinent point, not their expected denial of having been swayed by it. "Would any man among them have risked casting a vote for acquittal," he asked the judges, "and then ventured into that foaming mob below? Why, the defendant and his co-counsel had been advised by the court to absent themselves from the room at the time the verdict was read lest the populace act violently in the event of acquittal or a hung jury. Would the wrath of the people have been any less likely to be directed against the jurymen than against their beneficiaries? The action of the trial court itself in exiling the defendant and his counsel confirmed its own powerlessness before that mob, which no jury could have withstood."

The force of father's argument seemed to me irresistible. The Georgia Supreme Court nevertheless resisted it. In February of 1914, it found some of the testimony admitted by the trial court to be irregular, some not, but none of so momentous a character as could be said to have been decisive in a trial of such duration. Besides, ample rebuttal had been permitted to all the testimony admitted under protest. As to the occasional outbursts of partisanship by the spectators, the Georgia court was not greatly exercised:

> . . . The court below directed the sheriff to find out who was making the noise, and, presumably from what otherwise appears in the record, the action by the court was deemed satisfactory at the time, and the orderly progress of the case was resumed without any further action being requested.
>
> The general rule is that the conduct of a spectator during a trial will not be ground for a reversal of the judgment unless a ruling on such conduct is invoked from the judge at the time it occurs. The applause by the spectators, under the circumstances described in the record of the Berg trial, is but an irregularity not calcu-

lated to be substantially harmful to the defendant. And
even if the irregularity should be regarded as of more
moment than we give it, we think the action of the
court, as a manifestation of judicial disapproval, was a
sufficient cure for any possible harmful effect of the irregularity, and deemed so sufficient by the counsel who,
at the time, made no request for further action by the
court.

The court doubted as well father's claim of the coercive effect of
the street mob at the time of the verdict. "In order that the occurrence complained of shall have the effect of absolutely nullifying
the poll of the jury taken before they dispersed, it must appear
that its operation upon the minds of the jury, or some of them,
was of such a controlling character that they were prevented, or
likely to have been prevented, from giving a truthful answer to
the questions of the court. We find that the affidavits of jurors
submitted in regard to this occurrence are sufficient to show that
there was no likelihood that there was any such result. Under
such circumstances, we hold the occurrence complained of to be a
mere irregularity. . . ." The appeal of the motion for a new trial
was denied.

Before a new execution date could be scheduled, father again
moved for a re-trial, this time on the basis of new evidence. Its
gravamen served to point the finger of guilt away from Noah and
toward Vernon Pike.

Plato Layne, who by then was working as gardener and handy-
man for Amanda Baxter, came forward, upon father's urging, with
an affidavit telling of Mo Easter's visit to his quarters on the afternoon of the murder and his remarks at the saloon regarding the
alleged illicit activities that Pike had directed in the basement of
the factory prior to his dismissal. The testimony had not been introduced at the trial because Noah had been unwilling to risk
Pike's certain counterclaim that he had come upon the superintendent in his office one Saturday with a young woman kneeling
before him "in that unspeakable position." With a rope already
around his neck, Noah could no longer be squeamish about such a
charge and told father not to hesitate. Yoked to Plato's additional
testimony was the disclosure by a clerk at Rosen's Pharmacy that
he remembered now, ten months after the fact, that the murdered

411

girl had come into the drugstore late on Friday, the day before the crime. He remembered, he said, because she was carrying a big box, the kind you might pack a dress in, and was accompanied by a tall young man in a checked suit and derby who closely resembled the photographs he saw afterward of Vernon Pike. "They were quite friendly, like sweethearts," the clerk stated. "The young lady went to make a telephone call, and the gentleman said he would order them both something sweet to drink. As she left the table, she said, 'All right, make it anything but a Juby.' I made them each a lemon phosphate."

Pike's likely involvement with the Dugan girl had been apparent all along, but he was no fool. Father made a renewed effort at undercover investigation of that gaunt country boy's whereabouts on the day of the murder. All trails led back to the tavern called the Eye of the Storm, which Pike frequented and from which he apparently drew his clientele for the fornication emporium he ran at the factory on Saturdays. Those who had enjoyed his service were not about to risk Pike's disclosure of the fact by undermining his alibi—if he were indeed not telling the truth. One chap admitted remembering that Pike talked that Saturday about the early-season crowd he had found the day prior at Tybee Beach, where he had taken a girl friend, but that was the extent of it. Still, the new revelations made the circumstantial case against Pike, in father's view, at least as incriminating as the one against Noah, and probably a good deal more so. All that was missing was a motive—and a perjurer like Mo Easter.

Judge Vickery denied the new motion, holding that the fresh evidence did not shed any material light on the events during the day of the murder itself. Father again appealed to the state supreme court, and again he lost. Nearly a year had passed since the jury had voted to convict Noah Berg. The prisoner weighed no more than one hundred twenty-five pounds by then.

Father saw one last hope. He filed a motion to have the results of the trial set aside because of the involuntary absence from the courtroom of the defendant and his co-counsel during the reception of the verdict. That right could not be waived, as the court had in effect ordered the defendant to do, without dissipating the guarantee by the state of Georgia to a trial by jury and by the Fourteenth Amendment to the United States Constitution to due process of law. "Not only was the defendant thus deprived because he was kept out of the courtroom when the verdict was rendered," father argued, "but the entire proceedings became *coram non judice*, because of mob domination, to which the presiding judge succumbed and which in effect wrought a dissolution of the court." The very fact that the judge had moved to curb the right of the defendant instead of the excesses of the mob was sufficient cause to nullify that entire proceeding.

I thought it a dubious premise since father and Archie had yielded to the judge's suggestion to stay away at the time the verdict came down instead of protesting the very idea and seizing upon it as evidence of his submission to the mob. "I am seizing upon it now," said father. "That is why we yielded at the time—and unwillingly, as we stated. It gives us this ground for appeal."

But it was far too nuanced a position for either the Superior Court or the Georgia Supreme Court to embrace. The high court of the state ruled: "Such objections must be raised in due season if the orderly process of adjudication is ever to be conducted." Father was too late in his eleventh-hour effort, said the Georgia longbeards.

Father appealed on every ground he could think of to the United States District Court for the Southern District of Georgia. The Fourteenth Amendment was, after all, the essential federal guarantee against prejudicial procedures in state courts of law. It was also our last hope.

The federal court heard the appeal and promptly affirmed the ruling of the Georgia courts. Father took his case to the Supreme Court of the United States. He had never been there before.

I left aside my studies at Columbia to come to Washington for the argument before the nation's highest court. I did not let father know ahead of time that I would be on hand. The dear man would have enough to worry about without fawning members of the family under his feet at every turn. Yet I would not have missed the occasion for anything. I hung in the back of that long, echoing catacomb in the depths of the Capitol building, where the Justices had met since the Senate abandoned it as its meeting place upon completion of the new wing in 1860, the year before father was born.

He looked perfectly grand that first time he came before that august body. He wore a rented morning coat and a boutonniere, as was the custom of that day, and stood so straight and was so full of his cause that I thought it impossible he would not carry the day. Then I looked up with him at that mammoth figure of the Chief Justice of the United States, the honorable—and deplorable, as my law-student friends at Columbia had called him—Edward Douglas White. There seemed to be no end to him. I had read of his ancestral plantation down in Louisiana and his heroic lobbying efforts in behalf of his fellow sugar barons while he served in the United States Senate. His partaking of the pleasures of the French Quarter of New Orleans was likewise legendary, and his fondness for *haute cuisine* unmistakably signaled by the rivulets of black silk that cascaded down his honorable corpulence. McKinley and Taft, from the photographs I had seen, were as mere blades of grass—well, credit Taft for a clump, perhaps—in comparison to this mass of Southern gentility and retrogressive social philosophy.

Most members of that august Court, I had learned, traditionally looked with the healthiest regard upon the sanctity of private property and trod gingerly, if at all, upon the privileges of capital. In none was that worshipful attitude more deeply inculcated than the Chief Justice. Like so many of his colleagues, moreover, who stemmed from small towns and rural areas, he cherished the rights and prerogatives of these native places and fiercely resented the intrusions upon them that the reformist champions of federal supremacy had lately sponsored. Another transplanted Southerner, Wilson, now headed the executive branch of the national government and was acting with alarmingly unregional vigor to improve the public health and morals of the nation by a sweeping set of legislative initiatives. Washington, for the first time, had chosen to use its power to tax and to regulate interstate commerce in a broad assault upon such undeniable evils as food adulteration, child labor, prostitution, and narcotics traffic. And even the arch-conservative Chief Justice had gone along with these measures. But what likelihood was there, if any, of the Court's intruding upon the judicial activities of the state of Georgia in the matter of Noah Berg, whose case had thrice been duly deliberated upon by the highest tribunal within the sovereignty and thrice dismissed? Even the most progressive member of the Supreme Court, Justice Oliver Wendell Holmes, was known to prefer avoiding interference with the judicial machinery of the several states except in cases of the most flagrant abuse. Thus, father said at the outset of the hour allotted to him, the disregard of the appellant's rights had been flagrant indeed.

"It is our contention," he said, gripping the lectern that stood directly beneath that formidable tier of Justices, "that a trial court within our system of laws surrenders its jurisdiction over any case it hears when it falls under the domination of a mob, and the rulings of the appellate courts of any state as to the fact of such domination can be reviewed by this Court and remanded for corrective actions." His hands let go of the lectern as his jitters subsided, and he scanned that bulwark of the judiciary above him without fear. "Whatever disagreement there may be, your honors, as to the scope of the phrase 'due process of law,' there can be no doubt that it embraces the fundamental conception of a fair trial, with opportunity of the defendant or his counsel to be heard at every point. Mob law does not become due process of law by securing the assent of a terrorized jury." The phrases flowed from him now with clarity and power. "We are not speaking in this case of mere disorder, or mere irregularities in procedure, as the Georgia Supreme Court has held, but of a case where the processes of justice have been actually and shamefully subverted."

He seemed to gain strength as he proceeded, and by the way the Justices followed him, I supposed him to be doing very well indeed. He came then to the point in his argument where he insisted that the Georgia high court had erred in declining to consider the merits of the appellant's claim that he had been denied due process by being excluded from the courtroom at the time of the verdict. "It is immaterial that this objection was not raised in the original motion for a new trial," father asserted. "What is material is not the timing of the motion but the fact that Berg's absence constituted an infraction of the guarantees of the Fourteenth Amendment—a usurpation of a right that cannot be waived, directly or indirectly, expressly or implicitly, before or after the rendition of the verdict. The arbitrary ruling of the Georgia appellate court cannot deprive the appellant of his constitutional right to attack the judgment as a nullity."

Suddenly, there was the angular Justice Holmes, hair and mustaches of snowy white, leaning forward and begging father's pardon and asking in his reedy voice, "Could you kindly tell us, Mr. Adler, just where in the Fourteenth Amendment it states that a

415

defendant is required to be present in court at the reception of the verdict? I don't recall that language."

And this came from our prime candidate for an ally among those grim arbiters. I held my breath and prayed father had prepared himself for this sort of colloquy.

"Well, sir, it is not there in so many words, I grant you," he said after an instant's reflection. "But it is implicit in the words 'due process.' A man who is not there cannot defend himself—and surely he cannot if his counsel are likewise absent."

"Do you mean to suggest in all seriousness, counselor," Justice Holmes persisted, "that the outcome of the trial could in any way have been affected by the defendant's presence, or that of his counsel, at the time the verdict was reported to the court? Surely, the damage, as you see it, had already been done by then."

"The thrust of our argument is not so much that the outcome might have been altered," father answered, "but that that denial of a basic right was prompted by the court's submission to the spirit of the mob. All the forms of due process may be preserved, we hold, yet in aggregate these may be little more than an empty shell if the court cannot keep its own house in order."

"Thank you, counselor," the Justice said and sat back.

There were a number of other brief questions from the bench, most of them in quest of clarification of the record. Overall, the Court seemed to have received father with cordiality and attentiveness. Having delivered his statement and encountered few interruptions, he ended his remarks with more than twenty minutes of his allotted hour still remaining. He told me later he had seen the United States Solicitor General, John Davis, yield the floor similarly the day before when father had come to the Court to watch its manner of functioning, and the Justices had seemed grateful that the principal advocate for the federal government knew enough to sit down when he had said all he needed to.

The indefatigable Vincent Tunney, on the other hand, reviewed the record exhaustively, giving far too many citations in support of his case and nagging the Court not to lay hands where it had no cause to:

> In all of these proceedings, your honors, the state of Georgia has accorded to Noah Berg the fullest right and opportunity to be heard according to the established

modes of procedure. We have granted him due process of law in every respect, and now he must pay the penalty for the crime of which he has been adjudged guilty.

Noah Berg's worst luck was that so able a prosecutor had taken it into his head to send him to the grave. Father offered only brief rebuttal. "Due process of law," he said, "means not merely the outward gestures but the inner substance of fairness. I would ask simply how the spirit of the law could have thrived in that alien ground where the presiding magistrate was unequipped or unwilling to protect the lives of the defendant, his counsel, and presumably the jury itself against a mob poised to do violence in the event the accused was freed."

The Supreme Court gave its ruling on the twelfth day of April 1915. Mother sent the text to me in the mail. For the majority, Chief Justice White wrote: "The essential question before us is not the guilt or innocence of the prisoner, or the truth of any particular fact asserted by him, but whether the state, taking into account the entire course of its procedure, has deprived him of due process of law. This familiar phrase does not mean that the operations of the state government of Georgia, or of any state, shall be conducted without error or fault in any particular case, nor that the federal courts may substitute their judgment for that of the state courts, or exercise any general review over their proceedings, but only that the fundamental rights of the prisoner shall not be taken from him arbitrarily or without the right to be heard according to the usual course of law in such cases. We find no such deprivation of fundamental rights in the case of the appellant Berg."

Justice Holmes dissented, and was joined by progressive Justice Charles Evans Hughes, who was to run the following year for the presidency and nearly win. "The single question in our minds," wrote the old Yankee jurist, "is whether a petition alleging that the trial took place in the midst of a mob savagely and manifestly intent on a single result, is shown on its face to be unwarranted. This is not a matter for polite presumptions; we must look facts in the face. Any judge who has sat with juries knows that, in spite of forms, they are extremely likely to be impregnated by the environing atmosphere. And when we find the judgment of the expert on the spot, of the judge whose business it was to preserve not only the form but the substance of due process, to have been that if one juryman yielded to a reasonable doubt as to the guilt of the prisoner, neither prisoner nor counsel would be safe from the rage of the crowd, then we think the presumption overwhelming that the jury responded to the passions of the mob."

But Holmes and Hughes were just two, even if the two best. In that turgid and majestic language it prefers, the court of last resort ruled, by a vote of seven to two, that Noah Berg had exhausted his last possible remedy. For a day after receiving the opinion, father moved about the house as if shell-shocked, my mother reported to me and urged that I come home as soon as my studies permitted. I would be needed, at any rate, to lend him strength at the time of the hanging, scheduled for the twenty-first of June.

III

Having done his best to win justice for Noah Berg, father subsided and let Rabbi Weisz try to gain the doomed man mercy. The rabbi met with a good deal more success.

He started by approaching the B'nai B'rith, which enlisted its members all over the South, and then the North, and then spiritual leaders of other faiths, and then social reformers—Jane Addams was prominent in the growing list—and editorial writers and politicians. Few outside Georgia doubted that Noah had been railroaded, and many likened his plight to that of Captain Dreyfus. The petition-gatherers went to work and within a month began dispatching thousands upon thousands of signatures to Governor Slaton in Atlanta, asking that Noah's sentence be commuted to life imprisonment. Father thought nothing would come of it until word arrived that the state legislatures of Tennessee and Texas had passed resolutions asking that Noah's life be spared. "My God!" he said and went right to his office and got to work trying to marshall the citizenry of Georgia behind the effort. By the first of June, ten thousand Georgians had signed, including Judge Vickery. "He told me not to take it as a sign of judicial repentance," father reported with bittersweet satisfaction.

Only up in Thomson, outside of Augusta, was the cry for blood raised. But it was raised so loud and so savagely there that it could not be ignored. Tom Watson, like a mad old terrier, had seized upon the Berg case as if it were a choice bone and would not let it go. His public utterances were largely restricted now to the pages of his weekly magazine, *The Jeffersonian,* in which he devoted hundreds of pages to the Berg case. During the trial itself, relatively little of an inflammatory nature was printed in it; Watson must have felt the jury would do its Aryan duty. But once father began his efforts for a re-trial and one of the Atlanta papers came out in support, Watson's magazine became a weekly hate sheet directed at but a single result. Georgia was once again being manipulated by a "gigantic conspiracy of big money" that aimed to corrupt the courts, the governor, and the newspapers of the state in order to save the life of "this wealthy pervert." For Berg, it was well known, "belongs to the Jewish aristocracy, which has determined that no member of its race should have his blood spilled for the death of a mere working-class Gentile." As for Jean Dugan:

> Yes, she was only a factory girl: there was no glamour of fashion or wealth about her. She had to work in the sweatshop to help her poor and ailing parents. She had no rich family to send her to college, no kinsmen ready to raise and spend thousands of dollars to spare her. And so while the Sodomite who took her sweet young life yet basks in the warmth of Today, the poor child's dainty flesh has fed the worms. . . .

Having in earlier volumes of his fecal sheet smeared the negroes and the Catholics and several dozen other favored whipping boys of the region, Watson exhibited a practiced virulence in turning now upon the Jews. The lechery of the Pope's clergy was as nothing, he wrote, compared to the arch-fiendish Jewish businessmen who routinely corrupted the daughters of Gentiles who worked for them, and Noah Berg was in that mold:

> . . . Here we have the typical young libertine Jew who is dreaded and detested by the city authorities of the North for the very reason that Jews of this type have an utter contempt of the Anglo-Saxon law and a ravenous appetite for the forbidden fruit—a lustful eagerness enhanced by the racial novelty of ravishing a daughter of the uncircumcised. Is it not plain, to look upon him,

that this Berg is a lascivious beast, guilty of the crime that caused the Almighty to level the Cities of the Plain? Note in the accompanying photograph, if you will, those bulging, satyr eyes, the protruding, fearfully sensual lips, the animal jaw. . . .

The accompanying picture was indeed of Noah Berg, but he looked more the frightened rabbit than a randy primate. That scarcely mattered to Tom Watson. The more scum he printed, the more copies of his vile *Jeff* got sold. Circulation was approaching one hundred thousand, most of it in Georgia. He used the issue as target practice for all his favorite shibboleths—regional pride, chivalry toward white womanhood, racial hatred, class consciousness, agrarian depression, and the impacted rage of all the dispossessed souls in the land. In rural places and working-class districts, where remnants of his long-dispersed Populist camp still lingered, *The Jeffersonian* was eagerly consumed, just as news of the Berg trial itself had been a hungrily sought after commodity while it was in progress. The longer the date of Noah's execution was put off by the maneuverings of his defenders, the more torrid Watson's fulminations became:

> How much longer is the innocent blood of little Jean Dugan to cry in vain to Heaven for vengeance?
> Now is the time to have a Vigilante Committee APPOINT ITS OWN SENTRIES TO WATCH THAT DESPERATE CRIMINAL—whose money and whose resources seem *so insolently determined that this crime shall go unpunished.*
> If Berg's rich protectors keep on lying about his case and seeking to deny justice, SOMETHING BAD WILL HAPPEN! If our Governor seriously entertains the pleaders for this murdering pervert's mortal soul, let the cry be heard in all the counties: RISE, PEOPLE OF GEORGIA!

"I looked up to no man of my own generation more than Tom Watson when I was young," said father. "How he must loathe himself now, to spew such filth into the air and care nothing for the consequences. I can think of no one in my time who has fallen so low from such a height."

Father went to see the governor a week before the scheduled execution. Complicating his task was the fact that Governor Slaton's term was due to expire the day before the hanging, and the forces ranged against Noah argued that any grant of clemency ought properly be left to the incoming governor. The new man, however, had had the strong endorsement of Tom Watson, and for weeks the *Jeff* had praised the governor-elect as "a man strong enough to withstand the corrupt triumvirate of Yankee, Carpetbagger, and Jew that has taken up Noah Berg's venal cause."

"Mr. Watson has given me his pledge of support for the United States Senate if I keep out of this," the governor told father. "And his support these days is a mighty valuable thing, Mr. Adler."

"More's the pity," said father. "I myself would shy from aspiring to a trophy purchased at such a price. You need no such bargains to prevail, Governor, but that is merely my private view. And I have no such influence as Watson's. All I can say is that there is a substantial body of evidence that casts reasonable doubt upon the guilt of Noah Berg, and the state of Georgia, in its magnanimity, should spare him."

"I am considering the matter with great care," the governor said.

Two days before the execution was set, Noah was ordered removed from the Chatham County jailhouse, where he had been under heavy guard, to the state prison at Milledgeville in the dead center of the state. The following day the governor announced that he had commuted Noah's sentence to life imprisonment; he gave no explanation why.

So vast an outcry was raised that the state militia was called out to guard the governor's quarters during his last hours in office. Rabbi Weisz held a special service at the temple to give thanks for the governor's action and offer prayers for his well-being. But he needed temporal forces more than divine blessing when a mob five thousand strong marched, with knives and dirks, hatchets and pistols, and a large basket of dynamite, to his home on the first day he was again a private citizen and sought to eviscerate him. Martial law had to be declared to save his life; and sixteen soldiers were injured in the rescue.

The next issue of *The Jeffersonian* burst with apoplectic prose:

Our grand old State HAS BEEN RAPED!
We have violated, AND WE ARE ASHAMED!
The great Seal of the State has been pilfered, LIKE A
THIEF IN THE NIGHT!
We have been betrayed! The breath of some leprous
monster has passed over us, we feel like crying, in horror
and despair, "Unclean! UNCLEAN!"

Fed by such hydrophobic sentiment, the lower orders of Georgia yeomanry, and not a small segment of its more privileged ranks, reacted harshly against the clemency decision. Slaton, in the interest of survival, decided to take an extended vacation and was last seen heading for the Hawaiian Islands. But the Jews of Georgia could not leave like that, and they began to suffer. Handbills were distributed in front of "the Jew store" in every little town in the state with messages like "Can't you buy clothing from an AMERICAN?" Synagogues, including Mickve Israel, had hate messages painted on their walls in tar. And many Jewish families found their credit suspended or painfully tightened. Most of father's remaining Gentile clientele left him then, and his young associate, a Methodist, confessed sheepishly that he thought there might be more opportunity for him with the firm on the floor above. "No doubt," father said and offered his hand.

So gorged with enmity was the Georgia air that the warden at the state prison required all his guards to sleep armed upon the front porch of the main building lest any harm come from the outside to their most famous inmate. Of graver immediate peril, it turned out, was the threat to him from within those walls. At about eleven o'clock one night in the middle of July, another prisoner convicted of murder and serving a life term stole out of his bunk, slipped across the large sleeping room, and drew a kitchen knife he had smuggled from the mess across the throat of Noah Berg. Gurgling blood, the victim cried out and sent his assailant scuttling, but that single stroke had almost produced decapitation. Only the quick work of another prisoner, who happened to be a doctor, saved Noah's life. He was placed in a private room adjoining the warden's office, where he recuperated for a month under 'round-the-clock guard.

Tom Watson was so exhilarated by the murderous assault that he urged a petition be circulated throughout the South seeking parole for the man who had tried to kill Noah Berg. He wrote in his magazine for August 12, "*The next Berg case in Georgia will never reach the Courthouse.* THE NEXT JEW WHO DOES WHAT BERG DID IS GOING TO GET EXACTLY THE SAME THING THAT WE GIVE TO NEGRO RAPISTS."

That was too much for father. Watson's writings, he wrote the new governor, were clearly felonious—a violation of the state code that outlawed the publication of literature tending to incite riot. The governor did not write back. Father took the sole step remaining to him. He and mother collected Amanda Baxter and drove with her out to the Jubilation Plantation to try to prevail upon Tom Watson's principal ally in the Savannah area to have that poisoned pen stilled. I went with them.

"Billy's a mite under the weather just now," Cissy Baxter told us in the foyer and pointedly failed to ask us into the parlor.

"Billy's been a mite under the weather for fifteen years," said Mandy. "I'll see him anyway."

"He's truly indisposed," said Cissy Baxter, a trembling hand climbing to her cheek. "I know he wouldn't like to be seen this way, Mandy. Tomorrow maybe."

"Tomorrow he'll be worse. This can't wait." And she pushed on past her sister-in-law up the main stairway.

You could hear them arguing up there, mostly her voice, hard and wounding. I was afraid for her, having heard what I had about the manic-depressive William Doak Baxter, eccentric now beyond redemption and likely as not to turn upon any tormentor as he once had upon his brutish uncle. But Mandy came down five minutes later looking florid and furious. "I'm to tell you," she said, turning to father, "that all you Jews must learn to take your medicine before you can hope to be regarded truly as white men. He cares nothing for Noah Berg—or you—or me, for that matter. Or himself." She looked at Cissy and said, "My God, how long has he been like that? The man reeks! Can you do nothing with him?"

"Nothing," his wife said. "He stays like that for weeks at a time, and then he just gets up and takes his guns and goes out to hunt for a day or two, and when he comes back he's just fine, just as good and kind as always. We have dinners and dances and he tends to the crops and his finances and his philanthropies—oh, my, yes, he is a charitable soul—and he even looks after the chil-

423

dren's welfare a bit. Everything is glorious for a time, and we even make love—and then, without any warning, he falls off the world again. God in heaven, Mandy, what am I to do with him?" And she threw herself in tears upon her haughty sister-in-law's silken bosom.

By telephone the next morning, Amanda Baxter summoned me to her home on East St. Julian Street, which I had never before visited. She had some news she wanted to give me, she said, and needed my help in a matter of mutual interest.

"Forgive me for having been so cryptic on the line," she said upon my arrival, "but the operators often listen in." It was Noah Berg's fate she wished to speak of and did not want to trouble father after the emotional ordeal he had undergone. "Ever since the trial," she said, "I have been convinced of Berg's innocence and of —of a savagery that has seemed to take hold of the people and prevented a civilized disposition of his case." There was a hesitation in her manner at the start of what she had to report, as if by commiserating too directly to those in Noah's camp she would assume responsibility not only for this single instance of persecution of our people by hers but for the entire toll of activities exacted over two millennia. I said nothing either to lighten or to compound her task.

"I have read over the newspaper accounts of the trial many times, looking to discover some revelation—some slip of the tongue—some little ignored alleyway that might be followed," she said, "and I believe I may have found one." The post-trial disclosure that Jean Dugan and Vernon Pike had come together to the Rosen Pharmacy late in the day on the Friday before the murder forged a link in Amanda Baxter's mind. The drugstore clerk had remembered the girl made a telephone call while she was there. "To whom might that call have been?" Amanda asked me.

"Why, I can't conceive," I said.

"Exactly. Jean Dugan was a poor working girl, not in the custom of just ringing someone up. And it could not have been her mother she was calling since there was no phone in the Dugan home. And the chances were that most of her girl friends, who came from similarly poor homes, did not have such a luxury at their disposal either."

"Probably not," I said. "Then who?"

"Who, indeed? Perhaps her place of employment—to someone who she knew would be there then."

"But why should she have called the factory?" I wondered.

"To find out, perhaps, if she could collect her pay the next day?"

"No," I said, roped in now by her deductions. "A notice had been posted all week that the factory would pay off as usual on Saturday to anyone absent at the regular time—that came out at the trial."

"Quite so," she said. "But then I went back over my scrapbook and re-read the testimony. Bryce Woodcock, that comely Galahad, was paying off the girls as usual, you will recall, but then he was said by the witness Prudence Jordan to have been interrupted in that task for a moment to take a phone call. It was then, during his brief absence from the paymaster's window, that Noah Berg evidently passed through the outer office in the superintendent's suite and was asked by the Ferguson girl about whether she might pick up the pay envelope for a friend. My attention was drawn, like everyone else's, to the alleged exchange between Berg and the Ferguson girl—what, if anything, was really said and was there any way he might in fact have known that the Dugan girl would be in the next day for her envelope? No one has bothered to ask who telephoned Bryce Woodcock at that moment."

"You mean it was Jean Dugan?"

"I mean that I thought it might well have been," she said. "And this morning, my dear, I went down to Rosen's Pharmacy and spoke with the clerk in question to find out precisely when the girl and Pike came by. He is not a very acute fellow, I must confess, but he said he thought it was about half past six, going on to a quarter of seven. I then rang up Joe Dettwiler, who seems to have become hard of hearing since his retirement. But he heard me well enough to say that the factory always paid off between six and seven on Friday nights, with the workers from the various departments coming by at specified intervals."

"So," I said, "it might have been he she was talking to. But why?"

"Use your imagination, my dear."

"They were sweet on each other—is that what you're saying?"

"They might have been."

"But she was seeing Pike—they'd been together all day at the beach, I thought."

"But Pike was leaving Savannah, going back home or up to Macon, and she was young and pretty, and Bryce Woodcock is handsome and well-bred and went to Georgia Tech, Joe Dettwiler tells me."

"And since Woodcock couldn't reach her on the phone, she reached him—is that it?"

"That might have been it. The next day was a holiday and perhaps they had made plans together, vague ones, at any rate, and she had bought a nice dress—."

"Pike!" I cried. "We must find Pike and ask him who Jean Dugan telephoned!"

She smiled at my impulsive excitement. "You're right," she said, "but in the first place that is quite impossible. Joe Dettwiler says Pike hasn't been seen in Georgia since the trial ended—he headed out to Oklahoma, Joe thinks, and changed his name—and given the suspicions that were raised about him, it's no wonder. In the second place, even if Vernon Pike were in this room right now, he probably couldn't tell us whom Jean Dugan called. She went to phone while he ordered the sodas, so all he would know was whom she *said* she was going to call—and if in fact the call was to Bryce Woodcock, she would likely not have told him that, would she?"

"Because she was two-timing Pike?"

"In a manner of speaking. It depends on what the true nature of Pike's relationship was to the girl. And there is only one person who might be persuaded to tell us that—and everything else we want to know. I want you to come visit Mo Easter with me this afternoon."

That black unworthy had been released from prison a month earlier, shortly after and as if in reaction to the governor's commutation of Noah's death sentence. Easter had served two years and three months of a four-year sentence as an accessory after the fact in the Dugan girl's murder. He had not thrived on the rockpile. He returned in broken health and spirit to a shack in the Yamacraw section of the city where he was living with his woman and a baby that had materialized in his absence. White folks were infrequent visitors there, especially a pair of white women who came by on horseback, which Amanda felt was a trifle less conspicuous means of arrival than the chauffeured Cadillac by which she generally traveled in her later years. It took some asking around to locate Easter's shack; plainly, the neighbors sought to spare him renewed onslaughts from the white community. His woman came to the rickety door, sized us up quickly, and said that her man was not home and she did not know when he would be back. Amanda said we would wait. After an hour, Mo Easter came out to see what we wanted. He wore a tattered shirt and soiled trousers and no shoes, and scarcely resembled the alert witness whose vivid testimony had doomed Noah Berg to a life behind bars.

"We've brought you a gift," said Amanda and took out a packet from her purse.

"What fo'?" he asked, his stubbled face pinched with suspicion.

"Because we think you were unduly punished, Mo, and deserve a fresh start."

He walked us over to the bank of a small creek that served as a privy for those people—for the children, anyway, several of whom emptied their bladders into it a few dozen yards downstream from us during the course of our stay. He found a clean, dry spot and asked us to sit on the ground. Then he squatted beside us and asked, "What kinder present is it you brung?"

"Money," said Amanda. "Isn't that what you'd like best?"

"Yes, ma'am," he said, his caution still unrelenting.

She handed him the packet and said, "There is three thousand dollars in here, Mo, and it is yours to keep. You can count it if you'd like." The negro just looked at the proffered envelope. "I'd like you to take it," she said.

"What do I got to do for it?"

"You don't *have* to do anything."

"Dat's a whole lot o' money for nothin'," he said.

Amanda looked contrite. "All right," she said, "I guess you see right through me. What I'm after is some help. But the money is yours whether or not you decide to give it."

"What kind o' help, ma'am—'cause if it got to do with de killing, I ain't got nuthin' more to say. I done my time. I hurts still."

"But you're free, Mo," she said, "and Mr. Berg isn't. You can take this money and go somewhere and start a new life. You can

427

get a nice cottage and some land or start up a business with it. Your family can be comfortable, for a change—if you'll just help us. We think you did what you did in court because you had no choice."

He considered carefully what she said. Then he asked, "You think dat?"

"Yes," she said, "I do."

He nodded a few times but said nothing. Then he took the packet and tore it open and peered in. Cautiously he poked a finger at the bundle of bills. "Three thousand, huh?" he said. And Amanda said yes. "I never had more'n a hunnert at one time before," he said. He shut the packet in obvious awe and drummed it against his knee for a while. "An' I kin keep it no matter what?" And Amanda said yes. "An' you ain't gonna go run to the police and tell nuthin'?" Amanda said no, not ever. "How I know dat?" he asked. "You don't care nuthin' for a nobody nigger."

"I care for Plato Layne," she said, "and some people think he's that. He works at my place."

Mo's eyes widened. "Plato work for you now? Is dat a fac'?" Amanda said it was and that she only wanted to get to the bottom of the killing while there was still time. "Time fo' what?" Mo asked. To save Noah Berg's life, Amanda said. "Dey already saved it, ain't they?" said Mo, and Amanda said Noah was hardly safe in jail or anywhere so long as most folks believed he was the murderer.

He stood up and looked into the stream for a long while. Then he put the money in his hip pocket and said, "I'm thinkin' to ask my woman what to do—if'n it's all right with you." Amanda said that would be fine, and Mo went to his cabin. For an instant, I was sure he would go right out a back window and never reappear. And then I saw that none of those pitiful shanties had anything so elegant as a window, front or back, and felt bad for having even conjured the thought. Then Mandy said, "I wonder if we'll ever see him again," and I loved her.

He must have stayed in there fifteen minutes, and when he came out, uncertainty remained on his furrowed forehead. "She say dat's one whole lotta money," he reported, "and it mus' be a trick. I tell her you don' seem tricksters, an' she say I'm gonna get right back into trouble. I say I already got trouble, an' maybe dis here money kin fix it. She don't think so. Leastways she ain't shore."

Amanda got to her feet and said we were leaving and that the money was his unconditionally, but that if he wanted to help, he could come to her home, and she told him where it was. Then we left. I was firmly convinced that would be the end of it and expressed consternation at the strategy Amanda devised. "No," she said, "he'll come. This way, he sees we trust him—he's got the money, after all. No one's ever trusted him before in his life, probably."

She asked me to spend the rest of the day with her and to dine at her place, and I gladly did. She reminisced with great exuberance about father and mother, withholding from me, of course, any clue of the true nature of her relationship to them both. It was well after eight, and she was playing Chopin for me when a servant appeared to say that Mo Easter was in the kitchen asking for her.

He had scrubbed up for the occasion, and the transformation was remarkable. It was clear now how Tunney and the police had groomed and polished him to the point of presentability at the trial. He said he had been thinking all day since Amanda's visit and had talked with the preacher in their settlement, and the preacher said her coming to him now, after he had come out of jail, was nothing short of providential and that he should accept the money with gratitude, do what was asked in return, and get out of town fast. "We leavin' at sun-up," he said, pointedly not saying where he was headed.

"Will you answer my questions, Mo?" she asked him. He would, he said, so long as she promised again never to tell the police—or anyone else who would tell them. That seemed a stiff condition to me, but what choice was there? Amanda readily agreed. Then she asked him to sit down and try to relax and think as clearly as he knew how. He sat, but just barely, looking as if he were ready to spring into the air at any second. Amanda waited in the hope he would compose himself, but the longer she waited, the more jumpy Mo became. Finally, before he thought the better of it and flew the coop, she began the interrogation. It took the form at first of her narrative and his mumbled assent.

She said Miss Dugan had in fact come downstairs from the su-

429

perintendent's office that Saturday, just after noon, hadn't she, and Mo said yes.

She said there was someone waiting down there for her on the first-floor landing, wasn't there, and Mo said yes.

She said this someone else had talked to him at length that morning, hadn't he, about the sort of sexual enterprise that Vernon Pike had run in the basement of the factory, and Mo said that was so.

"And this someone asked you about whether Miss Dugan took part in Pike's little business, didn't he?" and Mo said yes and that he said he didn't know for sure but thought that she arranged for some of her girl friends to go to the basement "on accounta dey needed de money awful bad."

"And then Miss Dugan and this other man went into the coatroom on the first floor after she got her pay, didn't they, Mo, and wound up having some sort of a fight?" And Mo said yes.

"Was the fight because he wanted her to help him start up Pike's business in the basement again, Mo, or because he wanted to take her down there himself and have his way with her?" It was hard for him to hear through the door, said Mo, but it was "kinder both."

"And then Miss Dugan complained and threatened to go up to Mr. Berg's office and tell him about Mr. Woodcock's offensive behavior, didn't she, Mo?"

"I didn't say nuthin' about no Mr. Woodcock," Mo said at once.

"No, you didn't," said Amanda, "I said it. Are you contradicting me, Mo?"

He fell silent, his eyes fixed to the floor.

"But you heard Miss Dugan raise her voice, didn't you, Mo, and threaten to tell on him if he didn't let her out of that room right fast?"

"It was kinder like that," he said. "She said she thought he was some gentleman but she seen now he was a beast jus' like her stepdaddy. I remember her usin' that word—'stepdaddy'—and thinkin' it was funny. Then Mr. Woodcock, he—" And Mo stopped, seeing that he had let the name out.

Amanda waited a respectful moment and then said, "Go on, Mo."

Mo closed his eyes and sucked in a deep breath and then spilled all his terrible secret. "He musta said somethin' else to her, an' she gave out a kinder yelp—dat musta been when he knocked her in de face and sent her flyin' against de coat hooks. In a minute he come flyin' outa dere hisself and tole me what he done to her. He said, 'Dat little whore play cute wif me—she want money from me to go downstairs, so I got angry and hit her.' Then he say he want me to help him take her down de scuttle-hole. Now I didn't want to do dat, ma'am, not nohow, I swear to mercy—."

"Of course you didn't, Mo," said Amanda. "You didn't have any choice."

"No choice," he echoed.

"Who went first down the scuttle-hole, Mo?"

"Him. He made me go look out the front door and den up the stairs, and when I tell him all clear, he hurry-up dragged her out from de coatroom right to de trap-door. Dat's when I see she is bleedin' and fainted. He goes on down de ladder, an' I shoves him her body head first, an' he takes it and I gotta hold her arms down 'gainst her sides so as she'd fit through, an' when she's mostly on down there, I took up her feet and we gwine down de ladder together very careful." The white man then told Mo to go upstairs on lookout while he himself tried to figure out how to dispose of the girl and cleaned up the bloodstains in the coatroom and on the ladder.

"It must have been then that he took the coat hanger and went back down and strangled her," said Amanda.

"Must a' been," said Mo. "She shore wairn't dead when I seen her last—leastways her tongue weren't pokin' outa her mouf like dey said at de trial, and I seen nuthin' of no wire hanger 'round her neck. I didn't know he was fixin' to kill her, ma'am, I shore didn't, and he didn't tell me she was gone right den." The two of them waited then behind crates on the first floor until they saw Noah go out to dinner; all the while, Woodcock must have been hatching his plot. After a spell of waiting, he told Mo that the girl was dead and that they were in the thing together, but he had wealth and connections and he had no intention of hanging. He said he needed Mo's help, though, and would repay him for it. "But he never pay me nuthin', that lyin' son-o'-bitch—he jus' use me and throwed me away."

"Because he could always blame you for the killing," Amanda

prompted him, "and if he paid you anything for your help, he was afraid he'd never be able to stop paying you—isn't that it, Mo?"

"Dat's how I figure it," Mo said. "Dat's why I come here." The rest of the story he offered freely. The pair of them went upstairs after Noah had left at a little past one, and first Woodcock opened up the punch clock and ran off a fake time slip but didn't say what for. Then he fixed up Mo's time slip so that it would look as if he had worked openly at the factory that morning. Next, the assistant superintendent wrote out the note blaming a negro for the girl's death, took pains that the impression made by the pencil on the top sheet caused indentations on the sheet below, and left the pad in a prominent position on Berg's desk. "He tole me to go on down and push dis paper into de girl's hand," Mo said, "but I say no-sir, I ain't goin' down dere for anythin' on earth, so he went hisself."

In his agitation, Woodcock had failed to notice when he first cleaned up the coatroom that the dead girl's purse had been thrown into a corner. Only when he checked the room over before going up to Berg's office to carry out his plot did he spy the purse. It would be a useful addition to the evidence he intended to plant against the superintendent, he must have decided, and when he got to the second floor, he placed the purse in the factory safe, but in his preoccupation with the other elements in the complex trap he was setting, he evidently forgot to shut the safe door. When Woodcock went back to the basement to plant the note, Mo noticed the purse and grasped then who the victim of the plot was intended to be, and he did not like it. "Mr. Berg been nice to me," he said. "He give me work even knowin' I jus' been on the city gang. So I snatched up dat purse and stuck it in my drawers and pushed de safe door closed so he wouldn't notice nothin.'" And he tore the top few sheets from the notepad and ripped them into tiny pieces and dropped them down the incinerator in the hall, where he awaited Woodcock's return. The young white man then made him agree to two final chores. He was to go to Plato Layne's quarters, steal a shirt of his, soak it in blood— "He tole me to git de blood from a chicken from de hen house down de road and he give me a dollar for it," said Mo—and slip back in that night while Plato was working at the factory and put it with his things. "I tole him I didn't have no grudge 'gainst Plato—fac', I hardly know who he was—but he say to me it's a trick an' Plato's punch slip show he was on de job so not to worry. I say so what for do I need to put de shirt in his place, and he say not to ask so many questions. Then he say I gotta go down to de factory 'round three o'clock at night and rattle on de coal bin so as Plato'd be sure to go on down to de basement t' find de girl." Mo stopped short and looked up at the two of us, fright brimming in his eyes over his own retelling. "I had to do it, ma'am," he said. "He'd have tole the cops I done it if I didn't go along wif him, sure as yo' sittin' there."

Afterward, Amanda and I surmised that when Woodcock discovered on Sunday that two of the prime clues he planted to point the finger of guilt toward Noah—namely, the purse and the notepad with its telltale indentations—had somehow gone astray, he decided to add to his dirty handiwork. He planned that it would be discovered on whatever day the factory resumed regular production. That turned out to be Wednesday. Perhaps he collected a jarful of blood from the same hen house Mo had patronized or he might have gone at dawn to the city meat market, but it would have been no great trick for him to reach the factory before anyone else that Wednesday, spread the blood and then a great deal of bleach on the floor of the cloakroom next to the superintendent's office, and thus add a key link to the incriminating evidence against Noah. Even less trouble must have been his substitution on Monday of the counterfeit time card he had made out for Plato Layne in place of the real one that he more than likely had pocketed during the hurly-burly of the investigation on Sunday.

The net of it was this: When Mo Easter was brought down to police headquarters and the girl's purse found in his room, the negro's choice was to go along with the circumstantial case that the police had been building against Noah Berg or to tell the truth and risk having Woodcock turn around and blame the murder on him. "You were caught between the devil and the deep blue sea, weren't you, Mo?" Amanda had said, and he said that surely was how it felt.

Next morning, I was back at Mandy Baxter's side when she rang up the factory and chatted cozily with Superintendent Bryce Woodcock. He was due to leave the following month for a far more important job in the sales section at corporation headquarters in Atlanta; might he come by for a bon voyage supper that evening? she wondered. Young Woodcock, ambitious and eager for a patron of such eminence, said he would be delighted.

We spent the day reviewing his testimony at the trial, and only then were its highly ambiguous intentions apparent to us. Appearing as a steadfast defender of his office superior, he nevertheless managed to let out enough unsavory hints about Noah to add to the weight of suspicion against him. He was, we agreed, some shrewd article.

In the flesh, Bryce Woodcock was every bit as slick. He could have charmed the tusks off an elephant, that toothsome young man with the courtly manners. But Amanda Baxter was not about to let him evade her clutches. There was much sherry and wine and merriment, much talk of the company's past and boundless future, of life and the beauty of the women in Atlanta, where Woodcock was headed. Only when the after-dinner drinks were served did the talk touch upon Noah Berg, his trial, and his brush with death at the state prison. "There is just one thing I continue to be curious about, Mr. Woodcock, and that is the nature of your talk on the telephone with poor Miss Dugan on the day before the crime. How sad you must have felt after learning of the tragedy."

He looked for an instant as if someone had dumped a wagonload of cotton on him. "Why, yes," he said, struggling to make a rapid recovery, "I felt horrid. She was a nice young lady—very able and diligent."

"And a lovely face," said Amanda. "A madonna's face, I've always thought."

"Yes," he said, sipping at his empty cognac decanter.

"Why *did* she call, exactly, Mr. Woodcock?" Amanda then persisted.

Great turmoil was written upon his handsome face. Trying hard to fathom how much we knew, he paused revealingly.

"Oh, don't be alarmed," Amanda said. "I wouldn't dream of reporting it to the authorities. I'm just curious, since the lawyers never pressed you on the matter in court."

"I don't quite understand why you're so involved at this late date," he said.

"An old woman's curiosity, if you will, Mr. Woodcock," she said airily. "You know the idle rich have nothing better to do than stir mischief. I gather, young man, that you were sweet on the dear child."

Woodcock's brows shot upward and then dove back into place. "I can't imagine how you'd devise such a notion, Miss Baxter. I knew her a little, of course, but—"

"Oh, well, I grant you that the girl was considerably beneath your station, Mr. Woodcock, but such sentimental slumming is not unheard of among the children of the wealthy." He frowned at that, and she said brassily her source for the information was Vernon Pike.

"That can't be so, Miss Baxter," he said, very wary now. "Pike's out West, I hear—Kansas or Oklahoma, I think I heard someone say."

Amanda remained breezy about the whole subject. "Yes, but he told someone who told someone else who told someone in whom I have the utmost confidence. Word does travel, you know, Mr. Woodcock."

He looked glum. To protest too vigorously would have been a giveaway; too little, a confession. He said he could not think why Pike would have told such a story—"except to deflect attention from his own involvement with the girl. They were closer than ever came out at the trial."

"Yes," Amanda said, "so I've gathered. But come now, you still haven't told us why she telephoned the factory that Friday. There's no denying that, you know." She delivered her hemlock with a smile

"Well, it's true," he said, "she did call in, but I never volunteered the information because it did not seem to be in any way connected to the crime."

"Wouldn't that have been better left for the authorities to decide?"

"Perhaps," he said with enough sheepishness to seem genuine, "but I suppose I preferred not to get involved any more than I had to. I did my best to answer all the questions put to me as thoroughly as possible, but I did not want to say more. That was perhaps craven of me—I see that now—but the police were flailing around in so many directions that I was not eager for them to turn in mine."

"Yes," said Amanda, "quite. And now what was it the girl

called you about? To see if she might pick up her pay on the morrow, no doubt?"

He seemed to grow flustered and altogether uncertain of our motives. "Yes," he said, "I think that was the nub of it."

"Come, come, Mr. Woodcock, you know that can't be so," said Amanda with mock sternness. "A notice had been up all week to that effect. Surely she called to make firm the plans you and she had had for the holiday—when and where you should meet—to watch the parade perhaps?"

"Yes, all right—it was the parade. She was to join me right after work to watch the parade."

"I thought you told us you were not sweet on her?"

"I meant that we were not sweethearts, Miss Baxter. She was considerably younger than I, after all."

"Yes, but she kept company with older blokes like Pike—and you didn't much like her seeing him, did you, Mr. Woodcock?" There was a metallic edge to her voice now, and he did not miss it.

"That was her business and his," he said.

"But he was leaving town," she said, "and that left her to you."

"I fear you're badly overstating the situation, ma'am."

"I'm glad to learn that, Mr. Woodcock. But the fact remains, then, that you knew what time Miss Dugan was due in the vicinity of the factory that Saturday."

"Approximately," he said. "We were to meet at the five-and-dime."

"Yes, you couldn't meet at the factory or else Mr. Berg would have discovered your interest in her—?"

"You make it all sound too sinister, ma'am. It was at most an innocent flirtation."

"Perhaps not so innocent, Mr. Woodcock," she said with a hard smile. "No doubt you would have risked being pressed into overtime duty by Mr. Berg if you had reported to work as usual that day, and so you contrived a sickness for the occasion and assured that your pleasure-taking would not be interrupted by so demanding a boss."

Woodcock laughed aloud. "You astonish me, Miss Baxter. Who would've thought someone as removed from the event as yourself stayed up late to fret about it so. Well, yes, I admit it— my illness was a fraud. It was a nice day, if a bit brisk, and I simply did not want to be cooped in that office, especially on the day when Berg worked up his production figures. He could be insufferable then."

"So I understand," said Amanda. "And so you never did see Jean Dugan that day then, did you?"

"No," he said. "I never did. I waited at the five-and-dime for an hour or more. I thought she had forgotten—or could not get away from home."

"Or had found someone else to watch the parade with?"

"Perhaps," he said. "I don't recall thinking that, however."

"I'm sure," said Amanda. "You are too gallant a gentleman for that."

I flew home from East St. Julian Street and told father everything that had transpired during my two days with Amanda Baxter. He seemed thoroughly astonished at the developments. Nor did he much doubt the truth of what I reported. All Mo Easter had had to do on the witness stand, he saw, was to substitute one white man for another in his narrative and add a few embellishments that the police had handed to him. Woodcock's courtroom performance, too, was now more explicable. "He appeared to be such an admirable young man," said father, "yet a shade too candid on the stand. Well, it's late. We'll have to decide what to do about all this in the morning. No doubt you'll have me tossing half the night now."

IV

Father was not the only Georgian who passed a restless night.

When the belltower tolled two o'clock at the Sumter County Courthouse in the market town of Americus, the best part of two hundred miles due west of Savannah and not far from the Alabama border, a number of darkened automobiles converged on the courthouse square. By all later newspaper accounts, the motorized caravan consisted of eight cars, drawn one each from the surrounding hamlets of Smithville, Archery, Sumter, Leslie, Andersonville, Plains, and Eagle Pond; the front car came from Americus itself and was reported to be driven by a leading county official. Indeed, they were all said to be prominent citizens of their own small farming communities, devout followers of Christ, staunch defenders of the fallen Confederacy, and would-be avengers of its past and present shame. They had pledged to undertake their mission of that dark night because the pride of Georgia demanded it of them, it was said, and they asked only anonymity in carrying it out. There were twenty-five of them, and each swore to the rest that he would never reveal the name of a single member of their brotherhood, even unto the pain of death.

They traveled upstate over a carefully mapped route, north through Ellaville and Butler until the road swung east and they followed it into Macon, where they skirted the center of the city and continued on northeastward, on through the crossroads at Stevens Pottery. Now their voices grew muffled, and when they came to Milledgeville, they hushed altogether. Several in their band had come there to the state prison three days earlier to learn the layout of the grounds and buildings, the size of the complement of guards, and the extent of communications with the outside world. They learned, too, that Noah Berg had convalesced from his severe throat wound and was due to be returned the next night to sleeping quarters with the other prisoners.

With seemingly rehearsed precision, the invaders went about their assignments. All of them were armed with shotguns; only five of them bothered wearing masks. Two went to cut the telephone lines. Another pair punctured the gasoline tanks of every vehicle on the prison grounds. The rest split into three units. One went to the quarters of the superintendent of the prison, who unhesitatingly answered the harsh rapping on the door, promptly had his arms pinioned and wrists handcuffed, and yielded up the keys to the inner prison without vocal protest. The second group captured the warden in like fashion and marched him out at gunpoint to the main building, where the third group confronted a pair of drowsing guards, who upon seeing that their superiors were held prisoner by the armed strangers put up feeble resistance.

Having escaped with his life twice recently at intervals of a month, Noah Berg must have been sleeping fitfully at best on his prison cot. Perhaps, for the instant, he thought it but a dream when the door slammed open and three dark forms fell upon him. One grabbed his wrists and handcuffed them. A second seized a fistful of his hair and wrenched him out of bed. The third drove a gun butt into his vital organs. Then they picked him up and carried him out into the back seat of the lead car of the convoy, which stood waiting at the curb with engines running. The two prison sentries, the warden, and the superintendent were given a cigarette apiece, directed inside the main building, and then locked in. As if in formation, the eight vehicles veered onto the roadway and shot off into the night. So orderly had been the intrusion that few men other than those in bunks immediately adjacent to the captured prisoner were awakened by it.

One of the eight cars continued on east, toward Augusta. Its passengers fired off their rifles and howled rebel yells as they passed through settled areas in the hope of luring any pursuing vehicles after them. The main group of cars swung south, proceeding about twenty miles along the main road to a general store, where a local car was waiting for them. The guide vehicle led the line of them, gun barrels bristling out of every window, through a series of back roads in the vicinity of Gordon at the western end of Wilkinson County, where Jean Dugan was born and raised and buried now on a hillside above a grove of large oaks. They drove past Frey's ginnery, which was identified by the first soft rays of dawn, and took a steadily narrowing road that dwindled into a path winding through that grove of oaks near where Jean Dugan lay. There they stopped their cars and tied Noah Berg's legs with bundling cord and tested the new steel cuffs upon his wrists. And then they dragged him into the center of the grove, not a quarter of a mile from the house where Jean Dugan had spent her girlhood.

He wore only a nightshirt of plain homespun, the required prison garb, but it had his initials upon the left breast, embroidered for him by his wife Naomi, who would come to visit him each week. A robe of crocus sack was affixed to the hem of his nightshirt to cover his lower portions, and a handkerchief was fitted over his eyes as a blindfold. Around his neck they dropped a circle of hemp and fitted it up tight underneath his chin. They asked him if now he would confess to having raped and slain the little Dugan girl, the girl who was nearly as big as he was, but Noah Berg did not confess. Perhaps he was praying for God to rescue him a third time. No heavenly sign came, however, to that woodland thicket which the rosy sunrise could not penetrate, and the rope was thrown over a stout branch of that giant oak, and two masked men took up the loose end and held it and then tugged hard upon it. Noah Berg flew into the air and was drawn slowly upward toward the branch, his head snapped backward by the thick rope. Blood flowed from his throat, where the healed knife wound had reopened, and his body flayed the air in spastic agonies of strangulation. The blood had reached the initials on his nightshirt and his body gave only a small, occasional jerk when the men holding the rope tied it around the trunk of the tree, turned their backs on the form dangling above them, and led the way back to the parked cars. At intervals now, the vehicles moved out of the grove and off into the new day.

The body hung swinging in a slight breeze when Elwood Frey, who owned the cotton gin at the head of the road and remembered the night Jean Dugan was born, ventured into the thicket. Frey reached up and touched the body and found that it was still warm and had a slight pulse, he told the city reporters later that morning, but by the time he went to phone the sheriff and came back to the big oak, the pulse was gone.

The town and countryside hurried down to the grove in rigs and autos to gaze, some in horror, some in exultation, all in awe, at the swaying dead man. Soon there were hundreds of onlookers, and a native fiddler who sang of the life and death of Jean Dugan, and a photographer who took pictures, as many and as fast as he could, of the hanging body and sold the good ones for ten dollars apiece to the city papers and a few blurry ones as souvenirs to members of the crowd.

Down the path on which the lynchers had come and gone now hurried a hatless, coatless man who paused on the outer fringes of the throng to empty the contents of his pistol into the air in fanatic jubilation. Then he pushed into the center of the assemblage, threw himself wildly upon his knees, and began ranting to the heavens. Women in the crowd edged away from him, sensing what was coming. Suddenly the zealot leaped up, began to reload his gun, and called for the absolute extinction of all that remained of "the fiend who killed our little girl." By now, though, the sheriff had arrived and he restrained the shouting man, whose ravings had begun to stir sympathetic rumbles from the crowd as more than one man called for cremation of the corpse.

"Jean Dugan's life has been paid for," said the sheriff. "We need no more such work." So saying, he opened his pocket knife, reached up, and slashed the heavy rope. The body fell to the ground, crumpling, as the muscles relaxed after their long suspension. The crowd surged forward, and one man planted his heel hard upon the face of the victim and pushed down fiercely, gritting his teeth until the vein in his temple stood taut. The sheriff pulled the defiler aside and summoned the local undertaker, who speedily scooped the body into a basket and carted it off to his establishment. The sheriff accompanied the pine box bearing the remains of Noah Berg to the local rail depot and rode with it on the first train through, which happened to be bound for Atlanta. There, state authorities took charge of the corpse and telephoned the news of his fate to his wife and family.

My father was summoned to the Klein home a few minutes before nine, and it fell to him to make the travel and funeral arrangements. He telephoned Archie Ruskin in Atlanta to look after the body until the family could arrive. "And please," father said, "no embalming."

"They embalm everyone," said Archie. "It prevents putrefication, haven't you heard?"

"Jews are not pharaohs," said father, "no embalming. And no religious service, even though you have a very enterprising rabbi up there." He said they would leave Savannah on the noon train and take the Queen of Dixie from Atlanta to New York that night if Archie would book the space.

So many thousands besieged the funeral home on Peachtree where the body lay in Atlanta that the authorities decided to allow an orderly procession to view the remains for three hours during the afternoon. Agony was still branded on that distorted face and terror in those half-open dead eyes as the quick and the ghoulish trooped by the bier and looked upon him with quiet satisfaction. Some lingered to savor the sight of the slain beast until an officer moved them along to make way for the restless thousands queued behind them.

Upon discovering the spectacle being made of Noah Berg even in death, father demanded that the viewing be halted at once. "Is his body a memento of some glorious triumph?" he asked the chief of police, who was overseeing the combustible crowd. The people seemed to think so, said the chief, "and they just wanted to see that the job had been done thoroughly. Our choice was to let them look or have them tear the body to pieces. I thought his family would rather have something whole to put in the ground."

I made that grim journey to Atlanta with father and stayed with

441

him long enough to visit Amory Austin at his estate outside of the city early in the evening. I recited to him the discoveries that Amanda Baxter had made. He expressed proper horrification over the now irreparable miscarriage of justice but added that he saw no point in dragging the company's name through the mud once more, especially since Mo Easter would never tell his latest revised story in a court of law. It was augered instead that an underling from Austin's staff would interview Woodcock in Savannah the next day, terminate his employment at once, and advise him in the most forceful possible language to leave the United States on the first available ocean-going craft, never to return. Amanda Baxter reported to me later that Woodcock had called her in a state of high distress, said he assumed her responsible for his plight, denied his guilt, and then made a beeline for the British trenches in France. I heard still later that he lasted just a month.

Father took the train from Atlanta that evening with Naomi, her parents, and Rabbi Weisz. Two Pinkertons rode in the baggage car to guard the casket bearing the body. Father telephoned the following night to say they had arrived safely in New York and that the interment would take place at dawn in Brooklyn. Noah was to be buried in his glasses.

At Mickve Israel the following Friday, Rabbi Weisz led the prayers. Only one fourth or so of the usual congregation was on hand. The rabbi rendered the entire service in Hebrew. I recited the *Kaddish* for the dead to myself in English. It contained, I noticed for the first time, not a word about death or resurrection— only adoration for God on highest. At the end of it I asked inwardly whether Noah would have been spared if I had cared for him more.

V

Father remained in New York for a week, visiting with Uncle Benny and their mother, who was to die a month later after fifty-one years of widowhood. Neither mother nor I responded with surprise when we had a letter from father, advising that he no longer wished to live in Savannah or the state of Georgia or anywhere else in the South. "It has been my home for nearly forty years," he wrote, "and its people can be exceedingly kind and generous and open, as many of them have been toward me, but all at once I feel more homeless than if our house had burned to the ground without a stick left standing."

Mother thought at first it was a natural enough phase for him to suffer in the aftermath of the Berg nightmare, but having myself become a Northerner by temperament (*i.e.*, too busy for civilities, too impatient to savor trivial delights, too hopeful to maunder over past glories or recent failures), I suspected that father's entire psychic metabolism had undergone a fundamental alteration. He had devoted himself too ardently to a place where the life of the mind had to answer, finally, to the demands of passion. Mother, a lifelong resident of Savannah, took it with admirable resilience the next spring when father announced to her that he had arranged to open a law office in Washington, D.C., and that there were some excellent buys to be had in small brick homes in Alexandria.

He had not, of course, just stuck a pin in a map and decided upon living wherever it landed. He had always been a man of eminently good sense, and even in his bruised state, he thought hard and well. Washington bridged the North and South, as father himself did, and it had become a very lively city under Mr. Wilson's regime. The power of the national government was growing, and there was increasing demand for knowledgeable lawyers to function there within and outside of the expanding bureaucracy. Among the enterprises in need of an enlightened representative to look after their interests from that ever more vital vantage point was the Jubilation Plantation Corporation. Amory Austin, entering his sixties, was no longer hopscotching across America with the same verve as earlier, and he recognized the merit in father's proposal. With the disposition of the Berg embarrassment, moreover, Austin had no hesitation in re-establishing ties to so able a champion. It was Seth Adler, after all, who had been wise enough in the first place to enlist him to run the company—and that had by no means been the extent of the man's contributions to its well-being over the years. Father, for his part, was not too proud to ask for the Washington assignment. He recognized the imprudence of starting up afresh at his relatively advanced age without a few substantial clients to bank on; he was, furthermore, the possessor still of a sizable amount of Jubilee stock, the value of which had made him a millionaire on paper several times over. It was to father's and the company's mutual interest, then, for him to take the title of special counsel without renewing day-to-day involvement with headquarters in Atlanta.

There was another reason for the transfer to Washington, I suspected, but father would never acknowledge it in so many words. He had been lifted from his profound gloom over the lynching of Noah Berg—and the state's failure to seek out its perpetrators despite extensive accounts in the newspapers of how the crime was carried out—by word that President Wilson had nominated the prominent social reformer Louis Brandeis, a Boston Jew, to the Supreme Court of the United States. Father held no lawyer in higher regard, and the Senate's confirmation of Brandeis, after a hard fight, meant that in America, a Jewish attorney might now aspire to the highest seat of judicial authority. I think he wanted to be in a city where all things were possible.

The great irony of it was that father contributed as much to the health and welfare of the Jubilation Plantation Corporation in his Washington years as he ever had in Georgia. Adding to the strength of the irony, his first vital contribution turned out to be a five-to-four opinion of the Supreme Court written by none other than Mr. Justice Brandeis.

People had been calling the drink "Juby" for short almost from the day it was invented. Amanda Baxter called it that herself, as if to make more of an animate organism out of it instead of a mere marketable object. But the company had trademarked only "Jubilee," on the notion that "Juby" was beneath dignity and might be tolerated in the most casual sort of references but not in advertising or other formal displays of the product. With the growing success of the company, moreover, Austin had become fearful that the trademark might suffer dilution if the nickname was put to common use and that consumers might become confused by rivals seeking to exploit the American preference for diminutives (an outgrowth, no doubt, of our egalitarian natures). And so the company's advertising started to pester the public. "Jubilee—ask for it by full name," it said. "Nicknames encourage substitution." Nobody paid much attention, and everyone knew what was meant by "Make mine a Juby." The company procrastinated until a West Coast outfit marketed a reddish-looking soda in a stubby hourglass bottle and called it "Joobee"; its sales soared. By the time Austin decided to seek an injunction, the wildcat rival had taken away nearly a third of Jubilee's business in the Far West. The legal problem came down to the defensibility of denying to another company the use of a name—or a phonetic version thereof—that Jubilee itself had publicly opposed for use in describing its own beverage. "A sticky wicket," said father as he looked on from afar while Jubilee's West Coast counsel lost the suit in the federal District Court and the Circuit Court of Appeals.

Father took the case to the Supreme Court only a few months after opening his Washington office late in 1916. It was called *Jubilation Plantation Corporation* v. *Joobee Company of America*; Justice Brandeis wrote for the majority in reversing the lower courts:

> . . . Of course no man or company is to be protected, as the appellee seeks, in the use of a device the very purpose of which is to defraud or swindle the public.
>
> Since 1900, the sales of the appellant corporation have increased at a very great rate. The nickname as well as the name of its product now characterizes a beverage to be had at almost any soda fountain. It means a single thing, coming from a single source, and well known to the community. . . .

That father scored so important a triumph so soon upon his arrival in the capital brought him more clients than he could handle. That he had done so on the strength of an opinion written by his co-religionist on the highest court in the land no doubt wiped away whatever residue of uneasiness remained in company headquarters in Atlanta over the Berg affair. Indeed, father's faith must have suddenly seemed a great asset to Austin and his hierarchy in 1917 when the nation mobilized for combat in Europe and the decision was announced in Washington to ration basic commodities under the supervision of the War Industries Board, whose chairman was Bernard Baruch, a Jew of Southern origins. Since sugar was the core ingredient in Jubilee syrup and sugar supplies to private industry were to be cut by 50 percent, the company's sales and profits appeared headed for a disastrous tumble. Father was asked to intervene with Mr. Baruch.

Although he did his best to argue that soft drinks were important to the morale of the nation, father got nowhere with the courtly Baruch. And then Congress made things worse by passing a penny-per-bottle federal excise tax on all soda sales for the duration of the war. The telephone wires crackled between Atlanta and Washington, and father was expected to make a major lobbying effort to overturn the new tax. Amanda Baxter, who corresponded with father and mother two or three times a year, wrote to warn that the company, and her brother Billy especially, thought that more vigorous representation of its interests in Washington might be in order.

"I shall be glad to step aside," father wrote back to her, "but my successor should be forewarned that there is in fact a war on and a certain modicum of patriotism is called for. The soda companies are not the only ones affected by these measures, and any transparent favor-seeking here now is severely frowned upon. As to that inconstant brother of yours, please tell him that you Gentiles must learn to take your medicine like everyone else. You will, no doubt, need to remind him of the circumstances wherein my intended irony resides." He went on to say that the sole piece of satisfaction that the war measures had brought him was news of the shutting down of Tom Watson's hate sheet on orders of the Attorney General. Watson, urging his readers to ignore the military conscription, denounced the war as Wilsonian insanity and a further selling out of the American masses.

The war ended before Jubilee suffered any substantial losses from the imposition of the sugar quota. But its effects in the immediate postwar period were very nearly catastrophic for the company. The price of sugar climbed from five cents a pound before American entry into the European conflict to a high of twenty-eight cents in 1920. One did not need to be a wizard to calculate the impact of such gyrations on Jubilee's fortunes. The basic mathematical formula upon which the company functioned was the sale of its syrup to the bottlers at a guaranteed price of $1.10 per gallon. That figure had been pegged at a time when sugar was in abundant supply and the stability of its price one of the eternal verities. But since each gallon jug of the treacly fluid consumed more than five pounds of sugar, its soaring price meant that the company would lose badly on each jug of syrup it sold so long as sugar costs remained at Himalayan heights. There were two alternatives: use other, cheaper sweeteners, regardless of how they affected the taste of the drink, or raise the price of the syrup to the bottlers and let them pass on the increase to the consumer.

The first possibility went entirely against the grain of the company, which had built its reputation on the quality and integrity of the product. The second option made far more sense; the only problem was that to raise the price was to violate the contracts each bottler held fixing the cost of the syrup at $1.10 per gallon "in perpetuity." At wit's end, Austin turned to father for help.

A contract entered into in good faith, father reasoned, was presumably of mutual, if not equal, benefit to both parties. But a contract in which unforeseen, and unforeseeable, circumstances prevent one party from honoring its side of the bargain except in a self-destructive fashion is no longer an agreement but a punitive arrangement by which the disadvantaged party is in actuality held as prisoner by the other side. Inevitably, the suffering party will be ruined and thus breach the agreement by ceasing to function. Ergo, one-sided contracts may be renegotiated at the insistence of the injured party. Father proposed, on the strength of this flawless logic, that new contracts be sent to the bottlers, calling for a graduated increase in the price of Jubilee syrup over the ensuing five years.

Steeled by father's resolve, Austin put the matter to an assemblage of the biggest bottlers. Most recognized the equity of his position; some threatened to sue, asking what good an agreement in perpetuity was if it would not be honored in foul weather as in fair. Pleading for reasonableness, Austin pressed the new contract, but when he met continued resistance, he grew impatient and made the mistake of unilaterally declaring the existing contracts void. A dozen suits were filed within a week. The company's operations were about to be snarled in what might have been years of costly litigation during which competitors would grab up Jubilee's fifty-million-dollar share of the market and not let go. To the rescue came father dear, as head of an emergency negotiating committee which methodically carpentered a new price formula adjusted to the cost of sugar. All but a handful of dissidents hailed the agreement and father's negotiating skills. The holdouts soon found their supply of syrup late in arriving and less than they needed; they caved in within six weeks.

Austin turned increasingly to father for objective appraisal of company policy. And a good thing. For the collective wisdom of the headquarters staff had produced a blueprint for the company's marketing program in the Twenties that proclaimed the principal growth sector of the population, and the one most promising for cultivation, to be the farm community. The statistical basis for this astonishing projection turned out, upon analysis, to be a statement by the president of a St. Louis bank that "the basic wealth of our country is founded in soil production" and that 70 percent of the dollars handled by *his* institution originated as farm dollars. To this crafty insight was added the finding of the U. S. Provost Marshal General's Draft Classification of Industrial Workers, taken during the height of the First World War, which discovered nearly fourteen million farmers and farm workers, by far the largest category in the survey. The conclusion to the canny corps of analysts surrounding Amory Austin in Atlanta was inescapable:

> . . . The farmers are there and so are their families, and they have a mighty thirst to quench as a result of their long hours of hard toil under the sun. Compare the number of farmers with the number of individuals in any other three classifications, and then remember that these farmers have large and growing families who not only yearn for the best but have the money to pay for it. This is where we must direct our best marketing efforts in the decade ahead.

"Pure poppycock," father wrote to Austin in his one-paragraph assessment of the sixty-page report. "The farming community is destined to shrink faster than any other part of our nation, in my view, as mechanization spreads with good economic times. The great phenomenon of the coming decade will be the bursting forth of the American automobile and the resulting spread of our cities and towns into the surrounding countryside. I would also suggest that industrial workers, whose ranks will swell in inverse ratio to the decline of the farm census, are capable of generating quite as large a thirst laboring indoors as the farmer achieves out of doors. But of course I have not researched this point extensively."

"You are returned to your pedestal as genius in the eyes of the powers that be in Atlanta," Mandy Baxter wrote to father soon thereafter, "and totally forgiven for your inability in wartime to have got the company exempted from its minimal duties." About the only sour note along the Southern front, she said, was that mad-dog Tom Watson, caged up in his fury at Hickory Hill and without a journal to ventilate his hatreds, threatened to run for the United States Senate and, given the usual fratricidal state of Georgia politics, might very well win.

The prospect that Watson might return to Washington after thirty years in the wilderness seemed preposterous to father. The man was a certifiable crackpot, he thought, at best merely irascible, at worst downright vicious. Did the republic, having become a recognized world power in the war, stand in need now of such ludicrous and irresponsible figures to write its laws?

The rest of the nation might just as well have skipped the privilege, but Georgia would not. Although the American Legion hotly fought him for his fervent opposition to the war, Watson won the enthusiastic backing of the Klan and easily routed his two opponents in the Senate race—the wishy-washy incumbent, Hoke Smith, his erstwhile ally, and the latest governor, none other than that slick ferret, Vincent Tunney, hero of the Noah Berg case to the Georgia masses. Tunney had at first been endorsed eagerly by Watson, but when the young governor declined to do the old Populist's bidding and turned out to be an advocate of the League of Nations and other enlightened policies, the sage of the know-nothings cut him to pieces. Watson carried 102 counties, twice as many as his opponents' combined total, and came back to Washington in triumph, if hardly in glory, in 1921 at the age of sixty-five.

"I do not expect you to be pleased at this development," Austin wrote to father, "but I trust you will let bygones be bygones and cultivate the man in the company's interests. He would be the natural spearhead, need I point out, of the long overdue effort to repeal the soda excise, which we were all led to believe was an emergency wartime measure. I trust you will give him the courtesy of a welcoming visit and broach this tax matter at the earliest felicitous moment."

Father would rather have kissed a rattlesnake. He wrote Austin that he was disinclined to pursue such a scoundrel and that if this reluctance jeopardized the best interests of the company, he was ready as always to step aside. The matter was dropped and, when Watson rapidly proved to be a truculent and thoroughly ineffectual member of the upper house, not renewed. Watson tilted at windmills most of the while, relieving his own pent-up frustrations but little benefiting the commonweal. Not all his positions

449

were lunatic, to be sure. He chastened the Republican majority for voting a twenty-five-million-dollar payment to Colombia, allegedly as reparations for the heavy-handed diplomacy that got America the Panama Canal; the treaty was a ruse, yelped Watson: "Let us confess what we are doing—that we are here to buy property for the Standard Oil Company." He thought it an outrage for America to withhold recognition of the Bolshevik government in Russia and demanded to know by what right we sought to dictate that nation's form of government. Why, President Washington had wasted no time in recognizing the revolutionary government of France, "whose garments dripped with blood" no less than the Soviets'. He flayed the militarists and denounced expenditures for a standing army of any more than 25,000 men, for why did the nation need a larger force, except for the basest of causes:

> . . . you are afraid of the millions of men and women and children who do not have enough to eat in this land of bounteous harvests; not enough to wear in the very cotton fields where their hands bring forth the staple that clothes the world. . . .

For every flash of the old idealism, though, he expended a dozen times the effort chasing phantom ogres. He drew headlines for prompting an inquiry into alleged brutality by officers toward enlisted men in the army during the war, but when the witnesses filed in to testify, there proved to be little of substance to the charges. Watson fell deeper into the thick melancholy that shrouded him during most of his second career at the Capitol. It was to last even more briefly than his first. He drank heavily, suffered painful attacks of asthma, and brooded for long hours over the deaths of all three of his children, two of them in early adulthood. Withal, he never missed a session of the Senate while he remained vertical.

I came to visit father and mother late in the summer of 1922 shortly before taking up the post I have held ever since on the faculty of Vassar College. On that trip, the three of us took a walk one day through the shade of Rock Creek Park to escape the worst effects of the sultry weather that marks Washington's summer climate. As we negotiated a turn in the path along a pleasing glen, we came upon another threesome seated upon a bench: a wizened little man in a white linen suit, gingerly balancing a child in a sailor outfit upon his meager lap; hovering maternally beside them was a largish woman in a lavender dress that had never been in style. As we neared, father took a step or two toward the rheumy-eyed old man, doffed his hat, and said pleasantly, "Senator Watson, I presume?"

The old man squinted up at him. "Do I know you, sir?" he asked.

"It's been some years," said father. "You advised me once why and how to become a lawyer. Seth Adler is my name, formerly of Savannah. This is my wife Ruth and daughter Judith."

"Why, yes," said Watson, tipping his hat in recognition but unable to unburden himself of the child in time to rise in formal greeting. "This fidgety tyke is my grandchild," he explained, "and perhaps you know my associate here, Mrs. Lytle." He turned to the woman. "Do you know Mr. Adler? He's one of the chosen people, if you recall the trial—."

"I know who Mr. Adler is, Senator," she said, nodding without a blink.

"Are you still looking out for the soda-water interests of Georgia?" Watson asked with a grin that showed his mouthful of dangerous-looking little teeth.

"In a desultory fashion, I'm afraid," father answered. "I have other clients."

"So I gather. I've heard several times from Mr. Austin in Atlanta. He tells me you are reluctant to pursue the Congress to end the soda tax." Watson smiled again. "I suspect it is me you are reluctant to pursue, Mr. Adler. And I cannot blame you. The problem with the Congress—I gather you know my position—is that it is filled with time-servers who believe their divine mission here is to seek favors in behalf of their most powerful constituents. I have not deigned to answer your Mr. Austin. Perhaps you might tell him that his efforts in my direction are misplaced."

"I'll do that," said father. "Good day, Senator—Mrs. Lytle."

Watson nodded briefly. Then after father had turned and headed back our way, the humbug Senator called after him. "Oh, Adler," he said, and father paused. "I greatly admire your Justice Brandeis. He's about the only courageous man in this whole bloody city of fools and knaves. I'd trade a hundred Herbert Hoovers for your one Louis Brandeis."

Father just looked at him for a moment. Then he said, "He is your Brandeis as well as mine, Senator," and continued on his way.

Watson succumbed to a cerebral hemorrhage the following month, shortly after placing in the *Congressional Record* several letters he had received from striking coal miners in Pennsylvania, where hundreds of mining families had been evicted from their homes. To the end he was a mixed bag, part avenging angel, part incorrigible hatemonger. The authentically saintly Eugene Debs eulogized him as "a heroic soul who fought the power of evil his whole life long in the interest of the common people, and they loved and honored him." And killed for him, he might have added. To me, the more apt tribute was the eight-foot-high floral crucifix that was sent to the funeral service at Thomson by the Ku Klux Klan, newly active in Georgia ever since rallying on Stone Mountain in the middle of the summer of 1915—about the time Noah Berg died.

VI

The inglorious demise of Tom Watson, once the piper of a brighter day for all the lowly, left father unmoved.

"You cannot rely on other men to do your own good works," he offered by way of epitaph.

"Today's prophet," I countered, "is tomorrow's fanatic." He liked mine better.

Lest I assumed that Watson's passing had materially cleansed American political rhetoric of intolerance, father sent me a magazine article published shortly thereafter. It dealt more or less with my field and was attributed to the Vice-President of the United States. Biological laws demonstrated, according to this writing of Calvin Coolidge, that the Nordic races deteriorated when mixed with other sorts. Having studied the subject for some years, I was under the impression that (a) there is no Nordic "race" and (b) the admixture of racial strains is generally far more beneficial to the mental and physical health of a people than inbreeding, leading me to conclude (c) that the Vice-President was a gentleman racist.

Fate promptly promoted Coolidge to the White House, where two years later he signed into law the notorious immigration bill drastically limiting the numbers who could henceforth come to these shores from Eastern Europe, where the preponderance of American Jewry had originated over the previous three decades. "America," said President Stoneface on that grand occasion, "must be kept American." "Somewhere in New Hampshire," father wrote me, "there must be a cave bleak enough to accommodate him."

Father's very next letter—I have saved them all—contained a surprise so complete and unsettling that I can still recall the sensation it provoked: dizziness. He had had a letter from his erstwhile associate Archie Ruskin in Atlanta (who, he noted without self-consciousness, "must be getting on in years now—pushing sixty-four or -five, I should say"). Archie enclosed a photostatic copy of a letter he himself had received two months earlier. "Its sender died the other week," he told father. "I thought you ought to see it. What comment is there to make but that life is an endless battering of astonishments when it is not utter tedium?"

Father had had a copy made of the copy and included it with his letter to me. It was headed "Savannah, April 3, 1924" and written in a large, flowing hand:

My dear Mr Ruskin:—

My sawbones says the cancer will spare me a month or a little more if I am lucky, but since the pain will only grow and the morphine softens my brain, I had best compose this while the power remains in me. I possess neither family nor wealth and so have nothing to leave behind but this acknowledgment. It is no treasure, but it is the truth. I ask your forgiveness for my burdening you with it and the merciful Lord's for its disclosures.

I never meant to harm the child. She was a bright fresh flower to me in my declining years. When her mother asked if I might help get her work at the factory, I jumped at the chance, never dreaming that my own weakness and the girl's needs would bring us together in carnal knowledge. My rooms were but a few blocks from her family's cottage, and I had watched with fondness when she passed by in the neighborhood and at church and saw her bloom into womanhood. The sight stirred

453

me at a level I did not suspect and have been ashamed of ever since.

I wish to declare that it was not I who deflowered her although I was her slayer as I was her lover. During her first year at the factory I offered from time to time and in total innocence (I wish to think) to give her a ride from work in my auto since our homes were so nearby. She shyly but gratefully declined until I wearied of asking. But one day she spied me at the close of work and asked directly if she might ride with me as one of the young men at the plant had made his intentions known to her and they were entirely dishonorable. In the course of time, my riding her home became a nightly ritual, although each of us took pains to disguise the fact—she from her family lest they disapprove, I (being a widower) from my underlings at the factory lest they brand me a molester of children.

As our contacts grew more frequent, so did our exchange of confidences and finally our intimacy. She was a greatly troubled girl. Her mother had become a constant scold as her stepfather's health worsened and the family funds vanished. Her stepfather, she said, had brutally taken her maidenhead while her mother was visiting family in the country. The morbid man said he would kill her if she told, and he took her after that with more kindness, saying he could not manage the act with the girl's mother and her pleasuring him that way was the only thing in life remaining to him. Her sense of sin, she told me, was made worse by the discovery that she enjoyed the sensation. Soon that enjoyment was transferred to another senior partner. I frankly relished those illicit hours with her in my room. A child in age, she was a woman in body and knew how to use it. It was I who insisted she have money from me as a payment of gratitude, not obligation. She said she did not want to take it, but the money was needed at home and she would credit it to overtime at the factory and I must verify the tale to her folks.

In time her head was turned by young bucks, and her

visits with me grew shorter and less frequent, although my need and eagerness for her held constant. When I fell sick, she visited rarely and then not at all. By that Saturday in April, I had been out for two weeks and sorely missed her sweet face and tender arms. I came down just after noontime to visit Berg at the factory and be brought up to date when who should I meet floating down the stairs but the young light of my life. She seemed scarcely to notice me. I must have blocked her path. She doubtless asked to pass, but in my ardor and my anger I could not have heard. What followed has always been a blur. I recall seizing her harshly by the wrist and drawing her after me to that room. Her struggle only fired my desire. She shouted that I was worse than her stepfather and called me a dirty name. It was not the insult I minded but that so foul a term fell from that milky mouth. She swore she would tell everything to her parents and to the company, and I did what was needed to silence her.

Afterward, I knew the nigger must have heard enough to hang me. I found him hiding in the corner of the packing room and told him straight out that he had to help me or he was a dead man. He did what I asked. What he told in court was largely true only he put it on the wrong man as he had to. The man he chose, or the cops did for him, was the same one I did. It was no problem to arrange as I knew the workings of the place and being the manager had all the keys and access needed. I even turned down the cellar light so the night nigger wouldn't see her body till late. I did not pick on Berg because he was a Jew but because he was forever showing his cleverness. He needed bringing down. Others must have agreed because it was not I who spread the bloody stains on the cloakroom floor the week afterward.

I could not but feel for Berg when I learned he wrote a kindly letter of bereavement to the girl's family—her mother showed me it—and proposed to me that the factory pay her burial expenses. He even gave me five dollars of his own when I said I would take up the collection. We bought her the finest casket there was to be had in Savannah, I stood by her at the graveside up there out of Macon, on the hillside above the oaks where later they strung up the Jew, and prayed her forgiveness. My own grave now beckons.

Your eternal servant,
JOS. A. DETTWILER

A thousand thoughts crowded my mind. Why had we none of us ever considered him the possible culprit? Because he was old and it was so plainly a crime of passion? But who else had had such ready access to the factory? Pike would have had when he worked there, but not after—and he had his alibi. The late Bryce Woodcock, then, as Amanda Baxter had brilliantly calculated. He was more interested in the girl than he had ever let on—that much she unearthed. But the rest was wishful on our part. She had manipulated Mo Easter just as the police had, and been manipulated in return. The police had offered him life; she, money. He told all of us the lies we wanted to hear. Woodcock told us the truth, finally, but we would not settle for it. All I could remember for days after reading Dettwiler's letter was how he had sat with us coolly in our living room as we debated who should defend Noah Berg against the charge of murder. Old Joe had been all for getting Tom Watson into the act. Why, he even came from Watson country.

Father, just then, was suffering one of his periodic attacks of certainty that all America was Watson country. He did not want to discuss the Dettwiler letter when I visited a few weeks later. He had written that chapter of his life and made too heavy an emotional investment to revise it. I wondered if the full impact of the letter had even registered with him. Mother assured me that it had. "What counts," she said, "is that Noah was not guilty. Who was doesn't matter."

That angered me. "But the same beastliness that killed Noah," I told her, "caused yet another innocent man to go to his grave thinking that others believed him a murderer. It's not enough to see every issue only in terms of how it affects the Jews."

Mother saw my point. But it was hard to get father to listen. He was too exercised by the publication and wide success, unto the millions of copies, of a book called *The International Jew:*

The World's Foremost Problem, whose principal patron and promoter was no one less than Henry Ford, the premier industrialist of the age. Ford's newspaper in Dearborn had earlier serialized the material in articles on the so-called "Protocols of the Elders of Zion," the gist of which was that the Jews had long been plotting the take-over of the globe, and the Great War was part and parcel of their international conspiracy.

"Listen," father insisted, reading to me from the book. " 'The Jew has not seemed to care to cultivate the friendship of the Gentile masses, due perhaps to the failures of experience, but due more likely to his inborn persuasion that he belongs to a superior race.' Oh, my Lord in heaven! Why, we're so superior we'll figure out any day now how to keep them from butchering us at regular intervals." He flipped through a few more pages. "Here," he said. " 'Had the Jew become an employée, a worker for other men, his dispersion would not probably have been so wide. But becoming a trader, his instincts drew him round the habitable earth.' Instincts, my big toe! It was the rumbling in his stomach. He became a trader because they wouldn't let him be a tiller or a maker. He worked for himself because no one else wanted him. Why, I know of a young Jew who once worked for other people down Savannah way. It was the general-store business, and this fellow did so well at it they offered him a partnership—provided, of course, he'd give up his faith. Then there was another young Jew down there, he went to work for a big soda company. And he did so well they hung him up with a rope."

For a time after that, father followed developments in Palestine with close attention. European Jews began flocking there after the San Remo conference had created a British protectorate of the Holy Land at the beginning of the Twenties, and father had heard good things about the burgeoning community of Tel Aviv. "They say it is a stimulating life over there," he reported and wondered what I thought of the notion of his and mother's relocating there.

"Little or nothing," I said. "It is a stimulating life here, too. Wherever Jews congregate, there will be anti-Jews. But here they are not greatly honored. This is your country."

Father said he wondered whether any man really had a country beyond the confines of his conscience. I reminded him that his own father had died for his country. "He was very young," said father. I never heard him say a more bitter word about America. Then his wavering spirits lifted anew when Henry Ford apologized, publicly and fully, for having foisted the patently idiotic "Protocols of the Elders of Zion" upon the American people. Father savored the apology as if it had been directed toward him personally. Ford's company, after all, epitomized the free-enterprise system that father so ardently favored, save for its wont to use and discard human beings like so many replaceable tin parts. But that callousness was beginning to soften, even as Henry Ford's virulent anti-semitism, and father understood well enough that America was not yet heaven and likely never would be.

In the last years of his life, I heard less and less from him about the pilloried circumstances of Judaism in America, aside from a periodic complaint that Fitzgerald or Mencken or another of the literary lions of the day seemed overly fond of giving the Jews an occasional, and entirely gratuitous, *zetz*. He abandoned attending synagogue, even on the High Holy Days, and said, when mother and I reprimanded him, that he would have supposed our own flawed characters provided us with quite enough ground for spiritual concern. Temporal matters interested him more. He took pleasure in the way Jubilee, to which he had sundered all ties but that of stock ownership, steered through the severest shoals of the Depression; the reason, he knew (though he never said it), was that he had helped build it into an extraordinarily solid industrial structure. His monument, though, he never thought it.

My husband, a microbiologist and devoted Al Smith supporter, proposed that we attend the inauguration of our manorial Dutchess County neighbor, Franklin Roosevelt. Father joined us and thereafter took a proprietary interest in the new President. He liked the way Roosevelt moved against the crueler aspects of the free-enterprise economy—and was more pleased still that his closest advisers included some men with names like Cohen and Hillman and Frankfurter and Morgenthau. "If there had been a few more Yiddish *kups* around *pisher* Harding and *shmendrick* Coolidge and *schlepper* Hoover," he said, "maybe we wouldn't have all fallen off the merry-go-round." That was easily the most ethnocentric sentence I ever heard him mutter.

In the final year of his life, no doubt to repair frayed ties to his forebearers, father made a pilgrimage to the little Swabian town of Ichenhausen, where his grandfather Solomon had grown up and then fled in the year 1819. Father had been advised that the coming to power of Chancellor Hitler had been a dour omen for the Jews, but he was determined to go, anyway. On his return, he reported with characteristic irony that the oppression he found was no worse than it had been in Grandpa Solly's day and of small worry. "The Jews may not hold public office or work in the civil service," he said, "but such work is notoriously unrewarding. They are banned from farming, which of course only gives backaches, and teaching, which only gives headaches. They are denied careers in journalism and the theater and radio, but these are the devil's work and merely distract the devout from *pilpul*. True, the Jews are not served in the groceries or the bakeries, but the food there is infamously stale, or in the butcher shops, where pigmeat is the national preference, or in the drugstores, where most of the counter space is devoted to cures for indigestion, the national pastime. And, of course, most of the hotels and inns are shut to the chosen people, but I am told the bedbugs are rife."

He never smiled during the recitation. At the end of it, though, he gave me a small kiss on the forehead and said, "Old Solly was right to leave that hellhole. And your grandfather Aaron was right to come here. Here is where I stay. You stay, too. America is just beginning."

He had worked hard and lived honorably and seen much and learned even more, and when he died in the middle of September 1934, he left behind a loving wife, adoring children, stock certificates in America's largest soda-pop company worth four million dollars (they had been worth twice that five years earlier and would be again), and a country he worshipped for having only once deserted him.

III

David's Epilogue

TWELVE

Yesterday's bicentennial celebration, which I joined remotely by way of our television set on this glorious if ever more crowded off-shore outpost, has stirred me belatedly to submit this entry by our family to the annals of the American past. A dozen years have passed since my Aunt Judith's death, I am astonished to discover, and because she bore no children (whether from want of fecundity or simple desire, I have no knowledge), the twin memoirs that she and my grandfather Seth composed have been in my possession ever since. Upon first reading them, I resolved to seek a publisher at the earliest opportunity. The moment, however, never seemed quite ripe before.

What is there to offer by way of postscript? Only a few notes on the passage of generations.

Had my father Elihu not pre-deceased her, I would have surely asked him to supply the lacunae in his sister Judith's otherwise admirable report by detailing his own relationship with his father. Suffice it to say here that they were close, and never more so than in Grandpa Seth's post-Savannah years. Daddy followed his father into the law, excelling at Harvard, then joining Archie Ruskin's firm in Atlanta for a few years before being called away to the First World War, throughout which he wore his grandfather Aaron's Congressional Medal around his neck along with a small, silver *mezzuzah*. Daddy, however, never did see combat, though his artillery unit was poised at dockside when the armistice was reached. On release from the service, he happily accepted his father's offer to form the partnership of Adler & Adler with offices

463

on Wisconsin Avenue in Georgetown. They prospered together for fifteen years until Seth's retirement. Daddy then shuttered the place and went to join the New Deal as Assistant Solicitor in the Department of the Interior, where he specialized in Indians. He was in and out of government service the rest of his life, able to stand on principle—and absorb the boot if need be—thanks to a not inconsiderable inheritance.

As Seth Adler's only grandchild, I was fated to follow the calling of the male members of the line, but the vagaries of politics drove me to seek a more stable vehicle for pursuing a career at law. Elected note editor of the *Yale Law Journal* a few months after Pearl Harbor, I stayed on at New Haven long enough to win my LL.B., donned the family Congressional Medal *cum mezzuzah*, and found myself a second lieutenant in the European theater for the duration. My heroism was limited, thanks to squinty vision, to collecting corpses from the battlefields of Tunisia and Sicily and later the Ardennes, but I will confess to three minutes of martial euphoria when our unit drove without resistance through the shattered village of Ichenhausen beyond the Rhine, with the wraith of Solomon Adler at my elbow. Aside from service as legal aide to Chester Bowles while he was governor of Connecticut and a sortie to Washington as a staff lawyer during one of the Kefauver Committee's well-publicized probes, I have been a denizen of Yale Law School, where I teach, write, and research. I have a slim but trenchant volume on the Fourteenth Amendment to my credit and a fat one on admiralty law, at which I happen to specialize. The sea, in fact, has all but possessed me. We live in Guilford, on the Sound, and keep a thirty-two-foot ketch, which I sail each summer to Nantucket, where we reside on the quiet end of the island. My wife Tony calls me, by turns, Admiral Adler or Professor Adler, depending on which activity has made me the more insufferable at the moment. She herself raises champion roses, makes exquisite jewelry in league with the local artisans' workshop (of which she is a *doyenne*), and keeps close track of our two far-flung offspring.

Our son Tommy was a victim—or beneficiary, if you will—of the nation's addled mission in Vietnam. Caught up in the antiwar fervor while a student at Columbia, he declined to be drafted when called. "It was easy for you," he told me. "You believed in what the country was fighting for. I would have, too, then. Not now. 'My country, right or wrong' is bullshit. Killing gooks for Christ is no different from gassing Jews for the Fatherland." He asked my blessing. I hung the medal that Tommy's great-great-grandfather won fighting for Abe Lincoln around the boy's neck and kissed him. He went to live outside Toronto for a year and then moved to Israel. He manages a plastics factory in Tel Aviv and saw action in the Sinai campaign of 1973. His mother and I have been over there twice; he seems happy enough, says he does not believe much in God, and contends that Israel is really America's fifty-first state, so we should not feel that he has abandoned us or his homeland.

Tommy's sister Vicky—Victoria Adler Bell—believes passionately in God and the almighty dollar (in that order, to be sure) and thinks America is running out of the kind of dynamism that made it rich and powerful (and brutal and arrogant, her brother would chip in). She is a graduate of the Wharton School of Business and Finance at the University of Pennsylvania, works as a securities analyst with a San Francisco brokerage firm, and is married to a lawyer with political ambitions. One of the joys of my mellow years is that our two children, although half a world apart geographically and ideologically, write to each other regularly—and to their parents, even, now and then.

This synopsis of his posterity to date would not likely have surprised Seth Adler. He would express muted satisfaction, I should think, judging by his own and his daughter's memoirs, over our varying but not ignoble works. But had he re-materialized for the nation's two hundredth birthday celebration yesterday, a few items would surely have stunned him.

The state of the Jews, for one thing. In America, since his time, they have advanced steadily to positions of leadership in every walk of life. It is true that for some years now none has sat on Grandpa Seth's revered Supreme Court, as Brandeis did in his time, but it must be borne in mind that the last Jew to do so was nominated for advancement to Chief Justice of the United States —a fulfillment denied to him by his own indiscretions as much as a blooming of latent anti-semitism. Meanwhile, Jews serve, as of this writing, as the United States Secretary of State, United States Attorney General, chairman of the Federal Reserve Board, governor of Pennsylvania and Maryland, senior senator of New York and Connecticut, mayor of New York City, president of the E. I. Du Pont de Nemours & Company, publisher of the *New York Times* and the Washington *Post*, president of Dartmouth College and Rutgers University, chairman of the board of the American Broadcasting Company and the Columbia Broadcasting System and the Radio Corporation of America, managing editor of *Time* and *Newsweek*, and the leading left-handed starter on the pitching staff of the New York Yankees. Thousands more have enriched the land as scholars, scientists, physicians, composers, painters, writers, entertainers, merchants, and manufacturers. Few that I know of were ardent supporters of the national crime in Vietnam; none that I know of was involved in Watergate. So much for thin-lipped Calvin Coolidge and the Jewish diseasing of the Nordic races.

Then there is the other state of the Jews that would astonish Grandpa Seth. Could he have conceived that the precarious survival of the State of Israel would have (1) become a collective mission of American Jewry beyond its prior obligation to this republic, (2) earned American Jews far greater dignity in the eyes of their countrymen than they had known before, and (3) been embraced as fundamental national policy by political leaders of every party and persuasion? Even to me, it is no less miraculous than the parting of the Red Sea that Israel's only constant friend on earth is America—but that one is enough. Can it be explained by the hateful contention the Jews of the United States have prospered so well that they hold the nation's will in thrall? Or is the explanation more nearly what Seth Adler died believing—that Jews are the most typical of Americans: a bit noisy and showy, perhaps, but proud and prudent and practical, generous and enterprising and liberty-loving?

Most startling of all to old Seth, I suspect, would be the prospect in the summer of 1976 that the next President of the United States is to be a Georgia farmer reared in the very same place that spawned the rabble who so savagely took the life of Noah Berg. Shades of Tom Watson! And our new hero even bears the initials of the saviour he so openly embraces. It is touching, and plainly a healing thing for the nation, that a good old boy who swabbed cotton bolls with arsenic in his family's fields, and had his hair shorn with mule clippers, and sold peanuts barefoot on the streets of a peanut-sized town, may be elevated by grit and wit to the White House, even when almost none of us had ever heard of him twelve months ago. While I am personally moved by reports that he overcame the navy's regulation against flat feet by pressing his arches endlessly over a bottle of Jubilee—or was it some other soda?—I cannot ignore that his father was a racist, that his sister is a fire-breathing Baptist evangelist who makes me fear I must genuflect to Jesus or she will wallop me with the cross, and that the candidate himself uses "Christian" as a synonym for "righteous."

But forgive me, Grandpa Seth, I am going to vote for this Georgian, though I wish he would have the grace to call himself James. There is lyncher's blood in us all, I suppose, and in this case it is well diluted by other strains. His father was less one of Tom Watson's groundlings than a highly enterprising farmer who did not stake his fate on cotton. His mother has been a healer of people of all colors and creeds. His principal mentor during his formative years was Judaism's chief contribution to the science of nuclear strategy. And he himself favored the comity of the races well before it was paid even lip service by the more generous of his fellow Georgians.

Is he then merely a mutant—or some new breed of open-minded and kindly-souled cracker? Well, the Jews of Atlanta issued a statement that as governor of their state, he named Jews to public positions they had never before held and is "a strongly committed Christian who is sensitive to the pluralistic character of this nation and of the contributions made to America by all religious, racial, ethnic and cultural groups." In short, what's good for the Jews is good for America. I've heard dumber things.

467

AUTHOR'S NOTE

This novel, which is a confluence of several stories, draws freely
upon many authentic historical events and personalities, but is
primarily a work of the imagination and all the principal characters with the exception of Tom Watson are inventions. The trial
of Noah Berg and its aftermath are based loosely upon the real ordeal of Leo M. Frank in Atlanta from 1913 to 1915. The larger
contours of the Frank case have been retained—Frank, like his
fictive counterpart, was a Jew transplanted from New York and
married to a Southern girl of his faith; he was the superintendent
of the National Pencil Company at the time of the murder of
Mary Phagan, and he died for it at the hands of a lynch mob after
being convicted on no more evidence than is mustered here
against Noah Berg. Both of Frank's lawyers were Christian, however, and I have no knowledge that his personality resembled that
of Noah Berg. Who really killed the Phagan girl has never been
conclusively determined.

Only a very few words and phrases in the courtroom testimony
are taken from the Frank trial, although I drew heavily on the
transcript as a point of departure. The judge did in fact enter the
courtroom at one point carrying that day's newspaper with the
headline exposed to the jury. One of the defense lawyers, in his
summation, did in fact declare that he would rather die than
harm a Jew. Street mobs did in fact howl at the jury. An Atlanta
streetcar motorman did in fact proclaim while on duty that the
defendant was "nothing but a damned Jew" who ought to be
strung up. But for the most part, I have orchestrated the trial to

meet my narrative needs. Anyone interested in pursuing the subject and discovering the full scope of my departure from the historical record may wish to consult the Atlanta *Constitution* starting with the issue of July 25, 1913; this was my principal historical source.

Elsewhere in the book, historical plausibility was a guiding principle when historical fact was lacking. All the public events involving Tom Watson are true, and his exact words (or very slight variations thereon) were used wherever possible. The scenes involving him in private confrontations with the fictional characters reflect Watson's known attitudes and public pronouncements, but I have of course taken some liberties. There is no record, for example, of his having invested in a soda company, but he certainly opposed Northern industrial marauders and approved of Southern initiatives. The incendiary words about Noah Berg attributed to him in *The Jeffersonian* closely follow the actual language he used in denunciation of Leo Frank and the commutation of his death sentence by the governor of Georgia. Indeed, the U. S. Attorney General was considering investigating Watson's part in inspiring and perhaps even directing the lynch gang.

Some miscellaneous items in the story that may strike the reader as inventions, and perhaps even implausible ones, are historically validated. The seemingly unfeeling remark in support of child labor attributed to Gus Griffin (cf. page 183) is an exact quotation of words spoken at about that time by Asa Candler, an Atlanta civic leader and president of the Coca-Cola Company. Jim Smith's convict-lease farm, Smithsonia, really existed, though it is doubtful he would have parted so readily with an inmate as he does, in an expansive mood here, with Plato Layne's father. Teddy Roosevelt really did appoint a commission to study health perils in the soda industry, Justice Holmes really wrote the Supreme Court's minority opinion in the appeal of the Leo Frank verdict (*Frank* v. *Mangum*, 237 U.S. 309), and Calvin Coolidge when Vice-President really did write an article about the ethnic threat to the purity of the Nordic races (he presumably being their finest flower). Oh, yes, at least four Jews won the Congressional Medal of Honor in the Civil War.

Temple Mickve Israel in Savannah lives. When I visited it in August 1975, I found a crumpled piece of paper on the floor of the main aisle. I opened it and read, handwritten, "Get history of the Congregation." And so I did, and set about writing the foregoing. Whoever composed that note, I thank. I wish to acknowledge my debt as well to the authors of the following books which were especially helpful to me: *Pills, Petticoats, and Plows: The Southern Country Store* by Thomas D. Clark; *Soda Pop* by Lawrence Dietz; *The Provincials: A Personal History of Jews in the South* by Eli N. Evans; *The Big Drink* by E. J. Kahn, Jr.; *Pilgrim People: A History of the Jews in America from 1492 to 1974* by Anita Libman Lebeson; *Documentary History of the Jews in the United States* edited by Morris U. Schappes; *Georgia: Unfinished State* by Hal Steed; *A Treatise on Beverages or, The Complete Practical Bottler* by Charles Herman Sulz; *The Principles of Scientific Management* by Frederick Winslow Taylor; *Tom Watson: Agrarian Rebel* by C. Vann Woodward; and *This Is My God* by Herman Wouk. Much of the dialogue on religion in the book grew from discussions with my son Matthew.

New Haven   R.K.

ABOUT THE AUTHOR

Richard Kluger was an editor and critic before turning to writing full-time in 1973. He was born in Paterson, New Jersey, in 1934, grew up on the west side of New York City, graduated from the Horace Mann School and Princeton University, and went to work for, in order, *The Wall Street Journal,* the New York *Post, Forbes* magazine, and the late New York *Herald Tribune,* on which he served as literary editor. Later he worked as executive editor at the publishing house of Simon and Schuster, editor-in-chief at Atheneum, and publisher at Charterhouse. He left publishing to write *Simple Justice,* his massive narrative of the Supreme Court's epochal decision in *Brown* v. *Board of Education,* the 1954 school segregation case, which was issued in 1976. *Members of the Tribe* is Mr. Kluger's third novel. He is married, has two sons, lives in an old house on a quiet street in New Haven, Connecticut, and voted for Jimmy Carter for President "not without misgivings."

DATE DUE